THE

PLINKO

BOUNCE

MARTIN CLARK

THE PLINKO BOUNCE

RARE BIRD
LOS ANGELES, CALIF.

READ OR DIE

THIS IS A GENUINE RARE BIRD BOOK

Rare Bird Books
6044 North Figueroa Street
Los Angeles, California 90042
rarebirdbooks.com

Set in Dante
Printed in the United States

10 9 8 7 6 5 4 3 2 1

Library of Congress Cataloging-in-Publication Data available upon request

Book Design by Hailie Johnson
Cover Design by Robert Schlofferman

For Deana H. Clark
and in memory of
Hazel Young Clark

Turn your light down low
Hear the four winds blow
Bow your head to pray
It ain't what you planned
You got one last stand
Let the music play

—Robert Earl Keen, "Let the Music Play"

CHAPTER ONE

JUDGE CHRISTINA LEVENTIS SENT the jury to begin their deliberations at 11:03 a.m., and she was so damn unhappy and agitated when she left the bench that she was already unzipping her robe before she reached her office, jerking out her arm from the sleeve while she was still striding across the courtroom, impatient, as if she were shedding a black polyester straitjacket.

As soon as the judge disappeared, Porter Bowman looked at his lawyer, Andy Hughes. "Judge Levin sure is pissed off," Bowman observed.

"*Leventis*," Andy corrected him. "It's written right there, Porter, on the nameplate beside her microphone. See it? And as many times as you've been in here, you ought to know her name by now."

"Well, whoever she is, I don't think it's fair she's actin' mad at me. If we lose, I wanna appeal. As much as we can. The Supreme Court if we have to. I ain't guilty of nothin'."

"I'm going to smoke a cigarette," Andy said. "Stay here. Don't leave this table. Don't move. Think you can manage that?"

Andy walked down the tight interior stairway of the Patrick County Courthouse, past the security desk and metal detector and through the heavy double doors. The July air was scorched and listless, the building's small yard baked. He turned a corner, heading for the alley across the street. He didn't think it was professional to loiter at the front entrance, beside the pencil-necked Smoker's Outpost ashtray where bailiffs, witnesses, clerks, and jittery defendants burned cigarettes and, more often than not, tossed the butts on the ground or underneath a giant holly bush.

Several of his public defender clients—the Reliables, the lawyers called them—hung around in the alley, occasionally sleeping there. Moonfaced

Dancin' Ben would cut a little jig, sort of a creaky soft-shoe, if you paid him a dollar. Pink Panther was as gentle as a baby lamb and could recite the books of the Bible in order until he became loaded, and then he pissed in public and panhandled at the grocery store, cursing and threatening shoppers who didn't see fit to give him cash. General Gene really had served in the army, though he never left Fayetteville and never made it past E-3 private. They'd been to every rehab, every shelter, every program, every church and halfway home, and they weren't fixable, weren't *ever* going to stop drinking and raising Cain, and they lived on the court dockets, with almost daily charges of drunk in public, curse and abuse, disorderly conduct, indecent exposure, littering, and assault and battery.

Today, Dancin' Ben was wearing a thrift-shop suit and a fat tie. He was seated in a lopsided metal folding chair, draining a forty-ounce Steel Reserve, eight percent alcohol, the big bottle only $2.50 and tax, strong fuel for cheap.

"You're looking sharp, Dancin' Man," Andy noted. "Why the shave and nice suit?"

"I'm meetin' ever mornin' with Dr. Cole over at his medical office. My momma set it up with him; she's a nurse at the clinic. He's ahelpin' me quit the drinkin'."

"Seems to be a work in progress, huh, Ben?" There was no barb or malice in Andy's tone. "It's not even noon, and you're already the man of Steel Reserve."

"Rome wont builded in no day, Mr. Hughes. Just beer—I'm leavin' the wine and vodka alone. Soon I'll go cold turkey." He peered at Andy. "Can you spare a cigarette?" He hesitated a beat. "And thanks, sir, for the good job you done me on that trespassin' charge last month. I always ask Judge McGarry if he'll 'point you as my lawyer—ain't no better public defender."

Andy tossed him a cigarette and noticed a gash along Ben's bony, pallid middle finger when he collected the gift. Forty-seven years old, he appeared sixty. "Well, I hope," Andy said sincerely, "you can sober up and stay out of trouble. It would be a relief for your mom. She's a fine lady."

"I will," Ben replied. "You hear 'bout Zeb?"

"Nope," Andy answered.

"He up and died on us." Ben trapped the beer between his biceps and ribs and lit the Marlboro Red. "They found him dead in his jail bunk. Three days ago. He was pullin' a month for shopliftin'. Nobody seen it comin'."

"Huh," Andy said. "Sorry. Zeb wasn't a bad person, even when he was drunk. He seemed to be the healthiest of all you guys. What was he, forty, maybe?"

"Yeah, he was pretty young." Ben tipped his head and jetted smoke toward the sky. "Never know when it'll be your time. Worst part is ol' Patches don't understand Zeb's gone for good. He's still there waitin' like usual."

Patches was Zebulon McAlexander's dog, a crackerjack blue heeler mix with different colored eyes who was the working member of their relationship: Toss spare change in Zeb's hat, and Patches would speak or roll over or play dead or shake hands or balance on two legs or—for the grand finale—leap high enough to snatch a treat from Zeb's shoulder. The loyal cur was so devoted that when Zeb was behind bars at the local jail, Patches always made his way downtown and stuck close to the building until his master served his time and was released.

"Maybe you or General Gene can adopt him and take care of him."

"Done asked," Ben said sadly, frowning, "and my sister won't let me. She has a sorry-ass cat at the trailer where I stay, and she ain't havin' none of it. There's feedin' him too. The money. Zeb drawed a check, and I don't. It'd be terrible if he's stuck in a cage at the pound. Worse, I heared from Deputy Ward they only give 'em two weeks before they put the needle to 'em."

"I don't think the rule's quite so rigid, especially for a celebrity like Patches. I'm sure he'll—"

"Mr. Hughes, the jury's ready," Ralph Howell, the circuit court bailiff, shouted from the top of the alley. The brick buildings on each side captured his words and caused a brief, faint echo.

"That was fast," Andy muttered.

"Tell Porter I'm rootin' for him," Ben volunteered. "I know he's innocent and don't deserve none of this."

Andy hotboxed the cigarette as he hurried toward the street, stubbed it against a wall, tossed it in a trash can, hustled to the courtroom, and beelined to the defense table.

"You good to go?" Bailiff Howell asked.

"Yes. Where's Porter?"

"I assumed he was with you," the bailiff responded. "He left a few seconds after you did."

"For heaven's sake," Andy blurted. "Great. Tell Judge Leventis I'll be right back. Sorry. He probably stepped outside for some air."

Howell grinned. "I'm not sure I'd call it 'air.'"

Andy dashed to the entrance. "You see a man in a green shirt and jeans come by here?" he asked a group of skinny, tattooed kids clustered by the door. "Bald guy?"

"No," the tallest kid answered, and the rest ignored the question.

"Mr. Hughes!" Bowman was waving from across the street.

"Get the hell over here, Porter," Andy commanded him. "The jury's back. I told you not to leave."

He sashayed across Main Street, in no hurry. "What do you think'll happen?" he asked when he finally ambled to where Andy was standing.

"No idea," Andy said tersely. "And you smell like booze. I *told* you to stay put. Couldn't you at least keep sober until we finish your trial?"

"I'm fine. Must be the mouthwash you're smellin'. Listerine."

Judge Leventis was still in a mood when the bailiff handed her the two verdict forms. She glared at Porter Bowman and instructed him to "please rise." She read from the first single sheet of paper. "In the Commonwealth of Virginia, County of Patrick: On the charge of littering, we the jury find the defendant not guilty. Signed by the foreperson, Dianna Mills. Dated July seventeenth, 2020." She paused. She picked up the second form. "In the Commonwealth of Virginia, County of Patrick: On the charge of drunk in public, we the jury find the defendant not guilty. Signed by the foreperson, Dianna Mills. Dated July seventeenth, 2020." She tossed the verdict on top of its file. "Ladies and gentlemen, thank you for your service. We're grateful. While all jury service is an important civic duty, I realize from watching your reactions today most of you were—understandably— not happy to be inconvenienced by these *extremely* minor cases; however, the defendant exercised his right to trial by jury, and we are duty-bound to honor that request. I apologize for any hardship and appreciate your attention to our Covid-19 guidelines. Please be careful as you return home or to your workplaces."

Andy was staring at the floor. His shoe was untied. The lace had lost its plastic tip and was starting to fray and unravel on one side. *Four years of college, three years of law school, law review at William and Mary, and this is my job, this is the penny-ante shit I have to do,* he thought, and closed his eyes for a moment. *Forty-three years old, stuck and stymied.*

"Damn right, Mr. Hughes," Bowman crowed. "We showed 'em who's boss."

"Yeah," Andy grunted, opening his eyes.

The clerk was sorting through Bowman's files, the jury members were meandering toward the stairs, Judge Leventis was studying her docket, and the assistant commonwealth's attorney, a quality man named Doug Reilly, came over to shake hands and exchange a few cordial words with Andy. Darrell Pruitt—an affable, professional veteran—was the arresting officer, and he was beside Reilly.

"Congratulations," Reilly said to Andy. "You always do great work for your clients." He nodded slightly. "No matter the case."

Officer Pruitt reached to shake hands with Andy but tried to keep his pandemic distance. "I don't feel so bad losin' to the best," he offered. "Maybe next time."

"Well, I got some bad feelings, you stupid fucker," Bowman bellowed, the recent alcohol beginning to saturate him and ignite his temper. "We made you look like the dumbass you are, Pruitt." Bowman wagged a finger at the deputy. "Dumbass," he repeated and cackled. "Put you in your place, little man."

Andy instinctively took a step away from the table and his client. He peeked at the judge, apprehensive.

"Ten days active for summary contempt," Judge Leventis said so quietly that it was difficult to hear. She didn't look up from her docket pages until she'd finished speaking. "Bailiff Howell, please take him to jail."

"Say what?" Bowman screeched. "I wont even talkin' to you. How's that legal? You been against me all day. Tried to railroad me."

"You received a fair trial, Mr. Bowman," the judge said.

"Well then screw you too, bitch," Bowman declared, the last word a maskless, spit-spray explosion.

"I'll consider that a freebie, sir," she said. "A twofer included in the ten days. Please take him to the jail," she repeated. "Before I ring him up again."

The bailiff and Officer Pruitt handcuffed Bowman, grabbed his pinned arms and guided him, jabbering and cursing and complaining and stiff-leg resisting, toward the holding cell behind the bench, and while Officer Pruitt was unlocking the metal door, Bowman twisted around and shouted to his lawyer: "We're appealin' this, Mr. Hughes. You file papers and get me out." He sucked a breath. "And call my grandma and see if she'll put some money on my canteen account at the jail." He balled his fist at the judge. "Crooked kangaroo."

"Well, there you go," Reilly said. The lanky commonwealth's attorney shook his head, chuckled. "You can always count on the Reliables. I don't know how you and your office deal with their nonsense day after day after day, Andy."

"The huge paycheck and free state Porsche make it all worthwhile," Andy joked.

"What did our boy Porter catch in lower court?" Reilly asked. "I've forgotten. Before he appealed and wasted everybody's morning over nothing?"

"Twenty-five-dollar fine on the drunk in public," Andy replied. "Five days suspended on the littering—no active time. Basically *zero*, since he'll never pay a penny of the fine and costs."

Reilly laughed. "Some folks just don't do well with prosperity. Only Porter Bowman could be found not guilty on appeal and wind up serving ten days more than he received in lower court." Reilly stepped closer. He laid a manila envelope on the old oak table. "Here's the last discovery information for Damian Bullins. We're still set for him to plead next Thursday, right?"

"Yes," Andy confirmed.

"See you then," Reilly said. "I'm sure we'll have a packed house for the show," he added as he walked off.

"Judge." Andy clasped his hands in front of his chest. "Apologies, ma'am. Sorry about the whole shebang. These guys know the system, and he was determined to appeal—for no real reason, other than he has nothing else to do and really nothing to lose—and I regret we wasted your time and the jury's time. I'm sorry about his conduct and language just now. You were gracious to only pop him with the ten days."

"No problem," Judge Leventis answered. She rocked forward. "I always enjoy having *you* in my court. I was a defense attorney once myself—I understand how it is." She arched her eyebrows. "As for not adding any more jail time, I often wonder, especially in really hot weather or really cold weather, whether I'm briar-patching certain defendants when I send them to a cot, three meals, TV, a never-ending card game and climate-controlled lodging."

***

TEN MINUTES LATER, SITTING in his 2018 Jeep Wrangler, his briefcase and suit coat on the passenger seat, the window rolled down, Andy called Brooke Scott at Patrick Henry Community College, where she worked in the financial-aid office. "My jury trial ended early," he told her. "Okay with you if I pick up Noah from the Y?"

"Sure," Brooke said. "You'll make my schedule easier."

"Appreciate it."

"How is it a jury trial's over before lunch, Andy? Did it settle?"

"No. It was a friggin' littering case with one of the Reliables. A wine bottle he allegedly left behind."

"Using all your Perry Mason muscles," she kidded him.

Andy had met Brooke at the FloydFest music festival in 2011, on a charmed summer Friday, the ground still damp from a stray shower, a rainbow anchored on opposite sides on the Blue Ridge Mountains. He spotted her in a beer tent, and they were so wrought for each other, so bullseye, that he dumbstruck stared and schoolboy smiled, and she welcomed it, took off her sunglasses and gave it straight back, their soundtrack a Taj Mahal song from the main stage. She was gorgeous, tall and agile, and he was every inch her match, six three and charismatic, the both of them dark-haired and rare, beautifully set apart from the common world.

They spent the festival together, had camp-lantern sex in her tent on Sunday night, then again in her SUV before they left the festival parking lot, the leather seats warm, a mountain breeze curling through the Honda in fits and starts. They began dating, and for a while it was as expected, came as billed, but three months later, in the fall, the leaves dying, the air chilly, they realized they were off-kilter once you dipped beneath the easy peaks and top-shelf romance. There was no nitty-gritty to them, no nuts and bolts, and they gave voice to the obvious at a bar in Roanoke, a sampler platter untouched on the table, both sipping water, both disheartened, as if they'd somehow been rooked, been cheated by fool's gold. Still, they were kind to each other at the melancholy end, and Andy sent her flowers—a cut arrangement, no roses—a few days later.

December 15, 2011, she called the public defender's office in Martinsville to inform him she was pregnant. She didn't hem and haw, just announced the news, subdued and measured.

"Oh, wow…wow," Andy spluttered. "Didn't expect this." He cleared his throat. Thought about shutting his office door. "So, well, so I'm glad you're telling me."

"Yeah," she answered. "I'm telling you."

Neither spoke for several seconds. Andy heard two lawyers chatting at the copier in the hallway.

"So…so…uh, what…what're you…what comes next?" he asked.

"You mean am I planning to have an abortion?" she said bluntly, her voice spiking on the last word.

"I suppose that's…a consideration." Andy could feel his neck coloring. His thoughts were scrambled, pinballing off his skull. His tongue was sandpaper dry against his front teeth. "Sorry," he said. "Sorry I'm so rattled. I'm just, you know, this is a bomb. Crazy sudden and unexpected and…the most important thing that could happen to me."

"If I were going to end my pregnancy, Andy, most likely I would've done it and put this behind me and not involved you. If I were certain about it. Positive."

"Yeah," he answered, slowly regaining his composure. "Not to be too personal—"

"This," she interrupted, "is about as personal as it gets, don't you think?"

"Not to be too personal," he repeated, "but you, uh, might decide you're not ready for a baby, right? Just asking. There's the *KEEP YOUR ROSARIES OFF MY OVARIES* sticker smack in the middle of your bumper. And, from our conversations, you were always very clear about…uh…a woman having a choice."

"Part of my right to choose is to pick what's best for me. Maybe I want to control my own life and body and not go through with this. Or maybe I want to have my kid. My damn business and nobody else's, either way." Her tone softened. "I'm thirty-five. Not getting any younger. If I were picking a man from the Wayfair baby-daddy catalog, I'd pick the Andy Hughes model—you're smart and considerate. Decent. Honest. Nice looking."

"I'll help a hundred percent, if need be. Support, money, insurance, you name it. I'll do my part, no problem."

"I'm sure. But I'm interested in more than an ATM with testicles, the mostly missing dude who pays exactly what he's supposed to and drops by for the occasional birthday party and calls his kid 'Sport' or 'Buddy' or 'Baby Doll.'"

"No offense, but how are you pregnant? What happened to the pills?"

"Obviously, Andy, they didn't work. They aren't infallible. To be honest, I forgot to take a couple when I was staying with my mom after her surgery."

"Okay," he replied.

"Believe me," she said firmly, "I'm as stunned as you are. And to answer the questions you're afraid to ask me right now: I'm not trying to 'trap' the ex-boyfriend *I* decided to dump, and I'll take a DNA test—wouldn't blame you for wanting to check, given the circumstances."

Andy gently laughed. "Our breakup was mutual, or so I like to think. Leave me a little dignity."

"True," she said. "We both agreed." Her voice broke. "Sorry. It's hard not to be emotional."

"Will you let me have tonight to think about all this? It's a lot. A whole lot. Life-changing. Double life-changing. Triple. Can I call you in the morning?"

He phoned that very same night, around seven, enthusiastic and certain, convicted, and he loved his boy Noah even before the lad was birthed, and with the exception of a few predictable snags and quarrels and reasonable disagreements and a single pitched battle over the car seat, Andy and Brooke were kind to each other and dedicated to their child and hellaciously wonderful parents, who, early on, even slipped a few times and wound up having more sex.

Noah Cheever Hughes, that was what they picked for the birth certificate, and it was perfect for the boy, handsome, spirited and a wink different.

Idling in the car line at the Martinsville YMCA, Andy spotted his son the moment he walked out of the building. He stretched across the console and opened the passenger-side door.

"Dad, Dad, Dad," Noah repeated, excited, darting to the Jeep from the sidewalk, eight years old, toting his backpack by a single strap. "Guess what? Guess what?" he said as he climbed in.

"I'm on pins and needles," Andy answered playfully. "No hug for me?"

"Howard saved my friend Butch's life," he exclaimed, talking nonstop through a rushed embrace. "It was *amazing*. He was bleeding to death. He fell off the diving board and busted his head. I heard you could see his brains. It was so scary."

"Wow," Andy replied, and it came out flat and curt. Howard Logan was a local physician who'd married Brooke three years ago. He was a steady man who kept an appropriate stepdad's distance from her and Andy where Noah was concerned. He was polite and civil to Andy, the ex who'd once shared a bed with his wife. He was tolerant and generous with the child—you couldn't ask for more under the circumstances.

"Yeah," Noah continued. "Howard's a hero. It's gonna be in the papers."

"Howard's a good doc." Andy forced the words. When he spoke, he was peering through the windshield at the brake lights in front of him.

"Yeah," Noah said. "It was so cool."

"Glad Butch is okay." Andy eased away from the curb.

"He's gonna be fine. Super. Like he was before."

"Yep," Andy said softly.

Blooded to his father, Noah, even at age eight, realized what he'd done, how he might've diminished his dad and bruised his feelings. "But you help people every day," he declared with false cheer. "Not just if they're hurt. I'd rather be a lawyer like you than a doctor."

"Both are excellent choices," Andy answered.

After grounders and fly balls at the sandlot, a trip to Pizza Hut for a parking-lot meal, a McDonald's soft-serve cone, a *Fortnite* showdown and the quid pro quo five minutes of Mark Twain's *Connecticut Yankee*, the bookmark now seventy-three pages deep, Noah was in bed asleep at eleven, and Andy sat at his computer, opened the file saved as RESIGNATION, changed the date *again*, and printed the three paragraphs. He signed the letter in black ink and slid it into his briefcase so he could deliver it to his boss on Monday.

Restless and distracted—even a trip to Noah's room to watch the precious child sleep didn't help—Andy bent open the metal clasp on the Damian Bullins envelope and began studying the discovery information the commonwealth's attorney had delivered earlier. Earbuds played Handel's *Water Music* while he read. On top was a photocopy of Bullins's nine-page confession. Because it was late, and because it had been a grueling day, Andy went through the first page three times, then removed the earbuds and read the initial paragraph out loud so he could be absolutely certain he wasn't mistaken. "Damn," he said when he finished. "Incredible."

CHAPTER TWO

THE FOLLOWING MONDAY MORNING, July 20, Andy was already in Vikram Kapil's office when his boss arrived with a fast-food bag, a large coffee and a leather satchel. Vikram's suit coat was missing, his sleeves were rolled almost to his elbows, his tie was loosened.

"Uh-oh," Vikram said jovially. "Never good if people are waiting for you at eight thirty." Vikram was a magnificent criminal lawyer, a genius at technical arguments, and better yet, he was a delightful man, well-liked by every judge and every attorney in the circuit. "I heard you put a *W* on the board for us Friday. Jury-trial win to boot. Congratulations."

"Yeah. It was a glorious day for justice."

Vikram reached in the bag. "You want part of a biscuit? Hash browns?"

"No, thanks."

"So how did you set one of the Reliables free?"

Andy crossed his legs at the ankle and relaxed in his chair. The chair was located on a strip of duct tape, seven measured feet distant from Vikram. "When Officer Pruitt discovered him, my client, Porter, was passed out, slumped against a wall, an empty wine bottle close by. Those are easy facts for the defendant. Of course, in a BS, nuisance case, there're no fingerprints—not worth the time, expense and trouble. 'No forensic evidence,' you hammer to the jury. The poor cop had to admit scads of other people are always drinking in the county parking lot on Orchard Street, and they discard bottles and cans, and Porter was simply 'sleeping.' I asked the cop if he thought this arrest was a wise use of police resources and tax dollars, rousting a man resting in a public space, even a man who'd had a few beers and wasn't steady on his feet once he stood—the commonwealth objected, but the jury got the practical point and let the guilty go free."

"Well, it's still darn fine work." Vikram ate a hash brown. "I understand it went to Hades in a handbasket afterward, though."

"Yep. We wound up worse off than we started."

"Not your fault." Vikram sipped his coffee. "What can I do for you bright and early on a Monday morning?"

Andy cleared his throat. He glanced at a Kapil family photo on the wall. Licked his lips. "Sorry, Vik, sorry…but I've reached the end of the line. I'm resigning. I'm fed up and frustrated—this crap, day after day, isn't why I went to law school."

"How long has it been?" Vikram asked. "Time flies when you're having fun."

"Seventeen years." Andy sighed. "Seventeen." He scooted forward, balanced on the edge of the chair. "I think the world of you and the people here. I'm just worn out and tired of defending guilty, ungrateful, shiftless, recidivist losers, most of them spouting off how they're 'gonna hire a *real* lawyer.'"

"More money help?" Vikram asked. "I think the commission is about to authorize an additional two thousand a year for senior PDs."

"It's not a money issue," Andy said. "It's a self-worth issue. On the other side of the equation, it breaks my heart every time I have to defend *another* Black kid who neglected to get a receipt for his Dollar Tree deodorant."

"Can I change your mind?" Vikram pressed. He set the coffee cup on his desk. "There's no replacing you. And on a personal level, I'll miss you."

"I've decided." Andy leaned over, opened his briefcase, removed the resignation letter, and put it on Vikram's jumbled desk. "You're a remarkable lawyer, an excellent boss, and an even better friend. Sorry."

"When're you quitting?" Vikram asked. "The date?"

"I'd never leave you in a bind," Andy promised. "My letter gives thirty-days' notice, but it'd be great if I could be gone sooner. I want to take Noah on a Montana trip before he starts school. I bought him a fly rod for Christmas. If thirty days isn't enough, I'll take vacation time for the trip and then come back until the transition is finished."

"I'll see what I can do," Vikram said, the words weary and solemn. "How many cases are you carrying?"

"A hundred and seventy-seven. Most in Henry County and Martinsville, maybe thirty in Patrick County."

"So where're you planning to go?" Vikram asked. "What's next?"

"Good question," Andy said. "Jim Haskins offered me a job with them—an improved salary and a better class of criminal. I might land there. Who knows? I need a change—I'm positive about that much."

"Bring me a list of your cases, and I'll start divvying them up."

"Speaking of which," Andy said, "take a look at this." He reached into the briefcase again, located the Damian Bullins confession, and passed it to Vikram. "Read the first page."

Vikram took a pair of cheap half-glasses from his shirt pocket. "Oh, wait, wow," he said after studying the paper.

"Yeah," Andy responded. "We're scheduled for a guilty plea on Thursday, but this will definitely delay us. Bullins was charged on a pocket indictment, and these pages just trickled in along with some other insignificant items. I had a typewritten summary of his confession, and I reviewed it with him, and he confirmed it was correct, recalled the cop Mirandizing him and admitted to me he killed the lady. But, still, in a first-degree murder case, it's our responsibility to turn over every stone, challenge every detail."

"What's the commonwealth have?" Vikram asked. "How strong is their evidence? I know the big picture—this story was in the news for days."

"Well, they have Damian himself. He's from Patrick County, Ararat, poor and white and raised by his alcoholic aunt. But he's very smart. And I mean *very* smart, though now it's more of a slick, self-serving con's cunning. Years ago, he was the community's darling. People were so proud of him. He graduated number one in his class, earned a free ride to Duke—"

"His first mistake," Vikram joshed.

"Didn't even make it to Christmas—he was convicted of a gun charge in Durham and expelled. There were drug and alcohol issues as well."

"Shame," Vikram said sincerely. "Not making excuses for him, but college can be overwhelming for small-town kids."

"Of course, initially, everybody and his brother tried to salvage him. Wanted to help. There was Damian 2.0 and 3.0 and 7.0, until he was basically a write-off. He pissed away great jobs and amazing opportunities. He has a vicious temper, a fierce self-destructive bent, and a meth-and-pill monkey the size of King Kong. Last time I represented him, Judge Leventis reduced a malicious wounding charge to assault and battery and sentenced him to twelve months. Damian stabbed a total stranger in a drug-store parking lot, a fracas that started over a pack of Nabs."

"So you've represented him before?"

"More than once, Vik." Andy shifted in his chair. "And you know how we often say about our clients: 'When he's sober, after a few weeks in jail, he's a different person, a nice-enough guy?' How we can, if we dig deep enough, find a speck of humanity in many defendants? Well, Damian Bullins is a waste and an asshole no matter what. A loser, probably a clinical sociopath, with a record and a history that make murder seem like the next logical progression on his resume."

Vikram removed the glasses. "I'm assuming we won't have to sort through a lengthy list of character witnesses at sentencing." He smirked.

"The murder-case rule's simple: Did the deceased deserve killing, and did the right SOB do the job? Damian Bullins definitely wasn't the right man for the job, and the victim…the lady he killed…" Andy trailed off, shook his head. "He killed Alicia Benson. She—"

"Was married to Cole Benson," Vikram interrupted. "And what catnip for the press, huh? The African American wife of a devout, high-profile Mormon multimillionaire is murdered in her own home. Too many unicorns in that tale to count."

"Four children. Girls. Thank heavens they were all at a church event the day she was killed. Mrs. Benson volunteered at a hospice in Mt. Airy and also tutored kids who struggled with math."

"And the defendant confessed?" Vikram asked.

"Yep. That would be what I just handed you. Confessed and signed every page."

Vikram began tapping a pen against his palm. "What's left without the confession? What's the commonwealth have against him if we can persuade the court to exclude his statement?"

"Security camera shows him entering the Benson house and leaving approximately six minutes later. Her blood was found on his pants. Absolute DNA match."

"So you and I are on the same page, Andy," Vikram said, "we're certain he's guilty, correct?"

"As certain as we can ever be. He was there, he confessed, her blood is on his pants. He confirmed the confession to me."

"Motive?" Vikram narrowed his eyes. "Why?"

"According to Bullins's statement, Cole Benson had hired him several months ago to do odd jobs—he'd painted a fence, cleaned out a shed, cut firewood, basically rough-labor work. He'd been at the Benson property nine or ten times. The day of the murder, he was jacked on meth and gin, hadn't slept the night before, and he drove there planning to steal tools or a chainsaw, but for whatever reason, he went directly into the house, happened on Alicia Benson, and demanded cash or her jewelry. She refused. He became enraged."

Vikram sighed. "Meth is wicked bad. I miss the good old days of homegrown pot, moonshine and trucker speed."

"Bullins shoved her, she fell, he threatened her, she still wouldn't give him anything, and he kicked her in the belly." Andy folded his arms across his chest. He glanced at the Kapil family picture again. "Instead of complying, she offered to *pray* for him and invited him to join her. Livid and high, he snatched a kitchen knife from the table and cut her throat. She was wearing an apron and peeling yellow apples for a pie. An apple fell off the table and landed in her blood. The crime-scene pictures look like Satan-o-rama."

"Jeez," Vikram said. "But evidently, he didn't take anything or rape her—it's charged as first degree, not capital murder."

"Correct," Andy confirmed. "He freaked out and immediately bolted. Benson found his wife's body when he returned home from his office around four forty-five p.m. The police interviewed Damian at his aunt's an hour and fifteen minutes later. He lives in a camper in her yard.

Uses a garden hose for water, and he's rigged a section of wire from her box for power. A complete deadbeat. He confessed right then and there."

"Was he coherent?" Vikram asked.

"The cops say he was, his signatures on the waiver and confession are normal—the handwriting, I mean—and his statement makes perfect sense and is consistent with the physical evidence."

"The murder weapon?"

"The knife," Andy replied, "was left there in the kitchen. No fingerprints, but Damian *gripped* it as opposed to handling it. There's a partial palm print, but it's not enough for a forensic match, or so says the examiner at the state lab. No recoverable touch DNA on it either."

"So, we—"

"As a bonus," Andy remarked, "when asked why he became so angry, angry enough to slit a defenseless woman's throat, our client nobly replied he 'didn't need some rich house n-g-r pitying' him." Andy spelled out the letters from the slur.

Vikram winced, hesitated. "So, we have an entirely different world minus the confession. No motive, no direct evidence, no witnesses, and a purely circumstantial case."

"Indeed, we do," Andy agreed.

"You think the commonwealth's aware they might have a problem?"

"I seriously doubt it," Andy answered. "I'm leaving here and driving to Patrick County so I can interview the investigator who took the statement. You want to go with me?"

"Can't," Vikram said. "District court DUI case at ten."

＊＊＊

MELVIN ELLIS HAD WORKED seven years for the Atlanta police before leaving the big city and its big crime and moving to Patrick County. The sheriff hired him in late 2019 and quickly promoted him to investigator. His small office at the jail complex was tidy and impersonal, and his desk was empty except for a stapler, calendar, cardboard blotter, and a coffee mug full of pens and pencils. The mug was black and encircled with a thin blue line. A file with "D. Bullins" Sharpied in black block letters was lying on the blotter. Ellis sat ramrod erect in a caster chair, his hands in his lap, his white short-sleeve dress shirt impeccably ironed and unbuttoned at the neck. He was small and wiry, bald with a barbered fringe of red hair. His mask was a KN95, which caused him to appear beaked.

"Thanks for seeing me," Andy told him.

"Sure," Ellis said. "Nice to finally meet you in person." They'd twice spoken about Damian Bullins by phone. "'Preciate the mask respect. My uncle's on a ventilator."

"Best of luck to him," Andy replied. "Hope this infernal plague ends soon." He reached into a pocket. "You mind if I record our conversation?" he asked.

"Don't know why you'd feel the need to tape us," Ellis grumbled.

"As I mentioned in my text, I'm here to talk about Damian Bullins. It's a *major* murder case. Recording protects us both later on if there's any dispute over what I said or what you said. Nothing personal. Sheriff Smith will tell you it's routine with me."

"So I guess we're startin' things off not trusting each other."

"If you'd prefer, I can ask another officer or the sheriff to sit in with us. Again, no offense meant. My memory's not always perfect, plus I'm trying to keep tabs on around a hundred seventy-five cases."

"Whatever." Ellis was brusque. "You tape me and I'll tape you, just in case, you know, like you say, there's a problem. It could be hard to hear important answers, or you might *accidently* delete something." He located his cell phone, tapped it several times, and placed it on his desk. "We'll have two copies."

What a dick, Andy thought. "Fine with me, and I hope there're no hard feelings, Investigator. I realize my client confessed, but I need to make sure every *i* is dotted and every *t* is crossed." He was switching on a small digital recorder as he spoke.

"Okay."

Andy began a series of questions, mostly feints and misdirection, and his voice never changed, remained monotone. He intended to signal that the interview was nothing but a required, for-show, butt-covering formality. He took notes on a legal pad, often scribbling while asking the next question. He rarely looked up. Once, he grinned, this when Ellis mentioned how discombobulated a young deputy was as they approached Damian Bullins's camper.

"So my client opened the door to this camper?" Andy asked. They were ten minutes into the interview.

"Yes, he did."

"He invited you in?" Andy asked.

"Yeah, but we had a search warrant and an arrest warrant anyhow. I already told you this when we talked on the phone." Ellis took a brown rubber band from his desk drawer and stretched it longwise, then let it shrink. "We knocked, and he came to the door."

"And you took a statement from him there, correct? The statement that begins with his Miranda warnings and lasts for nine pages, dated May fifth, 2020?"

"Yes."

"Do you have the original of that statement?" Andy inquired.

"Yeah, of course." Ellis fiddled with the rubber band. "And there's the usual version the secretary typed up so it's easier to read. We sent you the typed format in mid-May."

"Do you mind if I borrow your original to use today? I left my file and my copy in Martinsville, only brought my legal pad."

Ellis sighed, and the exhale was theatrical and exaggerated. He slid nine stapled sheets toward Andy. "Here you go."

"Thanks. Sorry for the trouble." Andy leaned forward, took the papers. "This is the original?" he asked as he flipped through the pages. "Appears to be. Nine pages in your handwriting, question and answer, signed numerous times by the defendant."

"Yep."

"So," Andy continued, "you were invited in, and Mr. Bullins gave you a statement?"

"Affirmative," the officer said.

"How did that happen?" Andy kept his voice low and level. "The details?"

"Well, Officer Hubbard and me went in, and your client, this Bullins joker, sat on a sofa, and right off, he said, 'No need for all this shit; I'm ready to go.'"

"The sequence is: You walk in—as you were entitled to do—you place him under arrest, he says he's ready to go—"

Ellis interrupted. "And, *immediately*, Mr. Hughes, I read him his rights."

"Okay. And those were his exact words: 'No need for all this shit; I'm ready to go?'"

"Exact words." Ellis raised his voice. "Wrote 'em down in my report later that night. Officer Hubbard heard him too."

"And you quickly read him his Miranda warnings from the preprinted section at the beginning of the statement. The statement you just gave me."

"I did, sir. Word for word." Ellis stretched the rubber band and held it taut. "He signed the waiver of rights, and he signed the bottom of every single page when I was done writin' down what he told us. Nine pages, ten signatures. Practically an autograph session."

"Did—"

"And, Mr. Hughes," Ellis pushed ahead, "after he indicated he wanted to talk, I asked him to tell me what happened there at the Benson house, and your client, Mr. Bullins, told me, pretty as you please, like he was describin' a picnic at the lake, how he slit Mrs. Benson's throat. Used the N-word on her." He twisted the rubber band. "The man murdered her for no reason other than pure meanness, okay?"

Andy stopped writing. He locked on to Ellis. "I've read the statement, sir. Sometimes my job is unpleasant. But I'm certain you, an experienced officer, understand I have to do my very best for any client, Mr. Bullins included."

"And I reckon you understand I have a job to do for the dead lady who can't look after herself no more and the community this man has terrorized for years. We all have our jobs and responsibilities."

"I appreciate the reminder," Andy said, still making eye contact, drilling every syllable. "Just a few more questions, and we'll be through."

"If I wanted," the cop bristled, "we can be through right this second. I don't have to talk to you. You have my notes and the confession and everything you're legally entitled to."

"Your choice. You want me to leave? Say the word, Investigator."

They stared at each other. The room was silent. A robin flew past the window behind Ellis and fluttered onto a car's roof.

"Make it snappy."

Andy continued: "Did my client say anything else after he signed the confession?"

"Negative," Ellis replied the instant Andy finished speaking. "Oh, wait, he asked if he could take a leak before we left his little camper."

"And you didn't record the statement?" Andy pressed.

"No."

"Why?"

"You tryin' to claim I made a mistake copyin' down what he told me?" Ellis craned his neck. "Listen, Mr. Hughes, the statement I wrote out is exact, your client signed it, and Coy Hubbard heard every single thing we said. Deputy Hubbard was right there with me."

"Not what I asked you," Andy replied. He was looking at his pad again, writing.

"What did you ask me?" Ellis was still pitched forward.

"Why didn't you *record* my client?"

"No law says I have to," Ellis answered. "Deputy Hubbard heard the confession, and since the suspect was talkin' freely and confessin' to a murder, I didn't think it'd be very smart to tell him to stop and be quiet while I pulled out a phone to record him and maybe spook him and shut him down from tellin' us what happened. Hope that makes sense."

"Fair enough," Andy said. "Makes sense." He pushed the statement to the cop's side of the desk.

"Bottom line is Mr. Bullins cut an innocent woman's throat." Ellis sat normally, reeled in his neck and shoulders. He returned the statement to his file.

Andy stood. "Appreciate your time." He offered a fist to bump, but the investigator remained motionless in his chair, cool and miffed. "Can't," he said smugly. "Corona."

As he was cranking his Jeep, Andy spotted Deputy Coy Hubbard driving into the jail parking lot. A Meadows of Dan farmboy, Hubbard was as patient as he was strong, and he was honest, deliberate and good-natured—an excellent policeman. Andy waved at him, switched off the ignition, and walked toward the cop's brown cruiser.

"Hey, Andy," Hubbard greeted him. "Mornin' to you." They met near the main entrance and shook hands, their arms fully extended, heads offset. Hubbard's hand was huge and rough, and a fingernail was partially missing, the damaged skin blackish-red underneath the jagged remainder.

"Morning to you, Coy. Glad I ran into you. Dispatcher said you were taking the day off."

"Storm last night tore down a poplar on my fence. My cows were loose. I planned to repair it and chase 'em back this mornin', but when I got there, my dad and my neighbors had already rounded 'em up 'cept for one stubborn heifer, so it didn't take the bunch of us no time to finish. I decided to come on in."

"Well, I'm pleased to hear everything's fixed and your cows are home. How in the world do you ever make any money farming? Seems to me it's nothing but expense and aggravation."

Hubbard laughed. "My wife keeps askin' me the same question."

"You have a few minutes to talk?"

"Yes, sir. Happy to. But how 'bout we get out of the sun and heat? You wanna come inside?"

"Won't take that long," Andy assured him. "Over there be okay?" He pointed at the shade underneath the canopied sally port doors.

"I'm assumin' you're here about Mr. Bullins some more," Hubbard volunteered as they walked side by side but several feet apart. This was their fourth time discussing the case.

"Yep," Andy replied. He didn't bother recording their conversation—they'd worked together for years, and he could count on Hubbard to always tell the truth, no matter whom it might benefit.

"What can I do for you?" Hubbard asked.

"When we first talked, you mentioned that you were there with Investigator Ellis the entire time at Bullins's camper."

"Yes, sir. I was." They'd reached the shade. Hubbard wiped his forehead with a red bandana handkerchief. "Heavens to Betsy, it's hot."

Andy was also sweating, his shirt turning damp across his belly. "I forgot to ask last time I interviewed you: Did you notice the blood on my client's pants?" The topic was more ruse and camouflage, intended to obscure the money question that would come later.

"Yeah, I did."

"One leg or both?" Andy asked.

"Both," Hubbard said.

"How high did the splatter go on the pants?"

Hubbard squeezed his eyes shut. Knotted his lips. "Not past his knees on either side. It wasn't much, but you could definitely see it."

"Let me backtrack just a bit. Sorry. Investigator Ellis said Bullins invited you in, then you guys began to serve the arrest warrant—"

"Like I told you before, he didn't make no fuss," Hubbard interjected. "Strange for Damian to be so cooperative. He's usually itchin' for a fight."

"Who physically cuffed him?"

"Me," Hubbard replied. "Honestly, everybody was on guard, and I just wanted to get him under control as fast as we could."

"Okay," Andy continued. "I understand Bullins told you he was submitting to the arrest—"

"That ain't precisely how he put it, but yeah." Hubbard adjusted his utility belt. "You know how he can be."

"Better than most," Andy said. "And then, immediately, while you're still making the arrest, Investigator Ellis Mirandized him."

"Correct."

"So you saw the blood on the pants as soon as you laid hands on Bullins."

Hubbard thought for a moment. "Pretty much. Yeah."

"Then while Ellis reads him his rights, you're cuffing him, patting him down, checking for weapons, focusing on the arrest process, concerned because it's Damian Bullins, and he's a suspect in a violent murder?"

"Yes."

Andy paused. He touched his cheek with his index finger. Debated whether to ask a few more questions and risk an unhelpful answer. "Had... uh...can you tell me the *exact* sequence? What Ellis was doing and what you were doing, how you guys matched up?"

Hubbard's expression became serious. He realized that somewhere in all the smoke and mirrors and thicket of questions there was a lawyer trap, but he was an honest cop, and he'd learned long ago the best answer was always the stone-solid truth, that fudging and trying to outfox attorneys never went well. He swatted at a yellow jacket, missed. "I remember I'd started searchin' Bullins when Investigator Ellis began readin' the rights. Ellis actually said, 'I'm gonna read you your Miranda rights,' and I seen he had a folder that he carried his papers and so forth in, but once he started readin', I was more worried about dealin' with The Bull than I was anything else. I was payin' full attention to the dangerous guy I was arrestin'. So I'm not positive about the specific times down to the second, but I'm positive Damian confessed. He owned up to it. I stood right there while he told us how he killed the poor Benson lady." Hubbard swung at the yellow jacket again. "Damn bee."

"Thanks, Coy. Appreciate the time."

"Sure." The officer abruptly stepped left and looked past Andy. "Don't know what in the world we're gonna do 'bout him," he remarked. Patches the dog had appeared from behind the jail and was lapping water from a silver bowl. Hubbard walked closer to the building, knelt, and dipped a finger in the water. "Already too warm. Need to refill it." He dumped the water and stood.

"No one here wants him?" Andy asked. "I heard he was recently orphaned."

"He don't want none of *us*," Hubbard answered. "Claude Baliles carried him home, and the crazy rascal left and come straight back here. Four-point-six miles. I measured it myself. Claude was worried to death, searched and called for the dog all night, and the next mornin' here's Patches, strolling down Commerce Street and barkin' when he got to the jail's door."

Andy laughed. "Well, you guys were a constant source of aggravation for his beloved master. He probably figured Claude for the enemy."

"In that case, Andy," Hubbard declared, "you oughta take him home with you. You and his daddy were best buds." He smiled. "I'm serious. Maybe you could adopt him. He's smart as a whip. You ever seen him do his tricks?"

"I have. He's impressive. We're old pals. I've probably invested fifty bucks in his dog-and-no-pony show over the years, and I've visited with him—a lot—while Zeb was waiting to sign paperwork after one of his trials ended." He whistled and the dog trotted to him. "A few months ago, I gave Patches a ride here, to the jail—remember when he was limping and dragging his leg? Unfortunately, though, it's not a great time for me right now. A new dog doesn't fit my circumstances, sorry to say." He petted Patches and repeated "good boy" in a friendly, singsong voice. "I miss having a pup around. It's been close to a year since Rufus died."

"Sheriff's gettin' impatient. Can't blame him. We ain't the pound, and I suppose there's all grades of complications and liability and whatnot if he bit someone."

"Oh, one last question, Coy, please."

"Is this the loaded one?" Hubbard asked amiably. "The reason why you truly come today?"

"I'll let you decide. I'm interested in your opinion—what do you make of Investigator Ellis? I just met him for the first time."

"Hmmm." Hubbard kicked at the pavement with the toe of his shiny cop shoe. "He's a different-natured fellow. Has his own style. Let's leave it there."

"Thanks." Andy tugged his damp shirt away from his belly. He crouched and said goodbye to the dog. "Stay out of the highway," he warned the mutt.

The Jeep's interior was blazing hot, and Andy dialed the fan to its highest speed. He slipped on sunglasses. He tuned the radio to the Sirius jazz channel, the real article, not the squishy spa junk, and he was clicking on his safety belts when he heard Coy Hubbard shout his name, and he checked the rear-view mirror, and the officer was running full tilt, waving his hands, and he was chasing Patches, who was hell-bent for the vehicle. The dog ended his frantic dash near the Jeep's front tire and plopped onto his haunches, then looked up with his mismatched eyes, his tongue in a Gatling-gun pant.

Hubbard slowed to a walk. "Come on, man," he said to Andy. "Even a heartless lawyer like you can't leave him behind now. Seriously."

Andy considered the dog, who sat there steadfast. He had no tail, only a nub, and his blue eye was encircled by black fur. "So this is the deal, Coy,"

Andy said. He turned off the engine. "I don't need to worry about him hitting the road and trying to make it back here—it's a heck of a lot farther than four-point-six miles from my house. I'll take him, but first, you and I are going to allow him to tour the jail complex and every cell and office and closet and room and shower and toilet in there, so maybe we can convince him Zeb's not around."

"Say what?"

"You heard me," Andy insisted. "We'll go together, you and I."

"We're holdin' almost two hundred inmates—"

"I'm sure Patches is familiar with many of them," Andy interrupted. "It'll be like Old Home Week."

"And I ain't comfortable just bustin' in to other people's private offices," Hubbard complained.

"Perhaps we could ask the magistrate for a search warrant."

"Sheriff's car's gone," Hubbard mused. "I'll have to see if Lieutenant Craddock will approve it."

"Well, Coy, I'm betting he won't," Andy said. "Me, I'd make the call myself. You're a shift supervisor with twenty years of service."

"But like you was sayin', Andy, a man would probably starve if farmin' was his only income. His wife and kids would go hungry too."

CHAPTER THREE

DURING THE LATE 1990S, when the textile mills shuttered and the Patrick and Henry County economies evaporated, the region's unemployment hit twenty percent, forty-hour workweeks vanished, and Trade Act classes at the community college became the rinky-dink consolation prize for the fired, the furloughed and the laid-off. People left the area in droves, main streets turned hollow and makeshift—a doodad "emporium" here, a Curves franchise there—and high-flying hustlers promised to build seven-figure grants into business juggernauts with hundreds of quality jobs, then ripped off desperately gullible local governments and disappeared, precious birthrights traded for a mess of pottage. Real estate values declined, tax liens piled up in the clerk's offices, and small-print foreclosure notices filled the classified ads.

In 2004, Andy Hughes purchased a modest brick rancher—fourteen hundred square feet—on a gravel road in Henry County, three miles off Route 58 and not far from the Patrick County line. The house was surrounded by an unruly yard and seven acres of hardwoods. List price was one hundred and six thousand. Andy offered ninety. The seller, the son of a deceased couple who'd lived there for decades, didn't bargain or dicker; he instructed the realtor to draw a contract and get a signature as quickly as possible.

The former owners had survived into their eighties on Social Security benefits and a meager DuPont pension, so the house was dated and obsolete and full of jerry-builds, leaks and shoddy repairs, but none of the failings concerned Andy. He'd grown up in Rhinelander, Wisconsin, his family full of carpenters, plumbers and masons, his dad a master electrician, and he might not be as superbly talented as the rest of his kin, but he could revive the place himself and do a dandy-fine job of it. Better yet, saws, hammers, pry bars, drills, chisels, nails, plywood and lumber were a wonderful cure for the public-defender woes that often ailed him. By 2009, the house, while Old-Dutch-brick commonplace on the outside, was a craftsman's marvel once you stepped through the door, so much so that the gang from his office gushed and oohed and aahed when they visited for a Christmas party. "Amazing," Vikram complimented him. "Well done."

Andy drove directly home from the sheriff's office, Patches riding shotgun beside him, the windows cracked although the air conditioner was dialed to high. Andy parked the Jeep, and the dog scrambled out behind him on the driver's side, circled and sniffed and wet an azalea bush, leg cocked high and proud, then returned to where his new owner was waiting for him in the grass.

"Come on," Andy encouraged him. "Let's see how you like it here." The dog followed him to the kitchen, where he filled a silver metal bowl with Ol' Roy kibble, both the bowl and the cheap food donations from Coy Hubbard. The dog wasn't interested in eating.

Andy phoned his office and told Cindy, the public defender's sole administrative assistant, he'd be working from home for the remainder of the day. He changed clothes, dressed in shorts, a Fela Kuti T-shirt and flip flops. He and Patches sat on the screened-in porch while blue jays, cardinals, nuthatches and finches swooped and tussled at the bird feeder. Two fans, one above on the ceiling, the other an ancient oscillating table model, kept them in a crosscut breeze. Andy opened Lexis on his laptop and began searching United States Supreme Court cases. He sent *Dickerson v. United States* to the printer in the den. Next, he located a Virginia case, *Timbers v. Commonwealth*, and printed it as well. "Money in the bank," he informed Patches.

At eleven o'clock, he quarter-folded a quilt and situated it in the corner of his bedroom, introduced the dog to his new pallet, then walked with him outside for fifteen minutes before Patches finally decided on a spot a few yards inside the wood line. Andy praised him, especially pleased that the dog had avoided the yard proper. The mutt back-kicked dirt and dead leaves and trotted for the house.

Patches wouldn't rest, wouldn't stay still, wouldn't lie on the quilt or the floor, and he paced ceaselessly, his toenails unhappy Morse code on the hardwood. He wasn't hungry, wasn't thirsty, wasn't whining—he simply refused to quit roaming around the room. "What?" Andy asked him at midnight, exasperated. He locked the dog in the den, but within minutes he heard pawing and scratching and a brief, sharp yelp, and he returned and discovered his new pet assaulting a custom-made hickory threshold, trying to dig an escape from the den onto the porch. "Ah…okay," he said. "You're not a house guy, is that the problem?"

He relocated the quilt, and Patches joined him on the porch, content now, sprawled on his side, his eyelids soon droopy, his front legs twitching when he finally fell deep asleep. Andy relaxed in a chaise longue, mindful and patient, planning to tiptoe back inside once the dog was for sure over his insomnia spell. An owl and symphonic bugs and the tree frogs from a tiny creek at the property's corner kept him company, and he watched a ribbon of cloud glide toward the moon, and…

He woke suddenly, groggy and startled, still in the chaise longue, still on the porch, just in time to see Patches hightail through the torn screen and flee into the dark. A flashlight hunt, calling, yelling, cajoling, whistling, clapping, rattling Ol' Roy in the metal bowl, a road search in both directions, none of it did a lick of good, and at three thirty in the morning, Andy surrendered, telephoned the sheriff's department, and asked them to be on the lookout for Patches. "Oh, no," the dispatcher said. "He's such a sweet boy."

He was still missing at sunrise. Andy was worried sick, skipped breakfast because he had no appetite. He called WHEO radio and asked them to include Patches on the Pet Patrol program, and he left word on his closest neighbor's answering machine. There was no sign of the lost dog along Route 58 as Andy drove—slower than normal—to meet with Damian Bullins at the jail.

● ● ●

BULLINS WAS DRESSED IN a baggy orange jumpsuit, white socks and orange slides. The jumpsuit was unbuttoned to his sternum. He was unshaven and chalky, his dark hair limp, and his several tattoos seemed faint, the ink somehow dulled by the coarse air and harsh fluorescent lights. He was double chained, restrained at his wrists and ankles, waiting at a small wooden table with a slick spot worn in its center, cardboard tucked under a short leg.

"I'm glad you're here," he said, the moment Andy entered the interview room. "Man, I'm gettin' no kinda medical care. None. I still haven't been to the doctor, and there's the growth on my side they found last time I was locked up, and I need to have it looked at. And I'm still sufferin' from trying to wean off meth by myself. I'm entitled to medicine. Valium or somethin'."

Andy bit his tongue. "Okay," was all he said. Inmates like Bullins, the benzo poachers, wanted to stay buzzed and blurred, same as they did while drifting through the community, and they found new pains and complaints almost every day in hopes of finagling a pill prescription from the jail's infirmary.

"Yeah. It's not fair how I'm bein' treated." He shook his head, dismayed.

"Well, Damian, we have bigger fish to fry. I have some information for you."

Bullins moved closer. The handcuff chain scraped against the table. "Okay. What?"

"The investigator made a mistake when he read your Miranda warnings."

"How?" Bullins's hands were stacked so that the BLUE in his BLUE DEVIL knuckle tat was visible. "How'd he make a mistake?"

Andy opened his file, laid the confession on the table. "I want you to listen to me, Damian, and keep your mouth shut. Am I clear? Just sit there and be quiet. If I need to know something I'll ask you."

"I knew the investigator was—"

"Already, Damian, you've violated the rule. Shut your mouth for once, please."

"Sorry, Mr. Hughes. I understand." He raised his manacled hands and pulled an imaginary zipper across his lips.

"I didn't want to talk with you until I'd interviewed the cops involved and done the legal research, and this is where we are: For whatever reason, there's a critical omission in the rights warning printed on the first page of the statement—the warnings Investigator Ellis read to you."

"Well, he read me my rights. You've asked me 'bout that."

Andy pointed a pen at Bullins. "Last reminder. Please listen and don't talk. You have a tendency to shoot yourself in the foot."

"Gotcha."

"Here's what Investigator Ellis read to you from his preprinted form: *Anything you say may be used against you as evidence in a court of law. You have the right to consult an attorney before speaking to the police and to have an attorney present during questioning now or in the future. If you cannot afford an attorney, one will be appointed for you at no cost to you. Do you understand these rights?*"

"Okay," Bullins mumbled, and it was barely audible.

"For some reason, Damian, the first and most important Constitutional protection isn't listed and wasn't read to you: You have the right to remain silent."

Bullins didn't respond. He fidgeted with his sleeve.

"I plan to speak with Mrs. Katt, the commonwealth's attorney, and I hope we can use this as leverage to reduce your punishment."

Bullins clumsily raised a hand.

"Okay, what?"

"If they screwed up my rights, then the case goes away, doesn't it? It's dismissed. I beat the charge."

"Nope," Andy said emphatically. "If we can win on a motion to suppress—and I think we can—then your *statement* is excluded from the commonwealth's case. The rights error isn't like a lottery ticket or a magic *Monopoly* card. The commonwealth can still rely on all its other evidence, but things change without your confession. They still have strong circumstantial evidence, enough for you to be convicted, but this is a complication for the prosecution."

Bullins began to speak and Andy talked over him: "Hope you feel better soon."

"Yeah. The first day I was here, I was pukin', which they still aren't doin' anything about, my sickness. Addiction is a disease, Mr. Hughes, same as the flu or cancer. I'm entitled to medicine and treatment. Valium or Xanax."

39

Andy ignored the bleating. "Don't breathe a word of this. Keep your mouth shut, and I'll be in touch after I meet with Mrs. Katt."

There was a knock on the door behind Andy—three loud, rapid bangs—and a deputy peeked in and apologized for interrupting. "His aunt's here with the readin' glasses that were such a big *emergency*. Sheriff said since we already got him outta population she can have five minutes of visitation when your legal meetin' is done. She was sick and missed seein' him on Sunday."

"We're finished," Andy declared.

"Hey, Aunt Connie," Damian chirped, and a stooped, wizened woman with a cane, a bald spot and a flesh-tone hearing aid hobbled into the room.

"Hey, Sweetie," she said. The cop closed the door and was gone. "I brung your glasses so you won't be blind no more." The booze smell steamrollered off her.

Damian tilted forward and grasped Andy's wrist. "Mr. Hughes, thank you," he said. "Thanks from the bottom of my heart." He tried his best to sound contrite. "I did what I did, and I'm guilty, I killed her, but it was the drugs and my addiction hurtin' Mrs. Benson, not me. Not the real me. You're a good Christian man to fight so hard for me."

"I doubt many people would share that opinion, Damian."

***

STEPHANIE KATT WAS A smart, talented and methodical prosecutor, nicknamed Amarillo Katt because she had the best poker face in the biz. Andy didn't make an appointment with her to discuss the Miranda-warnings mistake, instead just dropped by her office after leaving the jail and Damian Bullins. He discovered she was running a bank errand and was due back soon. He sat in the lobby and, while he waited, phoned both the dispatch center and animal control and inquired about Patches. There was no news. He posted an alert on his rarely used Facebook page and tagged several friends.

"Ah, Andy," Katt greeted him as she came through the entrance five minutes later. "Perfect timing. I need to speak with you, if you have a few seconds. I was planning to call. The Bullins case."

"Well, that's exactly why I'm here," he said. "Appreciate your seeing me."

He followed her down the hall to her office, and she closed the door and took a seat across from him on the visitors' side of the desk. She smoothed her blouse. "Sorry to hit you with this so late," she said, "but I think we may have a conflict."

"A conflict?" Andy repeated, surprised.

"Seems Doug Reilly's sister-in-law works for Cole Benson. She's the office manager—in other words, it's not an insignificant connection. I only heard about it over the weekend. Apologies. Doug just found out. His wife despises her brother and has nothing to do with him."

"Happens. Small world in these parts."

Katt's phone rang, and she waited for it to stop. "No matter how objectively and fairly we treat Damian Bullins, the day will come that *always* comes with these defendants. Always. No matter how many times they agree to plead guilty, no matter how completely guilty they are, and no matter how thoroughly the judge explains every tiny detail, usually the ink's not dry on the sentencing order before they're complaining and filing appeals, or asking for a rehearing, or jailhouse lawyering every perceived loophole you can imagine. This is a blockbuster murder, Damian's a pro, and I need everything to be as clean as possible. Even with a guilty plea and a confession, we both know this case will spend years bouncing around the appeals courts. A week after Damian's convicted, he'll be the king of frivolous excuses and swearing he's innocent."

"Yep," Andy said. "Prisoners become especially disenchanted when the years begin to register as years and not simply numbers on a piece of paper—eventually most want a mulligan. But two things come to mind...." He hesitated, flipped his hands palms up. "I was *about* to say we've discussed an open plea to second degree—and thanks again for not demanding murder one—so the judge would handle the sentencing, and your involvement would be minimal. Plus, we can always waive any potential conflict, and this is a stretch, pretty remote—the alienated sister-in-law of an assistant commonwealth's attorney on your staff is employed by the victim's husband."

"Appreciate the waiver offer," Katt said, "but then we open a can of worms and spotlight an appeal issue for Damian. And, ethically speaking, it's not that remote. I don't need a bar complaint, and Damian is just the kind of lowlife opportunist who'd sic them on me."

Andy steepled his fingers under his chin. "Well, Stephanie, I'm afraid I have a late-breaking complication as well. Have you checked the statement *closely*—not the typewritten version, but the original pages that contain the Miranda warnings? Especially the Miranda warnings."

"I haven't. No reason to. I interviewed Investigator Ellis, and he said your client was read his rights and was eager to talk. Coy Hubbard confirmed those facts. I reviewed the typewritten version. Very first line tells us: *The defendant was informed of his Constitutional rights.* You and I agreed to a plea, and there were no motions to suppress or objections regarding the legality of Damian's confession…or anything else, Andy."

Andy pulled his hands apart. "I hate to raise this now, but I only received a copy of Ellis's handwritten questions and answers and the actual Miranda warnings last Friday. As a precaution, a few weeks ago, I emailed Doug about getting a copy of the original. Not sure why it was so late in coming—"

"It was late," Katt said firmly, "because Investigator Ellis brought it to us late, along with three meaningless photos, a lab report on a random shotgun shell, and a second interview with Damian's pitiful aunt, who didn't see him come or go. Doug immediately gave you all of it. He looked over the original confession, and Damian's answers matched what we'd already seen." Her expression never changed, remained impenetrable. "Since you passed basic Criminal Procedure at William and Mary, I'm certain you quizzed your guilty client about admitting to the murder, and he confirmed Officer Ellis read him his rights."

"I'm not allowed to share my conversations with Mr. Bullins," Andy replied. He hinted at a smile. "I learned that rule in my William and Mary attorney-client-privilege training. You know I'm not suggesting you did anything intentional or underhanded." He gave her the statement. "See for yourself, Stephanie."

She studied the first page, then rolled the papers into a tube. "Interesting," she said cryptically.

"We both understand this is important. I *have* to file a motion to suppress. If you lose the confession, then your case is no longer a slam-dunk.

You have no obvious motive, no direct evidence, and some blood splatter on the defendant's pants. Her husband had even *more* blood on him—"

"Yeah, because he knelt hoping to help his murdered wife, then cradled her body while he wept and prayed to God."

"Just saying." Andy shrugged. "A jury won't learn about Damian's past and dreadful, violent record unless he's found guilty. Far as they'll know, he was a guy Cole Benson trusted enough to hire and bring to his property."

Katt unrolled the confession and returned it. Andy noticed her bracelet, crowded with charms celebrating her kids and family. "Damian walks in the Benson home, doesn't knock, has no reason to be there, no invitation or work project, then he hurries out minutes later with her blood on his pants. They're the only two people in the house, and she's dead. He's going to suggest *what* as a defense? She cut her own throat? Aliens? A vampire? The Invisible Man?"

"Motive, Stephanie? Why'd he do it? You'll lose his gin-and-meth admission. The jury won't know he was crazed on a Schedule Two. That's a big hit for the commonwealth."

"I'm confident they'll have all the explanation they need once they see the pictures of the bloodbath he left in the kitchen."

"Never know," Andy replied. "But at a minimum, we certainly have legit, impactful issues we didn't have last week."

"True," she agreed. "Which brings us to where we started. I'm going to withdraw and let the court appoint a special prosecutor. Especially with this wrinkle. This isn't simply a guilty plea any longer. I'm sure the confession will become a bargaining chip, and we might even end up trying the case."

"Damn, I wish you wouldn't. Can I change your mind?"

"I wish I didn't have to," Katt said, her voice and expression impassive.

"At least please find us a quality replacement," Andy urged her. "Dawn Futrell? Cliff Hapgood? I can work with Brett Nester."

"The problem, Andy, is there aren't a lot of volunteers for the gig. My colleagues aren't waiting in line behind the velvet rope, eager to take on a nasty murder case in addition to their own busy dockets. Pete Morley owes me a favor. We were law-school classmates, and I did a manslaughter case for him in 2017. I'll ask him."

"Peter-frigging-Morley? Seriously, Stephanie? Come on?"

"Seriously," she said.

"Thanks," Andy groused. "No need to waste time; might as well dive straight to the bottom of the barrel."

❈❈❈

LATER, AFTER A PLATE lunch at Checkered Pig, Andy tried a misdemeanor case in Henry County General District Court, then went to his office to meet with a series of clients, nine appointments scheduled over two hours. Probably three people would actually appear, and at least one of them would be so high that the conversation would be a waste of time, jibber-jabber and non sequiturs.

At four o'clock, following the expected streak of no-shows, Andy interviewed his first defendant, a timid young girl, Hannah, who, coached and prodded by her shiftless, felon "boyfriend," had embezzled cash from Food Lion, every penny of which she'd handed over to her Romeo. She was a shy, awkward eighteen-year-old, an honors student, only nine days an adult when she stole, and this had been her first-ever romance. She and her parents arrived on time, all three Sunday-best dressed, and Andy was touched by her story, and he vowed—his voice sincere, reassuring—he'd battle to keep her record clean and see that she received a second chance. She and her mom wept, and Andy accompanied them to the exit, gave them his cell number, encouraged them not to fret, and reminded them to begin saving a few dollars so they'd have restitution for the grocery store.

"You're still a big softie, Andy," Cindy said from the front desk. "We'll really miss you."

"Ah, word travels fast," he said, staring out the door, watching the family walk to their dinged minivan, the mom and daughter holding hands. "Poor girl. Why is it the most likable kids usually wind up with the short end of the judicial stick?"

"She's lucky she landed with you." Cindy held a pink phone message in his direction. "You know a Jerry Fain? He called, said he thinks he has your dog." She squinted at him. "I didn't realize you had a dog. I thought Rufus died."

44

"Oh, great, thank goodness. Jerry lives on my road, about a mile away as the crow flies. Nice guy. I *had* a dog—for less than a day—before he ran off last night. I posted a piece on Facebook and tagged everyone here—you didn't see it?"

"I haven't even had a chance to open the mail yet," she replied. "And I quit lookin' at Facebook months ago. It brings out the worst in the worst people. It's nothing but a bunch of loudmouths who can't spell 'cat' and have no manners and too much free time." She handed him the message.

Andy phoned immediately, standing there in the reception area, and Jerry Fain answered, jolly as always. "I hear you lost a dog," Fain declared as soon as he recognized Andy's voice.

"I did. Blue heeler mix."

"Well, I think he's here vacationing with us," Fain said. "He was in the pasture this morning, havin' a go at my donkeys, chasin' 'em and nippin' and barkin'. Heard he was missin' on the radio."

"Oh, Jerry, man, I'm sorry. His owner died, and he was hanging around the jail in Stuart, so I adopted him. The scoundrel tore out my porch screen in the middle of the night and went wandering. I hope he didn't hurt your animals."

"Nah, they had him outnumbered, and they were just playin', having fun as best I could tell. They're buddy-buddy now, nappin' in the shade together."

"I'll be there no later than six," Andy assured him. "I hate to ask, but do you think you could tie him or trap him in a stall so he doesn't go AWOL again? I'd appreciate it."

No other clients came to discuss their cases, so Andy collected Patches a few minutes after five thirty. The dog recognized him and barked and spun an ecstatic circle and shot to the end of his baling-twine tether. Andy thanked his neighbor, apologized for the trouble, and loaded Patches into the Jeep. The dog had a clear conscience about his travels, seemed unburdened, and as they left the Fain driveway, he almost knocked the Wrangler out of gear when he lunged to lick Andy's face and tried to worm and wiggle into the driver's seat beside him. He stank terribly because he'd rolled and frolicked in donkey shit, and there was a dried black smear on his side, but dry or not, some of the manure rubbed off on Andy's white dress shirt, another aggravation.

CHAPTER FOUR

THE MORNING WAS GRAY and damp when Andy arrived at his office on July 22, a scrubbed Patches leashed and obedient, cordial with every human he met, a friend to all. As man and dog were making their way to the breakroom's coffee pot, Curtis Matthews turned a corner in a rush, a file in one hand, a necktie in the other, a yellow stain on his shirt, his blazer missing a gold filigreed front button.

"I'll be damned," Curtis exclaimed. "Is that Patches, the Canine Prince of Patrick County?" He stopped, briefly petted the dog. "Here, hold my file," he instructed Andy.

"Certainly, Boy Wonder. Will you require the Batmobile as well?"

Curtis began a hasty Windsor knot that finished with the tie out of whack, the narrow end three inches past the wide end. "Close enough," he announced. "Late for a bond hearing. Most hick lawyers receive a goat or chickens or sourwood honey or maybe a bushel of corn for payment. How'd you score a Reliable's savant pup?"

"His owner died," Andy answered.

"Huh," Curtis replied, taking the file from Andy. "Hadn't heard about Zeb. Not crazy surprising, though. Last time I represented him, the poor sap was riding the opioid train—rare for his gang. They're usually just hall-of-fame alcoholics." He adjusted the slapdash knot. "Catch you later, Andy," he said as he was leaving. "We'll discuss why you can't resign."

"Hey, Curtis." Andy raised his voice. "See if your cousin who works for Fulton Brothers will bring his mini-excavator and dig a trench for me. I need a dog fence, the electric variety. So far, my free pet is in line to cost me around five hundred bucks, not to mention the lost sleep and today's babysitting responsibilities."

"Consider it done, *amigo*," Curtis said over his shoulder, almost at the exit.

A few minutes later, Andy was drinking black coffee at his desk and answering emails, and his phone buzzed, and Cindy informed him, her voice hushed, that a woman was waiting in the lobby and wanted to see him about the Bullins case. "It's his girlfriend," she whispered.

"Okay," Andy replied. "Bring her back, but remind her I have to be in court at nine-forty-five."

"Warning," Cindy said, continuing to whisper. "Live wire."

Misty Dawn Pack was hardscrabble bony, inked on both arms, her front tooth chipped. She wore a black bra underneath a thin pink tank top. Her jeans were soiled and threadbare in the knees. She plowed through the door, flopped down in a chair without any kind of introduction or greeting or small talk, and started her torrential spiel, anxious and high-strung. Behind her, Cindy mimicked a needle injection and mouthed "crazy."

"So, Mr. Hughes," she said, her sandals in the seat, her arms encircling her shins, "I'm Damian's fiancée, and I really, really, *really* need to tell you some important information which you don't know. About Damian, who's a good man. Very important, but you ain't heard none of it yet."

"Well, I'm eager to learn anything that might benefit my client." Andy was calm, polite. He'd seen this show before.

"There's more to the case than people are seein'."

"What do you want to tell me?" Andy flipped pages in a legal pad until he found a clean sheet. He took a ballpoint from his drawer. "I'm ready."

"Damian ain't the man people think he is. He's changed. Before all this, he was goin' to his drug classes and meetin' his probation officer regular, like he was supposed to. He was a great daddy to my kids, Montana and Harley. We call Harley 'Peanut.' He misses Damian so much. His own dad is in the penitentiary. It's gonna destroy him if we lose Damian. He already has special classes at school, and…yeah…that's something else I need a lawyer to look into, the—"

Andy cut her off. "If you're willing, and if we get to that point, I might call you as a witness to help Damian with sentencing. Can't do much for Peanut. Sorry. I only practice criminal law."

"I don't think Damian's guilty, Mr. Hughes. I think he's a fall guy. I know him better than anybody. I love him, and he loves me. He was workin' steady, helpin' me pay the bills. This is not even possible for him. Trust me. He couldn't kill this lady. Could not. He was not usin' no drugs! I'll take a hundred lie-detector tests. He's been clean for months. Both of us have."

"Do you have any specific evidence or facts or information?" Andy was patient. His tone was pleasant and professional. "I appreciate your opinion and your vouching for Damian, but we need facts for court."

She balled herself tighter in the chair. "Just what's in my heart," she said defiantly. "I know Damian Bullins better than anybody in the world, and I'm positive he didn't do this. Why ain't those facts?"

Andy dropped the pen on the pad, and it rolled off onto the desktop. "Ma'am," he said softly, "how long have you known Damian?"

Pack unwound herself and finally put her feet on the floor. "Goin' on eleven months. I—" Suddenly, her head jerked toward the wall. Her eyes popped wide. "Whoa, is that a dog?"

"Uh, yes." Patches was curled nose to tail beside a plant stand, where he'd been since Pack barreled in and started her ramble.

"Like a guard dog or protection?" she asked. "Where'd he come from?"

"A pet. He's harmless. He's been right there for a while."

"Yeah, okay. Cool. I'm just tore out of the frame over this murder charge against Damian. Can't keep my mind focused like I should."

"Ms. Pack," Andy said sympathetically, "I've known Damian Bullins for over *ten years*, and I say this with all due respect: Damian is exactly the type of person who'd commit this crime, and his prior conduct and convictions prove he's quite capable of violence. It might be beneficial for you to learn—and this is public record—that a meth-paranoid Damian beat a lady named Gayle Adkins black and blue and served jail time because of it. She was his 'fiancée' in 2016, and sadly, at his sentencing, she took an oath and testified he was a changed man and an irreplaceable father-figure to her son. She begged the judge to go easy on him. Sound familiar?"

"So how's it justice to keep draggin' up a person's past?" Pack snarled. "Can't nobody ever pay their debt?" She shook her head, angry. "Seems like you done made up your mind Damian's guilty, and you ain't doin' squat for him. A typical PD. It ain't for 'public defender,' it's initials for 'prison deliverer.'"

"Ms. Pack, my job is to do the best I can for my client. I wish I had better facts and evidence, but I don't. The commonwealth has a strong case against Damian."

"Here's somethin' else I'm sure you don't know. The first Sunday I went to visit him at the jail, he told me there was more to this than the police were revealin', more than people was aware of, so I think there are secrets or hidden truth which you aren't discoverin'."

"Did he tell you exactly what this huge secret is?"

"No, he couldn't," she said.

"Couldn't?" Andy paused. "Maybe, and this often happens, he simply hoped to save face with his girlfriend. Who wants to confess to a loved one that 'hey, I sliced an innocent mom's throat and took her life because I was high on drugs?' Usually the there's-more-to-it deflections involve a mysterious 'they' or 'two dudes who appeared out of the blue,' or, at the big-league level, an operative in a fedora and trench coat."

"Maybe," Pack huffed, "you should get off your smart ass and stop sidin' with the state and look into shit."

"Unless you have more to tell me, I need to be in court soon. I'm not allowed to discuss the particulars of Damian's case with you, but please know I've been investigating a situation that might prove to be very positive for him."

"How about obvious stuff, like maybe that colored Benson woman he's supposed to have stabbed was pregnant or hooked on drugs? Damian had been at their house hundreds of times, so maybe they had some relationship. A famous rich guy like her husband would do all he could to keep things on the down-low. You ever think 'bout that?"

Andy had heard enough. Misty Pack had finally pissed him off. He set his jaw hard, drew a bead on her. "Listen to me, Ms. Pack." He tried to smother his temper, but it still inflamed every syllable. "First, Damian had not been there 'hundreds of times.' Second, none of your obnoxious theories make any sense whatsoever. Third, the autopsy report showed no signs of recent sexual activity, she was not pregnant—especially by *your* boyfriend—and her toxicity screens were negative for drugs. More to the point, there's no chance this lady would ever touch Damian Bullins, not even with gloves, an N-95 mask *and* a ten-foot pole. You need to stop wasting my time with your shameful, worthless, misinformed slander. You're free to go. Have a nice day."

"Big surprise. The state pays you, and you work for them, not Damian. Screw you, bitch. You and your dumbass dog both. I'm gonna hire Damian a *real* lawyer."

❋❋❋

ANDY THOUGHT AND DEBATED and dithered until four o'clock, couldn't decide. Twice, he wandered down the hall but turned around. He went outside to smoke, lit a cigarette, paced on the sidewalk behind his office, inhaled a single draw, and threw the Marlboro away—a waste. The day had kicked off poorly, what with Misty Pack's asinine rantings, and then he'd lost a trial, a close grand larceny case, and bad things come in threes, so maybe tomorrow was a better choice, the juju rectified, the slate clean.

He'd decided to wait until his odds and omens improved and was leaving for thirty minutes of Cybex machines at the gym, but as he passed by Kellie Alison's office, the door was swung open—it'd been closed all afternoon—and she glanced up from her keyboard and saw him in the hall and called his name. "Andy. Hello. Come in, please. I heard the news this morning from Vikram. I'm so sorry. I can't believe it. I hope you're okay."

Andy tugged the leash, and he and Patches veered into the office. "Thanks. I'm fine."

"I'm guessing this is Patches," she said. "Cindy told me the whole story. How sweet." She spoke to the dog, her voice silly and playful: "What a handsome boy. Who's a handsome boy? And smart too, a smart fellow."

"Smart when he's not on the lam and terrorizing my neighbor's donkeys." Andy smiled. "I will say, to his credit, I'm pretty certain he's never been on a leash in his life, but he's learning quickly."

"How old is he?"

"Fourish, I think. I'm dropping him for a wellness check while I'm at the gym—maybe the vet can be more precise." He instructed the dog to sit. Patches immediately complied. "Speak." He touched the mutt's muzzle, same as he'd seen Zeb do, and Patches barked. "Lie down," was the last command, and Patches slid his front paws forward until his belly was flush against the carpet.

"Wow. I'm impressed. He lives up to his advance notices."

Andy stepped farther into the room. He leaned against the wall but didn't slouch or stoop. He looked sideways at the open door, concerned about privacy. "I'm glad I caught up with you. I wanted to see if you'd like to have dinner." He stood straight. He was holding the leash. "So we're, you know, so there's no misunderstanding, this is a romantic invite, not a colleagues-having-beer-and-nachos invite. I've wanted to ask you for a while, ever since the Eddie Duggan case."

"Thanks," she said. She had a bob of blonde hair, a sprite's fast green eyes, scant makeup, and—always—fancy painted nails. "It crossed my mind too. You and I, I mean."

"There's the issue of our both working here," Andy said, "but that'll soon be resolved. And I realize you're not too long separated—"

"Nine months," she volunteered. "Only three left until I can get my final divorce."

"I'm not sure about your circumstances, and it may be too early. If it is, how about you add me to the waiting list?"

"It's not very complicated," she answered, "and my marriage was essentially over years ago. There's no waiting list. I've tried a couple of computer dates, but ugh, Lord, they were total busts. If you can't order a skirt that fits or comfortable size-eight shoes online, then I'm not sure why you'd expect to locate a boyfriend there either."

Andy laughed. "True."

"So, yeah, okay, thanks. I'd enjoy it."

Andy noticed his breathing was a tick rapid. "Great. I have my son this weekend. I was thinking we try for next Wednesday. It's not a premium night, not Friday or Saturday, so there'll be less first-date pressure, and you won't feel like you squandered prime hours if I'm a boor and disappointment."

She grinned. "Last guy I dated was darn near a catfish. Not sure who that was in his profile picture, but the man who met me had lost significant hair and gained twenty pounds overnight. His lucrative 'sales job' was trading baseball cards and bobbleheads from his sofa. And here's a question for you: Worse to live with your mom, your kid, or in your car? He was bunking with his twenty-year-old son. Sad."

"I'd say sponging off mom is the gold standard for domestic failure."

"At least I know what you look like," she said. "You have a job. And a showplace house—well, inside. Though now I'm worried about the pooch. You're not the cad who borrows a dog so he can meet ladies in the park, are you? Suspicious you'd ask me on a date the same day you bring an adorable rescue pet to work."

***

ANDY DEPARTED KELLIE'S OFFICE in a much-improved mood, happy, infatuated, restored and rose-colored-glasses excited. Following the Eddie Duggan not-guilty verdict two weeks ago, he and Kellie had celebrated at the Martinsville Applebee's with a handful of friends, and the night was flirty and freewheeling. They held on to every glance, and brushed shoulders laughing at jokes and stories and Kellie's Alfred E. Neuman mask, and they left the restaurant together and hugged in the parking lot, bare-faced, her chest mashed into him, his palms pressing against her low back, wrapped together, a full-on, primed prelude, but nothing more happened, and he watched as she opened her car door, the interior light painting her face, the restaurant sign bright and juiced behind her. She looked at him and waved, then kissed her fingertips and bent her hand in his direction, blew.

"Nice," he said as soon as he closed her office door and was out of earshot.

He was chatting with Cindy, saying goodbye and small-talking about her kid's college plans, when Vikram appeared and invited him to his office.

"How goes it with the Bullins confession?" Vikram asked from behind his desk.

Andy kept standing, Patches on his haunches beside him. "Good and bad," he replied. "We're solid on a motion to suppress the statement."

"Yeah, I'd think so," Vikram said.

"The bad news is Stephanie believes she has a conflict, and she plans to ask for a special prosecutor, especially now that this isn't simply a guilty plea."

Vikram rubbed his chin. "Who? Who could she rope in to taking the job?"

Andy cocked an eyebrow. "Who's the worst prosecutor in the state?"

Vikram was always a gentleman, always charitable. No one in the office had ever heard him use profanity or speak ill of another person. "I'm not sure I can answer that," he said elliptically. "Depends."

"Peter Morley," Andy declared. "Can't get any worse."

"Well," Vikram said, the word ironic and deadpan, "Mr. Morley enjoys a certain reputation."

"No kidding," Andy grumbled. "You and I suddenly have new timetables and a raft of unnecessary problems. It'll be weeks before the order is entered appointing Morley. Then we'll have to find a day when his hair-and-makeup crew can come to Patrick County, and it'll take him forever to do a self-serving press release with the obligatory headshot. He'll want cameras in the courtroom for the motions—a complication—so nary a moment of his bluster and pointless preening goes unnoticed by potential voters. Seriously, Vik, it'll be a miracle if we hear the motion to suppress the statement this *year*."

"Unfortunately," Vikram said, "it will not serve Mr. Morley's...uh... interests to strike an early, objective compromise that reflects the risk to both sides. If the commonwealth loses its best evidence—the confession—this is no longer a *total* cakewalk."

"Morley'll force us to hold a hearing and then scapegoat Judge Leventis for following the law and excluding the statement. He'll have a press conference and spit fire and brimstone and promise an appeal and wag his finger at the cameras. But we will suffer months of delay until the rubber finally meets his vainglorious road, and he'll definitely stall like hell until after the votes are counted in his November election."

"So, Andy, where does this development leave us? This won't fit in thirty days, not even close."

"No doubt," Andy said softly.

"Thanks to the usual bureaucratic boondoggle and the pandemic draining the state treasury, I'm looking at a hiring freeze until at least 2021, then there'll be a delay and an advertising period, so best-case scenario, we're talking next spring before a new attorney is actually here—if I'm fortunate."

"I can't miss the trip with my son," Andy insisted. "I can't."

"I'll start spreading your cases around, easing your workload, especially the probation violations, and maybe, just maybe, you stay until we finish Bullins or the end of January 2021, whichever comes first? I'll cover for you so you can take your father-son trip. Heck, take two weeks—you've got plenty of vacation time."

"If I stay, Vik, I'm not going to be a freeloader. I'll pull my share." Andy switched the leash to his left hand. He half-smiled, curved a corner of his mouth. "Seems I'm losing ground," he said drolly. "Instead of setting off footloose and fancy-free to chase my midlife will-o'-the-wisp, I'm stuck with Patches the High-Maintenance Hound and more of the same old, same old public-defender grind."

"I'll do everything I can to make things tolerable for you."

"Well, here's a disclosure since it seems I'll be a PD for a few more months. I have a date with Kellie. You should know."

Vikram beamed. "Congrats. What took you so long?"

***

FRIDAY NIGHT, NOAH WAS enraptured by his new companion, Patches. They repeated the entire catalog of tricks over and over and over and over, nonstop, until Andy finally forced his son to let the dog rest. The mutt's history and pedigree were embellished and fairy-taled for a PG audience: Patches's late owner was a circus trainer, a colorful character who'd died unexpectedly, and Patches kept a long, noble vigil for him at the *hospital* before coming to live with his new master.

"Can he sleep with me in my room?" Noah pleaded at ten thirty.

"Nope, sorry. Dogs sleep outside. He has the excellent house I just bought for him and the Invisible Fence to keep him from escaping. More important, he doesn't want to stay in here—not how he was raised.

The scratched and gouged threshold we're replacing in the morning is a testament to his dislike of the indoors at night."

"Please," the child begged. "Why can't we just give him a chance?"

"Sorry."

"Can he at least come with us while I read my book? Then you can stick him in the yard to freeze to death."

"Seems fair. And I think he'll survive the artic July air. But he leaves when the lights go off. You're not going to slippery-slope me."

Father and son took turns reading, with Andy changing voices and inflections for the different *Connecticut Yankee* characters, and before he began his first section, Noah looked at the dog and said his name, and Patches sailed onto the bed lickety-split, and there he remained, stock-still and on his best behavior, the entire night, no problems, no barking, no pacing, no whimpering, a child and his loyal friend, the room at peace.

On Saturday morning, after a breakfast of frozen waffles, bacon and sliced bananas, Andy, Noah and Patches went to Andy's workshop—the house's former garage—and carpentered on a new threshold. Father and son donned safety glasses, and they both wore ear protection, a needless precaution in Andy's opinion, but the gear and preparation made a routine handyman's task seem much more mystical and impressive, and bare ears might draw a complaint from mom.

Andy cut a section of hickory to length then used the table saw to cut it to width and to height, and each time through, he allowed his boy to manage the tail end of the wood. The saw's motor sent the dog scurrying, and he watched from the yard, never quite sure about the racket and the fanged, whirling metal comet. Andy angled the blade to shape the sides and slope, and twice they carried their work to the porch and checked the fit against the jambs, and they kept measuring and trimming until the new strip was snug and perfect.

"Most people would just go to the hardware store and buy a cheapo and slap it down," Andy remarked as they were shaving shims.

"This is way better," Noah said enthusiastically.

They sat in ladder-backs with flat, faded cushions, and with a little help and advice from his dad, Noah hand-sanded the threshold, skipping the quicker belt-sander.

"Next," Andy said, "we'll take the drill and countersink our holes and use the cutter to make our plugs from oak so it'll appear this piece of art is actually pegged. Start the polyurethane coats."

Noah scrunched his nose and toe-kicked at the floor and declared with a child's quicksilver candor: "Seems like a lot more to do. I think I'll get Patches and play *Fortnite*, unless you *really* need me."

Andy belly-laughed. "Sorry."

"It's been, like, an *hour* already."

"Well," Andy replied, still amused, "I appreciate the help so far, especially the sanding, but this is a good time for you to take a well-earned union break. We're looking at several coats of poly, so this won't be ready to screw down and glue until next week. I'll save those honors for you, okay? You can use the drill and finish the job."

"Okay," he said, distracted, ready to switch on his video game. He pulled off the ear guards, but he kept the safety goggles in place and was still wearing them at noon, tranced in to the TV screen, folded forward, his thumbs frenetic and at war. Andy was collecting their breakfast plates and glasses from the kitchen table and wiping the sticky, viscous smears of maple syrup from around his son's spot, and he heard Noah rejoicing in the den.

"Victory Royale!" the boy exclaimed. "Yes." He was celebrating, hands raised, spaz-dancing to the game's vaguely synthed version of Rick Astley's "Never Gonna Give You Up." Noah's "skin" Midas joined the party from an electronic, Crayola landscape, freestyling to the earworm tune.

"Don't forget," Andy reminded him. "Tonight we're classic gaming. The big three: *Operation*, *Barrel of Monkeys* and *Rock 'Em Sock 'Em Robots*. We'll see how skilled you truly are, hotshot."

"Is 'classic' the same as 'dinosaur'?" He giggled. "I'm not worried about my skills." He kept right on dancing, gleeful in his goggles.

CHAPTER FIVE

PETER MORLEY PHONED THE public defender's office on Tuesday afternoon, July 28.

Morley was Dunford County's elected commonwealth's attorney, a grandstanding charlatan who'd announced he was running for the state senate and would be on the ballot in November. His failures and shameless blunders were legendary in Virginia legal circles. He'd been busted for creating a bogus online account to praise his take-no-prisoners stance against "gay privilege," and even better perhaps, he'd used the fake identity to float the moniker "Peter the Great." His refusal to follow his local judge's order not to open-carry a Desert Eagle pistol into the courtroom was on appeal to the Virginia Supreme Court. Most worrisome, though, was his habit of treating every case, from speeding to murder, as a political opportunity. Morley calculated life-changing business based on what would benefit *him*, always kept a finger in the wind and never stopped working the angles.

Still, like most accomplished grifters, Morley was blessed with his fair share of gifts. He was clever, handsome, glib, and had a knack for sensing issues that would incite large chunks of his community. He always came off as aw-shucks affable even when he was attacked by his enemies, and according to both conventional wisdom and every early poll, he was a shoo-in to be elected—a martyr, truth-speaker and Constitutional patriot to the majority of voters in his district.

"Thought I should touch base," he effused over the phone, "since we'll be spending some time together."

"I appreciate the call, Mr. Morley," Andy assured him. "Damian Bullins suddenly has a complicated case."

"Pete, please. Call me Pete. My dad was Mr. Morley."

"Thanks, I will. I go by Andy."

"I have an uncle named Andy. Makes the best Brunswick stew you'll ever taste. Remind me, and I'll have him send you a quart."

"Kind of you," Andy said. "So have you had a chance to talk to Mrs. Katt about the case?"

"Yeah, she gave me an overview. We were law-school classmates. I think the world of her. She's a great gal. She also sent a bunch of stuff I haven't had a chance to read yet."

"Stephanie's top-notch," Andy agreed.

"But looks like you're stuck with me—not as pretty and not nearly as smart. I owed her a big favor for taking a nasty manslaughter case off my hands. Couldn't turn her down when she asked me to help y'all finish this one."

And you couldn't turn down the national limelight in a winnable murder case, Andy thought, but instead he said, "I know she's grateful."

"I hear you're a heckuva an attorney for a public defender, Andy, but Steph tells me your guy's as guilty as homemade sin, and he has a train-wreck record. How about we negotiate a deal that's fair to us both and not waste hours and hours in court—why drag the deceased's husband through more torment?"

"I'm willing to listen to any reasonable offer, Pete," Andy said sincerely.

"I'm thinking I let him plead to second degree, and we knock six months off his guidelines."

Andy was alone in his office, but he rolled his eyes and took the receiver away from his ear and briefly held it against his chest. "Uh, Pete, a couple of things," he said when he returned the receiver to his face. "Mrs. Katt had already offered to amend from first to second degree before we discovered my client's confession will probably be suppressed. Also, as you know, the max for second degree is forty years. Damian's low-end on the guidelines is forty-three years and a few months, so your offer wouldn't change anything for him. Do you have a copy of the guidelines?"

"Yeah, I think so. Somewhere. I'll have to find them."

"Have you had a chance to review the rights waiver, the incomplete Miranda warnings the cop read to my client?"

"Stephanie told me there might be a small hiccup," Morley answered. "But nothing we can't cure in the long haul."

"I'm not certain what you mean by 'the long haul,'" Andy said, "but I think you'll lose the confession, and this case will become much more difficult to nail down. Not impossible for you to convict my client without the statement, I'll concede that, but the confession is your ace. If the judge grants our motion, I'd estimate you decline from a hundred percent and no risk to about a seventy-five or eighty percent chance of winning."

"So, okay, what're you looking for?" Morley asked.

"I'd recommend my client take the max, ten years, on manslaughter."

"Yeah, I'm sure you would," Morley answered, but he wasn't rude or belligerent. "Don't think I'm in a position to be quite so lenient. Sorry. Mr. Bullins is a confessed murderer with a terrible criminal history. Plus, we're talking about a hyper-technical minor paperwork glitch here."

"Understood," Andy replied. He opened his calendar. "I suppose we need to go ahead and set a hearing date for our motion to suppress the statement."

"Yeah," Morley said, "I suppose. I'm not free until December. The election and so forth. You mind if we wait until then? Or, hey, the first of the year would give me a chance to enjoy the holidays. Running a commonwealth's attorney's office and a senate campaign simultaneously will sure tucker out a fellow. It'd be wonderful if I could enjoy Christmas with my children. I'd consider it a favor."

"Pete, I don't mean to be difficult, but I can't wait six months to docket a basic hearing. I have an ethical duty to promptly tend to my client's business. Also, I'll be leaving the PD's office in early 2021, if not before—we need to do our best to resolve this while I'm still around. If you win the election, you'll be gone next year as well."

"You...realize I'm promising I'll remember your help, and you'll have a friend in Richmond if I'm elected. I'd really appreciate the courtesy."

The rank bribe irritated Andy, and he answered immediately and decisively. "Something this straightforward, forty-five days should be a gracious plenty. I'm thinking September."

"Sure." Morley was calm and cheery. "I hear you and absolutely respect your position. I'll have my secretary call and try to find a time in September. We'll make it happen, even though I'll have to move important events or cancel other trials."

"Thanks, Pete," Andy said unenthusiastically, knowing full well Morley would drop the iron curtain and go dark, and he'd have to chase after him and eventually involve Judge Leventis to simply schedule the case.

"Sorry to learn you're quitting," Morley offered. "Hope you're moving on to greener pastures."

***

ANDY PLANNED TO LEAVE directly from the office for his date with Kellie, so he was thoughtful and deliberate with his clothes on Wednesday morning. He removed a Peter Millar blue suit from the plastic dry-cleaner's covering, added a white Gitman Brothers shirt, a striped tie, new socks and triple-polished shoes, now with the thin, waxy laces replaced. He leaned close to the mirror while he shaved, careful to blade every whisker, and he brushed his teeth longer than normal, trimmed his nails, and almost forgot a bottle of cologne he'd set on the kitchen table so he could carry it along for later. He enjoyed the preparation, the sense of purpose, the attention to fine details.

At four thirty, he had just sprayed the cologne—a birthday gift from his adolescent nephew who'd snagged the bottle from a PacSun bargain rack—when Cindy ducked into his office.

"Wow," she teased him, fanning the air with her hand. "Puttin' on the Ritz. Fancy-schmancy cologne. I'm half expecting the room to turn black and white, and a voice with a smooth French accent will pronounce the virile name on the bottle. You'll ride a motorcycle into the desert or toss your tuxedo jacket over your shoulder and smolder at the camera."

Andy was standing near a corner. "Well, I don't have a three-day stubble, barely buttoned shirt and floundering motion-picture career, and it's not the month before Christmas, so sorry, it's just me here in my sad-sack public servant's office—you didn't magically pop into an *eau de toilette* commercial."

"Well, it smells nice. No kidding. Strong but nice."

"Thanks for the tip. I'm putting it on *now* for that very reason. It should be more subtle by six."

"Kellie's already left," she noted and grinned. "Fingers crossed for you both." She fanned some more. "Stephanie Katt's in the waiting room, asking to see you. I know you're on a schedule, and I wasn't sure exactly what to tell her. She said it's regarding Damian Bullins."

"Yeah, hmmm, okay. Bring her back, please." He turned toward his desk, stopped abruptly. "On second thought, maybe I'll meet with her in the conference room, where it smells like coffee, mold and stale Mi Ranchito takeout. I'll be right there."

"Have a wonderful time tonight," Cindy said.

Andy waited until he heard the two ladies pass his office, walked to the conference room, greeted Katt from a distance, and sat in a chair across the table, catercorner to her.

"Sorry to barge in on you," she said. "Cindy tells me you have plans—"

"No problem, Stephanie. I'm here for another hour. You want a bottled water, coffee?"

"No thanks," she replied. "I had to take my daughter to dance class, so I was in town. I have some face-to-face business."

"What's up?" Andy inquired.

"This is a little tricky for me," she answered. "For obvious reasons, I needed to investigate an erroneous form being used by our sheriff's office. The sheriff is very professional and thorough, and this Bullins lapse was a surprise."

"Yeah, I've always liked Sheriff Smith."

"I'm no longer handling the case. I'm conflicted out, so—"

"And thanks again," Andy interrupted, "for bringing us Peter Morley."

"So," she continued, "legally and ethically, I'm finished."

"Correct," Andy agreed.

"Still, I feel I have a duty to give you any information that's helpful to your client."

"And you're worried," Andy added, "that Morley will either forget to produce this information in discovery or intentionally hide it and make things even worse."

Katt's expression remained bland. "I'm worried about the truth, Andy." She changed position in her chair. "Three weeks before Damian Bullins's confession, Investigator Ellis discovered he was out of the forms the cops use to take a written statement. He asked the sheriff about it and was told to request the forms from Janice Hooper, a new secretary. Janice couldn't locate the template on her computer, so she borrowed the form from another officer, and when she typed it, she omitted the 'You have the right to remain silent' line. Basically, this was a clerical error. A mistake. Seven-word negligence."

"Okay. I'm not sure why it matters to me *how* this was fouled up, but I appreciate the explanation."

"Try to be a little more patient, Andy."

"Sorry. Yes ma'am. I'm all ears."

"With so much audio and video technology, we don't have the need for very many old-school, written statements. The questionable form was only distributed to one other cop and used twice. He didn't notice the problem either, nor did the defense attorneys, but the statements weren't critical to those cases. We've solved the mystery and fixed the error."

"Okay," Andy said. "So there's no doubt Ellis read from an incomplete set of warnings."

"Well," she replied. She peered at the ceiling. "Ellis claims he actually read the rights from a laminated pocket card and didn't rely on the form." She lowered her gaze, bunched her lips.

"Bullshit," Andy said angrily. "Total bullshit."

"But—and this is exculpatory, so you're legally entitled to know— Coy Hubbard didn't see any card. Also, he can't say exactly *which* rights were read. No surprise there, since he was preoccupied with your violent, sociopathic client."

"Of course Coy didn't see a card, Stephanie. There was no card. Ellis is lying."

"That'll be for the judge to decide," she said.

"Come on," Andy challenged her. "You don't believe him, do you?"

"Put it this way, Andy: I'd much rather argue your facts than the commonwealth's."

"What a worthless sonofabitch." Andy almost shouted. "Did you speak with Ellis yourself?"

"I did," Katt answered. "He recited the story about reading the rights from a card. He showed me a card. Many cops use a card or keep some kind of reminder with them."

"Of course, he spins this fantastical tale to you only *after* he's on notice his mistake has compromised a murder case."

"Naturally, as soon as you showed me the handwritten confession, I contacted the sheriff and asked him how this happened, so yeah, I wasn't the first to speak to Ellis."

"I wonder how long it took him to cook up such an obvious lie?"

"He informed me he acquired the card when he was in Atlanta. The Atlanta police department did in fact issue this kind of card to officers while he was employed there. I checked myself."

"And here we go, Stephanie, the classic easy out for the court. Damian Bullins is a vile, terrible man, who's guilty of murder, and all of a sudden an escape route conveniently appears for Judge Leventis, and hey, so what if she's forced to be intellectually dishonest and hold her nose and accept Ellis's maggot-rotten perjury to make justice happen—the guilty need to be punished. We ought to honor spilled blood on a kitchen floor, not some prissy, powdered-wig abstraction. Anyhow, we all realize Damian wanted to confess, he's heard those rights read before, probably knew them better than the police, and the omission of a warning about keeping quiet made no practical difference."

Katt stood. "For what it's worth, Andy, Melvin Ellis will never be called as a witness by my office again. I told the sheriff as much."

"I'd hope not."

"Maybe, Andy, I unintentionally did you a favor. Would you rather have a competent, skilled commonwealth's attorney on the other side of the courtroom or Peter the Great?"

***

"Early June was the worst for me," Kellie said. She finished the last of her wine and set the glass beside a bread plate. "The cicada racket, the virus and the George Floyd murder—it was like *Plan 9 from Outer Space* crossed with Moses versus Pharaoh and a visit to Room 101." They were seated at a two-top corner table, a garrison of empty space around them. The Third Bay Café was open again, but a full house still wasn't permitted.

"Yeah," Andy agreed. "Weird times. And the future hardly looks brighter come November: We have a choice between Caligula and Mr. Magoo. How'd we wind up with such dismal candidates?" He'd finished his salmon and asparagus and was considering a third beer. "I'm enjoying our night on the town—you want another glass of wine? Dessert?"

"Sure. But I better have one or the other, and I think I'll opt for the wine."

Andy ordered their drinks, and they stayed for thirty minutes more, cutting up, laughing, talking shop, and swapping bits and pieces of their histories—she reminisced about learning to drive a straight-gear Chevette, and they both recalled the tense, fretful nights before their first law-school exams. The check came in a black folder, and Andy opened it and paid with cash.

"I'll leave the tip," Kellie volunteered.

"Already done," he replied. "Twenty-five percent from a former busboy. I'm glad you mentioned it so I can boast about my largesse and impress you."

"Well, thanks. But I won't be impressed until I can confirm you didn't sneak back and pull a few bills from the pile."

"I've actually seen customers do that," Andy said. He stood and waited for Kellie to join him. "Not a lot of traditional post-dinner date options in these plague days—no movies, live music, bars, bowling or minor league baseball. I took a stab at chairs and a romantic firepit by the little creek near my house, but even with gallons of citronella, it's a mosquito free-for-all there. Patches and I can offer the screened-in porch, a ceiling fan, Veuve Clicquot, a respectable sunset view and Chet Baker."

"Ordinarily a quality effort and much appreciated. A solid seven or low eight on the Liz Barrett Browning scale." They were walking toward the door. She slipped her arm in his. "But I have my own love-shack plans for us. My pal Ben is the curator at the natural history museum, and even though they've been closed for months, I coaxed the door and security codes from him, and we can have our nightcaps with candles and the glow of emergency-exit lighting in the Hall of Ancient Life. Surrounded by the *Pteranodon* and the *Allosaurus*. We'll have the place to ourselves. Prehistoric VIP."

"Damn—I feel like a piker," Andy replied. "How cool. I've only been there once, for a reception. Thanks."

"The perks of a small town. Ben and his wife were the first people I met when I moved here. I didn't know what you might want to drink, so we'll have to tend to any alcohol needs on the way, and we are absolutely, a thousand percent sworn to secrecy."

They sat—tiny in the huge space—underneath a span of flying bones as the last window light expired and the dim, oversized night bulbs automatically took hold, at first shoulder to shoulder against a wall, then more comfortable in chairs borrowed from the gift shop, and they stayed until eleven o'clock, kissed while they were still seated on the floor, early, not long after she semicircled them with a sweep of candles.

She told him how she'd married too young and decided at age thirty that working as a scheduler for a busy dentist's office had become a millstone. She did two years at a Norfolk community college, finished her VCU sociology degree with mostly online classes, then graduated from Appalachian School of Law in Grundy, though she was quick to mention she'd also been accepted at the University of Virginia. Money was scarce, and her scores and grades were so elite that Appalachian allowed her to attend virtually for free, and remarkably, at thirty-eight years old, she became a new lawyer, minus the usual student debt. "It was either college or explore some serious boozing and an affair with my boss," she said. "He was big on 'drilling' double entendres."

"And your husband?" Andy wondered.

"He's a good-enough man, just not *my* man. He's exactly the same guy he was when he was nineteen, right down to the Eminem—I call it Mother Goose rap—and Velcro wallet. I definitely can't claim any kind of bait and switch. He changes jobs often but always works. For whatever reason, he had conniptions over me returning to school and trying to improve our circumstances. He was also unhappy with the divorce, wouldn't sign a separation agreement, hence the year-long wait. We're civil. I wish him well."

"The law's simply another job for you?" Andy asked. "Most latecomers to the legal system have causes or motivations—kids, poverty, race, the death penalty, the environment. Or learning the law so they can punish the insurance company executives who wouldn't pay for mom's cancer treatment."

"I was looking for something that paid over twelve-fifty an hour and didn't require me to wear hideous pink-raccoon scrubs every day, even though I worked on a calendar and computer, never touched a patient. This gig checks the boxes. We have great benefits and a state retirement plan. The work's meaningful and occasionally exciting."

"Well, that might change—the exciting part, I mean."

"Yeah, it might, but no matter how tedious it becomes, I'm convinced Vikram will never try to entice me into an Atlantic City root-canal convention."

"This was the best," he told her as they were leaving the museum and she was punching in numbers on the security keypad. "Not every day you have a private audience with a giant flying reptile. Thanks again. I had fun."

"Me too."

"What's next? This seems like a perfect spot for the storybook kiss if we're calling it a night."

She finished setting the alarm. "We only have sixty seconds to leave the building, so it would be more haiku than storybook." She pecked his cheek. "Let's go."

He drove across the empty parking lot to a side street, checked for traffic, and took an illegal-turn shortcut to her place. They shot straight through the numbered apartment door holding hands, didn't dillydally or pretend, and the sex was tangled and spectacular and intimate, well worth the wait, maybe even better because of the long, lovely prologue.

❖❖❖

ON AUGUST 3, FIRST thing, Andy buttonholed Vikram in the office hallway. "I need a favor, please," he informed his boss.

"Always happy to help, if I can," Vikram said.

"Can you or Cindy send an email to the lawyers here and find out who's had a case, any case, with my new pal, Investigator Melvin Ellis? I've asked Chris Corbett to quietly do the same for me in Patrick County."

"Sure. May I ask why?"

"Trolling for some impeachment evidence."

"Would you like to be more specific?" Vikram asked.

"I'll let you know if we ring the bell. Just trying to look around the corner and betting Ellis will double down on a big fat lie."

"The office gossip line tells me you and Kellie hit it off. I'm pleased to hear the report. Bad news is I'll be breaking up the Nick and Nora Charles team if you need a second chair for Mr. Bullins. You two were stellar on the Eddie Duggan trial, but you'll now get me, not her, for the Bullins case. There're too many complications on every side of the equation if you guys work together while in a romantic relationship."

"Okay. No quarrel from me. I understand the rules. And I appreciate your offer to help, especially given how much attention will be on this." Andy rested a hand on Vikram's shoulder. "You, sir, can tell Kellie she's pre-emptively fired from the biggest case any of us will ever see in our lifetimes."

"It's why I make the big bucks," Vikram said.

By Wednesday, Andy had a legal-pad list of twelve defendants whose cases involved Melvin Ellis, and he set to visiting them all, tracking down men and women at plants, trailer parks, bars, HUD apartments, a nursing home, and—bingo—at a small, immaculate modular house in Stuart, where the ceramic birdbath was encircled by landscaping bricks and orange lilies, and Lonnie Duncan's darling mom still tilled a modest summer garden, mostly squash, snap beans and Brandywine tomatoes. The wooden door was swung wide open, so when he rapped on the screen door, Andy could see a lady with a spatula busy above a frying pan. She greeted him wearing an apron, her hair in a bundle, stacked off her face and forehead.

"Ma'am, I'm very sorry to bother you at suppertime. Apologies. My name is Andy Hughes, and I'm a lawyer from Martinsville, and I'm interested in an older case involving a Mr. Lonnie Duncan."

"I'm Lois, his mother," she said pleasantly. "What can I do for you? Oh, can I please see some ID?"

CHAPTER SIX

ANDY WAITED UNTIL HE and Noah had finished playing Friday-evening catch in the yard to break the sad news. "I'm afraid we're going to have to delay our Montana trip for a while," he told his son. "It's too risky to fly on an airplane—the virus is dangerous. I know this probably seems like a huge disappointment to you, but I've made other great plans for us that might be even *better*."

Noah full-stopped from a carefree walk, a baseball wedged into his glove, his face pained, his mouth agape. They were standing near the front porch. "Then why can't we drive?" he pleaded. "Why?" The last word was soggy and fractured, a flimsy dam crumbling against a surge of tears.

"Montana's over *two thousand* miles away. Two thousand. We'd spend our whole vacation driving there and back. How fun is that?"

"You promised." The tears came in a torrent.

"I'd take you if I could, but Covid has changed the world. I'm sorry. I was looking forward to Missoula as much as you were."

"You're a liar," Noah blurted. His cheeks were red. He wiped at snot and tears. He threw his mitt on the ground and the ball rolled free. "You promised," he sobbed.

Andy reached to hug him, and the boy recoiled. "We'll still have our vacation, it'll just be closer, at a different place. Let me tell you where we—"

"It's not the same. I've practiced with my rod every day."

"We'll fish as much as you want, Noah."

"I hate this." He kicked his glove. "Lie!"

Noah refused food, wouldn't eat. He barely spoke another word, until he dramatically phoned his mom, who did the right thing and tried to reason with him, even hinted that she was the villain who'd put the kibosh on his travels, and when he wailed for her to come and pick him up, she refused and told him to act like a big boy and be nice to his dad. "I hate it here!" he exclaimed.

That night, after Noah cried himself to sleep, belly down, his face in a quicksand pillow, Andy called Vikram at his home, and then he exchanged several text messages with Brooke, and the next morning, he sat on his sullen son's bed with an atlas and detailed their route from Virginia to Missoula, four days to drive across the country, four days to fish and visit, five days to return, the extra day at the end a safety concession to Brooke.

They left as originally scheduled on August 12, Patches joining them, traveling in Brooke's 2019 Explorer with all the bells and whistles, this while she bumped about in Andy's Jeep for two weeks, the swap coming with five hundred dollars transferred to her checking account as payment for the extra wear and tear on her vehicle, money Andy insisted she accept even though she told him three times she didn't want it.

The ad hoc road trip was a hit, an unexpected father-and-son bonanza. They listened to the remainder of *Connecticut Yankee* on audio, along with every novelty song ever recorded, "Monster Mash" played to death in the heat of August. Far East Movement's "Like a G6" was also in heavy rotation, their Iowa soundtrack, Noah singing the refrain as "like a cheese stick." They took in all grades of roadside attractions—Salem Sue, the world's largest Holstein cow, Louis L'Amour Lane's gigantic buffalo, scenic overlooks and national monuments, tacky tourist traps, rock and crystal shops, local parks, and a windshield view of Mount Rushmore, which didn't make Noah's list of favorites when he was ranking them to pass the hours on the journey home.

Patches adapted well, soon learned not to fear elevators and not to fight his leash in hopes of meeting and sniffing other dogs at the rest areas. The mutt did remain uncertain about sleeping inside, even with Noah there—he ignored his padded bed and always dozed with his hindquarters mashed against their hotel-room door, occasionally growling at hallway footsteps or barking at a squeaky luggage cart.

Hot weather and bright, sunny skies didn't make for the best trout fishing, and after the drift boat and the big rivers became routine for him, Noah spent a fair amount of time on his iPad, occasionally prompted to look at an eagle or a bear or a moose or a diving osprey, and they were always off the water by noon so he wouldn't get too bored. But on the morning of the third day, a fat brown trout, not a trophy, but plenty large for a novice kid, slammed his foam fly, and with his dad and Guide Joe giving him more instruction than he needed, he landed the fish. His picture, holding his orange-speckled Bitterroot catch, was a delight, a revelation, his little boy's smile pure and rapturous.

CHAPTER SEVEN

WHEN JUDGE LEVENTIS SAW the multiple unanswered letters and emails attached to the defense motion requesting a hearing date for Damian Bullins, and when in response to that very motion, she received only a slipshod, sporadically literate letter from Morley's "paralegal" claiming he was not available "untill febrary," she herself phoned in late August and told his secretary he could appear either on September 18 or September 21, take your pick, and the choice wasn't negotiable. This *finally* prompted Morley to schedule a conference call, during which he was at his unctuous and slippery best and bellyached about the extreme hardship *any* 2020 date would cause him.

"You shouldn't have accepted the case if you can't manage it in a punctual and professional manner," Judge Leventis reminded him.

"Uh, yes ma'am. But could you at least give me until after November? I thought this was probably going to be a basic, half-hour guilty plea when I agreed to help Mrs. Katt—the Miranda issue drastically changes the landscape in terms of time and preparation."

"No," she replied curtly. "Mr. Hughes has been trying to schedule this since *July*. You've simply ignored his good-faith requests. Your job as a commonwealth's attorney trumps your political distractions. If you don't want to come, send an assistant. I checked: You have four other lawyers in your office."

And so, on September 21, the Peter the Great spectacle was dragooned into the Patrick County Courthouse in Stuart, Virginia, and the rubberneckers and national media came along in tow, the reporters and production trucks cramming Main Street full, the crowd large enough that

Leon's Coffee Shop sold completely out of food, even the vegetable-soup blocks from the freezer, thawed and heated on a seventy-degree day.

Andy insisted Damian Bullins be allowed to wear his street clothes, not convict orange, and he'd instructed his client to shave and shower before their ten o'clock hearing. In khakis, a polo shirt and brown shoes, his hair combed and parted, Bullins was neatly nondescript. Once in the courtroom, two masked deputies shadowed him, and a shock belt was concealed beneath his untucked shirt. While the deputies waited outside a witness-room door, Andy, Vikram and Bullins huddled around a table and discussed every scenario and possibility for the umpteenth time.

"Any questions, Damian?" Andy asked when they finished.

"No, sir. I understand." He was jail blanched, and the pale skin set off his eyes. "We can't let them cheat and take advantage of me."

"Yeah, well...okay," Andy replied. "Not sure that's how I'd put it." He closed his file. "And remember: The camera is always on you, Damian. Potential jurors are watching. Mind your manners. Keep your tattooed hands in your lap. Try not to look guilty or menacing."

"Yes, sir."

The ancient courtroom was stuffy and sweltering, the air-conditioning puny against the crowd—even at fifty percent capacity—and high ceiling, but Peter Morley was wearing a vest, and initially, Andy thought he was overheated and sweating. However, as soon as he caught a closer view, he determined the commonwealth's attorney's hair shimmer was from a generous product dousing. "Is he wearing some kind of makeup, Vik?" Andy asked his boss after solving the shiny hair mystery. "Seriously?"

"Maybe, possibly," Vikram answered. "But there's no doubt those are tasseled loafers. And never trust a lawyer—"

"With tassels on his shoes." Andy finished the rule quietly, leaning toward Vikram. They both flickered grins.

Cole Benson arrived dressed in a gray suit and subdued necktie, accompanied by the victim-witness coordinator and another man, older, also in a suit. Benson was tall and large and beefy and robust, his jacket stuffed through the shoulders, his pants snug at the thighs. His blond hair was short, almost a crewcut. A lighting fluke caused his hands and forehead to appear strangely white and stark as he walked through the gallery. His mask was stamped with a beehive, a twisted-straw skep.

He found a seat on the front bench, lowered the cloth mask to his chin, and surveyed the room, starting with the defense table and Damian Bullins and ending a hundred and eighty degrees later with a minimal nod at Peter Morley. While nothing leaked from his expression or commanding eyes—not hurt, not anger, not frustration—his staid, half-circle inspection of the killer's tableau in front of him was plenty powerful, and when he covered his face again, you understood, make no mistake, he was not a man to trifle with.

Judge Leventis welcomed the attorneys, acknowledged Bullins, recited several formalities, and asked Andy if he was ready to present the defendant's motion.

Andy stood. "Yes, Your Honor. Thank you. As the Court is aware from our memorandum, we've objected to the commonwealth's using a statement taken from my client, Mr. Bullins, in its case-in-chief. Once we contest the statement's admissibility, the *commonwealth* has the burden to show by clear and convincing evidence it was obtained in compliance with the Fifth Amendment and *Miranda v. Arizona*. Specifically, in this instance, my client was not informed of his most fundamental safeguard: the right to remain silent. We've filed our objection and argument in writing, and we now await the commonwealth's proof on this issue."

"Mr. Morley," the judge said politely, "are you ready to proceed?"

Morley was already on his feet. The counsel table in front of him was fortified with boxes and files and tubs, a grandstander's props and scenery, none of it necessary and most of it no doubt virgin to Morley, unread and untouched. He had an administrative assistant seated beside him, a stern lady with tightly braided hair and a paisley mask. He peacocked several steps toward the bench, making certain the national news cameras had a favorable, full-frame shot.

He unbuttoned his suit jacket. A gold watch chain was draped across the vest. "Judge Leventis and fellow counsel, good morning. I'm Peter Morley, from up the road in Dunford County, and I'm honored Mrs. Katt and the Virginia Supreme Court have chosen me to represent the people of Patrick

County in this murder case. I'm also honored to be here in Stuart, Virginia, in this venerable courthouse, seeking justice for Mr. Cole Benson and his four young daughters, and to be doing so beneath the imposing shadow—"

"Mr. Morley." Judge Leventis pitched forward in her chair and cocked her head. "I know where I am, and the shadow we need to concentrate on today is the one cast by the Constitution. So let's save your Cicero talents for a jury. Today you have a singular audience—me." She somehow managed to sound genial, not smartass, and she was signaling to everyone from the get-go that she ran the show and would run it by the book, no tomfoolery, no politicking.

Morley didn't miss a beat. "Exactly, Judge Leventis, and we look forward to demonstrating to *you*, ma'am, how we have more than complied with the Constitution, and we will respectfully urge the Court at the conclusion of the evidence to overrule the defendant's motion and allow his murder confession to be admitted at trial."

Morley called Melvin Ellis to testify, and the investigator made the journey down the center aisle to the witness stand. Andy watched him and was pleased. Ellis was tense and antsy, and he avoided glancing at the defense table or Judge Leventis, jitterbugged his gaze every which way, the cavernous room so quiet Andy could hear an occasional board squeak underneath the carpeted aisle and the feathered clicks of still cameras.

Morley did excellent work with Ellis on direct examination. By the time they reached the drum-roll questions, they were in a confident rhythm. Ellis seemed prepared and trustworthy, and Morley was all business, standing beside his chair, so familiar with the basic facts that he never once lost pace or checked his notes.

"You were the lead officer, then, when the police arrived at Mr. Bullins's trailer in Ararat?"

"Yes, sir," Ellis answered, his voice strong, his words crisp. "Though if we're bein' exact, it's a little travel camper, not a real mobile home."

"I appreciate your attention to detail," Morley replied. "Thank you." He ran his thumb across the watch chain. "Who served him with the warrants?"

"Mr. Bullins came to the door and opened it. He invited us in, then he sat on a couch, and I gave him both the search warrant and the arrest warrant."

"Did he say anything?" Morley inquired.

"Can I use his actual words? The profanity?"

"Yes, you may, Investigator," the judge told him.

Ellis primly pursed his lips. "Mr. Bullins said, and I quote: 'No need for all this shit; I'm ready to go.'"

"Who cuffed him and searched him?" Morley asked.

"Officer Coy Hubbard."

Morley eased a half-step closer to the witness stand. "What did you do, Investigator Ellis, while Officer Hubbard was physically arresting the defendant?"

"I immediately read him his rights. Immediately. Officer Hubbard heard me." Andy noticed he rushed the answer, stuck the sentences together.

"Tell us, please, Officer Ellis, the specifics of the Miranda warnings."

"I used a card," Ellis said. "A laminated card I always keep with me."

"Do you have that card with you today, Investigator?"

"I do," Ellis answered. He leaned left, wiggled his wallet free, unfolded it, removed the card, and held the laminated rectangle—about the size of a driver's license—toward Morley.

Andy cut his eyes enough to glimpse Bullins, who was perfectly composed and playacted just the right amount of astonishment at an answer he well knew was coming.

Morley took the card and pointed it in Andy's direction. "Would you like to see this, Mr. Hughes?" he asked, cocky and self-satisfied.

"Thanks," Andy replied. "I can see it from here."

"Investigator," Morley continued, "did you read the defendant his rights off of this very card?"

"I did," Ellis said. "I did." He sat taller and reinforced his voice.

"Would you please read for the record and Judge Leventis precisely what is on that card?"

Ellis held the card with both hands and recited its contents. It contained a complete, correct set of Miranda warnings.

"Thank you, sir," Morley said. "So there's no misunderstanding, you offered explicit notice to Mr. Bullins that he had the right to remain silent?"

"Yes," Ellis answered, his voice still a notch too loud.

Morley turned to get Bullins's statement from his assistant. He flipped through the pages, then passed them to Ellis. "Is this the original of the statement you took from the defendant there at his...uh...camper on May fifth, 2020? Nine pages."

"Correct," Ellis replied.

"Tell Judge Leventis, please, exactly how you obtained this."

"After I read Mr. Bullins his Miranda rights—all of 'em, mind you—I asked him what happened and some more questions. I wrote down the questions and his answers. I let him go over everything to make certain he agreed it was accurate, then had him sign the pages."

"Now, to be candid with the Court," Morley said, folding his arms across his chest, "we've learned since that day, the day you took the statement, the preprinted Miranda rights section on the form the defendant signed omits one warning. It doesn't include his right to remain silent."

"Yes, sir," Ellis answered somberly.

"However, as luck would have it—"

"Yeah," Ellis jumped in, bursting to recite his rehearsed deceit, "lucky for me and the dead lady, I relied on my card like I always do."

"So, sir, you read from the card, not—"

"Not the form they gave me at the sheriff's office. Just like I was trained to do in Atlanta at the academy."

Morley paused to unfasten a vest button, slowing their exchange so the investigator would quit spewing his answers. "And you didn't record the defendant because...?"

"Because," Ellis responded, "once he started talkin' and admittin' to what he'd done, I didn't want to risk spooking him by pullin' out a recorder or my phone. Officer Hubbard was right there the whole time. He also heard Mr. Bullins tell how he cut the poor woman's throat. It's not just me as a witness to what was said."

"Was Mr. Bullins coherent and competent during your few minutes of question and answer?"

"Yes. He was fine. He never had any trouble understandin' me, and his speech and demeanor was perfectly okay." Ellis licked his lips. He touched his scalp, where a sweat patch was taking shape above his red fringe of hair.

"Thank you, sir," Morley said. "We'd offer the Miranda card into evidence." He gestured at the investigator with a gameshow sweep of his arm and an open hand. "Your witness, Mr. Hughes. Those're all our questions, if it please the Court."

"Cross, Mr. Hughes," the judge said.

"Good morning, Investigator Ellis," Andy began, speaking as he rose from his seat.

"Morning to you too," Ellis said, the words forced, artificially bright.

"I think, sir, we can all agree you served an arrest warrant on the defendant."

"Yeah," the cop replied. "Yes. I served the warrant on him—"

"And he allowed Officer Hubbard to cuff him and was in custody when you questioned him."

"Yes, sir."

"You entered the camper with your gun drawn?"

"We did. Me and Officer Hubbard both. Officer Eggleston went around to the rear, and Officer Clement stayed right outside."

"Where were the warrants?" Andy asked.

"In my folder," Ellis answered. "I put the folder down on the little attached steps in case we had trouble. I wanted both hands available, okay?"

"That would be the leather folder you brought along today?"

"Not sure it's real leather," the cop said, "but yeah."

"Once you knew Mr. Bullins wasn't a threat or resisting—"

"Then I stepped directly outside and got my folder and served the papers on him," Ellis said.

"So, Officer, the warrants were in the folder as well as the form and blank pages you used to write down the defendant's statement?"

"Correct."

"And, as you just testified, Officer Ellis, you handed Mr. Bullins the warrants and then immediately read him his rights from a laminated card."

"Yes." Ellis owl-eyed the judge. "All his rights."

"Same as you always do?" Andy asked, almost before Ellis finished speaking.

"Same as always," Ellis stated.

"Where was the card when you reentered the camper with your folder?"

"With me," the cop said emphatically. "In my wallet. Exactly like how it was today."

"Was it in your hand when you first walked back inside to serve the defendant with the warrants?"

"No," Ellis answered. "Only the folder was in my hand."

"And, Officer Ellis, from the steps to the couch in the defendant's tiny camper, we're talking at most seven feet. Officer Hubbard measured it for me—six feet, seven inches. You and Coy Hubbard were right on top of each other, weren't you?"

"There was room enough," Ellis said. A sweat bead from the wet patch on his pale, freckled scalp almost nicked the corner of his eye before it trickled down his cheek.

"How many hands did you have on that day?" Andy inquired, the sarcasm unmistakable.

Morley hopped to his feet. "Judge, that's improper. He's badgering the witness."

"Judge," Andy responded, "I realize we're on TV this morning, but I hope Mr. Morley understands we're still using the genuine, honest-to-goodness Virginia rules of evidence, not the *Matlock* version currently in reruns. I am in fact badgering the witness—it's called cross-examination, and there's no law, statute, precedent or—"

"The objection is overruled," Judge Leventis declared. "And, Mr. Hughes, how about you try to stay on point and practice law minus the clever editorials? We'd all appreciate the courtesy. Leave the zingers to me."

"Will do, ma'am," Andy promised. "Officer, you may answer the question. Do I need to repeat it?"

"Two hands, obviously," Ellis said.

Andy pivoted toward Judge Leventis. "Ma'am, with your permission, I'm going to ask the investigator to demonstrate exactly how he alleges this happened. The defendant will take a seat in front of the jury box,

Officer Hubbard will reenact his search and the cuffing, and Investigator Ellis can actually show us how he removed the card and read from it. Officer Hubbard will measure and mark the relevant distances, and I'll have him confirm the same under oath before we begin. I'd request you return the Miranda card so the investigator can place it in his wallet. Where he *always* keeps it."

"Fine with me," the judge agreed.

The bailiff relocated a chair, and Damian Bullins sat in front of the empty jury box. Coy Hubbard was summoned from a witness room, accepted the oath, confirmed the camper's dimensions and measurements, and waited beside Bullins. Andy invited Ellis to bring his folder and join Hubbard.

"Okay." Andy was at the defense table, sitting adjacent to Vikram. "Let's assume, sir, you've finished serving the warrants, and Officer Hubbard is searching and cuffing. Please show us exactly what happened, how you went about reading the defendant his rights. And, Officer Hubbard, please begin your duties, same as you did there in the camper on May fifth, 2020."

"I was probably around half through when he started readin' the rights," Hubbard volunteered. "First thing I done, I checked under the sofa cushions for weapons."

Ellis was wired and jittery and irritated, and not particularly smart, so it wasn't until he reached for his wallet that he realized he'd been hogtied and gutted, and he hesitated, wallowed to a halt, as if he were a tin toy with its batteries drained dead, and for three or four seconds that registered as exponentially longer, he stood puzzled and exposed, the closed wallet in one hand, the folder occupying the other, the card buried. Flummoxed, he briefly peeked at the floor, clearly was thinking about squatting and laying the folder there, then his eyes skipped to the jury-box railing, and he finally tucked the folder underneath his left arm, this while Coy Hubbard worked his way around Bullins, patting the defendant's clothes from socks to collar, turning his pockets inside out, only inches away from Ellis and occasionally facing him.

With the folder still chicken-winged under his left arm, Ellis was forced to awkwardly use that hand—now free but mostly curtailed—to remove the card from his wallet, and as he was reading the Miranda warnings in a stagey voice, the smooth folder slipped a few inches farther down his ribs and he had to hastily bump it secure again, the wallet flopped wide open in his hand. He returned the card to his wallet, then crammed it back into his hip pocket.

Andy was slow to ask his next question, let the moment percolate. He turned a page on his yellow legal pad. He asked the judge to allow Coy Hubbard to leave the courtroom, and he waited for Ellis to sit down again in the witness stand. "And that's the story you want to tell Judge Leventis?" he asked, every syllable incredulous. "You're testifying under oath you went through all those contortions to remove a card when you had the Miranda warnings right there in front of you?"

"That's how it happened," Ellis replied. He licked his lips. "No big deal, not much to it."

"Did you consider putting the folder on the camper's floor, same as you just did here? Did you think about resting it on a jury-box railing there at the camper?"

"No, of course not," Ellis answered, his voice deflating. "I didn't, you know, consider it here today either," he lied.

Next, Andy gave the judge and Morley a transcript of the recorded conversation with Ellis, and he directed them to page twelve, "lines fifteen though seventeen, please," and he played the exchange for everyone to hear:

And you quickly read him his Miranda warnings from the preprinted section at the beginning of the statement? The statement you just gave me?

I did, sir. Word for word.

Andy tapped his laptop screen to stop the audio recording. He focused on the cop. "There was no mention, Officer Ellis, of your reading from any card when you went over this with me at your office, correct?"

"Ah, no, but...you didn't ask about it."

Andy stretched forward, planted his elbows on the table. "Why, Officer Ellis, would I ask about a card when you told me you read the rights 'word for word' from the preprinted form?"

"That's up to you," Ellis replied.

Andy jutted farther forward, nearly separated from his heavy wooden chair. "Of course, sir, you hadn't yet discovered the preprinted Miranda form was flawed when you confirmed to me you relied on it and read from it word for word. The sheriff hadn't alerted you. He spoke to you the next day, on July twenty-first?"

"I suppose, yeah, I hadn't talked to him yet when you recorded me, but none of it matters because I used my card."

Andy paused, thought for a moment, asked Vikram if he'd neglected anything important, and told the judge he was finished with the witness, whom he referred to as "Mr. Ellis," purposefully not acknowledging his police title.

Morley didn't relent, instead prodded a hemorrhaging Melvin Ellis through a handful of feeble rehabilitation questions, though to the commonwealth's attorney's credit, he pulled it off with a huckster's verve and fierce sincerity, never cracked, acted as if his sweaty newt witness were delivering the plain, righteous gospel. Still, by the time Judge Leventis excused him to return to the witness room, Melvin Ellis had become a "Flying Coyote," the term a public-defender's insult taken from the inevitable moment in Road Runner cartoons when Wile E. Coyote blunders off a cliff and hangs airborne for an instant—his eyes crazy kaleidoscopes—before plummeting to a disastrous, puff-of-dust splat.

Morley rested his case, didn't have any more witnesses or evidence, and Andy called Coy Hubbard to testify. Wearing a Western suit with dark piping, cowboy boots and a garnet tie tack, and speaking in a dignified mountain cadence, Hubbard put the lie to Ellis's fantastical claims about a Miranda card. "Never seen a card, no, sir," he said bluntly. "When Investigator Ellis was readin' Mr. Bullins his rights, I was focusin' on Bullins, but I do recall turnin' in Officer Ellis's direction a time or two, and he had a folder open and was lookin' down in it while he was readin'.'"

"Did you ever see that folder tucked under the investigator's arm?" Andy asked.

"No, sir."

"Was there ever a wallet in his hand?" Andy asked.

"Not that I seen, no, sir."

"Did he inform the defendant of his right to remain silent?"

"I can't honestly say one way or the other. I wasn't payin' close attention to the particulars. I had my full mind on The Bull...uh, Mr. Bullins."

Morley remained animated and cocksure, smiled and mugged as if he were invincible and pretended Coy Hubbard's truth didn't make a whit of difference, and he salvaged what he could when he questioned the deputy. He gestured at Damian Bullins. "You heard the defendant answer questions?"

"I did," Hubbard said.

"Is the handwritten Q&A prepared by Officer Ellis an accurate record of what was said there in the camper?"

"It's accurate," the cop replied. "What Officer Ellis wrote down is what Mr. Bullins told us."

Lois Duncan was the final witness to testify for the defendant, and she had a sweet, delicate disposition, her gray hair beauty-parlored into place, her lipstick of the variety that left red imprints on a tissue she kept in her purse. She described her son Lonnie, and she talked about his drug addiction, and how he'd stolen money from her, and forged her checks, and lost his temper and wrecked her home, and she told the courtroom only one policeman had ever seemed concerned about saving her boy: Mr. Melvin Ellis. Andy let her meander and reminisce, and after several minutes of rambling, he gently steered her toward the payoff.

"Now, Mrs. Duncan," Andy said, "do you recall the last time Investigator Ellis was in your home, in the kitchen, and your son admitted to stealing your prescription pills? In January of this year?"

"I do," she answered. "Officer Ellis made us a promise that if Lonnie told the truth and owned up to stealing the pills, he would speak for us in court and try to have my son sent for treatment instead of jail. And that's what he done. He fought for Lonnie."

"I understand," Andy said. "But in the past, sometimes you, as a mom who loved her son, sometimes you decided you just didn't want to testify against Lonnie and cause him trouble, correct?"

"That's true, sir. I'm a widow too."

"And sometimes Lonnie would admit things to you, then he'd change his story once you were in court."

"Occasionally," Mrs. Duncan answered.

"So Officer Ellis wisely wrote down Lonnie's confession when you three were there in the kitchen and he made you that deal. So Lonnie couldn't crawfish on you again. There was a record if you or Lonnie got cold feet."

"Yes. Yes, sir."

"And," Andy asked, "he read Lonnie his Constitutional rights?"

"Yes. Even though he was our friend, he done it like you're supposed to. Official. Didn't cut any corners."

"You were there and saw and heard everything?"

"Yes."

"Did Officer Ellis read those rights from a card, ma'am?" Andy asked.

"No," Mrs. Duncan said. "They was wrote on a paper he had in his folder. He read them off the paper, and Lonnie signed everything."

"Did you ever see a card that looked anything like this?" He showed her the card Morley had submitted into evidence.

"No, sir. There was never a card."

"Did Investigator Ellis ever remove his wallet?"

"No."

"Are you positive he read the rights from a sheet of paper?"

"I'm positive."

"Thank you, ma'am," Andy said sincerely. "Mr. Morley may have questions for you."

It wasn't much and it vanished quickly, but Morley finally showed a flash of distress—lines etched across his forehead and he narrowed his eyes. He stood there silent, thinking. Uncertain. He aimlessly opened and closed a file on the table. He stalled some more by rummaging around in a box of papers. "Ma'am, good morning to you," he said to Mrs. Duncan, evidently having decided to roll the dice.

"Same to you, sir," she replied.

"It's fair to say, ma'am, and I'm not trying to give you a hard time about your testimony and what you *believe* you recall, but the main person, the person the officer was reading the rights to, was your son, Lonnie?"

"Yes."

"And he might remember this differently?" Morley inquired.

Lois Duncan appeared bewildered, and she didn't respond.

"Lonnie might remember the card," Morley prompted her, "but Mr. Hughes didn't call him as a witness."

"Sir, my son is dead. The drugs, they were impossible for him." She said it matter-of-factly, no tears, no petition for pity in the answer, long ago wrung-out and reconciled to the gouge in her heart.

"Oh, no," Morley responded. "So sorry. We'll keep you in our prayers."

Andy joined the bailiff at the witness stand, and he gripped Mrs. Duncan's elbow, more a courtesy than a necessity, and he helped her balance as she made the step down from the chair. "Thank you for coming, ma'am," he told her, his voice normal so the microphone spread the words around the room. "I realize this had to be tough for you."

Andy's closing argument was concise, took five minutes, and he cited the law and highlighted the dreadful inconsistencies in Melvin Ellis's testimony. He was methodical and poised and polished thanks to plenty of mirror rehearsal and a meticulous critique from Vikram. As he returned to his seat at counsel table, he sensed Cole Benson watching him, fierce and enraged, but he left that situation alone, let it go. Benson had every right to despise him—from where the widower sat, Andy Hughes was a devil with a briefcase full of clever deception and crafty cant, a shyster trying to whitewash a killer's bloody sin.

Morley was flamboyant, pacing as he spoke, and he migrated to the first row of the gallery and rested a hand on Cole Benson's powerful shoulder, reminded everyone "justice isn't only about rules and technicalities, but it's about a husband's profound loss." Fifteen minutes into his oration, he finally mentioned Melvin Ellis, and—with a finger jab and tent-revival fervor—he urged the judge to believe the cop's story.

"Have you heard one person today testify this experienced officer did not read the defendant his complete Miranda warnings?" he thundered at Judge Leventis. "All the defendant has done is nibble around the edges with innuendo and ugly speculation and a silly little theater stunt." He removed his round watch from its vest slit, sprung open the gold cover. "I apologize for taking so much time," he said, "but I'm greatly moved by Mrs. Benson's death, and we're here this morning to consider accommodating a murderer because of a bogus claim about a Miranda warning, a warning that wouldn't have made any difference whatsoever to a man who was 'ready to go,' and wanted to confess. The commonwealth is confident this court has the facts to deliver a correct ruling." Morley took a seat, adjusted his pocket square, thumb-swiped his upper lip. Hot as it was, he buttoned his coat.

A spectator in the gallery coughed. A cloud shifted and sunlight bored through a window, spreading a checkered pattern across the vacant jury box. The bailiff discreetly moved so he was behind Bullins. A frail man with a leg brace limped closer to the front of the room. The air conditioning hummed from vents. A photographer changed her lens.

Judge Leventis sat so her shoulders were not touching her chair. She was facing Morley. "Simply put, someone did indeed tell me Officer Ellis failed to read a full, accurate set of Miranda warnings to the defendant. I heard Officer Ellis admit exactly that in his own recorded words. On audio, before he realized his form was inadequate, he confirmed he used this flawed, preprinted document and read from it 'word for word.' Officer Hubbard's honest and objective testimony makes clear to me there was no card used at the camper, and the investigator's demonstration of how he claims to have produced the card from his wallet bordered on slapstick and was not convincing. In a context where the commonwealth bears a heavy burden of proof, Lois Duncan's testimony further impeaches Investigator Ellis's version of events—"

"Judge, if I could—"

"Mr. Morley," Judge Leventis said calmly, "please do *not* interrupt me. You're free to add whatever you wish once I'm finished with my thoughts."

Morley stood and glowered and hitched his trousers and stepped forward, but he kept his mouth shut.

"According to the law, specifically *Miranda v. Arizona* and the Virginia case of *Timbers*, the defendant's motion is granted, and the commonwealth will not be allowed to present Mr. Bullins's statement in its case-in-chief. This is not a close call. Officer Ellis utterly lacked credibility." The judge collected the courtroom's old wooden gavel and gripped it with both hands. "I'm aware this is a murder case, and I'm aware there's a grieving family, and I've now read the defendant's statement, which is quite damning. However, the law is the law, and we don't bend it or ignore it merely because honoring it might yield an outcome we find unpleasant or unfair." She returned the gavel, quietly and gently, to its place on the bench, so carefully that it didn't make the slightest sound.

CHAPTER EIGHT

"DAMN, WE'RE HOME FREE!" Bullins exclaimed the moment he, Andy and Vikram were back in the witness room, the door shut, none of them seated. He pumped his fist. "Wow, sir, thanks. I'd shake your hand if we didn't have this disease goin' round. Thank you too, Mr. Kapil." Their masks were off, but they remained apart.

"You're welcome," Andy said indifferently. "Exactly what do you mean by 'home free,' Damian?"

"I should win my case now."

Andy laid his file on the table. He sighed. "Do you recall our many conversations at the jail on the subject of the motion to suppress?"

"Sure. Yeah." Bullins was excited, his hands busy, his features animated.

"Did I tell you the charge would completely go away if the judge ruled in our favor?" Andy pointed at Bullins. "In fact, Damian, I told you the exact opposite—the commonwealth still has plenty of evidence to convict you. Remember?"

"Sorta, I guess."

"I'm positive you do." Andy stopped pointing. "Our position is improved, and we can use this ruling to negotiate a favorable sentence for you. But the case is far from being over. I wouldn't make a reservation at the steakhouse for tomorrow night."

There was a knock on the door, and Curtis Matthews popped his head into the room. "Well done," he said to Andy. "I heard the widow lady's testimony and your final argument. You were on the money."

Kellie appeared beside Curtis. "Congratulations," she said. "Several reporters are waiting and want to talk to you."

"I'll pass," Andy replied. "I'm sure Peter the Great is talking enough for both of us."

"So the press is a no?" Curtis asked.

"Definitely," Andy answered. "I'll catch up with you guys as soon as I finish with Mr. Bullins. Shouldn't be too long. Meet you at the high school parking lot."

"Proud of you," Curtis said. He closed the door.

Bullins was in a rush, spoke the instant the door latch clicked. "I've been thinkin' about this, about that day, and the more I study on it, I believe I need to correct my statement, 'specially if the case won't be dismissed."

Vikram dropped his leather satchel on a chair. His mouth thinned. He tugged his tie away from his collar.

"Correct it how?" Andy asked.

Bullins half-sat on a stout wooden table, his knees bent, both brown shoes on the floor. "Well, since there's no statement, things are kinda open, and once my head cleared and my memory got better, I think I want to say, uh, the truth, Mr. Hughes...and Mr. Kapil...and the truth is Mrs. Benson was already dead when I found her. I need to tell...what really happened. And since my prior statement from when I was high and confused is thrown out, who can prove different?"

"Seems you've been giving your situation lots of productive thought," Andy said dryly.

"Yeah. I guess when I was stuck with the statement, it really didn't matter because I'd look like I was lyin' or makin' up shit just to save my own skin if I changed my story. But thanks to what you did today, I can tell my side and defend myself."

Andy glanced at Vikram, who grimaced. "Here's the rub, Damian," Andy told his client. "You need to pay very close attention to precisely what the judge said. The commonwealth isn't allowed to use your confession during its case-in-chief—in other words, when it first presents its evidence—but Peter Morley darn sure can use your statement as impeachment, to contradict you, if you take the stand and try to sell some rogue's nonsense. Understand?"

Bullins pushed away from the table, scratched his head. His mouth gaped for a second before he spoke. "Wait. Hold on. Even though it's throwed out because that asshole Ellis lied and broke the law, you're claimin' it isn't really out? How can that be?"

"The Walder-Harris Doctrine, Damian. I think it's a pretty reasonable rule. The commonwealth can't use a statement obtained in violation of your Constitutional rights, but the initial exclusion of the statement isn't a license for you to commit wholesale perjury if you decide to take the stand and peddle a totally different tale. In plain terms: The commonwealth can't ever use the statement *unless* you elect to take an oath and say something completely different. Then the court will allow it back into evidence. Almost common sense."

"All this rigmarole today didn't really help me with diddly," Bullins declared, angry, his neck beginning to splotch. "I need to be able to tell the whole truth. Bitch was dead when I got there, and I was confused and pressured and high and…kinda gave in to them. Said what the cops wanted to hear."

"I've explained why and how this helps you, Damian," Andy replied. "My goal is to see if we can negotiate a ten-year sentence. For murder. For killing an innocent mother of four darling girls."

"Andy has moved mountains for you, Mr. Bullins," Vikram noted. "You've received remarkable legal representation from him. With this ruling, there's a legitimate chance to reduce your punishment."

Andy locked on to Bullins. "I guess, Damian, your memory will have to become even sharper—the current version isn't quite the ace you imagined."

"This isn't right," Bullins fumed. "The whole crooked system is stacked against the little man." He twisted sideways, balled a fist, and hit the table. "Nothin' but bullshit. Bullshit!" He struck the table again.

"Anything else before I go?" Andy pulled a long breath, exhaled. "Calm down and don't cause the cops any problems. Watch your temper and don't say a word to anyone. Act like a man."

Bullins didn't respond. His hands were trembling, his neck flushed, his eyes inflamed.

Andy rapped on the door, and a uniformed state trooper opened it. "Please tell Ralph we're ready to leave," Andy instructed him.

"I'm right here," Bailiff Howell said. He walked into sight. "Waitin' on you, sir."

"Thanks, Ralph," Andy told him. "How about you take Vik and me out through the rear exit? I wouldn't want to interrupt Peter Morley's campaign speech on the front steps, and I don't have any interest in being interviewed. The less we say, the better."

"Sure thing," Howell replied. "Mr. Morley, he's a doozy, isn't he?"

Andy and Vikram hustled through the courthouse's backdoor and zipped toward the Jeep, and they were inside the vehicle, Andy cranking the motor, before an amoeba of cameras, men, women, microphones, and tape recorders spotted them and closed in, rapid and clamorous. Andy shifted into drive and left the media behind, shouting questions and jogging across the parking lot.

"What an absolute, depraved bastard," Andy said to Vikram as they were turning onto Main Street. "Damian completely distorts everything we've told him, then concocts a claptrap lie for us to push, then plays the victim when we tell him he can't scam the system. He's easily the worst person I've ever defended. He's truly enraged because he'll be punished for murder. The single decent thing he's ever done—accept responsibility for a brutal killing—goes by the boards as soon as he has a few weeks to feel sorry for himself and plot and scheme."

Vikram clicked his safety belt. "I was surprised. He was so angry and frustrated. Maniacally mad for no reason. We need to make certain a court or jury never catches a glimpse of that. And you be careful around him."

"You didn't even see his A-game, Vik. He was just warming up."

Vikram pulled slack in the shoulder harness. "I'm surprised he confessed to begin with. Not his style."

"Something that horrific, even if you're a career criminal, no doubt has an immediate and overwhelming impact on you. You've finally crossed the holy, inviolate line, and you're stranded and beast-marked forever. There's no possible fix or excuse. And Damian knew he'd be caught sooner or later. With most people, the murder guilt will haunt you, and the remorse will dominate your life. For Damian, his tiny flicker of conscience disappeared about the time the various drugs left his system and he learned he's staring at forty years. Same as we see every day, Vik. People admit their crimes, regret it, then lie and fudge and swear they've been wronged."

"Yep. Once, Elmo Wiggins, the burglary king, was arrested and confessed, and he quickly regretted his spasm of truth-telling, recanted, and advised me he could pray for forgiveness just as well at home as in jail." Vikram chuckled.

"At least Elmo was tolerable to be around. I never had an issue with him."

"Well, congrats again. You did some remarkable lawyering today."

Andy rolled down his window. "Strange profession ours, isn't it? We celebrate the lawyers who do the most injury to justice, who sucker punch the truth. Our deities are the men and women who slickster the notoriously guilty free and leave pitiable victims holding the bag. I'm literally fighting to deny a widower and semi-orphans their due." He flipped the blinker, and the green arrow flashed. "We're mechanics who sneak sugar into gas tanks, surgeons who do a victory dance after butchering a major artery."

Vikram peered at him. "You're difficult to please, Andy. One day your job is numbing and repetitive and inconsequential, and you decide to quit, and now you're unhappy because it's too profound. Don't ever think we're surgeons or mechanics or anything close—we don't have that much influence. We're the drones on the assembly belt, following the manual jot and tittle, and the machine spits out the product our superiors designed it to make."

"I suppose that's one way to look at it," Andy replied. "I'm not complaining either. I enjoy trying a real case. I do. This is incredible. It'd be more satisfying, though, if I had a client who deserved the help instead of a despicable killer." He shook his head. "Recently, Damian somehow convinced the green, hayseed jailer that he's a veteran who served at Ia Drang in the Air Cav—a total lie so he could receive a few extra inmate privileges. Damian was born in 1974. He didn't fight in Viet Nam. Just never stops with him."

"Says a lot about both the staffing at the jail and Mr. Bullins's brazen nature. You'd think he'd at least make the effort to claim the Gulf War or Afghanistan." Vikram frowned. He was watching the road. "So...so what comes next?"

"It's a safe bet," Andy answered, "Peter Morley's still busy raging at the feckless, liberal judge and the failures of the turnstile justice system and writing checks he knows he'll never have to cash—"

"Exactly," Vikram chimed in. "He'll appeal this, even though Judge Leventis ruled correctly, and by the time it winds through the high courts and her ruling is upheld, Senator Peter Morley will no longer be the commonwealth's attorney in Dunford County, and someone else will be left to pick up the pieces and actually finish the case."

"No doubt," Andy agreed. "We're officially at a standstill for months, dead in the water."

"Would it do any good," Vikram asked, "to contact Morley and see if we can make a deal as he's heading for the Capitol? He can blame the judge for tying his hands and boast about not dragging Mr. Benson and his daughters through months of torment. A chance for him to save face."

"Can't hurt, and I'm obligated to try," Andy answered. "Did you pay much attention to Benson? He's not a guy I'd ever want to cross."

"Curiously, from all I've read or heard, he has the reputation as a very generous, very ethical businessman."

***

CURTIS AND KELLIE WERE waiting in a corner of the Patrick County High School parking lot, outside, next to Curtis's Toyota sedan. The four of them kept their Covid-19 distance and talked about the hearing and Melvin Ellis's audacious lies, and when they were ready to leave, they decided Vikram would return to Martinsville with Curtis, and Kellie would stay with Andy.

"I'll be off the clock for the rest of the day," Andy informed Vikram. "And my morning tomorrow is blank, so I'll see you around noon."

"You've certainly earned a break," Vikram said. "What time did you quit preparing last night?"

"Ten or ten thirty," Andy answered. "In my own defense, I left tomorrow morning free in case we had to find something quickly for the judge or write a snap-brief."

"I, on the other hand," Kellie said, grinning, "drew down my tiny vacation allowance by seven hours because I'd seen the rehearsals and anticipated we might be able to relax a bit tonight and celebrate an office victory. I'll be there at noon, also."

"Call me if you guys need bail," Curtis joked. "Or extra muscle in a bar brawl."

Andy removed the roof panels from the Jeep, and he and Kellie drove to a grocery store and bought a six-pack of Miller High Life bottles along with two sub sandwiches from the deli and a bag of baked potato chips. They traveled thirty-five minutes to the Blue Ridge Parkway, stopped at The Saddle overlook near Meadows of Dan and, still wearing their nice clothes, walked a dirt trail for a few hundred yards, Kellie in the lead. They spread a ragged blanket in a brief opening on a high mountain ledge above a valley beginning to dot yellow and crimson and drank beer and watched hawks bounce and glide in the currents, the view for miles and miles, everything made miniature, wee roads, a bottle-cap lake and occasional matchbox patches of cleared land patterned into the earth beneath them.

They were mostly quiet; it wasn't a place for chitchat, and after his first beer, Andy reclined against a large rock and Kellie took off her shoes, rolled her slacks to her knees, and rested her head in his lap. "What a day," she said. "Nearly perfect."

They ate the sandwiches and drank four of the beers, two each, and they left the mountain and Andy drove them to Wild Magnolia, a Martinsville restaurant where the local lawyers unwound at the bar. They arrived at four thirty, and Willie Bourland and Roy Reid were already on stools, taking advantage of dollar-drafts.

"The TV star," Willie said good-naturedly when he spotted Andy and Kellie. "Just saw you on CNN."

"You signing autographs?" Roy asked. He slid off the stool and mock bowed. "All kidding aside," he said, "nice job."

"How about a victory shot on us?" Willie offered. "They have a bottle of Colonel Taylor's single barrel."

Andy glanced at Kellie. "Well, I—"

"I'll treat Kellie too," Willie said.

"Thanks, Willie, but I'm not a fan of room-temperature brown liquor," she answered. "I'll have a cold beer, please, if you're buying."

"Appreciate it, Willie," Andy said. "Sure."

Andy asked for his bourbon in a highball glass with a single ice cube, and more lawyers and a retired cop joined them, and Kellie's friend Anita from the clerk's office stopped by, and they picked teams and played a video trivia game and pestered the barkeep until he changed the music to a Spotify party mix, and nearly everyone sang the title lines of "Brick House" and "Big Poppa." Andy cashed in Kellie's shot of bourbon for himself, thanked Willie for the generosity, clinked his glass against her beer mug, and all of them, including a probation officer who'd wandered in, enjoyed a raucous, merry afternoon, friends and colleagues, the pandemic gloom temporarily suspended, though it was habit by now not to crowd your buddies too closely, and Roy made the rounds with hand-sanitizer squirts after the trivia contest ended.

At dusk, the bar celebration began to wane, and Andy and Kellie ordered a to-go box of wings and chicken tenders. Andy gunned the bottom of a final bourbon, his third. Kellie hadn't even finished her first beer, and she volunteered to drive. He handed her the key, no argument or protest. "I'm probably legal," he said, "but thanks, good idea. I'm a little buzzed."

They'd traveled a quarter mile on the country road to Andy's house, and he had his hand on Kellie's thigh, the windows cracked, the roof still open, a luminous crescent moon pinned against a clear sky, and he asked her to pull over.

"Where?" She rolled the radio knob, lowered the volume. "Why? You okay?"

"There," he said, "right there, on the shoulder, next to the fence."

She slowed and steered the Jeep into the grass, the passenger-side tires in a slight ditch when they stopped. The vehicle was uneven, slanted away from the pavement, the headlights on high, illuminating a churn of insects and a grayish streak of asphalt. Andy pulled the shift into park, set the handbrake, and slid closer to her. He kissed her, and she touched his face and neck, and in no time, his hands were underneath her blouse, and she was unbuttoning his shirt, and then she helped him with her bra, and they kept kissing and undressing until she was topless and his shirt was undone. They were wedged together, jammed between the two seats, her hip on the console. "I want to go to your house," she said. "So we'll have room."

"Drive like hell."

He kept kissing her while she drove the last few minutes, and he unhooked the clasp at the top of her pants and started on the zipper, and she arched and shimmied to help him strip her. She was naked except for her panties and a single sock when they arrived at his house, the yard dark, only a sixty-watt post light burning. He left his shirt in the Jeep, and he climbed out through her door, right behind her. They kissed some more, her bare back against the warm hood, and she unfastened his belt and pulled it through the loops, dropped it on the ground.

"Andy? Andy."

He separated from Kellie, peered at her face, confused. She pushed at him, jerked straight and rigid, covered her chest with her forearm. A silhouette moved on the small front stoop.

"Who's there?" Andy shouted. "Get in the Jeep," he instructed Kellie, and he put his hands on her hips and guided her toward the door.

"Andy, I'm so sorry. It's me, Brooke."

Kellie was in the driver's seat, the interior light shining, scrambling for her blouse.

"Damn, Brooke, what the hell are you doing, lurking on my friggin' porch? Hiding?"

"I'm so sorry," she repeated. "I have an emergency."

"Where's your Explorer? How'd you get here?"

"I pulled it behind the garage, so it's not obvious from the road. There's no room inside because of all your tools and shop stuff."

"How about you call me first?" Andy said. He looked behind him and could see the outlines of her SUV tucked close to the building.

"I did. I left you two messages."

"We didn't have service on the parkway," Kellie reminded him. "And you didn't take the phone with you when we were at the bar." She'd regained her blouse and was searching for her shoes.

"What's the emergency?" Andy asked. "Oh goodness, it's not Noah, is it?" His tone changed.

"Basically, yes," she answered.

"What? What's happened?" He reached across Kellie, grabbed his shirt and was buttoning it as he hurried toward Brooke. "Oh shit," he blurted when he was close enough to see her plainly. She was wearing gray sweatpants, a baggy PHCC T-shirt, a thin jacket and flip-flops. A cut split her eyebrow, and the skin around her cheekbone was discolored. "Oh my. You okay?"

"Now I am. Howard and I had a fight. I didn't have anywhere else to go or take our son. I didn't want to put him in a hotel, so I brought him here, but you weren't at home, so I've been waiting. He's in the den, playing video games."

"Yeah, I thought he was with you until tomorrow night—your birthday and all."

"Some birthday," she said ruefully. "Seems bland, reliable Howard has a CNA girlfriend roughly half his age."

"Sorry," Andy mumbled. "Never would've suspected it."

"His plan was for me to just tolerate it and overlook it and be happy to be his '1-A lady.'" She wiped her wrist across her nose. There was a blood smudge above the stenciled P on her shirt. She sad-laughed. "I had no idea. None. What an idiot."

"Have you called the cops?" Kellie asked. She was disheveled but dressed. She walked toward Andy, stopped slightly behind him. "I'm Kellie," she said. "Kellie Alison."

"I'm so sorry to show up here with no warning," Brooke replied, her voice fractured, strained. "Embarrassed. I—"

"No worries," Kellie assured her. She stepped forward so she was beside Andy. "You did the right thing. I understand. Appreciate your trying to phone us."

"Thanks," Brooke said softly. "Andy's mentioned you. From his office at..." She trailed off, didn't finish her thought.

"So *did* you call the cops?" Andy asked.

"No," Brooke answered. She wiped at her nose again. Rubbed the corner of her eye. "We were arguing, and it just got worse and worse and louder—"

"And why wouldn't it?" Kellie interrupted. "Given what your husband did."

Brooke was emotional, struggling not to cry. Her voice sputtered and quavered. "He told me...well, he said something awful, and I slapped him, my mistake, and...just like that he punched me and went off, yelling and screaming and making threats. When the quiet types lose it, they explode. I got Noah and left. I was afraid he'd come after us, so I hid the Explorer and waited in the dark."

"You should still report this," Andy encouraged her. "A provoked slap doesn't give him the legal right to bust open your head."

"Whatever," Brooke said. "Is it worth dragging our son to court and dealing with all the humiliation? He'll just say I hit him first, and he was trying to defend himself."

"He didn't do anything to Noah, did he?" Andy demanded. "If he did, court will be the least of his worries."

"Honestly, no," Brooke answered. "But once he said he ought to kill me, I was scared and left."

"First thing in the morning," Andy said, "you need to go see a lawyer. I'd suggest Janine Jacob or Hoyt Barrow. Make sure you photograph the injury too."

"Okay, yeah, I should," Brooke replied, without conviction. "Yeah."

"Short term," Andy said, "we...uh...need to figure this out for tonight."

Kellie spoke immediately. "You and your son stay here, Brooke." She tucked a loose section of blouse into her slacks. "I had no idea Noah was going to be here—"

"We've been trying to ease into an introduction," Andy explained. "Very carefully."

"He's had enough surprises for one night," Kellie said. "I'll take the Jeep to my apartment and drive it to the office tomorrow."

"Yeah, I agree." Andy stuck his hands in his pockets. "And…I'll stay on the sofa," he added awkwardly. "The sofa," he needlessly repeated. "We'll do our best to handle this with Noah in the morning. If that's okay by you, Kellie?"

"I suggested it, Andy," she said tersely. She paused. "Good luck, Brooke," she offered sympathetically. "Sorry to meet like this."

"Okay," was all Brooke could muster.

Andy draped an arm around Kellie, and they turned for the Jeep. His heel crunched gravel when he pivoted. He noticed his belt lying near a tire.

"What do you think I don't know?" Noah was on the porch, Patches planted next to him. He was upset, shouting, every word an attack. "Mom and Howard had a fight, and I hate him. Kellie's your new girlfriend. I'm not a dummy." He began sobbing, and he kneeled down and wrapped up the dog, and the tears—the worst Andy had ever experienced—sliced his parents' hearts. Kellie told him she'd be fine and to go take care of his boy.

❖❖❖

THE FOLLOWING MORNING, BOTH Brooke and Andy were awake before the sun rose, and they sat at the kitchen table, the room dim, and drank coffee, his black, hers with two-percent milk that was a day past its use-by date. Despite their cordial relationship, it was the first time they'd shared breakfast in years, and the first time she'd stayed over at his house since 2011. They'd spent the greater part of the night with their son, Brooke beside him on his single bed, comforting him, Andy sitting cross-legged on the floor, dumbfounded, at a loss for helpful words or a balm that would ease Noah's distress.

"It's probably not safe for you to live with your husband," Andy warned her. "More to the point," he said, "I don't want Noah in that environment." He hooked a finger around the handle of his mug. "You're telling me the truth? Howard didn't do or say anything to Noah?"

"No, he didn't. He was too busy unloading on me. But Noah heard and saw almost the whole fight. Sorry."

"I will drive over there right now," Andy declared, "and beat his ass if he so much as *looked* at my son the wrong way."

"He didn't bother Noah."

"What did he possibly say that caused you to slap him? If you didn't slug him when he admitted having an affair and evidently didn't plan to change his habits—what raises the ante from that?"

"It doesn't matter," she demurred.

"Legally and going forward in a divorce, it might make a difference. There's big provocation and minor provocation." Andy drank his coffee. He watched her over the rim of the mug.

"We were both yelling and screaming, and he told me I'd be seeing my 'budget' cut in half since…since my 'pussy contribution' wouldn't be nearly as much." Repeating the insult made her mad. Her face tightened, her eyes narrowed. "What an asshole."

"I'd say the slap was justified. As righteous as they come." He set his mug on the table.

"Yeah," she replied. "I don't really regret it."

"I'm not trying to meddle," Andy said, "but I hope you'll consider my advice and start tending to your situation this morning. I'll take photos. You need to see a lawyer *today*. Immediately. You should file for a protective order since he threatened to hurt you."

"Okay," she answered. She was staring out the window. The sky was starting to color, a band of brilliant orange pushing up from behind the mountains. "I will." The words were almost sough.

"Until you have a more permanent plan, you and Noah can live here for a few days, and I'll see if Kellie will let me stay at her apartment. I don't want Noah suffering any more upheaval and change—this whole revamped school thing is enough of a distraction for him."

"I'm not sure…I…well, maybe for just a couple days…until I can…"

"We'll figure it out," he said. "You might wind up with Patches, depending on the rules at Kellie's place."

"Thanks, Andy." Spills of window light captured the side of her face, and he could see the tears, so heavy that they soaked her cheek, curved at her jawline, and wet her neck.

He visited with Noah and told him how much he loved him and explained he was safe and would be living at the house for a while. Brooke lingered in the doorway and watched and listened, still wearing the same clothes, her cheekbone now mounded with yellow, purple and crimson swelling. He fed Patches, packed clothes and toiletries, checked the power on the Invisible Fence, ate a banana and a pear slice, and Vikram detoured to pick him up at eight thirty, hours earlier than he'd planned to leave for work.

The Jeep was in his parking spot at the PD's lot, and he said a hasty good morning to Cindy and took forty or fifty pink message slips from her as he dashed by her desk and down the hall. Kellie was in her office, a file spread on her desk, and she didn't notice him until he was well into the room. When she saw him, she slipped out white earbuds and raked through her hair with all five fingers.

"Morning," he said, halting next to a client chair.

"Morning," she replied.

"I'm sorry about last night. It was a mess."

"It is what it is," she said unhappily. She shrugged.

"Well, I appreciate your being so kind about everything."

"Okay." She was cupping the earbuds in her palm. "I feel sorry for Noah. Hope he's better."

"He's at least not weeping now." Andy thought about sitting but didn't. "It has to be hard for him."

"True."

"So, uh, yeah," Andy stammered. "Yeah. Thanks and apologies."

"You're welcome," she said, her voice a monotone. "No need to keep mentioning it."

"I won't." He cleared his throat. "Are you upset with me?"

"I'm not upset with *you*, Andy," she answered. "You didn't do anything to me. Nothing."

"I realize—"

She didn't allow him to finish. "Everyone involved did the right thing. You're a good dad, and you put your son first. You should. I have no issues with Brooke. But sometimes the slipstream of correct choices buffets the hell out of blameless people who're caught up in it, okay? You wind up naked and embarrassed in a coworker's front yard."

"Sure." He sighed. "Understood."

"Or, it's the same as...you know, if I catch pneumonia, it's not your fault, but I still feel sick and miserable. Can't help it." She opened a drawer, dropped in the earbuds. "We're not engaged or married or...anything. We're just dating. For around two months. And it's been great. But last night clarified the realities for me—there's a lot that would have to factor into our math if we keep seeing each other."

"I've had a great time with you too," Andy said. "I couldn't be happier. Your being so incredibly understanding about Brooke and Noah just adds to how much I like you."

"Jeez," she answered, "you sound like a glib cad at the end of a *Bachelorette* episode."

"I've never seen the show," Andy said. "How about this, then: I hope we can stay together and keep going. So far, from all I can tell, that would make me the luckiest man on the planet."

"Is your ex still at your house?" she asked.

"Yeah, until we can find a safe spot for her and Noah. I hope she'll be gone in a few days."

"Me too." Kellie cold-smiled her dismay at him. "Are you planning on staying there with them?"

"Ah, no...I'm not." Andy shuffled his feet. He coughed. "I figured I'd rent a hotel room for a couple of days," he fibbed. "Or maybe see about crashing at Curtis's place."

"Curtis has a wife and two kids," she noted.

"Well, it would only be temporary."

"Seems like you have a plan."

He looked at the floor, frustrated. "Doing the best I can."

"I'm not trying to be a bitch. Like I said, it's more about your circumstances than you as a boyfriend."

Andy moped in his office, the door shut, thumbing through the stack of messages, unable to concentrate, and the phone buzzed nonstop until he told Cindy he was too busy for calls. He went outside, lit a cigarette with a blue plastic lighter, and leaned against the side of a building, one leg stork-bent so his shoe sole pressed against the wall. He smoked the Marlboro to the butt. He needed to quit the habit, and maybe he would when he retired from the PD's office. He'd also missed six straight days at the gym, preoccupied with the Bullins case. He pushed away from the wall, decided he'd change clothes and drive to the fitness center and see if lifting weights and jogging on the treadmill would improve his mood.

He met Kellie as he rounded the building's brick corner and stepped onto the sidewalk. She stopped but wasn't close to him. "You can stay at my place," she said. "You'll have to drive me there anyway since I brought your Jeep here. Probably better to see how it goes than for me to fret about it for days." She was already turning for the office door while she spoke, so the last few words were faded and difficult to hear.

CHAPTER NINE

"FIRST THINGS FIRST," CINDY challenged Andy. "What did you do to Kellie? What happened?"

"Nothing. We had a bad night. My son and his mom are stuck at my house. It puts a strain on everyone." Andy had enjoyed an hour at the gym, showered at Kellie's, eaten lunch, and returned to work. "By the way, this is a law office, not TMZ, so you don't need to waste your energy on relationship sleuthing."

"Congrats on the Bullins ruling," she said.

"Thanks."

"Related to Mr. Bullins, among the messages I handed you earlier is one from Debbie Tatum. She's with social services in Patrick County."

"Social services?"

"Debbie phoned us yesterday. An anonymous female called social services claiming she had important information about Cole Benson."

"Was it Damian's idiot girlfriend again?" Andy asked.

"Nope, don't think so. According to Debbie, this lady was younger and well spoken, though it seemed as if maybe she was tryin' to disguise her voice. She gave Debbie a witness's name and address."

"A witness? To what?"

"No idea," Cindy replied.

"Did this woman sound sane? It'll be crackpot city for a couple of weeks given all the media coverage."

"Far as I know," Cindy answered. "I wrote down Debbie's number and also the tipster's number that Debbie copied from caller ID."

"Thanks. I'll take a look."

She raised her hand and pointed two fingers at her own eyes, then flashed the sideways *V* at Andy. "Watching you. Be good to Kellie."

Andy located the message and separated it from the pile on his desk. "Heather Farris," he said aloud. The address was an hour away in Winston-Salem, North Carolina. He called the number Debbie Tatum had provided and no one answered, nor was there a voicemail. A Google search came up empty, except for a Facebook link that took him to a page belonging to an attractive young woman whose profile picture showed her smiling and holding a Pomeranian with a rhinestone collar. She didn't appear to be a criminal, druggie, or lowlife, such as would have any connection with Damian Bullins. She'd listed her occupation as "student."

The public defender's office of seven lawyers shared a single part-time investigator, a savvy, boisterous former cop named Ted Utley. Paid for only twenty hours per week, he often worked triple that, and once a case caught his attention, he never let loose until he was satisfied he'd discovered every last speck of truth. Andy collected the message and went to Ted's office, where he found him with his feet on a credenza, engrossed in a NASCAR magazine. "Here's a prediction for you, Counselor," he told Andy, still reading his magazine. "Bill Elliott's boy Chase is the real item. He'll be the champ this year. You wait and see."

"I'll contact my bookie," Andy replied.

"What can I do for you, Mr. Hughes?" A robust seventy-three years old, Ted called all his public defender colleagues "mister" or "missus" no matter how often they'd asked him to use their familiar names.

"I need for you to please check on a lady named Heather Farris."

"Check for what?" Ted closed his magazine and tossed it on the credenza.

"I'm not certain. Supposedly, she has information about Cole Benson. An anonymous tip, so it's probably a dead end, but as you're well aware, we have to explore every lead."

"Yep," Ted agreed.

"The address is on this message." Andy stretched across the desk and handed the pink paper square to Ted. "There's a Facebook page that seems to match her as well."

"I'll nose around first thing in the morning."

"Thanks. Appreciate it."

"Say, what did you do to hurt Missus Alison's feelings? I hear you guys had a spat. She's a keeper. You'd be wise to make it right with her."

***

THREE DAYS LATER, ON September 25, a crisp autumn Friday, Andy traveled from Kellie's apartment to his own house so he could share breakfast with Brooke and Noah. While Noah was still in his room, Brooke detailed her plans and progress. She'd secured a protective order, she'd signed a six-months' lease for a rental home off Mulberry Road, and she liked her lawyer, Ms. Jacob, whom she described as a quiet warrior. Howard's attorney had agreed the cheating doc would temporarily pay for the new rental house and keep Brooke on his health-care insurance.

"I'd say you're in decent shape all things considered," Andy commented. "I can help a little too, if you run into a money pinch or Noah needs something extra."

"Thanks," she said. She was scooping bacon from the skillet with a plastic spatula and spreading it on a paper towel. She laid the last brown strip on the towel and looked at Andy intently. She took a breath, string-blinked. "But here's what's happening. Noah wants to stay with you. And I understand why. He announced that the new place is 'crappy' and 'scary.'"

"Well, is it?"

"Of course not, Andy. Why the hell would you even ask me?"

"I've not ever been there, so how would I know?"

"It's a nice, safe home—it's not Howard's forty-five hundred square feet and infinity pool, and not your *Garden & Gun* country-hip centerfold, but it's just fine."

"Okay, sure." He studied her. "Good to know."

"But I need you to…to…swear you won't use this whole nasty divorce to sandbag me, to try and take my son away from me."

"Why would I do that?" he asked, every syllable earnest.

"Because you love him, and he's exceptional and the most important thing in your life."

"We've been fair to each other so far, and I intend to continue. You're a good mom and a good person. Noah needs two parents."

"You can't sell me out," she said, "and cave in to him and isolate me because he's reluctant to stay at a new house and angry with me because of Howard."

"I'll do whatever it takes to keep us as equal parents, Brooke."

"So I have your word?" She was still focused on him, edgy and determined.

"Yes, absolutely," Andy vowed. "Here," he said reaching in her direction, "shake on it."

Their breakfast went well, and Noah seemed normal and content, in that he was grumpy and pasted to his iPad and had to be prompted three times to finish his orange juice and scrambled eggs. Patches stationed himself beside the table, his nose frantic each time the bacon plate was moved. Andy slipped him a single crispy scrap, but only after they'd finished eating and cleared the dishes—nothing worse than a dog table-begging, he reminded his son. He left with coffee in a Yeti Rambler, and he'd just pulled on to Route 58 when his phone played Ernie Ford's "Sixteen Tons."

"Morning, Boss," he said to Vikram.

"Morning," Vikram replied. "Where are you?"

"On 58, driving to work. Had breakfast at my house. My exile should end soon, I think, although there's a lot to like about staying with Kellie."

"You'll probably want to do a one-eighty and head for the Patrick County jail."

"Why?"

"Mr. Bullins has already phoned the office five times, claiming he has an emergency. He started last night. His girlfriend…sorry…his *fiancée* has also been haranguing us. We're informed Damian needs to speak to you or me in person. Immediately. Cindy thought I had court in Patrick County this morning so she called me first. My case there was continued late yesterday, and you're his lawyer anyway, so I wanted to give you the great news."

"Yeah, I'm sure it's critical," Andy scoffed. "He's probably prescribed yellow Valium instead of the more potent blue pills and wants me to sue the sheriff."

"What's on your schedule today?" Vikram asked.

"Guilty pleas with an agreement on five grand larcenies. Dawn Futrell's handling it for the commonwealth. Cut and dried, but I'm not due in court until eleven thirty." He glanced at the Jeep's clock. "I suppose I'll go see him now. May as well bite the bullet. Damn. No doubt it'll be a total fiasco. Cover for me if I'm late for my cases, okay?"

"Will do."

The thirty-minute trip to the jail was pleasant, the hardwoods starting to gussy-up in bright hues, the sky blue and fresh, the traffic modest, the only delay a tractor and hay baler driven by a man with a battered straw hat, sunglasses and a plaid shirt, who waved at Andy as he passed by in the fast lane. Andy couldn't help but listen when the canned news show on the radio mentioned his name and did a piece on the Benson murder. He left a voicemail for Kellie, told her he was thinking about her and would fetch them a pizza from Leonardo's—a favorite—for lunch.

Like many inmates, once free of dope, fed a jail diet, and confined by concrete and cinder blocks, Damian had gained weight, enough that it was noticeable. His belly spiked against his orange jumpsuit, and his face was fleshy and rounded. He arrived in the interview room, chained as usual, but wearing glasses and carrying a file thick with papers protruding willy-nilly.

"Man, finally, you're here." He sat, situated his folder on the table, and bent eagerly toward Andy. "We need to talk."

"What's so urgent, Damian?" Andy asked. "You can sit normally, please. No need for you to be in my face." Only Andy was wearing a mask.

"Sorry." He scooted the chair farther away. The legs scraped against the floor. "This is hard for me to say, Mr. Hughes, really tough, and I've been holdin' it a secret for a long time, but there's more I need to tell you 'bout Mrs. Benson."

"Well, Damian, you've already enlightened us as to how she was dead when you found her. Is there more to the story?"

"Yes. Yes, sir."

"Okay," Andy replied. "Quit beating around the bush. Just tell me version number three."

"I know this'll seem...seem...crazy, but, sir, I swear on the sacred name of Jesus, it's true." Damian drummed his fingers on the sloppy file. "Even better, I got the proof right here."

"Great." Andy made a point of checking his watch, raising his wrist to eye level.

"So, like I told you, poor Mrs. Benson was dead when I found her. But that didn't surprise me, you see. I knew she was. It was planned. Staged. And I agreed to take the fall."

Andy couldn't help himself. He reflexively bumped back in his seat and reset his head. "Say what?" He crossed his arms, incredulous.

"Yeah, yeah, crazy, right? But Mr. Benson, Cole, hired me to show up and confess."

"Bullshit, Damian," Andy snapped. He laughed. "Sure."

"Okay, I don't blame you for not believin' me. I don't—"

"You're telling me that you signed up for a murder you didn't commit—and signed up for the rest of your life in prison—for a paycheck? I guess you could use the money to buy unlimited canteen candy and postage stamps."

"Hear me out, please." Bullins waved his bound hands, fingers spread, palms apparent. "You have a son, and—"

Andy interrupted him again. "Do *not* mention my son," he warned, "or anything about me or my life outside of the legal job I'm doing for you."

"No, no, sorry, I just meant that as a dad you'd understand how much I love my boy and wanna help him."

"Yeah, I've seen that affection in action. Last time we were in court on the issue, you owed almost seventy grand in support arrears and hadn't paid a dime in years."

"No doubt," Bullins answered pensively. "I've failed my son as a father, and this, well, this gave me a chance to even the score and make up for my past mistakes. Mr. Benson agreed to pay for Damian Jr.'s school at NC State—we call my son DJ—then hire him for a job at a hundred thousand a year until he'd paid him a million. DJ didn't know nothin' 'bout our secret deal. He wasn't part of it except for gettin' the money. He's totally innocent."

"Nobody will ever believe you. I damn well don't. This is a Hail Mary, Frankenstein's monster of a lie, cobbled together to fit your current needs.

Long term, it's the kind of untruth and cowardly denial that'll make your situation worse by implicating an innocent victim. I know you, Damian—you're far too selfish and narcissistic to make any kind of sacrifice for another person. Never happen. Not you. You wouldn't spend a weekend in jail for your son, much less decades."

Bullins bowed his head, playacted sorrow and shame, and spoke while he was still slumped, gazing at the floor. "You're right, Mr. Hughes. See, I thought I was dyin'. Didn't have too much time left. Honestly, I probably wouldn't have done it otherwise."

"Why would you think you were dying?" Andy asked impatiently.

He changed position so Andy could see his face. "Remember how I told you in one of our first meetings I wasn't gettin' the medical treatment I was entitled to? Remember? I have this growth on my side. I definitely told you 'bout it. Last time I was at the jail, in 2018, the doctor was worried it might be cancer, then, after I pulled my sentence and was at home, it kept growin' bigger, and I was sick a lot, so I thought I had cancer."

"You mentioned a growth to me," Andy said. "So what? And, of course, you don't have cancer, correct? You just assumed you had a terminal illness—come on. And while you were free, I'm certain you didn't follow up with a physician."

"Man, no money, no insurance. But I really thought I was a goner." He removed the glasses, hung them in the neck of his orange jumpsuit. "They cut some of it out three weeks ago, and it turns out I'm okay. It's a…" He opened his file, removed a paper. "'Benign lipoma.'" He peered at Andy as soon as he finished reading. "There's proof for you. Medical records. My fiancée went by and got 'em straight from Dr. Owens's nurse. If you go back farther, the doctor mentions the cancer in a different report."

"Proof of what, Damian?"

"Proof of my story, my defense."

"But now you've decided to come clean." Andy's mask slipped below his nose, and he adjusted it. "I'm sure you have a compelling reason for this sudden change of heart."

"Yeah, I do. This dude Benson screwed me over. He made the first payment to DJ's college, then after I helped him, he crapped on me. He ain't paid another dime. The next semester's due, and Benson has refused to help. So, I mean, yeah, I know Mrs. Benson is dead, and that's awful, and what I agreed to might've been stupid, and I admit I done wrong in coverin' up the truth 'bout a killin', but here I sit, not dying and cheated outta the money for my son—I'm a victim too, Mr. Hughes. I was a sucker for a rich, powerful man."

"You're telling me Cole Benson paid for your kid's college?" Andy asked.

"I'm tellin' you, sir, he promised he would take care of DJ if I showed up and confessed to killin' his wife. And I did what he asked 'cause I thought I was dying, and I could finally be a father to DJ. Heck, my boy'd have college paid for and a million-dollar start, and I'd maybe spend a few months in a penitentiary hospital, which would be better than sufferin' in my camper, sick with no meds or food or insurance. But devious Mr. Mormon, he hoodooed me and only paid once, then forgot me and our deal. My fiancée wrote him for me, sent an email, and he's ignored us, treated me like dirt." He opened the file. "Here's the smokin' gun." He held up a sheet of paper, shook it. "This come direct from DJ's file at NC State. Copy of a check for $4,660 paid to the school for DJ. He has scholarships, and this was the amount left on his fall tuition for 2020."

"Let me see," Andy said.

"It's wrote from, you know, another company, a business trick, so Benson could hide what he was doin'. I'm sure if you track it all down, it'll come back to Cole. You would know how to get to the bottom of it, cut through the legal mumbo jumbo, but he damn well sent the money."

Andy took the paper, which showed a check copy from a company called Nephi26 Inc. "Damian Bullins Jr. #4570120" was written in the memo section. Andy was silent while he pondered the check. When he stopped studying the image, he focused on the ceiling, his chin angled, the copy on his lap. "And, Damian," he said, almost whispering, "Cole Benson murdered his wife because…"

"The *because* ain't our problem," Bullins insisted, the angst act instantly gone. He *voila* gestured with his hands, smug and satisfied with himself and his clever deceit. "Reasonable doubt, right, sir? You've said it yourself, like when we had the coke possession case with Judge Williams in 2013, and you reminded him that ten percent doubt and ninety percent certainty equals not guilty." He held up his index finger. "This, the true truth, won't require me to have to take the stand either. The illegal statement they pressured outta me stays gone. You can just show the check and my doctor records and tell what happened."

"Since you're an apprentice attorney these days, I'm sure you understand I can't just 'tell what happened.'"

"You have my word, on a stack of Bibles, this is true. Anyone can see why I did what I did and was slow to let the cat out of the bag. Cole paid for my son's school. I thought I had cancer, and this was a chance to do right by DJ, to take care of him. Cole made the first payment, roped me in, then welched on me, and here I sit. His chump. Lady was killed but not by me. As smart a lawyer as you are, you won't have any trouble makin' this stick."

Andy didn't reply. He sat there mute, his expression icy and impenetrable, the check copy still resting on his thighs. He noticed footsteps as someone passed by the door behind him. He could hear Damian breathing. He could smell him, a sourness that traced marrow deep.

"What?" Damian finally squawked. "You not gonna say nothin'?"

Andy placed the paper in the center of the table. "Here's your evidence." He stood and turned for the door.

"You're goin' to help me, right?" Bullins pleaded, his voice strained, uncertain. "You're my lawyer, and I didn't kill Cole's wife, and I've showed you the facts, clear as day, and you need to do your job and fight for me."

Andy opened the door and walked off, didn't answer, didn't stop, didn't hurry, didn't acknowledge his client.

●●●

Forty-five minutes later, as he was winding through the cloverleaf at the outskirts of Martinsville, Andy's phone buzzed, and Ted Utley's name and number flashed on the screen.

"What's up, Clouseau?" he asked.

"I kinda see myself more as Joe Mannix or Jim Rockford," Utley replied. "Or Easy Rawlins. The dashing gumshoe who solves the crime and woos the pretty ladies."

"No doubt," Andy chuckled.

"I have news about Heather Farris."

"That was fast," Andy noted.

"Wife wanted to go to the mall in Winston. There's a sale. Shoes. Lady already has more shoes than Carter's got liver pills, but happy wife, happy life, so we left early and I dropped her off and did a little explorin'."

"I hope you're not planning on charging the state mileage," Andy teased him.

"Moseyed over to Missus Farris's apartments. Nice location. Chatted with the mailman. A complex like hers, he's there most mornings for around thirty minutes. Sees a lot."

"That's smart, Ted. I'd never think to quiz the postman."

"He says this Heather's nice as can be, left him a Christmas gift the last two years and seems to stay close to home. Rides a bike, walks her itty-bitty dog. No drinkin' or drugs as best he can tell. Very peppy and sweet."

"Okay."

"I asked about the routine stuff, job, family, kids, boyfriends, and I learn she has a steady fellow, older gent, who the mailman has seen four or five times."

"Older gent?" Andy asked. He was stopped at a red light.

"Older than her," Ted explained. "Big guy. Crewcut."

"Damn. Here we go," Andy said. "Seriously? Let me guess."

"Ding, ding, ding, ding," Ted quipped. "I showed him a picture of Cole Benson, pulled it up on my phone, and he was like, 'yeah, could be.' He wasn't positive and obviously couldn't provide a name. But the busybody, retiree neighbor from down the hall was gung ho to tell the world every darn thing she knows about 'Heather the Tramp.' I asked her if she'd be kind enough to take a look at a picture, and she nearly bites my head off: 'I don't need a picture. It's Cole Benson, the Mormon millionaire whose wife was killed.'"

"You're the master, Ted."

"Appreciate the respect, Mr. Hughes, but this wasn't Cold War spyin' at the Kremlin. The neighbor lady—by the way, her name is Bessie Reed—was spillin' her guts while I was still puttin' her at ease with my carefully worded introduction and charmin' manner. Hadn't even displayed the badge, and she was lettin' it fly."

"You think she might be our tipster?"

"No, sir. I asked her 'bout the phone call to social services. Not her."

Andy's light turned green. "Can you run the caller ID number, find out who our mysterious benefactor is? Huge-ass coincidence we receive this adultery info the very same day our boy Damian engineers a tale making Benson's affair suddenly relevant. See if you can discover a name—or a location, even—for the number used to call social services."

"I'll try, Mr. Hughes, but the number definitely has a prepaid, throwaway feel, and tracking those rascals is as hard as eatin' mashed potatoes from a Dr. Pepper bottle."

CHAPTER TEN

"GIVE THE DEVIL HIS infernal due," Andy said. "It's a creative and cunning lie." He'd arrived at work and was sitting in Vikram's office. He'd repeated Bullins's most recent account of the murder to his boss. He'd also told him about Benson and Heather Farris. A boxed Leonardo's pizza was on the floor beside Andy, along with a small white bag of napkins, packaged oregano, and plastic knives and forks.

"Well," Vikram mused, "he's much smarter than the average criminal, and he's thoroughly experienced with the system." He pinched his chin with a thumb and forefinger. "He's been very careful as to how he's orchestrated this. He's adamant he's offering the truth, and the facts in isolation, such as the medical records or Mr. Benson's lady friend, are completely accurate, and if we can somehow link the check to Benson, that's also simply an objective data point—"

"Plus attorney-client privilege keeps everyone except you, me and Kellie from discovering the evolution of his story—no one else, especially a judge or jury, will ever learn this is his third iteration and the last two versions were tailored to fit his shifting legal situation."

While Andy was speaking, Vikram rolled his chair to a bookshelf behind his desk. He removed a thick black volume. "Triple checking, but this is a rule we all know well." He read from the Virginia Rules of Professional Conduct: "'The prohibition against offering false evidence only applies if the lawyer knows the evidence is false. A lawyer's reasonable belief or suspicion that evidence is false does not preclude its presentation to the trier of fact. A lawyer should resolve doubts about the veracity of testimony or other evidence in favor of the client.'" He closed the book.

"Yep," Andy agreed. "We're *required* to sell Damian's version of events as best we can, especially since his story can be tied to other true, genuine evidence. You and I don't sign the verdict form. Ultimately, a jury makes the call as to who's lying and who isn't."

Vikram was back at his desk, facing Andy. "The shrewd part of Damian's newest account is it doesn't conflict with his confession to the cops or his many admissions of guilt to you. He doesn't deny confessing, doesn't deny his several conversations with you accepting responsibly for the murder—he's only explaining *why* he confessed. A court veteran like Mr. Bullins understands he can't just outright lie to us and then have us vouch for a falsehood at trial. But this is ethically quite clean." He smiled weakly. "For us, for lawyers."

"So, Vik, it seems our legal dilemma is how we assemble this defense for a jury without Damian testifying. Me, I'd rather build the Damian-as-fall-guy tale indirectly so the confession's still excluded. Better if we don't get bogged down explaining the confession and its nasty, persuasive details, and we can stay on offense."

"Yeah," Vikram said, "any jury that hears the confession will believe it's the truth. Far too much venom and far too many horrible specifics for it to be a fake. It needs to stay gone."

"If we can somehow pull that off, all the commonwealth would have remaining is Damian's presence at the crime scene and the blood splatters on his pants. The jury would have no confession and a narrative suggesting Cole Benson had a reason for—and hand in—his wife's murder. We aim for a not-guilty verdict, a longshot, but more realistically, an obstruction of justice conviction—twelve months max. And if Damian never testifies, the jury won't be aware of his lengthy list of convictions unless and until they find him guilty."

"What can I do to help?" Vikram volunteered.

"Nothing right now, but thanks. I'll start trying to solve the Nephi riddle."

"Keep me posted."

Andy finished his circuit court larceny cases at noon. He sent a text to Kellie letting her know he was on his way for lunch, rewarmed the pizza in the breakroom's microwave, took it to her office, and they ate the slices straight from the box.

"A serpent slithering through skins and a rich man with a side piece," she said after Andy told her about Bullins's newest fiction and Cole Benson's Winston-Salem girlfriend. She wiped her hands on a paper napkin that was already crumpled and streaked with red sauce. "Potentially a very useful combo for our side."

"Yeah," Andy replied. "I'll start with the check. Then I'll interview the doctor—let's see what he actually told Damian. Also, I need to discover what kind of video the sheriff's office has from the Benson house. I've never had any reason to watch more than the few moments before Damian arrived until he hurried out several minutes later."

"How was your breakfast?" she asked. "With Noah?" She was still cross with him, but each day her disposition was slightly better.

"Good," he answered. "Brooke has rented a place of her own and will be gone this weekend, though I think Noah's reluctant to move to their new house."

"Can't blame him," she said.

"I've really grown to like freeloading at your place—okay if I just stay?" He grinned at her.

"I'm glad things will be more normal again soon." She tossed the dirty, wadded napkin at him. "Thanks for the pizza."

Locating the online information for Nephi26 took less than ten minutes. Utah's public records disclosed that Nephi26 was a corporation in good standing. Its registered agent was Howland Kimball. Andy used his credit card to pay a three-buck fee and downloaded the business's recent filings, which showed a two-member board of directors: Cole Benson and Arlie Hatch. Benson was also the president. He printed the document, put a copy in the Bullins file, and emailed the forms to Vikram.

***

ON OCTOBER 1, ANDY had returned to his home. He was awake at 6:00 a.m., and he let Patches inside while he made coffee and cooked breakfast. He'd not smoked a cigarette in eight days, and though he rarely lit up in the mornings, for some reason, today, sitting in pajama pants and a long-sleeve T-shirt at the kitchen table, sipping coffee, the house quiet and orange embers still alive in the fireplace, the dog curled near his feet, he craved a Marlboro. Like most nicotiners, he knew there was buried treasure, a single in a suit coat pocket, old and stale, left over from an interrupted trip to the office parking lot weeks ago. He slid on a fleece jacket and took Patches outside and tossed his ball in the dawn light, hoping to distract himself, but he kept thinking about the damn cig until he finally marched to the closet, patted his coat pocket, found the smoke, crushed it in his palm, and flushed the paper-and-tobacco clump down the toilet.

He drove to the Patrick County jail, where he'd scheduled a meeting with Coy Hubbard at eight sharp. The deputy was waiting for him in the lobby, and they bumped fists and exchanged dampered hellos through masks. They were standing near the receptionist's bulletproof window, which was plastered with signs and notices and a flyer offering a used sofa and recliner for sale, a blurry picture of the furniture at the top of the paper, a fringe of tear-off contact numbers at the bottom.

"Appreciate your seeing me," Andy said. "I doubt Officer Ellis would return my calls or be anxious to help me."

"Well," Hubbard replied, "he ain't gonna be helpin' nobody these days. Sheriff was so put out with him over his testimony at the hearin' that he busted him down to jailer and stuck him on third shift. Mr. Ellis quit three days ago. He's not officially gone; he's burnin' vacation time for a while, but he's no longer with us."

"Good riddance," Andy answered. "Guy's a liar. Sheriff should've fired his ass the moment court was over that morning."

"He wanted to, but I hear Mr. Morley felt it would be better for the case if Ellis was still employed with us, so the sheriff hid him where he couldn't cause too much trouble. Once the trial is finished, sheriff would cut him loose. Least that's my impression."

"Well, Coy, I appreciate your testifying truthfully. Thanks."

"Yeah," Hubbard said. "But, you know, it ain't made me real popular with a few folks in the community. And Melvin Ellis gave me a cussin' and a tongue lashin' like you've never heard. Course, I'm only number two on his list. He hates you somethin' fierce."

"Perfect—I'm the villain because he failed at his job and then committed obvious perjury."

Hubbard's mask was riding up his chin, and he tugged it down. "What mischief you brewin' for us today?"

"I'd like to watch the security-camera footage from the Benson house. So far, I've only seen the section where Damian comes and goes."

"How much of it are you wantin', Andy?"

"From the time Cole Benson leaves until my client arrives. Several hours, if you have it."

"I'm not sure what we have. Ellis was runnin' the show. Sheriff transferred the case to Investigator Wilson."

"Oh, okay. Gary, right? Is he here?"

"Probably not yet," Hubbard said. "As best I can remember, the Bensons had a very good system."

"Why don't you just ask him if he'll make me a copy of everything you have?"

"I will," Hubbard answered. "I'll have him text you, and y'all can make arrangements." The skin around his eyes crinkled. "How's my old buddy Patches?"

"King of the world," Andy said. "He's doing well after the wanderlust and delinquent start."

"I'll be darned if we ain't started to miss him 'round here."

"One more thing, please. As much as I dread it, can you have the jailer bring Damian to the interview room? I need, literally, five minutes."

"If I ever break over and get in trouble," Hubbard said, "I sure hope somehow you'd be my lawyer. Especially if I'm as guilty as Judas Iscariot, like most of your clients."

"I'd do the work for free," Andy replied. "Somehow."

Ten minutes later, Andy was standing in the interview room, and the jailer brought in Bullins, shackled as usual, his hair a greasy swirl and pillow-flat on one side, his folder clutched at his chest.

"No need to sit," Andy immediately told him.

"Okay," Bullins answered.

"I'm guessing—in your fat file folder—there's a copy of the email your girlfriend sent to Cole Benson."

"Oh yeah," he said enthusiastically. "Can I put my papers on the table so I can look through 'em?"

"Yes."

"See, after I helped Cole, and he cheated me—"

"Just find the email, Damian. I don't need you to repeat your story."

"Well, Cole, you see, he—"

"Find the email." Andy bristled. "And keep quiet, please."

"You're still my lawyer, and you're gonna help me beat this?" Bullins asked. He was sorting through papers so manically that several fell from the table, and he accidentally tore off the corner from a yellow legal sheet covered in pencil scrawl.

"Yes. I'm still your lawyer, and I'll give you the best defense I can."

"I knew I could count on you," Damian said.

"You don't have to rush," Andy told him.

"It's here somewhere. I wrote down the message and gave it to my fiancée to send from her email since, you know, I'm in jail and don't have a computer or phone."

"I'm sure you did." Andy cocked an eyebrow. "May I assume this email was sent only *after* your suppression hearing on the twenty-first?"

"Uh, yeah, but I'm not sure why it matters. I waited and gave Cole every chance, and he was right there in court, actin' like nothing ever went on between us, so I emailed and reminded him." He snatched a paper from the topsy-turvy pile. "Here. Found it."

Andy took the email and read it:

Cole: You need to remember our agreement and take care of DJ and pay like you promised. A million and college. I've done my part. DB

"Never heard a peep," Bullins complained. "Nothing."

"Assuming, Damian, there is such a deal, today is October first. I seriously doubt second semester tuition is due. I also seriously doubt any murderer worth his salt would send you an email confirmation of his guilt."

119

"Did the holier-than-thou prick sittin' there in court look like he was of a mind to help my boy?" Damian was organizing his papers, lining up corners and tapping the stack against the table. "What else am I supposed to do? Call him on the recorded jail line?" He collected the several papers from the floor. "Did you find anything 'bout the check?" he asked.

"Yeah," Andy said. "Took me a whopping five minutes to learn from online *public records* Cole Benson is the president of Nephi26. He really did some quality corporate camouflage to hide himself."

"If it was a clean deal, how come he didn't write the check from his own personal account? Huh? Why the dummy company? A jury'll be suspicious."

"Yeah, well, depends on how bright the jury is."

"Does the email help us?" Damian asked.

"Question, Damian: You aware of any reason why Benson would want his wife dead? You have any suggestions for me?"

"You looked at insurance?" Damian offered. "Bet he got hisself a nice check."

"He's already crazy wealthy. Anything else?" Andy was pressing, fishing, trying to discover if Damian was connected to the Heather Farris tip.

"Like I said before, Mr. Hughes, that ain't our legal responsibility. Who knows why he wanted her killed."

On his way back to Martinsville, Andy detoured by the clerk's office, where his pal Vicki was working at the main desk. She greeted him and smiled, and before he asked her, she reached beneath the counter and located the Bullins file. "Here," she said. "Did I guess right? It's such a hot item, we keep it convenient so we don't have to traipse to the file drawer a hundred times a day."

"Yep," Andy answered. "Thanks. I need to check the commonwealth's appeal notice. You okay?"

"Living the dream," she said good-naturedly. "Saw you on TV. You still planning to leave the PD's office?"

"Yes," Andy replied, "if I can ever shake free of this case."

"You have a new job waiting?" She handed him the file.

"Not yet. Any openings here? I'm a team player, a self-starter, and I can pass a drug test."

"None today. But you're welcome to submit an application, and we'll keep it around for the next vacancy. There's the summer intern program too."

He laughed and so did she. He moved to the end of the counter and began flipping through the file. He reached the last paper, an indictment, frowned, and began his hunt again, this time studying each page more deliberately. "Huh," he said when he finished a second search, "is this current? Everything here?"

"You better believe it."

"There's no appeal notice. Did Peter Morley not file a notice?"

"All I can tell you," Vicki answered, "is that as of this very second, every paper we have is in the file. I'm positive. We treat this case like it's the Holy Grail."

"Strange," Andy muttered. "Thanks." He pushed the file so she could reach it. "I'll let you know about the application."

He phoned Morley's office from his Jeep, identified himself, mentioned the Damian Bullins case, and was shrilly informed by the lady who answered that "Mr. Morley is unavailable."

"Any idea when he'll be *available*?"

"He's extremely busy. I'll leave him a message."

"Yeah." He paused. "Actually, no need to bother him. I'm certain he has a lot on his plate, most of it far more important than a murder case."

"Have a blessed day," she remarked. "I'll tell him you called."

***

THAT SAME EVENING, NOAH came to visit, and after tomato soup and cheese bread, he joined his dad in the workshop, where they planned to install a radiant heat mat in the doghouse they'd been building for Patches. The house itself was a beauty with cedar-shake sides and real shingles. It was chilly enough, around fifty degrees, that Andy had made a fire in the woodstove, and Patches was stretched out on his belly close to the warmth, his muzzle resting on a paw.

"So tell me, please, Noah," Andy said to the boy, "what's our rule for anything and everything that involves electricity?"

"We always respect electricity," Noah intoned, bored and disinterested, "because it's dangerous and can kill people. Uncle Lawrence was almost electrocuted."

"Exactly. And we always triple inspect any electrical work or wiring."

"Uh-huh," Noah answered dully. "You've told me a million, zillion times."

"So our project today, with cold weather due soon, is to make certain Patches is cozy in his new house, which we'll locate on the front porch, next to a power source." Andy was unrolling a black mat as he spoke. "You remember I showed you how to rig a pigtail? Well, this'll require a double pigtail. I've already got our wire nuts, and I'll let you watch me do the first connection, then you can do the other one, okay?"

"I guess."

"Don't sound so excited," Andy kidded him. He playfully exaggerated the words.

"I hate mom's new house," Noah declared. "And I hate Howard."

Andy released the mat and the ends quickly coiled toward each other. "Have a seat," he said, pointing at one of the ladder-backs. "Let's take a break."

Noah kept standing, didn't budge.

"Son, listen. I've seen the house. It's a great place. Even if it isn't, your complaining hurts your mom's feelings and makes her life harder than it ought to be right now. She needs you to *help* her, same as she's always helped you. As for Howard, you have every right to dislike him. You should. He'll be punished for what he did to Brooke. I promise."

"Why can't I stay with you?"

"You do stay with me, Noah. Roughly half the time. Some whole weeks in the summer. Some Thursday evenings all the way until Monday morning. Holidays."

"It's not enough. Don't you want me to be here?"

"You're my world. I couldn't love you any wider or deeper. And because I love you so much, I understand how important it is for you to have two parents. I miss you every single second I can't see you—it makes me heartsick when you leave. But that's the price I choose to pay to make certain you have both a mom and dad—a family. I wish, maybe as a favor to me, you'd try to be happier at your new place."

"I hate it there," he replied, completely unmoved by his father's encouragement.

"Sorry. How about we enjoy our weekend and worry with all this later?"

Noah yanked off his little-boy work gloves and dropped them on the floor. "Come on, Patches," he said, on the cusp of sobbing. He and the dog left for the house, and Noah locked them in his room and wouldn't respond to knocks or iPad messages or questions shouted through the door, so after a while, Andy had to push a finish nail into the knob's small hole and trip the mechanism. Noah and the dog were on the bed, the boy glum, Patches lying lengthwise beside him. "I'll be in the den, okay?" Andy offered. "It'd be wonderful if you'd come and hang out with me. We could play *Fortnite* or watch a movie. Or finish the doghouse. Or whatever you want to do."

CHAPTER ELEVEN

"Good morning, Andy. Hope you're well and prosperous on such a fine day." Peter Morley's greeting was a wash of ooze, purr and smarm.

"Yeah, same to you, Pete." Andy was at his office on Monday, October 5, loading six misdemeanor files into his briefcase, on his way to general district court.

"Understand you called last week. Sorry for the delay responding. Stump speeches and rubber chicken are keepin' me busy. Swamped with trials too." As always, and despite the debacle with Melvin Ellis, Morley sounded blithe and buoyant, full of himself.

"No worries," Andy said.

"What can I do for you?"

"I'm curious—did you decide not to appeal Judge Leventis's decision? I stopped by the clerk's office, and there's no notice in the file."

"Judge Leventis entered her order on the twenty-second. We have ten days to file our paperwork. I had one of my office ladies drive it down Friday afternoon. You must've been there earlier, before she delivered it."

Andy smiled. He stifled a chuckle. "I'm fairly certain you only had seven days. Not ten. I think you missed the deadline."

"No, it's ten," Morley insisted. "Ten days."

"Where are you, Pete?" Andy asked.

"In my office, at my desk."

"Pull 19.2-400," Andy suggested.

"Okay. Bear with me. I'm opening it on my computer." Morley was silent while he located the code section. "Wow," he said after several seconds. "I was positive it's ten days. When did the statute change?"

"Far as I know, it's always been seven," Andy replied.

"Well, hmmmm, seems like you and I have a problem," Morley said. "Gave it to my assistant, Arthur, to handle—can't count on anyone. Should've done it myself."

"Respectfully, Pete, it seems to me the problem is yours exclusively. We didn't blow a deadline. No offense."

"I guess we'll just have to take it directly on up to the Supreme Court. Or, most likely, the Court of Appeals will allow me to file late."

"You and I both know those options are embarrassing dead ends." Andy was firm but not rude. "How about this? You and I keep the mistake between us for a couple of days while I investigate a few loose ends, then we meet and see if we can hash out a deal? Fair or unfair, Judge Leventis has tied your hands and given you ample reason to accept a manslaughter plea. Blame her."

"So you intend to keep this under wraps?" Morley asked, tentative and uneasy.

"For now. At least until you and I can have a good-faith discussion about a plea agreement. But, so you won't think I'm sandbagging you, please understand if we don't make a deal, then I plan to ask the judge to schedule this case ASAP, before you and I leave and two new lawyers have to start from scratch and reinvent the wheel. I'm thinking mid-December."

"There's no possibility I—or any lawyer—could be prepared to try this case in December. Setting it then would be brutally unfair to the commonwealth and the murdered woman's husband and kids."

"It's only October, Pete, and you've already had the case for weeks, since August. It's a large case in terms of publicity but a very simple case in terms of the facts and the law. A December trial date will give you over two months more to prepare. You should start getting ready *today*." Andy sharpened his tone. "So there's no dispute about my position, I'll put this in an email and send it to you. I definitely plan to ask for a December date if we don't settle this, and I'm betting Judge Leventis will allow it."

"Do what you have to do," Morley snarled. "But don't you dare think Peter Morley'll be strong-armed or blackmailed."

"Of course—given your reputation, who would even consider such as that?"

ARLIE HATCH WAS THE second name connected to Nephi26, and a few minutes of Google research revealed Hatch was the well-dressed gentleman who'd accompanied Cole Benson to the recent court hearing. Hatch was a Salt Lake City lawyer with numerous connections to the Mormon Church. After finishing his six district-court cases and eating a sandwich and an apple at his desk, Andy collected Vikram, and they went to the conference room, set the boxy taupe phone with worn, faded pushbuttons to speaker, and called Hatch at his law firm in Utah, where it was still morning. Andy explained to a receptionist who he was and why he was in hopes of talking to Hatch, and following several minutes of scratchy hold music, Hatch came on the line.

"Arlie Hatch," he said warily.

"Mr. Hatch, good morning to you."

"And you also. Is this in fact Mr. Hughes, the Virginia attorney?"

"Yes," Andy answered. "Appreciate your taking the call—"

"To make certain you are who you claim to be, could you please tell me the first name of the judge at our last hearing?"

"Christina," Andy immediately replied.

"The name," Hatch continued, "of your associate there at counsel table?"

"Vikram Kapil," Andy said.

"And finally, the name of the widow who testified?"

"Uh…oh…Lois Duncan, mother of Lonnie."

"Thank you, Mr. Hughes. I'm surprised to hear from you. What business do we have?"

"I'm interested in Nephi26. According to the state's records, you and Mr. Benson are officers and directors."

"Correct," Hatch said. "No secret about that. Why is our corporation your concern?"

"Nephi26 wrote a check to North Carolina State University to help my client's son pay his college tuition. Young man's name is Damian Bullins Jr."

"Oh, I see." Hatch paused. "I wouldn't be surprised."

"Why would Mr. Benson's Utah corporation write a check to help Damian's son?"

"I'll inquire about the specifics for you. I assume this gift happened before your client murdered Mrs. Benson. Correct?"

"The check," Andy answered, "was written before the offense date stated in the indictment, yes."

"Then it is one of many similar checks." Hatch sounded relieved. "Nephi26 has quietly distributed over six million dollars so far this year. We plan to hit seven million."

"What does Nephi26 do?" Andy asked.

"Nephi, Mr. Hughes, was a prophet who wrote the first two books of the Book of Mormon. Second Nephi, chapter twenty-six, verse thirty, is a scripture that addresses our obligation to do charity for the Lord and love our fellow man. It is a holy instruction Mr. Benson takes seriously. A faith duty. In simple terms, Nephi26 is a charity funded exclusively by Cole Benson that gives away millions of dollars to help others. As the Bible admonishes us, this is done quietly and without fanfare or publicity."

"Strictly a charity?" Andy asked. "Nothing else?"

"Strictly a charity. You're welcome to inspect our records and ledgers."

"Much appreciated," Andy said. "And thanks for the explanation."

"Yes."

"Just a couple of other quick questions, please." Andy bent closer to the phone. "Do you know anything about Mr. Benson's relationship with a lady named Heather Farris?"

"The name's not familiar to me," Hatch said coolly. "So no."

"Would it be possible for you to let him know I contacted you and asked about her?"

"Is this business or personal?" Hatch sounded irritated. "Or more Nephi money?"

"I suppose I'll let you and Mr. Benson determine how it's characterized." Andy glanced at Vikram, who was jotting notes. "As an aside—and I did my best to research this—your church basically ended plural marriage in 1904."

"Absolutely. As a matter of doctrine, we celebrate and insist on spousal monogamy and excommunicate anyone who does not honor that marital teaching and claims to have more than one wife."

"Last question, and I'm grateful for your time. Did my client, Damian Bullins, send an email to Mr. Benson? And, of course, my apologies if he did. I just recently heard about the possibility."

"Remarkably, Mr. Benson did in fact receive a strange and cryptic email that purported to be from 'DB'—those are your client's initials. We were mystified how Mr. Bullins could email from jail, so we weren't sure if it was genuine. Sadly, Mr. Benson, whose beloved wife was slaughtered in her own kitchen, receives all kinds of messages, many of them provocative or hateful or racist. Some attack his faith. Some are simply crazy."

"I'm sorry," Andy said sincerely. "From everything I've heard, Mr. Benson is a quality man."

"He is indeed," Hatch noted. "Candidly, I'm not a criminal lawyer. My work on behalf of Mr. Benson is almost all civil and business related, so my involvement in the murder case is limited. His secretary forwards the various emails to me. We print hardcopies, then my staff creates an attachment containing any messages that reference the trial or the murder, and every week, we email the information to law enforcement, Mrs. Katt and Mr. Morley."

"Obviously, no one responds to the messages."

"Not on our end of things," Hatch confirmed.

"Thanks so much for speaking with me," Andy said. "I recognize how awkward and unpleasant this has to be for you. More than most, you, I hope, can understand I'm simply doing my job."

"I understand you represent the man who killed my friend Cole's wife."

"Fair enough," Andy answered. "Thanks again for your time."

"Before you go," Hatch said, "a question for *you* please. Do you plan on taking this case to trial now that you have a favorable ruling from the judge? Your inquiries seem very preparatory, more than routine."

"We aren't certain. Honestly, Mr. Hatch, I hope to negotiate a plea with Mr. Morley, but who knows if that'll happen."

"Feel free to include me in any of those discussions," Hatch said. "Neither Mr. Benson nor I have heard a peep from Mr. Morley since the unfortunate day in court. We were relieved to learn he'll be replaced by the time the case makes it back from the various appeals."

***

THAT EVENING, KELLIE CAME to visit Andy, and they ate egg rolls and chicken fried rice on TV trays in front of the fireplace and drank half a bottle of red wine. As best Andy could tell, she was no longer cross with him, and she decided to spend the night at his house, a first. She'd never seen *Casablanca*, and he streamed it on the den's big-screen, but by the time Major Strasser arrived and was quizzing Rick at the café, Andy was kissing her, and it went on from there, and when they finished having sex, they were entangled on the hardwood floor, naked and happy, closer to the warm brick hearth than the sofa.

She was little-cat-feet quiet the next morning, and Andy never heard her leave the bedroom. He found her in the kitchen at 6:45 a.m., seated at the table, drinking orange juice, and when she sensed he was there, she glanced up from her phone, and she was emotional, her eyes brimming, her cheeks colored pink.

"Oh goodness," he said. "You okay? What's wrong?"

"Nothing." She quavered the word. "I'm fine." She laughed. "You caught me."

"You seem upset."

"Actually, just the opposite. Especially now, with this crazy pandemic, I've cut down on my Internet time. Every visit to the ether can be a depressing doomscroll if you're not careful."

"True. I've always avoided social media and the whole nine yards anyway. I can only imagine how dismal it's become."

She dabbed the corner of her eye with a paper napkin. "It's not *all* bad, Andy. These days, I try to block the noise and gloom and politics and bickering and banal bullshit. Every morning, I read something worthwhile and bright—these days it's a poet named Honorée Jeffers. Takes about three minutes."

"Okay."

"Then I watch an animal video. They're all over Facebook—the dog missing for a year is reunited with its owner, the construction guys shepherd a mother goose and her babies across the interstate, a pelican is freed from a tangle of fishing line, the kids save a deer who's fallen through the pond ice. Anything with Jane Goodall. People with darling pet possums—they're such homely creatures they're cute. You even root for the tourists rolling beached sharks back into the ocean. There're tons of three-minute clips online. You ever see any of this?"

"Uh, not really."

"They're the sweetest, best stories and always have a happy ending. When you startled me, I'd just finished watching a baby elephant rescued from a water hole. It's how you should begin your day. With an inoculation of wonderful. Here, I'll play it again. Watch."

"Oh, yeah," Andy said when the elephant video ended, "that *will* cause some happy tears. Great stuff. Thanks for the tip. Even my go-to entertainment choices are lousy right now—the Red Sox were an embarrassment and Pat Metheny's stuck at home and can't tour."

❊❊❊

Five hours later, DeMarcus Hampton arrived in Martinsville. Since Cindy had met him before and knew who he was, she allowed him to sneak down the hall and surprise Andy. DeMarcus didn't knock or announce himself, just flung open the office door and stood at the threshold, his suit immaculate, Ahmaud Arbery stenciled in white block letters on his dark-blue mask. "Damn, brother," he announced, "I'm stunned: It's nearly noon, and there you are, sober and working. Still employed. A miracle."

"DeMarcus!" Andy exclaimed. He dug in his pocket, found his own mask, looped it over his ears, and started for his friend. "Hold your breath and turn your head left," Andy instructed him. "I gotta hug you, fool."

DeMarcus came forward, arms spread wide, and they wrapped each other up and slapped backs. "Sit down, D," Andy said, pulling away and exhaling. "What a treat. Why in the world are you haunting my office here in Southside Virginia on an ordinary October morning?"

Andy and DeMarcus had shared an apartment for their last year of law school at William and Mary, and they remained big pals. After graduation, DeMarcus clerked for Justice Kennedy, then went to work in Richmond for Harold, Edwards and Slate, where he became the huge, influential firm's first Black managing partner and won several seven-figure verdicts in blockbuster civil cases, including one whopper against a pharmaceutical company whose blood-pressure medication was more carcinogen than cure.

"I had a summary judgment hearing in Danville," DeMarcus explained. "So why not drive a few extra miles and visit you? Man, it's been a while—last I saw you was January, and we barely even had time for a beer. This pandemic, if nothing else, has given me a better perspective on the value of time spent with friends."

"Danville, huh?" Andy laughed. "You sporting the Arbery mask in the last capitol of the Confederacy?"

"Oh hell yeah, Andy. Talk about a safe harbor. Nobody there much knows who he was or how he was murdered. I swear to you this is true: A polite, helpful bailiff, nice as he could be, asked me if I was Mr. Arbery. I kid you not. Told him I wasn't, and he seemed bewildered. Informed me he was trying to locate the lawyer for the next case, a Mr. Hampton, but thought he'd check with me since I was the only person in a coat and tie waiting to enter the courtroom."

"Hope your hearing went well," Andy said.

"It did. We won. Smart judge, well prepared, didn't waste time." DeMarcus shooed Andy away, flicked both hands at him. "Quit crowding me and passing the plague."

Andy returned to the chair behind his desk, but DeMarcus kept standing and retreated a step so he was closer to the door. "Can I buy you lunch?" Andy asked. "How long are you here? You're welcome to spend the night. It'd be great to catch up. And I'd love for you to see my house. I've done a lot of work since you were last there."

"Lunch, for sure. Thanks. But I'll drive home to Richmond after we eat." DeMarcus adjusted his jacket sleeves so that both silver cuff links were visible. "I do have some business, though. An offer for you."

"Oh, here we go. I should've known there's a catch when a powerful city-slicker lawyer in a bespoke suit arrives unannounced."

"Well, this is favorable business, not an ambush," DeMarcus assured him.

"Why am I skeptical?"

"You and I both realize," DeMarcus began, "it's rare for famous lawyers—the bold-print names, the people who're known to the public—to actually be worth a damn. Most of them fluke into a very winnable case and ride it forever or master the art of the snappy thirty-second TV interview."

"True," Andy agreed. "We see it every day on a smaller scale. The high-flying hired gun from Roanoke or Norfolk is full of bluster and worthless theatrics, and nine times out of ten, my colleagues here at the PD's office would provide a far better defense for a fraction of the price."

"You, though, Andy, are the exception to the rule. You're suddenly front-page news, and you are a phenomenal, brilliant attorney."

"Keep going, D." Andy grinned. "Don't stop."

"My firm wants to establish a full-service, robust criminal-defense practice. We're just kind of dabbling right now, hit and miss. Last we talked, you mentioned leaving here. How about you come and work with us?"

"Say what?" Andy blurted.

"We'll put you in a corner office, top floor, pay you half a million a year to start, make you a partner after fifteen months, and give you a three-percent equity share. Health care and retirement, of course. In five years, you'll be taking home two mil, easy. As a bonus, you'll definitely be representing a better class of criminal, you'll be appreciated, and you won't have impossible caseloads to manage."

"You're serious?" Andy asked.

"Why wouldn't I be?"

"So…I'd have to relocate to Richmond?" Andy rocked his chair forward. The springs creaked.

"Yes. And leave Southside and all its charms and opportunity behind. We'd also expect you to travel occasionally. We have offices in Norfolk, Abingdon and DC."

"Wow…damn, thanks. I have a girlfriend here and a dog, but the big, critical variable is my boy, my son. Noah. He lives nearby, and right now there's a lot of upheaval in his life. I don't want to make matters worse for him, and I don't want to surrender a single, solitary second with him. He spends half his time with me, and that's the highlight of my life. He's an amazing kid."

"Listen, Andy, you'd be in Richmond, three hours away. Not Shanghai. Your son might benefit from an occasional visit to the state's capitol, where we have all grades of experiences not available in Martinsville or Henry County."

"I'm grateful, D, I am. Thanks. It's a tremendous offer, and I appreciate it. Let me think on it for a few days, okay? And, no matter what, I won't be leaving this office until February, unless I finish Damian Bullins's case before then."

"Understood," DeMarcus said. "I've not formally taken this to my firm yet, but I've talked with several partners, and I feel certain we can make a deal happen. We'd be honored to have you on board, and it'll be a great, and lucrative, fit for everyone."

***

By Thursday, a laggard hot spell was dawdling across most of Virginia. Andy left work a few minutes before five with plans for a long gym visit, assuming the machines and treadmills weren't too crowded and the obnoxious toad who grunted and groaned and volcanoed spit with every repetition wasn't there. He'd survived fifteen cold-turkey days without a cigarette, and the tobacco demon was losing its grip on him, or so it seemed. Whistling and happy, he was still a ways from his Jeep when he noticed the lady, and she was staring directly at him, walking with purpose and clearly intending to cut him off.

"Mr. Hughes," she said, the two words oddly casual. She was nicely dressed in a blazer, white blouse, jeans and fashionable, no-regrets shoes. "Could I please speak with you?"

"Sorry," Andy answered. "I don't think I recognize you. Is this about a case?"

"We've never met, and yes, it's about a case. My sister's case. Alicia Benson's case."

She was stopped in front of him, now only an arm's length distant, and he was boxed in by a row of cars on his right. He was nonplussed, didn't answer immediately. "You realize, ma'am," he finally said, "I represent the *defendant* charged with her murder."

She smirked, but it softened into a wan smile. "Yeah, Mr. Hughes. Of course I know who you are and that your client, Damian Bullins, murdered my baby sister."

Andy reflexively checked her hands for weapons and then darted his eyes to her waistband.

"My mace is in my purse, which is in the car."

"Okay," he said. "Good." He glanced over his shoulder at his office. "Would you like to go inside?"

"No. If I'd wanted to schedule an appointment, I wouldn't be approaching you in the parking lot. This'll do just fine, and I prefer speaking here to a more visible, on-the-record meeting. For a number of reasons."

"Okay, and so we're on the same page, you're definitely aware my job is to do all I can ethically and legally to help my client, Damian Bullins? Normally, you should speak with the commonwealth's attorney if you have questions or information about the case." A lady from a Main Street shop walked past, spoke to Andy, and aimed her key fob at a SUV.

"Since I have a doctorate degree and manage a company with four hundred employees, you can rest assured I understand the basics of the criminal justice system."

"You mind telling me your name?"

"Audrey Clayton. I kept my maiden name when I married."

"What can I do for you, Ms. Clayton?" Andy asked. "Why're you here?"

The sun was beginning to pin her down, and she sidestepped to avoid the glare. "I'm here, Mr. Hughes, because shit rolls downhill. You mentioned Heather Farris to Arlie Hatch, who told my brother-in-law, who then discussed her with me, among other topics."

"Ah, plumbers' rules. Do you know the rest of the guidance?"

"Sorry?" She tightened her expression.

"Basic rules of plumbing: Hot goes on the left, cold on the right, and shit rolls downhill."

"Thanks for the tutorial," she said.

"You're suggesting, ma'am, Cole Benson sent you to waylay me so we can chat about Miss Farris?"

"Believe me, Cole didn't send me," she replied emphatically. "He'd never involve me." She moved again to dodge the sun. "How'd you discover Heather?"

"Honestly," Andy answered, "social services received an anonymous tip. From a woman. Could be you, I suppose. Are you our secret caller?"

"I'm not, but I'm pretty certain I know who is." A kid with a cell phone stuck against his ear passed by her.

"If Cole Benson didn't encourage you to—"

She pointed at him and interrupted. "I'm here to *remind* you my sister left behind four darling girls and to *inform* you Alicia was well acquainted with Cole's adultery and tolerated it, even, you might say, incorporated the infidelity into her life." She lowered her index finger. "She considered it a 'for worse' occurrence covered by her marital vows and was determined to overcome it, no matter what. She loved Cole, and Cole, strange as it might sound, loved her. Loved her on his own terms, obviously. Me, I'd have castrated him, and I thought the whole situation was insane, but my sister accepted it as a powerful man's foible and an impediment she'd be able to endure if need be."

"How, pray tell, do you come to such a place in a *marriage*?"

"Well, say what you will, there's still some vestige of 'sister wives' in their wacky, golden-tablets religion. But Cole never misled her. He told her right from the jump he was seeing another woman, and he convinced her that she and the children would always be his number-one priority—"

"Seems to be a lot of that going around," Andy remarked.

"Pardon?"

"A friend of mine recently had a very similar experience with her wealthy husband," Andy explained. "But he's a Presbyterian doctor—no golden tablets or New York parlays with angels."

"At any rate," she said, "as unfair and unfortunate as the situation was for my sister, Cole Benson had the best of both worlds, and no motive to hurt Alicia. None. Zero. From my perspective—"

"It's always possible she had a change of heart and gave him an ultimatum."

"From my perspective," Audrey continued, "Cole was a wretched, selfish, hypocritical husband, but he didn't kill my sister—there was no 'change of heart'—and your trying to sell that defense for your soulless client will gain you nothing and perhaps only push the oldest girl, Clara, who's sixteen, almost seventeen, into further confusion. Thanks to the Internet and its ugly gossip and speculation, and thanks to Cole's boneheaded, rushed introduction of his concubine to his daughters, Clara's convinced her dad might not be the man she once thought, and she's extremely angry with him."

"Tough situation," Andy said.

Audrey hesitated until Andy looked her in the face. "Most important, she's motivated by a hope she and her sisters can come and live with me and my husband. I imagine she believes revealing her dad as a past adulterer and current sinner might help her chances of leaving him and staying with me, especially with the church community."

"She's my tipster?"

"I'd wager she is, Mr. Hughes."

Andy cocked his head. "And your reason—"

"My reason for this visit," she declared, "is to promise that, if need be, I'll eagerly raise my right hand and tell a jury *exactly* what I just told you. If you make Cole out to be a murderer, I'll fight the idea tooth and nail. He was an unfaithful husband, but, one, he cared for my sister and he loves his kids, and, two, she was irreplaceable—Cole was a 1950s, never-changed-a-diaper breadwinner, and now he's left without a maid, cook, homework tutor, chauffeur, landscaper and business-party hostess. The girls are miserable, lost, and completely overwhelming him."

"You understand, Ms. Clayton, my sworn duty is to raise any legitimate evidence—"

"Regardless of who is ruined as collateral damage," she finished the thought.

"Exactly. Wish it were otherwise."

"Which is why I came here. I realize your allegiance is to your client, not four girls you've never met. My pitch to you isn't moral, it's legal. If—if—Cole's adultery has become part of your defense, I'm telling you I'll blow you out of the water in court. Simple as that. Don't try it."

"I understand," Andy replied. He was peering at the pavement. He noticed ants swarming a speck of bread crust. "Do you want the kids to live with you?"

"Yes, absolutely. I do. Right now, it's in their best interest."

"Suddenly we have lots of motives, twists, crosscurrents and leverage in the math, Ms. Clayton."

"I have only one motive," she said abruptly. "Doing right by my sister's children."

"Later, Andy," Curtis Matthews shouted as he was crossing the street. "Take care."

Andy briefly waved at Curtis but didn't say anything. "I don't doubt that," he assured Audrey. "Before you go, if I could, I'd like to ask you something. How did an African-American lady like your sister wind up in the Mormon Church and married to Cole Benson?"

"Alicia and I were placed in Chicago foster care—never knew our dad, and our mom lost custody when I was four and Alicia was only two. Alicia was born drug-positive. We were both adopted by the Claytons, devout Mormons, who are some of the best people I've ever known. We love them with our full hearts. We were raised in Nauvoo, Illinois, the middle of nowhere, in the Latter-day Saints community. There's much to recommend the LDS faith and culture—honesty, family, hard work, clean living, sobriety and self-sacrifice. There's also much I find discouraging as an adult Black woman."

"I didn't mean to come off as hostile toward Mormons or their beliefs," Andy noted. "I apologize if it seemed I was being critical. You just don't see many Black Mormons, especially in a mixed marriage."

"Our parents, the Claytons, are White, so it's possible that's why the notion wasn't completely foreign to my sister."

"By all accounts," Andy said, "Alicia was an admirable lady in every respect. I'm sorry to meet you under these circumstances."

"She was pure, unalloyed goodness. Angelic. A joy. I'd left the church far behind by my sophomore year of college at Marquette, but for whatever reason, Alicia found even greater comfort in the LDS doctrines, and as the years progressed, especially after she met Cole, she lived a content, simple life of decency, devoted to her kids, her marriage and her faith."

Andy didn't speak. He put his hands in his pockets, struggled for words that didn't come.

"And, of course," Audrey's voice cracked, overloaded with anger, "despite all her praying and sacrifice and her godly heart and pious beliefs, she's dead, her throat slashed, while a swaggering sinner like Cole Benson roams the earth with his dumbass girlfriend and your client, a life-long criminal, catches what many would term 'divine intervention' and receives the break of all breaks in court, inching him closer to truly getting away with murder."

CHAPTER TWELVE

OCTOBER 12 WAS COLUMBUS Day, and Peter Morley was scheduled to attend a pig-pickin' fundraiser at noon, then he was filming a campaign commercial for regional TV, and he was speaking to a Rotary Club at six, so it was eight o'clock at night, overcast and blustery, when he met Andy at the Dunford County commonwealth's attorney's office. "You'd think the dimwit would be driving here to Martinsville with his hat in hand," Kellie had remarked as Andy was loading an ecstatic Patches for the ninety-minute trip.

Several people were in the lobby when Andy and the dog arrived, all of them, it appeared, dedicated to Morley's senate race, and they were cold-calling voters, folding glossy mailers, and typing up a storm on a bank of laptops. The staffers were friendly, especially with Patches, but there wasn't a mask in sight, nothing but bare noses and mouths, and Andy hurried past them and located Morley, who was pacing his office and jabbering on his cellphone. He waved and beckoned Andy into the room. Andy only entered far enough to shut the door, and he instructed Patches to sit, tweaked his leash.

Morley kept Andy waiting there, ignored, until he finished the call. "Sorry, but that was Congressman Arnold—been trying to connect with him for a week." He tossed the phone onto his desk. "Pull up a chair, and let's see what we can do about this Bullins case. Beautiful dog, by the way. What's his name?"

"Thanks, Pete, but my mask and Patches and I will just stay socially distanced over here."

"Faith over fear," Morley declared. "But I completely respect your decision to cover your face. That's your *right*, same as I have my right to choose."

"Whatever." Andy didn't conceal his irritation.

"Hey, listen, you were kind enough to drive from Martinsville to meet with me, and if it'll make you more comfortable, I'm happy to wear a covering." He opened a desk drawer, located a cloth mask with an American flag motif, removed its plastic wrapper, and put it on. "Brand new," he said. "No problem."

Andy and Patches didn't budge. "Thanks for the accommodation."

Morley plopped down behind his desk. He unbuttoned a cuff and rolled his shirt sleeve to his elbow. "So you'll be aware, I've drafted a request to the Court of Appeals to allow a late filing. We're optimistic they'll grant it." He rolled the other sleeve as well.

"I'm optimistic they won't," Andy calmly replied. "Let me tell you where we are and what we have. Ordinarily, I'd keep this quiet and land-mine you at trial. But, your knowing our facts isn't going to change them or give you any tactical advantage, and I'm fairly certain Mr. Benson and his private counsel already have an idea what's coming. Have you spoken with either of them lately?"

"Uh, no. I think Cole left a couple messages, but I wanted to meet with you so I'd have a clear picture before I talked to him. I did have my secretary email to let him know about this discussion. I'll definitely reach out to him tomorrow."

"Here's the short version, Pete. We can prove Benson was having an affair with a young woman by the name of Heather. We can prove his wife became aware of this affair—"

"Whoa!" Morley blurted. "Cole Benson was cheating on his wife? Seriously?"

"Seriously," Andy answered. "Why don't you ask him about it when you return his call tomorrow? I understand social services, trying to be fair, also gave you the same tip and info we used to track down the girlfriend."

"Well...uh, that's unfortunate, and surprising, but it doesn't much matter for our case. So what if he was?" Morley shrugged. "As for tips and leads, we've had more than I can count. Can't chase them all."

"Bullins contends Cole Benson in fact killed Mrs. Benson, and Bullins says he confessed only to take the blame off Benson. Benson promised

Bullins money, which would go to Bullins's son, and we can prove Benson made the first payment."

Morley wrinkled his forehead. "None of that makes any sense," he scoffed. "No sense at all, Andy. I mean, hell, the last person I'd hire to help me conceal a murder is Damian Bullins. And why involve anyone else to begin with? I'd just kill her and create an alibi and keep my mouth shut."

"Husband's always the prime suspect," Andy answered, his response practiced and the best he could concoct. "Cole would have a black cloud ruining his reputation and business. He'd suffer a high-profile, open murder investigation that would last forever, and he always ran the risk news of his girlfriend would surface and he'd be under even more scrutiny."

Morley raised his hands, flipped up his palms. "What do you accomplish by getting paid for taking the fall if you wind up in jail?"

"My client thought he had terminal cancer, and this was a chance to finally support his son. From Cole Benson's perspective, the cancer meant his accomplice wouldn't be around to double-cross him. Apparently, Benson made the first payment, then welched on the deal. After some medical tests, it turns out the growth in Bullins's belly wasn't malignant."

"Sounds crazy," Morley said. "Ridiculous. Impossible. I look forward to shredding your client when he takes the stand to tell such a flimsy lie."

Patches exhaled, sloshed his tongue across his lips and lay down, his belly flat against the floor, his front legs extended. Andy dropped the leash. "Then you'll be disappointed, Pete. I can promise you Damian will never get anywhere near the witness stand. I'll swear-in Cole Benson, and after I have him confirm his adultery, I'll read him an email my client sent him, an email that references the plan and payment. I'll quiz him about it and acquaint the jury with Bullins's defense and his story that way, through the backdoor. Benson received the email and didn't reply or deny it, and that, as a matter of evidence, is an adoption by silence. I'll be able to get our full version of events to the twelve folks deciding the case while Mr. Bullins stays glued to his chair at counsel table."

"I have to admit," Morley said, "you've been busy and given this some serious thought."

"We've scanned the relevant documents, and I emailed them to you before I left work today. You should have Bullins's medical records regarding the mass in his belly, his email to Benson, our investigator's notes on the girlfriend, and the check Benson sent from a Utah corporation to pay tuition for Damian's kid. We can buttress every component of my client's narrative with facts or supporting records."

Morley scowled. "I don't believe any of it, and neither do you. Pardon my French, but it's bullshit."

"Let's not forget your case will be even more complicated and incomplete since we'll be careful to make sure Bullins's confession remains excluded. We'll use phrases like 'show up and take the blame,' or 'act as the murderer,' or 'be there for the killing.' This will be a murky mess by the end of the trial with a great big guilty finger pointing at Cole Benson, who was cheating on his murdered wife."

"What do you want? What're you offering on a plea?"

"Oh," Andy said, "before I forget, I've been in contact with Vince Christopher, the forensic expert. Do you know him?"

"Can't say that I...oh, wait, yeah, is he the guy who used to work for the state lab? Retired and started his own business?"

"Yeah," Andy replied. "He's an expert on blood-splatter evidence—"

"He's an expert on getting paid," Morley complained. "Write the whore a check, and he'll testify exactly how you need him to. Has he *ever*, since he retired from his state job—even once—been a commonwealth's witness? He's a total fraud."

"You guys have a whole lab full of experts," Andy said, "so why would he have the chance to work for the commonwealth these days? We've used him before, and juries love him. I had him take a quick look at the photos and autopsy, and we plan to ask the court for funds to hire him as our expert. I copied you with our request to Judge Leventis. His initial, tentative opinion is the blood on Bullins's pants is consistent with *both* a discharge from the wound to her neck and a mechanical application. Of course, he needs to examine the actual pants and crime scene, do some tests and a more involved investigation, but we anticipate he'll conclude it's impossible to tell whether the blood-splatter is real or manufactured."

"So back to my question, Andy: What're you looking for in terms of a plea bargain?"

"Obstruction of justice."

"Come on." Morley shook his head, squeezed shut his eyes. Grimaced. "I'd be tarred and feathered." His nose peeked out from above the flag mask. "No possible way I can agree to a misdemeanor and twelve months. Ten years on voluntary manslaughter was bad enough. Give me something realistic."

Andy stepped forward, a single stride. His voice changed so the words were adversarial, an I'm-tired-of-mollycoddling-you challenge. "Here's what also might invite tar and feathers: Negligently missing a crucial appeal date and losing a nationally televised murder trial, where you leave the grieving husband's reputation in tatters." Andy reached down and grabbed the leash loop, then stood as tall as he could and leveled his shoulders. "The better option is for you to persuade Cole Benson to join the plea-deal program. Then you announce an agreement, blame the judge—and Melvin Ellis—for putting you behind the eight ball, cryptically mention 'other defense evidence' that's come to light, and sail off to the senate."

"Andy," Morley replied, his dander rising, his hands balled on his desk, "I'm aware of how I'm viewed by you and many others—your prerogative. I graduated Phi Beta Kappa from Washington and Lee and was law review at T. C. Williams. I seriously doubt your resume is as strong. I've built a persona that's colorful and controversial but necessary to accomplish important goals, goals I believe in my heart of hearts are fundamental. I have core values and standards, some of which we might even share. If you want to take a shot at humiliating me because of late paperwork, have at it. Maybe I screwed up. But, understand this: I won't sell out Alicia Benson to save my own hide. You do what you have to do."

"I will," Andy shot back. "Sorry we didn't make any progress. First thing in the morning, I'll formally file my motion to set us for trial." He located his phone, swiped, and tapped it twice. "I just copied you with the motion. Thanks for working me into your hectic schedule."

***

143

"NOAH'S FAILING HIS SCHOOL assignments, and he's becoming more and more sullen with me," Brooke informed Andy. "I can't do anything with him." She appeared exhausted, her skin pale, her hair pulled and gathered with a clunky plastic clip, her eyes punch drunk.

They were seated at a table in the community college's library, a few minutes past noon on the day after Andy's trip to Dunford County. He knew as soon as he received a text asking him to please come by the college he'd be hearing difficult news about his son. There was limited privacy in Brooke's office, so they occasionally met in the rear of the library and sat across from each other and hunched forward and kept their voices muted.

"Yeah, I'm not surprised," Andy said. "Honestly, he's not all joy and giggles with me."

"I'm so afraid I'm losing him." She was on the verge of tears. "This is a nightmare."

"Has Howard bothered you? How goes the separation and divorce?"

"Fine, I guess. The lawyers are trying to make a deal. Mostly, Howard seems happy we're gone and he can have sex with his new girlfriend. Rumor has it he informed people that paying me off will be an 'opportunity cost' and well worth it."

"Wow, sorry. Doesn't matter now, but like I mentioned, I was fooled too, always thought he was a quality guy, decent enough. And lucky to marry you. I'd never have predicted he'd be such an ogre underneath the thinning hair, jug ears, pleated Dockers and tiny, almost-invisible teeth."

She sniffed and wiped a wrist across her eyes and attempted a smile. "Amazing how quickly you can hit bottom."

"What can I do?"

"I realize this is a big ask, but I think it might help if tomorrow evening when you pick up Noah, maybe the three of us could go for a meal, do something together to validate *us* as parents. You and I on the same side. A pizza or burger, thirty minutes."

"Hmmm. I'll help, but I can't do it *this* Wednesday. How about next week, any day?"

"Why not tomorrow, Andy?"

"It doesn't fit with my schedule," he replied.

"Huh?"

"It's not a good time," he said.

"It's an ordinary Wednesday in the middle of October."

"Any time next week," he answered impatiently.

"Fine, Andy," she huffed. "No hurry. It's only our son and his welfare. We'll go whenever it's max convenient for you."

"So, okay, here's the bottom line, since you're making me out to be a jerk and an indifferent dad. Kellie and I have dinner planned Thursday, and I have a small gift for her, and if I tell her about this tonight—as I should— then all my sincere efforts might be misconstrued as a bribe or the fruits of a guilty conscience."

"Why didn't you just say so?" She rolled her eyes and pressed her palms against her temples. "I'm not a china doll. More power to you. I'm glad for you." She quit pressing her head. "I am."

"I didn't want to sort of underscore my good fortune while you're at the opposite end of the spectrum."

"Take this however you want," she said, "and I don't mean to sound smug, but your romantic doings and social life are of no interest to me, none, unless and until they affect Noah. Don't be so vain. We're *years* past my caring." There was no hostility or scorn in her tone, only a weary honesty. "We'll go next week. Sure."

"Just trying to do the best I can, Brooke." He rested both hands on the table. "While we're on the topic of Noah, it seems maybe my *professional* life might be the biggest complication coming our way."

"Huh? Why?"

He told her about DeMarcus's visit and the employment offer in Richmond. He concluded by emphasizing how fortunate he was: "I can earn millions of dollars from a nearly perfect job."

"Have you decided to accept it? To move to Richmond?"

"I'm still trying to puzzle through the pieces," he answered. "The timing couldn't be worse, and the opportunity couldn't be better. There's already so much upheaval in Noah's life right now. If I accept the job, I become a weekend father. Maybe you and I could share weeks in the summer, but no matter how we arrange the schedule, I'll lose time with my son, and that's the most valuable thing in my world. To make matters worse, he'll think I'm leaving him behind. Abandoning him."

"Maybe you could work remotely?" she suggested.

"Not long term, and it's impossible to prepare for a big trial by Zoom or a conference call. They're not offering to hire me and pay me large dollars to piddle around my den in T-shirts and fleece slippers and literally phone it in."

"Keep me informed, please," she requested.

"Of course," he promised.

❖❖❖

THURSDAY NIGHT, ANDY COOKED Kellie dinner—spaghetti with store-bought sauce, a tossed salad and broiled Texas toast from a frozen package. He opened the pricey bottle of wine he'd been hoarding since early 2018, spread a white tablecloth, lit candles, and set a vase of fresh florist flowers near her knife and spoon. For kicks, he'd mail-ordered a dog collar with a black bow tie attached, so Patches came formal to the meal.

"This is nice," Kellie said as she was finishing her salad. "Thanks."

"But wait, there's more."

She pushed her salad bowl to the side. "More? And I only pay shipping and handling for the bonus bric-a-brac?"

"I have a gift for you," Andy said.

"Now we're talking." She smiled. "Who doesn't love a surprise gift?"

He'd taped the present underneath the table to hide it, and he retrieved it and held it for her to see.

"Dang," she said. "No mistaking the box, that color blue. And it's large enough that I'm certain it's not a ring, in which case I'd be forced to make a momentous, life-altering decision on the spot. With regret, I'd turn you down, and nerves and anxiety and bruised feelings would ruin the remainder of our evening."

"Hope you like it."

She opened the box and removed a silver bracelet completely encircled with small hearts, each with *Tiffany* engraved on it. "Oh, it's lovely. Beautiful. Thank you, Andy."

"My pleasure," he said. "So you like it?"

"I do." She laid the bracelet across her wrist and had him come and help her hook the clasp. She kissed his cheek.

"There's a catch, naturally," he said, still next to her.

"It's a nice present, so I suppose you have some goodwill to burn."

He grinned. "Don't forget the fancy, romantic, restaurant-quality dinner. Should be points there too."

"The fact you *did it* is so sweet and adorable, how you made spaghetti, the single guy's go-to date staple. Kitchen magic for the take-out, stove-averse bachelor. Maybe we're finishing our gourmet romp with Neapolitan ice cream or some Mrs. Smith's? Fruit cocktail cups?"

"Nope. I have a cookie selection from the bakery in Collinsville and orange sherbet."

"Moon shot. Even better. So what's the rub?"

He sat down again. "I want us to just date each other. Exclusively. Boyfriend and girlfriend, as corny and trite as that sounds."

She briefly widened her eyes, amused. "Guess I'm a little behind. I thought we *were* a couple."

"Yeah, yeah, yeah," he stammered, "we are—and have been—but I wanted to tell you, rather than assuming. Thought I should."

"I'm happy you did. I'm all for it."

"I mean…hell, you're the cold siren who claims she would 'turn me down.'"

"Oftentimes, the first lotto ticket isn't a jackpot winner. Your dedicated players keep the faith and return to the convenience store with more cash, despite earlier setbacks."

***

"WHAT YEAR IS IT?" Judge Leventis asked Peter Morley's secretary the next morning, Friday. She and Andy were seated in her office.

"It's 2020, ma'am," came the reply over the phone's speaker.

"Exactly," the judge said. "Which means conversations are possible from almost anywhere at any time. Especially during these pandemic days, when we've all learned how to do business without the need to convene in person. Mr. Morley, wherever he is and however busy he might think he is, needs to simply power his cell or push the green button on his laptop and join us for a virtual hearing."

"I'm available twenty-four-seven, whenever," Andy volunteered. "Moreover, I told Pete on Monday this was going to happen, and we don't have time to waste."

"When might we expect him to join us?" the judge demanded. "For five minutes. By phone or Zoom or Skype?"

"I'm not sure," the beleaguered lady answered.

"You're his administrative assistant, correct?" the judge asked.

"Yes, ma'am."

"You have his calendar," the judge said.

"Uh, yes, yes, but …with everything so busy, I'm not sure …oh, gracious, here he is, he just walked through the door, let me see—"

"There's no 'see' in the equation," Judge Leventis snapped. "Hand him the phone."

A few moments later, Morley's voice was on the speaker. "Judge Leventis, good morning. And cheers to you, Andy. Sorry for the confusion. School buses delayed me driving here, and we're already up to our armpits in alligators."

The judge began bouncing the pink eraser of a pencil against her desk. "Mr. Hughes and my assistant Leigh have been trying for three days to have you return a call or reply to an email. Is there a reason we go through this song and dance whenever counsel or my office attempts to reach you? A reason I have to burn my time hunting you down?"

"Sorry, Judge. My apologies to you both. Won't happen again. Let me give you my cell number."

"I already have it," Andy said. "I left you three messages. You ignored them all."

"Something must've glitched then," Morley hedged. "Don't remember any messages from you, Andy. But I've been in the sticks campaigning, where the service isn't great, and my battery drained yesterday and the phone died, and I—"

"Well you're with us now, finally," Judge Leventis said.

"Yeah, I understand Andy wants to schedule a motions date so he can argue this case is ready for trial and we should set it, even though your ruling's still on appeal."

"It's not going to be on appeal much longer," Andy stated. "Judge, they missed the filing date. Here's the commonwealth's appeal notice from the clerk's office, and the timestamp shows it's late. No offense to Mr. Morley, but the appeal is over and done." He gave her the paper. "Also, here's a case directly on point, *Whitt v. Commonwealth*. There's no curing a late appeal and no possible extension of the filing period." He held several stapled sheets in her direction, and she took them and turned to the final page.

"Judge," Morley answered, "we can still request to submit a late appeal, and we can still take this to the Supreme Court."

"As I understand the law," the judge said, "once you miss the filing cutoff, any appeal is lost for good."

"And, Mr. Morley," Andy said, "while you're tilting at those windmills and wasting time and purposefully delaying this case in hopes you can hand it off to someone else, we can set a date for a jury trial, and you can prepare for a trial two freaking months away, and if lightning strikes and an appeals court allows you to fix your blunder *and* overturns this court's obviously correct ruling, then so be it, we'll postpone the case. We should set this now and move it later if you catch a double miracle."

"Hang on, Mr. Hughes," Morley griped. "I didn't realize we were planning to decide this on the merits today, over the phone, with me not having a chance to prepare. I need a formal hearing and time to write my response."

"It's a scheduling matter," the judge said, annoyed. She dropped the pencil. "What kind of hearing do you need? How about you simply tell me why you can't be here, ready to go, in December. Your election will be over in a few days, we've already had a lengthy preview of the case thanks to the suppression motion, and you've had the file since the summer."

"Judge," Morley said, "honestly, we're being rushed for no reason other than Mr. Hughes's desire to quit as a PD soon. This is a huge case. As big as they come. What's the hurry?"

"A huge case with simple facts," Andy replied. "We can try it in three days, maybe four. We might spend more time seating a jury than actually hearing evidence."

"Yeah," Morley said, "it'll take a week to seat a jury in a case with this much publicity."

"We're in Patrick County," Andy answered. "Not Florida or California. The biggest trial before this was Dennis Stockton's capital murder case. Major media attention. The jury was seated before lunch. True story. In our case, not very many local people will be personally acquainted with the victim and her family, and Mr. Benson works in North Carolina. Also, Mr. Morley, you'll have completed questionnaires so you won't have to ask a lot of questions."

"I don't see why we shouldn't calendar it," the judge declared. "Seems to me the appeal is a dead end now, and the state has two *more* months to get ready. Never takes very long to seat a Patrick County jury. What days do you have available, Mr. Hughes?"

"Note our strong objection," Morley said.

"Noted. Leigh's been recording us, so it's preserved."

"Judge," Andy added, "once we schedule this, I'd like to ask the court for funds to hire a blood-splatter expert and also a subpoena for Mrs. Benson's emails and texts."

"Just never ends with you, does it?" Morley whined. "What's next? The kids' report cards?"

"Yeah, Mr. Morley," Andy chided him, "all the time and effort we're putting in, you'd think this was like a murder case or something."

150

CHAPTER THIRTEEN

"I'll save the days on my calendar," Vikram said when Andy returned to their office and informed him Damian Bullins would be tried by a jury in Patrick County Circuit Court on December sixteenth, seventeenth and eighteenth. Saturday the nineteenth was a possibility if the case ran long. "No offer or movement from Mr. Morley?" They were in the breakroom, each with a Styrofoam cup of coffee, and Vikram was picking at the icing from a dry carrot cake slice with a white, disposable fork.

"None," Andy answered. "I lowballed him, asked for obstruction of justice in hopes he'd counter with voluntary manslaughter and ten years. He just indignantly burst into flames and lectured me about his integrity."

"Perhaps he'll be more flexible nearer to the trial date. Who knows with him?"

Andy sawed his thumb across his chin. He made a clicking noise with his tongue and teeth. "Man, Vik, it's weird where we are, but we have, well, we have a shot, a chance, of Damian avoiding any real damage if we draw the right jury."

"A lot of pennies from heaven have landed for us. We're certainly ahead in the breaks and flukes and dumb-luck score."

"You ever watch *The Price is Right*?" Andy asked.

"Once or twice," Vikram answered. "Can't claim to be a regular viewer."

"Remember when I was at home a few years ago, recovering from knee surgery? I was stuck in bed for a while, and I watched loads of daytime TV."

"More of your chronic malingering," Vikram kidded him.

"One of *The Price is Right* bits is a game called Plinko. You drop a big plastic disc at the top of a giant vertical pegboard, and it falls and bounces and pings and ricochets and clips against this maze of pegs until it winds up at the bottom, where it stops on a money amount."

"Sounds like slow-motion pinball with no bells and no flippers."

"The crazy-ass thing is the disc never seems to take the same route—you can drop it on the far left, and the son of a gun might end up at the money amount on the bottom far right. Or it might just as easily travel so it lands in the slot directly below where it was dropped. Or somewhere in-between. Every trip down the board is wildly random." Andy drank his coffee, noticed the cup left behind a brown ring. "On rare occasions, in our cut-and-dried, predictable, turn-the-crank justice system, we catch a Plinko case where a secretary mistypes a basic Miranda form and the bounces start and the whole infallible process goes haywire, becomes a chaotic spectacle, and there's no telling what the payoff will be."

"I love that game," Kellie said, walking into the room. "Plinko and Safe Crackers are epic." She opened the fridge and found a bottled water. "Your best bet is always to drop the disc three slots over from the end. Play the odds. Trust me, I've spent many hours with Bob and Drew."

"I'm hooked," Vikram said. "I assume YouTube will enlighten me?"

"Definitely," Kellie assured him.

"Before we get too excited about our legal house of cards," Andy noted, "we need to do some checking and find out where Cole was on the day our client killed Alicia Benson. All the misdirection and Nephi payments and innuendo and affairs are worthless if Cole can establish an alibi. For instance, if he was in meetings with people or his secretary recalls he never left the office, then we have a problem."

"True," Vikram agreed.

"I think I'll see what Ted can discover," Andy said. "If the world's best sleuth fails, I might try another call to Arlie Hatch."

❖❖❖

DeMarcus phoned half an hour later. "Come on, Andy, don't make me beg," he said right off the bat, no greeting or small talk. He chuckled, and the warning was entirely amicable.

"Sorry, D," Andy replied.

"It's been over a week since I offered to make you rich and handed you a dream job on a silver platter."

"I'm grateful, my friend, I am. You know I am." Andy took a deep breath. "I don't have any plans right now beyond leaving here—not as if I'm weighing my hundreds of options. I'm just kind of treading water, and your offer is beyond generous, more than I deserve, but I can't figure any way to be fair to you guys and to my son. He's very, uh, well…there's a lot on him right now, and he has to come first. That could change, but I realize you and your firm can't wait forever for me to accept your invite to the prom."

"I understand. Noah's a great young man, and you need to do what's best for him. Makes perfect sense to me."

"Keep me on your list," Andy said. "Maybe our lives will stabilize."

"Let me sweeten the pot." DeMarcus dragged the word *sweeten*.

"Huh? How?"

"I need your promise you'll hold this in complete confidence," DeMarcus told him.

"Sure. I will."

"We're very close to merging with Frith, Anderson and Peake in Roanoke. We have an office in Abingdon, but we'd like to have a western footprint closer to Richmond. You think you could possibly work there?"

"Hell yeah, I could," Andy exclaimed. "It's under an hour for me to drive to Roanoke—I can just hop on 220. And the folks at the firm are excellent lawyers and nice people. I met Phil Anderson when he was bar president."

"We'd still expect you in Richmond at least once a month, and your cases might take you anywhere in the state, but you'd be able to keep your castle there in Hooterville, and your boy's world would change very little, if at all."

"Absolutely," Andy said enthusiastically. "Thanks. Wow. We're scheduled to try Damian Bullins before the end of the year, so most likely, I'd be able to start in January."

"The dominoes all need to fall just right," DeMarcus said, "and again, please keep this strictly between us, but we might be able to pull this off. I'll stay in touch, and if you agree, I'll formally take this to our committee, make you a written offer, and we'll go to work together. January might be a little optimistic, but you should be my partner by early spring."

❋ ❋ ❋

"When, exactly, do you make time to work on our cases?" Andy asked Ted Utley later that day. "Have I ever walked in here and found you with an actual office file open? Or putting together one of those dramatic poster-board charts with yarn connecting pictures of the villains?"

Ted was seated at his desk, bent over a folded newspaper, circling classified ads with a red pen. He kept scanning the fine print, didn't look up when he spoke. "What the hell does 'serious inquiries only' mean, Mr. Hughes? Like the world is full of bored pranksters who call about your used chainsaw and wanna pay you in turnips?"

"Not certain, Ted. I suppose it means the seller isn't in the mood to dicker."

"Good luck with that. Only a chump pays askin' price." Ted whipped another quick red circle. He flipped the paper, ran his finger down a column, and then set aside the pen. "Can I help you with somethin'?"

"Yes," Andy answered. "Thanks. I'm not sure how available this information is, and short term, we have to be very invisible, but I need to learn where Cole Benson was on—"

"On the day his wife was killed," Ted finished the sentence. "Otherwise you roll craps with your whole Cole-murdered-his-own-wife defense. And don't worry: At my age, I pretty much only truck in the short term."

"Nicely put, as always." Andy grinned. "You're the master, so I'm in hopes you might be able to nose around for me and make sure he doesn't have an unshakable alibi."

"Oh, he doesn't," Ted replied.

"And you know this how?"

"You gave me the security disc which the sheriff's office sent, right? The video from the Benson house on May fifth. Told me to go through every second before you watched for yourself. Cole's office is in Mt. Airy. Restaurants were Covid closed in North Carolina. On the day Mrs. Benson died, he comes home around noon, leaves roughly forty minutes later.

154

I wrote the precise timestamps in my notebook. I'm assumin' he ate lunch. Their house is close to the state line, at the edge of Patrick County. Eleven miles to his office in North Carolina."

"Bang. The dice stay on fire."

"I wouldn't get too excited 'bout it. He's neat as a pin when he leaves. Same clothes, every hair in place—well, he has a buzz cut—but no blood, no nothing, calm as baby Jesus on Mary's breast. We both know he didn't hurt Mrs. Benson."

"But he's there, Ted."

"Yeah, for the whole wide world to see. Why would he drive right into his own security camera if he was plannin' to kill his wife? Why would he be anywhere near there? He'd pack a bologna sandwich and make certain he was with people every second of the day—last thing he'd do is cruise by for a murder cameo. He'd either kill her before he left home, or he'd park well away from the cameras if he came back intendin' to do her harm."

"Have you finished the entire video?"

"Nope. Not yet. I'm only a part-timer. Twenty hours a week, no benefits. I'll let you know when I'm done."

"You ever watch *The Price is Right*?" Andy asked. "The Plinko game?"

"It's rigged as rigged can be," Ted said. "They tie monofilament fishin' line—which you can't spot on TV—and guide that puck wherever they want it to go. Don't believe everything you see."

❧❧❧

ON TUESDAY, OCTOBER 20, Kellie's case was scheduled immediately before Andy's, and they rode together from the PD's office to the Henry County Courthouse.

"So you'll know," he informed her, "Noah's struggling with his mom's divorce, and the three of us are planning to eat together tomorrow, maybe at her new place. Show my support for her and fly the parental unity flag."

"I hope it helps him...and Brooke," Kellie replied. "What a shitty thing this Howard jerk has done to her and Noah. I wonder if the good doctor ever gave any thought to the boy when he was plotting his affair?" She sighed. "You men," she said, but it didn't come off as mean or jaded.

"I appreciate your understanding." Andy was relieved. His hands were tense, strangling the wheel, and he relaxed them.

"Sure. There's nothing to 'understand.' He needs his mom and dad. He shouldn't *ever* feel as if he's being ditched for some strange woman—one childhood dose of that is plenty for life. You take care of him."

At court, Andy sat on the lawyers' bench and watched Kellie claw and scrap for her client, a seventh-offense shoplifter caught red-handed by the store's security guard. The defendant had stuffed her purse with AA batteries, a shirt, a lighter and a lint roller. She'd also left her old shoes in a box, returned the box to the shelf, and was wearing new sneakers when she was stopped and asked to empty her purse. She hadn't made bail on the felony, so she sat beside Kellie in an orange jumpsuit and spent most of her time mouthing silent words to her frazzled mom in the gallery and pantomiming messages about a power bill. She rarely paid any attention to the testimony or the attorneys' questions.

Roy Reid was sitting next to Andy, and he cupped a hand over his mouth and whispered: "Kellie's amazing. A natural. A helluva lot better than you and I were as rookies."

"Yep," Andy answered. "If she doesn't burn out, she'll be a star. To watch her, you'd think she's done this for decades. Truth is, she's probably better than we are *now*."

Despite her tenacious efforts, Kellie didn't win, and her client's felony was certified to circuit court. Andy's case was called, and he did all he could to defend his client from a second-offense-drunk-driving charge, but the commonwealth had the goods and a .19 blood-alcohol test to boot, and the judge found Luther NMN Hopkins guilty and sentenced him to jail. As he was organizing his file and clearing the table for Roy, Andy watched Hopkins stand and lose his balance, and he noticed the man's pants, a wet, dark half-circle in the rear, and he knew to check the chair, and his client had pissed, and urine was yellow-dripping onto the carpet, spilling off both sides of the seat.

"How can you possibly walk away from glorious mornings like this?" Kellie deadpanned on the return ride from the courthouse to their office.

"Yeah, I'll probably regret my decision forever." They stopped at a red light, and he twisted sideways and caught her eye.

"What?" she asked. "Why're you staring at me?"

"I wouldn't call it staring," he said. "What time is it? I don't have to be back until one."

She looked straight ahead, smiled. "No."

"Your apartment is only—"

"Ten minutes from here."

"We could—"

"We *could* do all kinds of things, Andy."

"And talk about regrets, a few months from now, when you're making the forlorn trip—"

"I'll appreciate the solitude and privacy."

"...the forlorn trip alone from another glum day in district court, you'll think, *what I'd give if crazy, sweetheart Andy were here and we could take a romantic detour to my apartment like we used to.*"

"Well, since you put it like that, John Donne," she laughed. "I'd be a fool to lose the moment—so long as you promise to overlook the mess in my bedroom. And the kitchen sink. The last few days have been hectic."

❖❖❖

Lynn Dylan-Haley was Andy's first boss at the public defender's office. She'd hired him in 2003, and he'd worked for her until she left in 2016 to run the legal show for her husband's multimillion-dollar businesses. Despite making money hand over fist, and despite being rid of the PD's many aggravations and impossible clients, she eventually grew restless. She became bored with filing routine SCC forms and weary of scouring thirty-page boilerplate contracts to ensure every semicolon was in its proper place. In 2018, she opened a small office in Martinsville, and in addition to her corporate jobs for Haley's Comets, LLC, she began taking on various criminal cases, picking and choosing, sometimes working for free, just because she missed court and trials and the rush of winning an occasional not-guilty verdict. She stayed in touch with her former colleagues, often inviting them to lunch or to stop by her office for a cappuccino from the imported five-grand machine. She was, as Vikram once said, "a good egg."

There was nothing unusual about her dropping by the PD's office, so Andy didn't think anything was out of the ordinary when, the next afternoon, Lynn rapped on his door and poked her head into his office and asked if he was free to talk.

"Always have time for you, Boss," he said, genuinely pleased by the visit. "Come in."

"Don't mean to ambush you, Andy," she replied, "but I'm here on business, for a client. I can come back."

"A client?" Andy asked. "Do we represent co-defendants?"

She stepped over the threshold so he could fully see her. "Not exactly." She gestured toward the hallway, and a man appeared. "This is Mr. Hatch. Arlie Hatch. I think you've spoken to him over the phone."

Hatch nodded. "Mr. Hughes," he said solemnly. "Hope we're not barging in."

"No, not at all. Not being rude, but do you guys want to chat from over there, or should I mask up?"

"Whatever you prefer," Hatch answered.

"I vote for both," Lynn said. She and Hatch had already covered their faces.

"Fine by me." Hatch dragged a chair away from Andy's desk, and Lynn took a seat in it. He then pulled over a second chair to use himself. "Thanks for your time, Mr. Hughes."

"Mr. Hatch was in Mt. Airy meeting with his client and friend, Mr. Benson, then he traveled to Martinsville to meet with me, and I told him there was a chance you'd be available."

"No worries, Lynn," Andy said. "You're always welcome. What can I do for you folks?"

"As I mentioned during our phone conversation," Hatch answered, "I'm no expert on Virginia criminal law. Far from it, I'm afraid. Mr. Benson does not have complete faith in Peter Morley, so we've hired Mrs. Dylan-Haley to help us navigate this process. We felt we would benefit from the advice of a smart, local, experienced lawyer."

"Well, you're three for three with Lynn," Andy replied.

"That's kind of you," she said humbly.

Hatch was rigid in his chair, dressed in a dark suit and narrow tie. "Communication with Mr. Morley has been an issue, and frankly, so has his performance. Once he explained to us that he'd decided against the appeal and this case was set for December, we felt it wise to retain Mrs. Dylan-Haley. Of course, thanks to her, we've now discovered—despite the spin and deception in his press release—Morley managed to miss a basic filing deadline and bungled the appeal. Contrary to his public pronouncements, he didn't elect to forego the appeal because he feels confident in the commonwealth's case and wants to bring 'swift and satisfactory closure to the Benson family.'"

Andy held his forefinger close to his thumb. "Yeah. His statement was just a *tad* self-serving and fundamentally dishonest. But we didn't see any gain for our client by taking Peter the Great to task on it, and it's such an obscure procedural point the press probably won't discover the mistake on their own."

"In fairness to Mr. Morley," Lynn said, "there's no real loss. I read the transcript, and the critical error was made long before he was involved. The investigator screwed up the Miranda warnings, then lied about it at the hearing, and all the king's horses and all the king's men weren't going to fix that disaster. Mr. Morley was given an impossible task, especially with my friend Andy working the file for the PD's office."

Andy focused on Hatch. "He only appealed to save face and, more important from his perspective, so he could delay the trial long enough to win his election, resign as commonwealth's attorney, and hand over this beast of a case to some other unlucky sap."

"He's not the man we want representing our interests in such a deeply personal matter," Hatch said dourly. "Alicia Benson was murdered, and our lawyer is more interested in fleeing his obligations than gaining justice for her and Cole and the girls. We anticipated he'd be gone by the time this case is tried, but now it seems we've been locked in to a date, and we're stuck with an advocate who wishes he were elsewhere."

"I'd say that's an accurate summary," Andy noted. Concerned his mask had muffled his words, he repeated the phrase *accurate summary*.

"Are you willing to tell us what you have?" Lynn asked. "Where you're going? Did you make Morley an offer?"

"I did," Andy answered. "Most recently, obstruction of justice and twelve months. He turned me down."

"I would've too," Lynn said. "Twelve months on a misdemeanor? *Obstruction?* If that's your best offer, the commonwealth has nothing to lose by trying the case. Bullins has probably already served enough time to satisfy twelve misdemeanor months. The commonwealth would be playing with house money. Then there's the whole issue of who he's shielding. Yeah, I'd have hard passed on your offer too."

"But, Lynn," Andy answered, "you'd be a thoughtful professional, and you'd counter, and we'd engage in a meaningful, good-faith negotiation. Also, you'd be prepared and be familiar with the facts and law and understand your strengths and weaknesses. You wouldn't be distracted and wholly unaware of details and documents. There's the difference. Morley's simply marking time until he can hit the exit."

"Brass tacks, Andy," Lynn said, squaring herself toward him, "are you and Vik planning to use Mr. Benson's relationship with Heather Farris as part of your defense?"

"Yes," Andy replied. "As of right now, yes."

"Meaning," she said, "you plan to suggest he somehow had a role in his own wife's death?"

"Correct," Andy answered. He leaned forward when he spoke.

"Try my best, that's where I lose the thread. If every spouse who made bad marital choices was a murderer, we'd have people stacked in jails like cordwood. What's the link, the evidence, the connection? Certainly you're not planning to argue Mr. Benson was in league with a psychotic, drug-addled felon?"

"We have a theory of the case that'll get us to a jury." Andy was intentionally cryptic.

Hatch's hands were so tightly wadded in his lap that his fingertips were packed with blood and deep, vivid red. His eyes had soured, and the skin at their corners was creased. "From our viewpoint, this seems more and more like extortion. If we don't agree to allow a murderer to skip away with a wrist slap, you, Mr. Hughes, plan to ruin Mr. Benson's good name, damage his businesses, and poison his relationship with his daughters. Am I understanding? No one in this room truly believes Cole would raise a hand against his wife."

"Until a few days ago, no one in this room would've believed Mr. Benson cheated on his wife," Andy replied, his tone constrained. "But he did."

"Damian Bullins confessed, he's on video coming and going, and he was covered in her blood," Hatch stated. "He's a violent felon who was high on drugs. I mean, come on. Seriously?"

"As you understand, Mr. Hatch," Andy said, "it doesn't matter what *we* think. It doesn't matter what happened or how guilty Damian is or isn't. All that counts is what twelve strangers from Patrick County, Virginia, picked at random, with no training or particular qualifications for their task, decide in a pell-mell scrum behind closed doors."

"The truth *always* matters," Hatch insisted. "And proving the truth is much easier than proving a lie. The truth is very much our ally."

Andy shifted his focus from Hatch to Lynn. "I think Mrs. Dylan-Haley will confirm I'm a serious attorney, not a highwayman or blackmailer. We anticipate being able to present a factually accurate, reasonable, ethically sound defense. For what it's worth, it pains me that our evidence and theory of the case will probably cause hardship for four innocent girls. I'm a father myself."

"Andy would never leak this or flog it only for leverage," Lynn confirmed. "But we're right back to where we started: How does Mr. Benson's affair possibly help your defense? How is it even admissible?"

"Lynn," Andy answered, "I think at this point I'm completely on the giving end of the equation and not receiving anything in return. Why're we having this conversation? Why would I show you all my cards now?"

"If you have a viable defense," she replied, "we're certainly open to encouraging Mr. Benson to accept an appropriate plea arrangement. I see from the files you've subpoenaed Mrs. Benson's texts and emails. Is there some suggestion she was in touch with Bullins?"

"Is that accurate, Mr. Hatch?" Andy inquired. "Would you and Mr. Benson tell Peter Morley to take a plea that's less than optimum for the victim's family?"

"Mr. Benson is a wealthy businessman because of his ability to make difficult decisions objectively and dispassionately."

"This isn't a business decision," Andy reminded him. "I saw Mr. Benson in court, and he was enraged. Angry. He controlled it well, and I don't blame him for being vengeful, but we're not talking about the bulk discount on a tractor-trailer load of widgets here. He lost his wife and the mother of his four daughters."

"We'll listen with an open mind," Hatch said, "but rest assured, if it costs him every penny he has, and no matter how embarrassing his moral failures—assuming you can prove an affair and a judge allows it as evidence—Cole Benson is determined Alicia will receive justice and an animal like Damian Bullins will be punished."

"We can't really engage, Andy," Lynn said, "if you don't give us a reason to consider a plea. We'd be buying a five-dollar grab bag from the closeout bin."

"Well, I've already explained the big picture to Morley, and he has all our documents."

"He hasn't returned my calls yet," Lynn noted, "so I'm not aware of that information."

"Nor has he shared your trial strategy with Cole or me," Hatch said. "Good Lord. Unbelievable."

"Okay, Lynn, here's the short version. Before you leave, I can give you the same copies I gave Morley if you'd like."

"Thanks," she said.

In a deliberate monotone, with his arms folded across his chest, he told Lynn and Hatch about the medical records, the cancer scare, the tuition check, the million-dollar deal for Damian Jr., the email, the blood-splatter expert, and, of course, Heather Farris. "We can prove Mr. Benson had a motive to kill his wife and that he was there at the home around noon on the day she was murdered. We can—"

"Damian will never testify, right?" Lynn interrupted. "You'll just ask Mr. Benson about the email."

"Yes," he answered.

Hatch's neck reddened. "There's no possible way you'll be able to peddle that...well, that poppycock—and you both know what I really want to say—to a jury. It's crazy. Lunacy. Desperate. Untrue and the worst kind of grasping at straws."

Andy unfolded his arms. He noticed he'd missed a button underneath his tie and fastened it. "Lynn, if you're being objective, I think you'll agree we have enough to make it to a jury, to have them decide whose version to believe."

"Probably." She slid to the chair's edge, jutted forward. "Ah, the subpoena for her texts and emails—you're fishing for some mention of her unhappiness. Something to demonstrate she knew about the affair and she'd put Cole on terms. She'd had enough."

"Could be," Andy answered.

"No sane, rational person would ever believe a word of this," Hatch declared.

"Well, we have one other thing in our favor," Andy said. "Cole Benson will bust the EDR gauge."

"A gauge? Sorry..." Hatch was frustrated. His knee sewing-machine jigged. "The *what?*"

"The Eldorado Rule," Andy replied. "Mrs. Dylan-Haley trained me, and it's her rule—she can explain."

The room went silent. Lynn was wearing a bejeweled peacock brooch, and she rearranged it before speaking. "One summer day when I was a girl growing up over in Ridgeway, our neighbor, who had a DuPont supervisor's job, drove home a brand-spanking-new Eldorado Cadillac. I first saw it through the screen door, and my daddy was pleased for him, excited, and we all went outside and circled around the car, and I got to sit behind the steering wheel and blow the horn. My parents took a picture. Think about that for a moment."

"Okay," Hatch said, bewildered. "I am."

"There was once a time, Mr. Hatch, when we accepted things as they came, with no concerns about subtext or shady motives or dark secrets or 'doing my own research online'—Walter Cronkite delivered the news in black and white, good people truly were good people, the Rockefellers and their successes were admired, and the bachelor teacher who helped your boy one-on-one after school was like family. People were presumed honest, their intentions virtuous."

"But *now*," Andy said on cue.

"But now," Lynn went on, "there is no black and white. There're shades of envy, suspicion, grievance, jealousy and distrust, and we're always wary of conspiracies, ulterior motives, clay feet, flaws, deceit and double-dealing, especially where the rich and famous are concerned—"

"Every charitable donation is a tax dodge, every act of kindness is a photo op," Andy chimed in. "I know that line by heart."

"People—our jurors—are conditioned to *expect* the worst, to ferret it out, to never accept the obvious and honorable at face value. *60 Minutes*, *48 Hours*, Internet chatrooms, politicians, Madoffs and Fyre Festivals, tobacco executives, unholy priests, and Jack Ruby and Lee Harvey Oswald have done a number on us—somewhere along the way, we've seen the garden serpent, all of us, and many folks are spooked forever, never get over it. For them, the reversal becomes the norm. They'll labor and strain until they can piece together a Byzantine contrivance, even if the truth is plain and easy—and true. Think OJ or Casey Anthony. They'll *start* this case by trying to find what's *really* going on with this strange, rich *Mormon*, a foreigner in an evangelical land, and my friend Andy will do his best to encourage them on their righteous pursuit."

"So now," Andy said, "you wheel in a new Caddy...."

Lynn pivoted toward Hatch. Their knees almost touched. "And the neighbors immediately begin to speculate—drugs, embezzlement, showing off for a mistress—or they seethe because you have the nice ride and they don't, and they hunt for ways to tear you down, eager to believe the worst and happy to add fuel to the gossip bonfires. Sorry, but that's simply how it is. And how it'll be with a jury trial."

"Point taken," Hatch said somberly.

"Cadillac doesn't even manufacture the Eldorado any longer," Andy noted. "An era ended. Last model year was 2002."

"Thanks for seeing us," Lynn said. "I'll go over the information with Mr. Hatch and Mr. Benson, and we'll be in touch. Maybe we can find some common ground. Tell sweet Noah hello for me."

CHAPTER FOURTEEN

WEDNESDAY EVENING, ANDY, BROOKE and Noah shared Chinese food at Brooke's rental house. The adults were artificially voluble and cheery, kept their happy talk constant, barely stopping to chew and swallow. Noah seemed noncommittal about the whole forced effort—he was neither grumpy nor engaged, simply ate his meal and answered the leading questions his parents put to him using his politely bored voice.

"I have some great news," Andy offered when they were clearing the table. "Looks like I'll be accepting a new job soon. With Harold, Edwards and Slate. More money, better work. I'll be a partner in a big firm."

Brooke was holding a stack of dirty plates and she set them on the table, slowly lowering them, and surprise flooded her features and caused her to briefly freeze in place, as if she'd been unplugged. "So, yeah, okay," she said after the gobsmacked pause, "you mentioned the job, Andy, the new possibility, and you've decided to take it?"

"I have," he replied. "I'm excited. It's not formally done yet, not official, but if all goes well, we've agreed I won't have to move, and my main office will be in Roanoke. I'll visit Richmond once or twice a month, but otherwise I'll spend most every night at my house."

"Wow," she said. She exhaled a thick breath and collected the plates again. "How'd you persuade them to give you such a sweet deal?"

"A long story, and some of it's confidential, but with any luck I should be on the payroll by spring. Won't be any significant changes around here. How's that sound to you, Noah?"

The boy, eight years old, whimsical and impossible to decipher, replied over his shoulder as he was walking away to fetch his backpack, not even facing his mom and dad, apparently not concerned in the least: "Okay, I guess. We need to get to your house so I can see Patches."

●●●

ON NOVEMBER 3, ELECTION DAY, Peter Morley won a seat in the Virginia Senate. He received nearly seventy percent of the vote. Andy and Kellie drank beer and snacked on baby carrots, celery, broccoli, dip, cheese cubes, mixed nuts, and chicken fingers and watched the returns at his house. They were both impressed by how composed and articulate Morley was when he spoke on TV.

"Hell, I'd vote for him," Kellie said after the senator-elect finished his speechifying. "Maybe politics is his bag. His niche. He's a natural, and he comes off as smart and reasonable. Very charismatic. He's better on camera than a lot of the national bigshots. Almost classy. Maybe you're being too hard on him." She winked.

"Yeah, he's about as classy as a hickey on a thirty-year-old's neck or the champagne room at the Interstate 81 strip club."

The next morning was cold, and a frost had sparkled the grass and stamped tiny icy intricacies—whorls, doilies, lattices—across the Jeep's windows and windshield. The hardwood leaves had peaked, so the oaks and poplars were beset with gaps and bare spots, but runs of determined yellow, orange and crimson still held on to their branches, dying slow and pretty. Andy dialed the Jeep's heat knob as far into the red as it would go, routed the air to the defrost vent, and Bluetoothed a Miles Davis playlist for the trip to town, where he'd scheduled an early meeting with Lynn Dylan-Haley.

"I skipped my coffee this morning," Andy informed Lynn when she met him in her lobby. "But you better believe I came with my mug. I figure to at least wrangle a java treat out of you before you beat me to a pulp."

While she made him a cappuccino, they chatted about their kids and a colleague who'd recently suffered a health scare. "Here you go," Lynn said. "It's hot—be careful. There's sugar if you want some."

"Thanks." He was seated on a small sofa, and he set his Elvis-meets-Nixon mug on an end table's magazine. "This sounds weird, coming from me, the rookie you hired and trained, but I'm proud of you. You rang the bell. Good on you."

"I've been fortunate." She moved books and files from an upholstered wingchair, wiggled it cockeyed to the table, and sat down.

Andy crossed his legs. "Where are we with Mr. Benson?"

"I wish I had better news," Lynn said sincerely. "I finally met Peter Morley. He's a different bird, isn't he? He's intelligent and charming, but you get the impression when he speaks to you that every period or comma is simply an opportunity for him to silently snap-poll your reactions and calibrate his message."

"His strong suit is people skills," Andy said sardonically.

"At any rate, our conversation was very general, and he's still not quite up to speed on some of the smaller details and case law and tactical possibilities. I did my best to educate him."

"He'll be a dandy-fine senator," Andy said.

"I really didn't learn much from him other than he's anxious to somehow avoid a trial. The most bizarre thing was his asking me if I wanted to take over the case, to either run it myself or be appointed as his deputy."

"Wow." Andy took hold of the mug and encircled it with both hands. "You're kidding?"

"Nope. I explained to him the monumental ethical and due-process complications with that scheme, suggested he read *Cantrell* and the Supreme Court opinions on the topic, and bless his heart, for a few seconds, he just kinda looked at me, like a guppy with its nose mashed against a glass bowl. As you and I understand, I'm limited in what I can do since I'm employed by the victim's husband and not the commonwealth. I felt a little iffy even meeting with Morley."

"No issues on my part," Andy assured her. He chuckled. "You've been with the guy for five minutes, and he's trying to pawn off a godawful murder case on you. Sheesh." He tasted the coffee.

"As for Cole Benson, I Zoomed with him and Mr. Hatch, whom I've really grown to like, and gave them my best take on the case and trial, warts and all. Mr. Benson was gracious and noncommittal. He didn't seem anxious to compromise."

"Should I make another offer to Morley?" Andy asked. "Think that'll help?"

"Perhaps. Can't hurt, I suppose. Benson and Hatch are convinced the whole crazy tale is so far-fetched no one will believe it, and Damian will be convicted. The only downside for Mr. Benson is the damage to his reputation, and he's willing to take the hit if it means his wife's killer is punished. Of course, there's also the impact on his kids, especially the oldest daughter. He's in a tough spot."

"I'll phone Morley this morning, make a more realistic offer."

"Are you planning to ask for a change of venue, Andy? Move the trial?"

"No," he replied. "Not yet. We're as well off in Patrick County as anywhere for many of the EDR reasons you discussed with Hatch. By the way, did you explain to them the pig-in-a-poke nature of our jury-trial format? Is Cole aware the jury won't know sentencing ranges until *after* a guilty verdict? If they buy into Damian's defense and only convict him of obstruction of justice, they'll be handed a verdict form that allows them to give him a max of twelve months."

"I told Mr. Benson about Virginia's process. A trial only on guilt or innocence, then, if the defendant is found guilty, a sentencing phase, where the jury learns for the *first time* the specific punishment options. High end for this variety of obstruction is twelve months. He wasn't moved by the information."

"Let's stay in touch," Andy suggested. "People tend to become more flexible closer to trial." He sipped his coffee, held the mug toward Lynn. "You think, Boss, you might barista another one of these for me? I'd brew it myself, but your machine is too complicated for an amateur, and if I break something, the repairs would cost me a month's pay. Also—is that a donut box over there?"

●●●

Two hours later, at the jail, Damian Bullins cruised into the interview room with a shaggy beard and a new Holy Bible.

"Damian," Andy said, after they were situated across from each other at the battered table, "what's the most important thing in your life? What do you care about most?"

169

Bullins's blue surgical mask cut a rectangle into his beard, and Andy could see the contours of his mouth when he spoke. "For sure, Mr. Hughes, being a servant to my lord and savior Jesus Christ is by far the most important. Next would be my son. Then, I guess, there's being a good fiancé to Misty—she's really been a rock for me."

"We both know, Damian, none of that's true. What you care about more than anything is saving your own ass. Your top priority is *you*."

"Why do you always want to put me down?" Bullins demanded, his temper flaring. "I get tired of you always thinkin' poorly of me and talkin' shit to me like I'm a dog." The skin exposed above his mask flushed. "Half the time I think you'll be happy if they fry me."

"Electrocution is not a commonwealth option in your case," Andy said, his voice tamped down. "Virginia is currently a lethal injection state, but forty years is the worst outcome for second-degree murder. If the charge remains at first degree, a life sentence is the most severe punishment. And anytime you question my abilities or intentions, feel free to ask Judge Leventis for a new lawyer."

Damian glared and sulked, simmering, but he didn't respond. His ragged breathing pulled and pushed against the mask, concaving the blue covering, then flattening it out again.

"I asked you for a reason," Andy said. He was tense and on guard, concerned Damian might erupt and come across the table. He eyed the shiny chain that bound his client's wrists. "I have critical information in your case. This fact loses much of its value and some of its potency if it becomes confirmed public knowledge. I also have an obligation to reveal it to you. But understand, Damian, if you spread this, or the media runs with it, you lose ground. Don't tell anyone, not your girlfriend, not your aunt, not your inmate buddies. No one. This remains sealed away until we're in front of a jury. Can I be any clearer?"

"Uh-huh," he muttered, still brooding.

"We now have a motive for Cole Benson to kill his wife. We can prove he was having an affair."

"Damn," Damian blurted, instantly shedding his ill mood and jerking forward, transformed, his hands frenetic, his eyes dancing. "Damn! I should've known it. Hypocrite. I told you, he's crooked as hell."

"Do you understand why it's best the whole world not hear about this until trial?"

"I do. Yeah. Mr. Goody Two-Shoes doesn't want people seein' the dirty laundry on his line, and this'll give us a bargainin' chip. A huge advantage."

"Yes," Andy said. "Exactly. So if you care about yourself and want to minimize your time behind bars, you'll keep this strictly between us. As big as this murder is, there's already speculation of all kinds online, and Cindy, my assistant, came across a picture of Cole and his girlfriend on a gossip site, but this particular truth hasn't appeared in legit media yet."

"Yes, sir. Done. Don't you worry. Thank you. Sorry I was, well, not myself and was rude to you. You go nuts in here, lose your spirit."

"Item next," Andy continued. "I told you about our blood-splatter expert. The judge has approved payment, and Mr. Christopher, the forensic scientist, will be available to testify for you. I assume his final testimony will match his preliminary opinion."

"Awesome," Bullins said, suddenly genial and enthusiastic, almost manic.

Andy then spent ten minutes methodically recapping every aspect of Bullins's case, and when he finished the summary, he checked a handwritten list to make sure he'd not omitted any important details. "Do you have questions?" he asked at the end.

"No, sir," Damian answered. "I'm with you a hundred percent."

"I plan to contact the commonwealth's attorney today and make him a serious offer. You understand exactly where we are with your defense. Tell me, please, what you'll accept in terms of a deal. No need for us to negotiate a sentence and have you reject it."

Damian's hands were resting on either side of the Good Book, the manacle chain draped across the cover. "Man, to me, it looks like we kinda have them over a barrel. Thanks to you and all you've done."

Andy squelched a smart-aleck reply. "What's your bottom line, Damian?"

"Why're we even considerin' a plea agreement when we're gonna win?"

"There's a *chance* we *might* win," Andy said. "There's a much better chance you'll catch forty years. I'd urge you to consider a compromise. And listen: With your past record, we don't give a damn what the conviction is for—first degree, second, manslaughter, accessory, obstruction of justice—who cares as long as your punishment is acceptable."

"Okay," he answered. His orange jail slides were steadily tapping the concrete floor. "I'd settle for five years. I really don't want to do that much; I think we'll win. I think they'll give me obstruction of justice, and I'll be free as a bird."

"I doubt I'll make much progress if that's your number," Andy said, a vein of frustration in his tone.

"What do you think I should offer?" Bullins asked.

"Me, I'd be satisfied with the ten years we discussed before, a credit for time served so far, and the last two years at the therapeutic community program to help you with your substance-abuse issues. But ultimately, Damian, it's your choice."

Bullins's feet gained speed, amped enough that his shackles jangled. "I killed the woman, but why...I mean, *even if*—you know, 'even if' is what I was meaning to say—even if I killed Mrs. Benson, which I didn't, why would I agree to serve time I wouldn't get otherwise? Why would I piss away ten years if I don't have to, if a jury's gonna see this in my favor? I *took the blame* for a murder I didn't commit, so why should I plead guilty when I'm innocent and let a rich scumbag like Cole walk all over me?" He raised his hands, pointed at Andy with both index fingers. "Shit," he declared, "tell the bastards I'll take three years. Let's see how Cole enjoys havin' his name drug through the mud. I'll betcha he'll cave."

"Not for three years, he won't," Andy said sharply. "You're acting as if we're positive a jury will buy into your rather complicated story. Odds are, you'll be found guilty of second degree murder. On a bad day, first degree."

"Well, that's his problem, not mine," Bullins snapped, emboldened and hyper, his cheeks and forehead starting to color again.

"Actually, Damian, it's altogether your problem."

❋❋❋

"I WAS THINKING," ANDY told Vikram around three o'clock, after they'd failed to locate Peter Morley despite trying both his cell and work numbers, "when I left Damian there at the jail, pumped up on his own bullshit, I've created a monster, bit by bit, court ruling by court ruling, but then it dawned on me: I simply connected Frankenstein's neck bolts to a bigger generator."

"Or gave Dracula a tanker full of type-O blood," Vikram suggested. "The man truly has an empty soul and a scoundrel's willingness to say or do anything for his own benefit."

They were in Andy's office, and Cindy's voice came over his desk phone. "Mr. Morley returning your call," she announced. "A minor miracle."

"Andy," Morley said, "hope you're safe and healthy. I was on the phone with my sister in Charlottesville. Called you the second I finished with her. Don't need Judge Leventis taking me to the woodshed again."

"Thanks," Andy said. "Congrats on the election. You mind if I put you on speaker? Vikram's here with me."

"Sure." Morley paused. "We ready? Can you hear me, Vikram?"

"I can," Vikram replied. "My congratulations as well."

"Appreciate it. I'm excited to have a chance to do the people's business. Humbled by the incredible support—seventy percent of the vote."

Andy located a legal pad so he could take notes. "I'd hoped we could have a more focused and productive plea negotiation now that the election is behind you."

"I'm open to discussing an agreed outcome," Morley said. "Absolutely. I apologize if I haven't been totally engaged with you, Andy. I promise this is now at the top of my list. Believe it or not, I spent an hour with the file early this morning. Mrs. Dylan-Haley has been a tremendous resource for me. I'm up to speed. I've asked my chief deputy, Stella Hespell, to help me try the case. She's a champ. Makes sense to bring her in—trial could still be delayed, there's a high possibility of appeal, and she'll succeed me when I leave the office. First woman and first African American to hold the job. I'm gratified she and I could make history together."

"Do you have a specific recommendation in mind?" Andy inquired. "A number?"

"I'm not in the habit of bidding against myself," Morley said. "You tell me your proposal, and we'll go from there. I will say, though, there's no chance we'll accept an obstruction of justice plea. You and I both…hey, hang on, Stella just walked in, and we're switching to speaker also."

"Sure," Andy said.

"Mr. Hughes and Mr. Kapil, good morning. I'm Stella Hespell. I look forward to working with you. Are you able to hear me?"

"We go by Andy and Vikram, please," Andy told her. "No 'mister' needed. We can hear you just fine."

"And I prefer just plain Stella," she replied.

"Welcome," Vikram said.

Evidently, Morley was closer to their phone than Stella. His voice was louder, sharper. "I was telling them, Stella, we're not in a position to consider an obstruction plea. We have no intention of implicating Mr. Benson in his wife's murder. Moreover, twelve months would be meaningless in this case."

"I understand," Andy said. "I'm not interested in Kabuki theater or used-car-dealing you, Pete. I would recommend to Damian he take second degree murder, five years active, thirty-five suspended, the last two years pulled at the therapeutic community. Probation for the rest of his life."

"I appreciate the offer," Morley answered, "but you've got to give me something to lose. Five years isn't enough. We'd roll the dice."

"Then you tell me," Andy replied.

"I'm not saying Mr. Benson would go along with me, not promising anything, Andy, but I'd discuss splitting the risk with him. Bullins gets twenty years. He's looking at forty with second degree, life if it's first degree. The indictment is still at first degree since he never pleaded guilty as once planned and took advantage of Mrs. Katt's generous offer to reduce the charge. Conceivably, he might wind up with a worse verdict than forty years."

"I'll certainly mention the possibility to him," Andy said, "but I'm not optimistic he'll accept twenty years. Would you perhaps mention ten years, our original offer, to Mr. Benson?"

"Of course. I will."

Vikram raised his voice for the speaker. "Please tell Mr. Benson—it might help convince him to accept a five-year deal—all Bullins is really doing is signing up for the max sentence on the installment plan—"

Stella laughed. "You guys use that expression too?" she asked.

Vikram smiled, chuckled. "Yeah. There's no chance, based on his history, Damian Bullins will comply with probation. He'll be released after five years, arrive home, and be high or drunk or committing new crimes within hours of his return to Patrick County, and he'll serve the remainder of this time in installments, with small breaks in between."

"I doubt it's legally possible or binding," Stella mused, "but I wonder if we could agree any probation violation, major or minor, would result in activating the full suspended thirty-five years?"

"Certainly would be fair," Andy said. "I'd agree, but it might not stick."

"See why Stella's taking over for me?" Morley asked. "She's smart as a whip."

***

"How LONG HAS IT been?" Kellie asked Andy as they were leaving the gym the following day, an overcast Thursday.

"Closing in on two months. Longest I've been without a cigarette in years." They were walking side by side, and he was holding her hand. "I think I'm past the worst cravings and withdrawal."

"You're bound to feel better."

"I do," he answered. "It's just an awful habit."

"I have a surprise for you," she said. They'd reached the Jeep, and he went with her to the passenger side and opened the door.

"Hmmm, could be good, could be bad." He grinned.

"I've booked us a room at Mountain Lake. I thought it might be fun to take a little vacation before you become totally immersed in the Bullins trial."

"When? When're we going?"

"Next weekend," she replied. She was sitting in the vehicle, the door still swung open. "Friday's the thirteenth, but I think we can reverse voodoo any bad vibes. Noah's with his mom, your calendar is wide open."

"Now that's some great girlfriend effort and engineering. Thanks. I'll be packed and ready. Just what the doctor ordered."

"Vikram mentioned the jury list had arrived, ninety names to research, and I know you'll be covered up soon, so I thought we could use a nice trip before all hell breaks loose."

"Like I said, I'm grateful and anxious to go, so thanks, but isn't the lake gone? Didn't it mysteriously drain? It's kind of Mountain Puddle these days, right?" He was standing in front of her, wearing a heavy coat, his gym bag strapped over his shoulder. "Doesn't matter to me—I'm happy to spend the days with you, doesn't matter where. We could shack up at the Collinsville Best Western as far as I'm concerned."

"The lake is in fact very tiny, but there still should be a few pretty leaves left, the drive up the mountain is beautiful, and I rented us a dog-friendly room with a fireplace and a balcony. The restaurant has takeout, I'm bringing Veuve Clicquot and your Terri Lyne Carrington playlist, and if you're any kind of boyfriend, we shouldn't spend too much time worrying about the water levels."

"Amen."

CHAPTER FIFTEEN

THE WEEK PRIOR TO Damian Bullins's trial, Andy received one hundred sixty-seven media requests seeking a comment or an interview, including inquiries from London and Tokyo. He, Vikram and Kellie prepared a bland, restrained press release, and he elected to do only three interviews. He appeared on Roanoke and Greensboro TV—where the local reporters couldn't believe they'd snagged such a whale of a catch—and also Fox News. The regional stations served Patrick County and the potential jurors who'd decide the case, and according to the tallies from the recent election, most of Damian's panel was definitely watching the fair and balanced national report at six o'clock. Andy's broadcast statements were cautious and vague, but he always emphasized Damian's innocence and hinted at a surprise, bombshell defense.

The conference room at the PD's office became littered with papers and files and pictures and forensic reports and law books and juror questionnaires and empty pizza boxes. Andy and Vikram contacted the old-guard lawyers in Patrick County to learn everything possible about the names on the jury list, and Ted Utley visited his cousin in Meadows of Dan and asked what, if anything, she knew about the randomly selected group of men and women. By Monday, December 14, Andy had solid and helpful information about all ninety people on the list.

"Here we go," he said aloud—even though he was alone in his office—on Tuesday afternoon, only hours before the trial began. He picked up the receiver. His palms were damp. A dose of adrenaline pinched his belly.

"Andy, it's Stella," she said. "Mr. Morley wanted me to let you know we haven't made any progress. We're stuck. We're too far apart, even if you and your client would agree to accept ten years, which I understand is a difficult sell for you. Our final package would be forty years, fifteen to serve on second degree, the balance suspended on the condition of probation for the rest of his life. We're all for him pulling the last two years in the drug-treatment program at Indian Creek. You and I would simply note on the record we both expect him to receive the full, remaining twenty-five years if he violates his probation in any form or fashion."

"That's a reasonable, fair offer," Andy told her. "Appreciate it. A reasonable defendant would accept it. Damian's not reasonable these days. Of course, I'll convey the terms to him. He'll reject the deal." Andy noticed how still and quiet the building was. The bustle and commotion and hallway traffic were suddenly, oddly gone. A light snow had turned to a nasty rain, and he heard car tires cutting through slush on the street outside his window. "We'll see you tomorrow, Stella. Good luck."

"You and Vikram have been real pros—good luck to you as well. Never know what a jury'll do."

"Oh," he said. "You got the batch of emails from Mrs. Benson's account, right? The info we subpoenaed. I mentioned them to Pete. I copied you with the three we plan to introduce as evidence."

"We have them," she answered. "Thanks." She briefly paused. "Let us know if your client changes his mind. The deal's available until we start the case."

"I will. But I'm pretty certain we're headed for a trial." He disconnected Stella, then phoned Bullins at the jail. He communicated the commonwealth's offer to his client, and Bullins barely allowed him to finish before speaking.

"No," Bullins declared. "Nope. Hell no. No way. I'm innocent, and the Lord is gonna deliver me. Well, with some help from his disciple Andy Hughes. I trust you. We're gonna beat this. I'll be a free man in a few days."

"Let me remind you one last time, Damian—fifteen years is a whole lot better than life. They've made us a damn fair offer."

"I saw you on TV, takin' up for me. Thanks. You're a good man. It's cool how famous I've gotten. That'll help us. Has to. You wouldn't believe how many ladies want to meet me once I'm released. I'm seein' some incredible letters and pictures from nice, respectable women, school teachers and corporate vice presidents."

"'Infamous' might be a better word choice, Damian. As for the women, perhaps you could have your beloved fiancée help you respond to all the fantastic mail. She could address envelopes for you." He heard a car horn blow, and the rain came harder and the wind whipped it against the window glass, turning the view briefly opaque. "See you in court."

CHAPTER SIXTEEN

BECAUSE OF THE PANDEMIC, the Patrick County courtroom had been overhauled for Bullins's trial. Richmond *finally* approved a safety plan that jigsawed the room with plexiglass dividers and wide yellow tape, and the jury was seated in the gallery, while five randomly selected members of the press—six feet apart and separated by the clear shields—filled in the former jury box. The witness stand was reversed to face the gallery and the jurors. Squirt bottles of hand sanitizer were everywhere, and only testifying witnesses and speaking lawyers were allowed to remove their masks for any length of time. Several fans pushed around the boiler-heated indoor air. A deputy periodically sprayed surfaces with disinfectant, and by nine thirty the whole joint smelled of bleach.

Andy learned early in his career that jury trials can be determined before the lawyers give opening statements or a single witness testifies, that honest people often see the world differently—there are forgivers and there are punishers, loophole sticklers and believers in rough justice, and no matter how much the judge talks about reasonable doubt or burdens of proof or presumptions of innocence, a defendant, to have any kind of not-guilty shot, needs a few jurors with open minds and sympathetic natures. Lawyer craft is no match for dreadnought biases or instincts hardwired over the course of decades.

The trial began on time, and Andy was apprehensive as he watched the clerk reach into an old wooden box at five minutes past nine o'clock and withdraw a random name. He was relieved when she announced the first prospective juror, Herman Akers, a retiree from Critz. She continued pulling out folded slips and reading names aloud, and Andy couldn't believe what was happening: The next nineteen people drawn—by lot, purely by chance—were impossibly favorable to Damian Bullins. Andy had rated every person on the list from *A* to *F*, and the first group of men and women was an all-star team for the defense, an incredible sixteen *A*'s, three *B*'s and a single *C*. Superstitious, he didn't turn the page in his pad or let go of his pen until the clerk finished and closed the box's lid.

Bullins was a pleasant, well-behaved defendant. He was clean-shaven and dressed in a gray suit—purchased by his aunt and girlfriend—a light blue shirt and a nice tie. He made occasional eye contact with the twenty potential jurors, but just like he and Andy had practiced, he never stared. He kept his hands quiet, and he chuckled at a panel member's corny joke about the local weather. He didn't *look* or *act* like a killer, and when the judge asked him to walk toward the center of the room and remove his mask so the jurors could see if they recognized him or had any relationship with him, he was shy and worried and innocent, a schoolboy being introduced to the principal on the first day of classes. "Being a sociopath has its advantages," Vikram whispered as they watched Bullins's spot-on performance.

Morley was full of strut and bombast and dotted with hair product, and he wore his American flag mask as well as an American flag lapel pin, prompting Ted Utley to observe "a pair of flag socks would give the stupid clown a patriotic trifecta." However, the commonwealth's attorney was now prepared and competent. Lynn's spoon-feeding and Stella Hespell's diligence and smarts had transformed him. Stella was a game-changer for her boss—she'd been raised in the county adjacent to Dunford, graduated from Yale Law, and declined golden tickets and six-figure salaries so she could return home and make her mark in a poor, rural region where no one who looked like her had ever been seated at the prosecutor's table.

The sheriff and his staff had helped Morley vet the jury list, and after the initial twenty citizens were assembled to be questioned about their impartiality and understanding of the law, Andy noticed Morley flash Stella a how-the-hell-did-this-happen look. Nevertheless, he was confident and conversational as he ticked off his voir dire questions, and he couldn't help himself and hammed it up when a lady mentioned she'd seen his campaign ads on TV.

"Did you win?" she inquired. "We aren't in your district down here."

"I did," he replied. "The Good Lord and the voters evidently decided I'd earned their trust."

Andy asked only basic questions, and he finished by planting the early seeds of Bullins's defense. A pair of pedestal fans low-humming behind him, he addressed the twenty people seated in the gallery and informed them his client might not testify. "Near the end of this case," he explained, "Judge Leventis will tell you, will instruct you, Mr. Bullins is under no obligation to take the stand. That's the law. Mr. Bullins doesn't have to prove anything, and he's presumed innocent. While that's the law, I understand it might be difficult for some of you to follow. You might want to hear Mr. Bullins testify, even though he has a Constitutional right not to. No worries if you think it's unfair or you can't commit to honor this part of our Constitution—we just need to know before we get started. Can you follow this important legal rule?"

The group murmured okays and yeses, and a younger lady who was employed as an IT tech at a call center said firmly, "I'll apply the law," and then a man in jeans and a bulky sweater raised his hand.

"Yes, sir," Andy acknowledged him. "I believe you're Mr. Morris, from Woolwine. Morning to you."

"Mornin' to you, sir," Morris replied. He'd also responded to a couple of Morley's inquiries. "If the judge tells me to do it, okay, I will, but well, you know, I couldn't help but think in the corner of my mind, if I was innocent, why wouldn't I want to say so?"

"I appreciate your honesty," Andy remarked. He stepped closer to the railing that separated the gallery.

"Y'all swore me to answer your questions truthfully," Morris volunteered, "and I'll try to uphold the laws for jury duty, anybody would, but I thought I ought to mention this 'cause it was kinda naggin' at me."

Andy moved to his left so Morris's clear divider wasn't between them. "I'll be glad to answer your very reasonable question as best I can. We believe we'll be able to present our defense, our facts, through the commonwealth's own witnesses and through other independent evidence. We believe you'll have all the details of Mr. Bullins's account, his full story, without him having to testify."

"Okay," Morris said from his seat on the second row. "Sure."

Andy gestured at Peter Morley. "More to the point, my friend Mr. Morley is a senator-elect who graduated at the top of his law-school class. He's one of the most famous lawyers in the state. His colleague, Ms. Hespell, graduated from Yale. She's a gifted attorney, probably brighter than I am. My client has a high-school diploma. Honestly, I worry about him being nervous and winding up lawyer-tricked by some of the most skilled professionals I've ever met and leaving you with a wrong impression. If we can tell you Damian's story accurately without taking that risk, I've advised him to stay put right here with me. We want you to have the truth, and his testifying might not help accomplish our goal. If my client can catch his lunch from the pier, I don't want him swimming with sharks." Several jurors laughed, and Andy put his hands in his pockets. "So...can I count on you, Mr. Morris, to go by what Judge Leventis tells you?"

"You can, yep. Thanks for answerin' my question."

The majority of the initial twenty people made it through the questioning and indicated they'd be objective and could come to court for each day of the trial. Ultimately, forty-seven Patrick County residents were examined by Judge Leventis and the lawyers, and by late afternoon, Damian Bullins had his jury, fourteen men and women, the required twelve plus two alternates.

Kellie spent the night at Andy's, and she gave him a final critique of his opening statement, and when she asked if he'd have trouble sleeping, he told her he'd rest just fine, that he always slept well before important trials. At ten thirty, they were in his bed, and she was lying with her cheek on his chest, her leg straddling his, their breathing almost in rhythm. He'd plugged in Patches's mat, petted him goodnight, and left him, as always, with his muzzle at the threshold of this heated house, alert and keeping watch, Zeb McAlexander's vagabond sidekick, still averse to staying inside unless he was at the foot of Noah's counterpane. Andy sensed Kellie shift, and he was barely awake, drifting and blurry, and suddenly he popped open his eyes and blurted, "Damnit. Damn."

"What?" Kellie asked. "What's wrong?"

"I promised DeMarcus I'd speak to this big-wheel journalist, a guy named Fredericks, and kind of give him an exclusive quote every day. D believes the publicity will be invaluable and also thinks this Fredericks fellow will do a feature piece on me and my plans to land at Harold, Edwards and Slate. I forgot. I need to at least send a text."

"Oh, okay. You scared me." She elbowed him. "The price of fame. You and Peter the Great locking horns. Godzilla versus Megalon."

CHAPTER SEVENTEEN

THE ANCIENT HEATING SYSTEM rioted during the night, and the courtroom was hot and stifling the next morning, seventy-seven degrees, and even with the air conditioner switched on, it was still sweltering when Peter Morley gave his opening statement. Judge Leventis allowed the lawyers to remove their suit jackets, so Morley spoke to the jury in a vest and pressed white shirt. His stage makeup was gone, a wise, obvious choice, but the watch chain and monogrammed French cuffs remained part of his shtick. He was polished, personable, and adored the spotlight, and he was always keenly aware of the pool TV camera.

Morley immediately had a difficult decision to make about Cole Benson's affair and how thoroughly, if at all, he should address the adultery and Bullins's claim he was duped by the real killer. Focusing too much on the defendant's version of events gave the story instant credibility; ignoring it might cause Morley to appear as if he were hiding the truth. He began by quoting Thomas Jefferson and John Adams on the importance of jury service, then he ably highlighted the commonwealth's anticipated evidence, described the video of Bullins entering the house and leaving, waved around the DNA report, and promised to scientifically demonstrate that the blood on the defendant's pants came from the deceased, Mrs. Alicia Benson. "Blood doesn't lie," he proclaimed. "But better yet, we literally have the murderer caught on video."

He didn't explicitly mention Cole Benson's affair or Bullins's defense. Near the end of his remarks, though, he did suggest, with pitch-perfect dismay in his voice, the defendant, as defendants are wont to do, was liable to throw the kitchen sink into evidence, or to fabricate who-knows-what self-serving lie, or to try the old trick of blaming others as a distraction, and he urged the jurors to always test these flimflams against their common sense. "Your common sense," he repeated. He concluded by thanking the jurors for their attention and rejoined Stella at the commonwealth's table.

"Thank you, Mr. Morley," the judge said when he was finished. "Opening statement, please, Mr. Hughes."

Andy greeted the judge and jurors with a simple "good morning," and he acknowledged Morley and Stella, and he told the jurors he appreciated their service and sacrifice. After the formalities and pleasantries, he was intentionally mute—almost a minute passed—while he turned his head and traced from left to right, making eye contact with each man and woman waiting to hear from him.

"I doubt you'll run across many defense lawyers who'll tell you this from the get-go," he finally said, "but my client is in fact guilty. He's just not guilty of murdering Alicia Benson. He's guilty of attempting to help his son, he's guilty of stupidity, he's guilty of a dying man's desperation, he's guilty of being manipulated by a powerful adulterer, and legally speaking, he's probably guilty of obstruction of justice—he intentionally hindered the commonwealth's investigation of this crime."

Andy hadn't removed his jacket, and now he took it off and draped it across the chair in the witness stand. "Here's what Mr. Bullins did, why he did it, and the evidence that'll convince you we're telling the absolute truth." Andy recited Damian's story, and every time he had the opportunity, he buttressed his words by mentioning the medical reports, or the Nephi26 check, or the email to Benson, or Heather Farris, or Alicia Benson's forlorn messages to her husband, or Vince Christopher, the forensic expert. He ended the defense's account by describing Bullins's arrest at his own small camper, "Damian, meek as a lamb, *conveniently* still dressed in the bloody pants." He glanced at Morley. "We *also* would encourage you to please rely on your common sense," Andy reiterated to the jurors.

He collected his suit coat, put it on, and faced the panel. "A last thought about common sense. At the end of this case, I'll ask you to reflect on two things. Number one, I'll ask you to consider what motive my client had to murder Mrs. Benson and what motive Mr. Benson had to murder

Mrs. Benson." Andy's lapel was slightly amiss, and he smoothed it flat. "Also, please be thinking about this as we explore Mr. Bullins's guilt or innocence: Why do people kill other people? In my experience, there're two main motives for virtually every murder. Thanks, and I look forward to working with you on this important case."

Vikram complimented him when he sat down at counsel table. "Nicely done," he said.

Andy took the measure of his fourteen-person audience, observing them without being too apparent about it. He could tell from their expressions and reactions they were, so far, inclined to give Bullins a fair shake. The fantastical defense was no longer crazy, jailbird junk. The black robe, the rituals, the suits and ties, the formal portraits of dead judges hung along the wall, the oak benches and intricate woodwork, the high plaster ceiling, the juror oaths and the soft, murky lighting—the reach and gravity of this ancient place were beginning to work alchemy on a lie.

The commonwealth called the coroner as its first witness, and Morley took him through several topics and offered Mrs. Benson's autopsy report as an exhibit. Andy didn't ask any questions and didn't object to the jury considering the report. According to the doctor, Alicia Benson's death was a homicide. He also described the bruising and contusion on her abdomen as being consistent with a recent to kick to her stomach.

"Oh, Dr. Lane," Andy said as the coroner was snapping shut his briefcase, "I almost forgot. Time of death please, sir, in your opinion as the expert who performed the autopsy."

Dr. Lane left his briefcase closed. He was balding, with a gray goatee, his speech brisk and clipped. "Based on body temperature, rigor mortis and the lividity, I'd put the time of death between noon to two thirty p.m. on May fifth, 2020."

Coy Hubbard had retrieved the surveillance video from the Benson house, and he was the next witness, sat on the stand in full brown uniform as the recording played for the jury and they saw Bullins enter the home and then rush out minutes later. An enlargement of a frame showed red droplets on his pants. Hubbard also gave the jury pictures of the crime scene, Mrs. Benson dead on the bloody floor, one eye completely sealed, the other slitted and fixed, her drained lips separated as if she'd died struggling to speak. In the last photograph, the camera angle made an apple appear to float in a pool of red.

"So," Morley asked the cop, "who contacted 911?"

"Mr. Cole Benson called," Hubbard replied. He was as laconic as always and seemed unaffected by the reporters and TV camera.

"When you arrived at the Benson house, Officer, was Mr. Benson there?"

"Yes," Hubbard said.

"How long have you been a deputy?" Morley asked.

"March seventh will be twenty-three years," Hubbard answered.

"What was Mr. Benson's demeanor when you found him with his dead wife?"

"He was cryin' and extremely upset. Tore up."

Morley tugged at his watch chain. "As a policeman with decades of experience, did you observe, hear, or discover anything whatsoever that caused you to believe his grief wasn't sincere?"

"No, sir. To me, Mr. Benson seemed truly upset. Emotional."

Morley finished his examination by asking Hubbard to describe Bullins's arrest and the splatters on each trouser leg. He had the deputy detail the painstaking procedures the Patrick County police took to preserve the evidence and ensure the bloody pants reached the forensic lab without any contamination. Morley returned to his table, but he didn't sit, instead stood behind his chair. He lowered his mask to sip water from a paper cup.

"Just a couple of things," Andy began. "And, oh, good morning." The room had cooled, and Andy was wearing his jacket.

"Mornin' to you, Mr. Hughes."

"You'd never met Mr. Benson until the day his wife was killed and you saw him there at the house."

"Correct," Hubbard said.

"So you really don't have any baseline, any points of comparison, in terms of evaluating whether he was genuinely emotional or simply playacting for you and the other cops?"

"I'd never met Mr. Benson before the day his wife was killed," Hubbard answered.

"Also, in response to Mr. Morley's question, you indicated your investigation and your review of the security video revealed Mrs. Benson was alone in the house when my client entered through the front door."

"Yes. That's right. She was by herself as best we could discover."

"But, sir, she wasn't by herself the entire day."

"She wasn't," Hubbard said.

"In fact—and let's please play the timestamped section of the video—Mr. Benson appears around noon, remains inside for approximately thirty-seven minutes, then leaves."

"Yes."

Andy pointed at a large screen. "There he is, Cole Benson, arriving and going inside at twelve-seventeen?"

"Correct," Hubbard said.

"And you've reviewed this video?"

"A bunch," Hubbard replied. "Several times."

"And Mr. Benson departs at twelve fifty-four, thirty-seven minutes later."

"Yes, sir."

"Well within the noon-to-two-thirty time-of-death range established by the medical examiner."

"Yes," Hubbard answered.

"Officer Hubbard, it seems to me you did most of the actual police work in this case. You were the lead in the field."

"Sort of, I guess."

"But, technically, you weren't in charge. Investigator Melvin Ellis was running the show."

"Yes, sir," Hubbard said, "he outranked me."

"When you arrested my client, were you aware of the video showing Mr. Benson entering and leaving around noon?"

"No." Hubbard looked at Andy when he spoke.

"To the best of your knowledge, was Officer Ellis aware of the section showing Mr. Benson's arrival at the murder scene?"

"No. We played the video there at the house, and we seen the defendant go in and run out. We went to his place, and there he sat with blood speckles on his pants. Didn't really see no need to watch any more video."

"Be that as it may," Andy said, "Mr. Ellis is no longer an investigator. He's been demoted and now serves as a jailer."

Morley was still standing, and Stella leapt from her chair, and they spoke simultaneously. "Objection," they both shouted. "Completely irrelevant and inadmissible," Stella added.

"Sustained," the judge snapped. "The jury is instructed to disregard the question and draw no inference from it." She glared at Andy. "I don't think that was inadvertent. Consider this a warning."

"My apologies to you and the jurors," Andy humbly replied. "And to Mr. Morley and Ms. Hespell." He flipped a legal-pad page. "Hours after the killing, Mr. Bullins hadn't even changed clothes, and the blood spray was visible, correct?"

"Yes, you could see it. It was more of, well, kind of a mist with a few bigger drops."

"And he was beyond cooperative with you? Surrendered?"

"He was cooperative," Hubbard confirmed, "and didn't make no fuss."

"You found a knife at the Benson home? In the kitchen? The defense and commonwealth have agreed it's the murder weapon."

"I took custody of the knife," Hubbard said. "Mr. Ellis located it there in the kitchen and bagged it as evidence and later gave it to me."

"Mr. Morley has been kind enough to stipulate the results of the lab analysis: There is no fingerprint or DNA match from the knife with my client."

"Right," Hubbard said.

Morley lowered his mask. "Also, we agreed to stipulate there is no DNA or print evidence linking Mr. Benson or anyone else. Other than Mrs. Benson's blood, there was not enough DNA or clear finger or palm prints to make a valid ID. Not unusual with a rough, carbon-fiber knife handle that's only been clutched in a palm."

"That's accurate," Andy replied. "I'll enter the lab reports, please—both for DNA and prints." He handed the papers to a bailiff, who took them to the judge. She marked them and asked the bailiff to provide them to the jury.

"Last questions, Officer Hubbard," Andy said after the bailiff had delivered the forensic reports. "Did Mr. Bullins have any kind of prior relationship with Mrs. Benson?"

"None we're aware of. Other than he done odd jobs around the property."

"He was hired by Mr. Benson?"

"As I understand it, yes, Mr. Benson hired him."

Andy rubbed his chin. "And prior to May fifth, there was no feud or quarrel or issue or dispute between Mrs. Benson and Damian Bullins? They were basically strangers."

"None we've found."

"Was anything stolen or missing from the Benson residence?" Andy asked.

"No."

"Was there any sign of forced entry?"

"No," Hubbard answered.

"Was there any evidence of sexual assault?" Andy asked.

"No, sir."

"When you arrived on the scene, Mr. Benson was covered in blood as well, wasn't he?"

"Yes, he was sittin' there on the floor, with his legs stuck straight out, kinda cradling her in his lap, cryin' like a baby. There was blood on him."

Morley spoke the instant Andy informed the judge he had no more questions. "But there wasn't a drop of blood on Mr. Benson when he casually left his house after lunch, wearing the same clothes he wore in. There was nothing unusual about him or his appearance, was there?"

"Nothing unusual," Hubbard agreed. "He left same as he come in, and there was no blood on him, even if we blow up the pictures as much as we can."

"Goodness," Vikram whispered next to Andy's ear. "I was worried Judge Leventis might go full Medusa on you for the Melvin Ellis mention."

"It was worth the risk and scolding," Andy said. "Adds another odd, loose end for the prosecution. Every drib and drab helps."

Morley finished his case with his trump-card witness, the commonwealth's lab expert, who educated the jury on DNA, its isolation and analysis, and left no doubt the blood on Damian Bullins's pants belonged to Alicia Benson.

Andy was brief with his cross-examination. "Ma'am," he asked her, "you don't know *how* this blood wound up on the defendant's pants, do you?"

"I do not," she replied.

The commonwealth rested its case-in-chief without calling Cole Benson to testify, a sound choice in Andy's opinion—Morley could listen to the defense, learn the particulars, then have Benson respond if there was enough evidence to cause concern. The judge adjourned court at four thirty and reminded everyone they'd start at nine the next morning.

As Andy was organizing his files and papers, preparing to leave for the day, he asked Bullins about the woman sitting with his aunt in the small section reserved for family.

"Oh, her name is Becky. Becky Adams. I told you I'd been gettin' some pretty interesting mail. Becky's been a big boost for me. No need to worry. She's a nurse in Spartanburg, South Carolina. Clean record, works regular."

"Why's she here, Damian?"

"After I'm released, I think we might try to see each other. We have a lot in common. It's cool to get to know someone by letters and calls." He touched Andy's forearm. "And, man, look at her. I'd be a fool if I turned down *that* ass."

Andy shook his head. "I'm sure your fiancée will be pleased with this development."

"Since she has to stay in the witness room, I doubt she'll find out."

"Ah, of course," Andy replied. "Just to be cautious, I'll have Ted Utley check Miss Adams's background."

Later that night, after they'd eaten a meal at Andy's kitchen table, Kellie showed him an article at the top of her phone's newsfeed, where Clifton Fredericks wrote that the defense's opening statement was a "tour de force, equal parts Perry Mason, Antonin Scalia, college professor and bare-knuckle brawler." Fredericks also noted Peter Morley was "Matlock rebooted, this iteration with Gucci instead of seersucker, and blessed with a ringmaster's flair."

CHAPTER EIGHTEEN

FRIDAY MORNING, DECEMBER 18, was frigid and bright. Two cardinals were boisterous on a courtroom window ledge, and jurors sat beside their haphazard stacks of winter coats, hats, scarves and gloves. Andy called the defense's first witness, Dr. Ricky Owens, to start day three of the trial, and Owens confirmed Damian's medical history, including the cancer reference in his records. On cross-examination, however, Stella quickly minimized the notion that any reasonable patient would've believed he was suffering from terminal cancer.

"Did you tell Mr. Bullins he had cancer?" she asked.

"I *never* told him he had cancer," Dr. Owens stressed, "and while I might've mentioned the word in passing, I didn't believe from my examination of the mass that it was life-threatening or malignant, nor did I communicate such a diagnosis to Mr. Bullins."

When Stella finished her questions, Andy did the best he could to repair the doctor's testimony. "But yet, sir," Andy said, "my client returned for a follow-up visit, the mass had increased in size, he complained of discomfort, and you were concerned enough to order a biopsy. To check for *cancer*, yes?"

"Yeah, okay. But only out of an extreme abundance of caution." The doctor swiveled in Bullins's direction. He'd been instructed by the judge not to mention he'd treated the defendant as a county inmate. "There're things I evidently can or can't say, but as Mr. Bullins's treating physician, it's my medical opinion he was exaggerating his symptoms."

"A draw if we're lucky," Kellie told Andy during the break that followed. He'd asked for her thoughts on Dr. Owens's testimony.

"You're being girlfriend generous," he replied. "I'd say Stella probably whipped my ass."

"Well," she said, "it's not easy to win over the doc when your client was a malingering doper looking for pills and any excuse to leave the jail for a short vacation."

A juror was tardy returning to her spot in the gallery, and Andy sat at his table waiting impassively, shoulder to shoulder with a killer, at the center of blindfolded Lady Justice's pageant. He was grounded and serene, and the people and voices and his own thoughts came to him honed and vivid, everything impeccably sorted. He shut his eyes for a moment. He felt—it was almost audible inside his skull—as if he were ordained for this place and this trial, understood the hundreds of shitty little cases and the hours of analyzing code sections and the years of hunting legal trapdoors for the guilty were all part of his path and purpose, his deliverance to what was coming next.

The stray juror appeared and apologized, and Andy stepped to the front of the defense table. "We call Cole Benson as an adverse witness," he said, and the pair of front-row jurors who'd been furiously taking notes since Wednesday exchanged a six-foot glance as if to say: finally.

As a potential witness, Benson had been excluded from the trial since it began, sequestered in a side room. Walking down the main aisle, he appeared to have gained weight, and his buzz cut was even more severe, almost to the scalp. Asked by the clerk if he would tell the whole truth, he affirmed the oath with his right hand held high.

Andy said a perfunctory hello to him but didn't feign any pointless civility. "Let's see, Mr. Benson, if we can establish some basic facts without wasting a lot of time."

"Sure," Benson replied. Judge Leventis signaled him, pointing at her own mask, and he removed his face covering.

"Are you acquainted with a Miss Heather Farris, born June eighth, 1997, who lives in Winston-Salem, North Carolina?"

"Yes, I am," Benson answered. He stared out at the jurors, his shoulders braced. His size and bulk made the witness-box space too compact—railings and dark-grained oak surrounded him on every side, almost touching him.

"Please tell us the nature of your relationship."

"Uh…we have a personal and intimate friendship." He and Morley and Stella had evidently decided this deflection was the least poisonous description available to him.

"Meaning," Andy said, still lingering at the front of the table, "you've committed adultery with her."

"Yes," Benson said. "We've had sexual intercourse."

"In plain English, she was your mistress while your wife was alive?"

"I'm not sure the term *mistress* is fair to her." Benson continued to sit awkwardly, the chair too small for him, but he didn't appear nervous or alarmed or rattled.

"You pay for her apartment, correct?"

"Yes," Benson said, "I do."

"Give her a cash allowance each month?" This was a guess, but Andy assumed he was correct since Farris was unemployed.

"I help her with her bills. So, yes, sir, I give her money."

"And this sexual, intimate friendship and this monetary arrangement were ongoing the day your wife was discovered dead?"

"Yes." Benson's voice was flat, emotionless.

"And you'd been committing adultery with Miss Farris for months before the day your wife was killed?" Andy asked.

"Yes."

"So there's no misunderstanding, Mr. Benson, you are a devout, practicing Mormon, is that accurate?"

Morley stood so violently that his thigh bumped a law book and knocked it off the table. "Objection. This man's faith isn't at issue here." He stomped a foot, slapped the table with an open hand. "Mr. Hughes's question is offensive and obnoxious."

"Judge Leventis," Andy responded, "I have complete respect for Mr. Benson's right to choose how he worships and how he navigates his faith journey. However, some Mormons believe in plural marriage, and since our defense involves Mr. Benson's motive to do harm to his wife, we need to establish Mr. Benson's adultery wasn't an accepted part of his marriage or a legitimate practice in his religion."

"Go ahead," the judge said. "Overruled. But let's limit your questions to that very narrow subject."

"Our church does not allow or condone plural marriage," Benson said. He deflated slightly, settled more into the chair. His shoulders sagged, but his voice was still strong, commanding, even as he admitted his failing. "My relationship with Heather was against the teachings of our church. I concede that."

"Your late wife, Alicia, was heartbroken and begged you to end your affair with Heather Farris, didn't she?"

"She knew about Heather because I told her," Benson answered, the words without inflection. "I never lied to Alicia, nor did I ever neglect her or my daughters. They were paramount as my family. This may sound strange to you, but I loved my wife, the mother of my children, and deeply cared for her."

Andy picked up a thin file he'd positioned on the table. He removed three sheets of paper and asked the judge if he could show the documents to Benson. Benson scanned the papers, and Andy inquired if he was familiar with the emails he was holding.

"Yes. You obtained them from our service provider, and Miss Hespell gave me copies several days ago."

"Well, Mr. Benson, more important, you also received them from your wife, didn't you?"

"Yes, she sent them to me."

Andy read from his copy. "She wrote to you: *This is hell on earth, Cole, and I'm not sure how much more I can stand.*"

"Yes, she did," Benson admitted.

Andy read from the other messages, quoted Alicia Benson's anguished pleas to her husband to quit his cheating. She also advised him she wanted to see their bishop for counseling.

"All those emails, all those discussions," Andy said, "are evidence of her strong disagreement with your affair."

"To some extent," Benson answered, "but the last one was written seven months before she was killed. Seven months. We did in fact seek counseling together, and the situation, while not perfect by any means, and admittedly unorthodox, was an accepted part of our relationship. Alicia described it as a disappointing pain she was learning to tolerate but hoped to be rid of. A 'worse' in the 'for better or for worse' part of our wedding vows."

"I want to make certain the jury understands your explanation," Andy challenged him. "Even though you'd made her life hell on earth, even though you were selfishly damaging your marriage and family, she was going to endure your adultery *forever*, just kinda let it slide for as long as you wanted to sleep with your girlfriend?"

"We were at that point, yes. I spent almost every weeknight at home with Alicia and the girls, and we were a family, from school functions to vacations to just sitting on the porch together. I loved Alicia and I love my daughters."

"You're telling us that she never had a bellyful of your infidelity? Never gave you a choice? An ultimatum?"

"Yes, sir, that's *exactly* what I'm telling you. There's no mention of a divorce in any of her texts or emails, and you've scoured every single sentence. Her sister will confirm Alicia had no desire to leave. The day before she was murdered, Alicia had booked a family beach trip for June. Rented a house at Emerald Isle. I have the confirmation and paperwork to prove it. There was never any threat to leave or a divorce demand. Never. We were doing the best we could."

Andy didn't let on he was surprised to learn about the beach trip. Nothing registered in his face or voice. "But when your wife scheduled this vacation, you were still having an affair with Heather and had no plans to stop?"

"Yeah."

Andy then hammered through the rest of Damian's defense, asking short bursts of questions end to end, quick but not hurried, smothering and tightly tailored to elicit only yes or no responses. His tone never varied, and his volume never increased even when, once or twice, Benson became forceful or attempted to avoid a direct answer. In a span of ten minutes, the jury heard about and received both the Nephi26 check benefiting Damian Bullins Jr. and Damian's email to Benson reminding him of their "agreement." Andy also had Benson confirm his trip home for lunch and his past employment of Bullins, whom he trusted enough to hire for jobs at his residence, near his wife and children.

After he'd covered every aspect of Damian's story, Andy cocked his head and faintly smiled. He glanced at the clock on the wall. "I've been trying cases for years," he said to Benson, "and I've never had anyone break down on the stand and TV-confess just because the oath suddenly worked some special magic. I don't expect you to own up to killing your wife, but I still need to ask."

Morley objected to the editorializing, and the judge immediately sustained.

"I didn't kill my wife," Benson snapped.

"Well," Andy said, "you know Damian Bullins, and you hired him to do work for you at your home."

"Odd jobs, for gosh sakes."

"And did you hire him to take the blame for your wife's death?"

"Of course not," Benson answered. "No!"

"But you did pay for his son's tuition," Andy said.

"I did," Benson replied, composed and insistent, "but with my charity that's helped and assisted hundreds of people over the years. I felt sorry for the young man because his father was unable to be there for him."

"Did you promise to hire Damian Jr. and pay him a million dollars as the email reminded you?"

"Absolutely not."

"And you were aware Mr. Bullins believed he was dying?"

"No," Benson declared. "I never had any discussion with Damian about his health. Zero. None."

"You were home around noon on the day your wife was killed."

"For lunch. Same as I did most every day, since all the restaurants were closed. Alicia was very much alive when I left."

"You had a mistress on the day your wife was murdered."

"We've already been over my circumstances. Yes."

"The jury has seen the email Damian's girlfriend sent you on his behalf. He reminds you of an 'agreement' and states he's done his 'part.'

You received the email, thought it was from Mr. Bullins, but inexplicably buried it in a routine attachment instead of alerting the cops, correct?"

"Mr. Hughes," Benson said, exasperated, "I'm the person who had the email sent to the sheriff and the prosecutor. I gave it to my lawyer. Along with the bushel baskets of other crank junk I received." He focused on a clump of jurors. "First, who would ever write that kind of message if there really were a conspiracy? Second, why would I send the note to the authorities if I were involved? None of this makes sense."

"You'd send it because you had no other choice, maybe?" Andy said. "If you omitted it or concealed it, it would stick out like a sore thumb. What else are you going to do once your fall guy learns he's not dying and basically wants you to make payments that'll sound alarms and raise red flags and make you look guilty?"

"I suppose, sir, you, as a skilled attorney, can spin and twist anything, no matter how proper or decent, and make it seem corrupt. Regardless of what an innocent man does, you'll criticize him. I can't win."

"So, I have to ask," Andy said, "did you cut your wife's throat there in the kitchen?"

"No. I did not." Benson allowed his anger to etch into the denial. He glowered at Andy, and Andy gave it straight back to him, locked in.

Stella, not Morley, examined Cole Benson for the commonwealth, and it was apparent to Andy they'd practiced their presentation. Benson had a CEO's ability to dominate a large room and communicate to an important audience, and Stella talk-show-host nudged and guided him through a point-by-point rebuttal of Bullins's version of events. Benson was organized and sounded sincere, and he dabbed his eyes with a white handkerchief when Stella showed him a collection of family pictures, the last photo taken at a church covered-dish a few days prior to the murder, six big smiles and mom and dad with their arms around each other's waists.

Benson concluded each series of answers with a baffled expression and a shrewd question: *Why would I drive home and appear on my own security camera if I were planning to kill my wife and knew the patsy was going to be there a few hours later? How did I exit the house with no blood on my clothes? Why would I even hire someone to begin with, especially a man I barely knew?*

If I'd truly agreed to pay Damian Jr., why wouldn't I follow through rather than risk Mr. Bullins reporting me?

"Thank you, Mr. Benson," Stella said after reviewing her notes to make certain she'd been thorough. "I realize this has to be difficult for you. If Mr. Hughes has any further questions, please answer them."

Almost in unison, fourteen heads hinged toward Andy and Damian Bullins. Andy tented his hands in front of his face, finger to finger, his thumbs beneath his chin. He spoke through his disposable blue mask. "Mr. Benson," he asked from the table, "do you regret the affair with your girlfriend?"

"I do, yes," Benson replied. "It was selfish, and if I'd known your client was going to kill my wife, I'd never have made Alicia's life so difficult."

"Makes sense," Andy said. "Sure. You're remorseful?"

"Yes," Benson said.

Andy collapsed his hands. "So remorseful, sir, and so distraught and so respectful of your wife, what was it, all of a week before you brought your twenty-three-year-old girlfriend to your home and jammed her down your kids' throats? How long was it before you managed to contain your huge grief and introduce your mistress to your shell-shocked young daughters?" He stripped off his mask.

For the first time in almost an hour of testifying, Benson hesitated. He squirmed in the chair, buffaloed, and his suit jacket wrapped tighter around him. "I..." he fumbled. "Well, I wish I'd perhaps waited a bit longer. In retrospect—"

"Please answer my question, Mr. Benson. When your scheme made it appear to the world you were off the hook and my client was responsible for killing your wife, how long did you wait before trotting out your girlfriend and introducing her to your kids? How many days past your wife's funeral?"

"I'm not positive," Benson answered, growing incensed.

"You mentioned your sister-in-law. Do I need to ask her to give me a number?"

"It was about a week. But I was overwhelmed and needed help, and Heather is a good woman, from our faith community, and sooner or later I hoped to bring her into my daughters' lives. I trusted her, and I didn't feel comfortable dragging a total stranger into our world."

"Obviously, you'd have been waiting a long time to publicly reveal your girlfriend if the murder remained unsolved, if a stooge like Damian Bullins weren't arrested?"

"I wasn't able to run a global business and care for four kids by myself. Alicia was a fantastic and irreplaceable mother and spouse. This was sudden and unexpected. All Heather did was help with some housework, laundry and occasional meals. I never, ever introduced her as my girlfriend, and I was very careful not to give any indication of our romantic relationship to my children." He laid his hands on the railing. He still wore a wedding ring. "For gosh sakes, Mr. Hughes, doesn't this demonstrate why I *wouldn't* harm my Alicia? Her death made my life a total wreck. She held our household together."

Following an hour's adjournment for lunch, the jurors listened to the defense's final witness, Dr. Vince Christopher. Christopher brought along a video showing how it was possible to re-create the blood-splatter pattern from Bullins's trousers with ordinary kitchen items like a basting brush or a whisk or even a damp dishrag. "In my expert opinion, this blood splatter could've been mechanically applied," he concluded.

The commonwealth responded with its own expert, who disagreed with Dr. Christopher and informed the jury he was convinced the splatter originated "organically, from the severed artery in Mrs. Benson's neck."

Morley ended his case with Audrey Clayton. She was the last witness the jury heard from, and she was emotional and animated when she testified she'd spoken by phone with her sister two nights before the murder, and there was no hint or mention or whiff of Alicia Benson leaving her husband. "She was absolutely, one-hundred percent committed to her marriage." As promised, Clayton passionately repeated what she'd described to Andy in their parking-lot conversation. "Let me put it bluntly," she said, a tear on her cheek. "Cole Benson was a jerk and a terrible, selfish husband, but he had no reason to kill the goose who was laying his golden eggs. He had the best of both worlds, could play the great Mormon patriarch for the community and sleep with his young blonde girlfriend whenever he liked. He didn't kill my sister. Why would he?"

Clayton was bright and infuriated, and Andy realized he could only gain so much ground with her. "Ma'am," he asked, "you encouraged your sister again and again and again to leave her husband?"

"I did. He was mistreating her. Demeaning her. Alicia and I were very close, dear sisters and best friends, and despite my encouraging her otherwise, she was determined she'd keep her husband and her family. She was tough—"

"But you—"

"Let me finish my answer, please, Mr. Hughes. She was tough as nails when it came to her marriage. Alicia was sweet and quiet, meek, but she was a fighter, not a quitter, if her family was involved."

"But you," Andy continued, "her very closest confidante on this planet, insisted she ought to divorce her husband?"

"Yes. She should've."

"How do you know, over those last few days, she didn't come to accept your advice and inform Cole she was leaving? Everyone has a breaking point—often, it only takes a grain of sand or a single harsh word to finally tip the balance."

"Planning a beach trip and baking apple pies for your spouse hardly seem indicative of a woman who was packing her bags."

"How long was it after your sister's death that Heather showed up at the Benson home?"

"Far too soon. A matter of days. Poor, ignorant Cole phoned me to ask where the iron was and which settings to use on his kids' clothes. No surprise he was scrambling for a maid."

"Seems he got a twofer, right? There're businesses in Winston-Salem and Mt. Airy that could've helped him with household chores, though that's the limit of their services."

"Sure. It was, as I said, not a wise choice for any number of reasons."

"So much so, his oldest daughter now lives mostly with you."

"She does," Audrey confirmed. "She's seventeen, virtually an adult."

"At least part of her deciding to leave her dad's home is based on her reaction to his contact with Heather Farris. She's extremely upset with him."

"Part, yes. But Cole loves his daughters very much."

"Nice to see you again, ma'am," Andy said. "Thanks for your time today, and I appreciate your meeting with me in the past. I'm truly sorry about your sister. We can agree she was a wonderful, exceptional lady."

"We can," Audrey replied. "She was the best of the best."

The cavernous room was quiet except for steam rattling the ancient heating pipes and a muffled cough from a rear row, and as Audrey Clayton gathered her purse and left the witness stand, Andy addressed the judge, spoke precisely, solemnly: "The defense has nothing further."

"Nor does the commonwealth," Morley stated.

"Ladies and gentlemen," the judge announced, "you now have all the evidence. Next, I'll read your final instructions and the lawyers will give you their closing arguments. Realistically, you're looking at beginning your deliberations around seven tonight, depending on whatever supper arrangements we make. Do you want to keep working, or come back tomorrow, on Saturday? We discussed the Saturday possibility when we started on Wednesday. Within reason, I'll honor whatever you decide to do."

The jurors left for the reconfigured law library—the only nearby space large enough to socially distance fourteen people—and returned several minutes later. Wearing the same loud, lumpy sweater he'd arrived in on Wednesday, Mr. Morris spoke for the group and informed the judge they hoped to go home, eat a hot meal, enjoy a good night's sleep, and "get crackin' fresh first thing tomorrow."

"A prudent decision, I think," Judge Leventis said. As she'd done at the conclusion of every day, she ordered them to not discuss the case with anyone and to avoid all news reports and social media. She reminded them, as usual, she'd examine them in the morning to make certain nothing irregular had occurred that might affect their impartiality.

"Looks like your buddy Mr. Morris will be our foreman," Vikram said to Andy.

"Looks like," Andy replied. "I'm okay with him."

"What do you think?" Damian asked, his voice strained. "Her bitch sister didn't help, but otherwise, seems you're doin' a great job. Thanks, sir."

"I promise this isn't a lawyer's hedge," Andy said, "but it's impossible to tell. You have a chance. I don't have a crystal ball. If I thought we were too far behind to have any hope, I'd warn you."

"And you're sure I shouldn't testify?" Damian asked.

"In the end, it's your choice. But either of those lawyers will take you apart, and as a bonus, the jury will learn about your nice long list of prior felony convictions."

"Bringin' up my past record seems unfair. I've—"

Vikram interrupted and was uncharacteristically acerbic—even he was vexed by three straight days of Damian Bullins. "Complains the defendant whose confession has been excluded on a paperwork technicality and whose methamphetamine usage on the day of the murder has been lawyered out of the evidence. Yeah, I can see why you'd feel you're being mistreated."

CHAPTER NINETEEN

SATURDAY MORNING WAS GRAY and sullen, thirty-five degrees, a patchy rain occasionally underscoring the weather's sulk. The carpet at the courtroom's entrance was soon dark, dampened by wet shoes and dripping umbrellas, and a deputy was dispatched to pick up an elderly juror from Meadows of Dan who was worried about ice on the roads.

Judge Leventis read the jurors their final instructions, and she reminded them that they were *only* to determine guilt or innocence during this phase of the trial and shouldn't concern themselves with sentencing or punishment. There were three possible verdicts: first degree murder, second degree murder, or obstruction of justice.

The commonwealth was permitted to address the jury twice, to argue first and last, with the defendant's closing statement sandwiched in-between. Stella spoke to the jury for half an hour, and she did a bang-up job, was eloquent and accessible, and she described the defense as a "total fiction, a terrible lie cobbled together from a staged, preposterous email and the absurd suggestion a harmless lump was perceived as deadly, despite the treating doctor testifying he informed Mr. Bullins otherwise." She asked the jury for a first-degree murder conviction. "This killing was willful and deliberate," she stressed. "And taking Alicia's knife from her, physically subduing her, kicking her in the stomach, and cutting her throat from one side to the other, these acts show premeditation."

Andy began by thanking the jury for their time and complimenting Morley and Stella on their professionalism. Early in his remarks, while the jury was alert and eager and impressionable, he let go with the first outright attack on Benson: "No man who is genuinely grieving the death of his wife, who's shocked and surprised by her sudden, horrific murder, brings her rival, his mistress, into the family home and pushes her on his daughters. You should have the same reaction to Cole Benson as his oldest child did: You should break with him."

Andy spoke for fifty minutes. Before sitting down, he told the jury—saving his strongest argument for last—he hoped they'd think back to his remarks on Wednesday. "If you recall," he said from the middle of the courtroom, "I asked you to always hold the commonwealth's case up against this critical question: What motive did my client have to harm a total stranger, and what motive did Cole Benson have to harm his wife? From everything you've learned, especially from Officer Hubbard, we now know Mr. Bullins had *no reason* to kill Alicia Benson. None. No reason to kick her or cut her throat from ear to ear. However, it's clear Cole Benson, as demonstrated by his own admissions and actions, was extremely eager to move his girlfriend into a larger role. He showed you his unmistakable motive. He showed you why he'd have reason to be frustrated and enraged and violent—his wife had been an impediment for him and his mistress for months."

Benson was seated in a folding chair diagonal to Morley, and he bowed, covered his face, and shook his head. Andy glimpsed him in the periphery, enraged and on the cusp of erupting, victimized and understandably furious, his pants leg hiked so there was a pale band of skin above his dress sock.

"The other consideration I asked you to keep in mind," Andy continued, "is a focus on *why* murder happens. In my experience, two things are at the root of almost every killing." He held up a finger. He paused. He looked directly at Cole Benson. "Sex." He held up two fingers. He angled them to point toward the gallery. "And money. Here, ladies and gentlemen, you have them both. Cole Benson had a young mistress, and a divorce would be expensive. Not to mention embarrassing, since he'd no longer be the 'great Mormon patriarch,' to use Audrey Clayton's term."

"This is a purely circumstantial case, and the commonwealth wants you to arbitrarily convict my client for doing exactly what Cole Benson did. Two men entered the Benson house during the time Alicia was killed, but only her husband had multiple reasons to want her gone, and he needed a fall guy so he wouldn't be dogged by an open murder case for years and years and scrutinized as a suspect once the cops discovered his mistress. On behalf of Mr. Bullins, we'd respectfully urge you to find him guilty of the crime he actually committed: obstruction of justice. Thank you."

From the first syllable he uttered to the jury, Morley's disposition was dramatically different. The flashy showman broke character and became earnest and genuinely invested. Even a glib operator like Morley was moved by Cole Benson's plight and the case's ugly reversal, and his hour with the jurors was raw and frank. Every person in the courtroom who experienced his stem-winder believed Peter Morley was desperately convinced of his truth, bone-and-marrow convinced, and his argument to convict didn't come off as typical lawyer's song and dance—it was personal and heartfelt, pained, and all the more powerful because of it.

His voice gritty, his words bathed in conscience, he explained Andy's sleight of hand, the defense's trickery and misdirection. "Essentially, a very clever attorney is asking you to find Cole Benson—a devout, good man, with a long history of community service—guilty of adultery, adultery he never concealed or denied. Mr. Hughes hopes to fool you into forgetting about an innocent dead woman because her husband made a mistake. Don't put the wrong person on trial. Don't lose track of why we're here and let a stone-cold killer go free."

Morley was so focused that he shed his usual affectations. He bore down on the jury, and he finished his argument with his belt buckle against the gallery's railing, close and urgent. "This tale the defense has patched together is a cruel farce and full of gaps. Tell me, please: Have you heard any evidence of when and how and where this alleged agreement to help Damian Jr. was made? No, you haven't. The only direct evidence you have on the subject is Mr. Benson's denial under oath. Do you have any confirmation of this alleged plot other than a contrived email from a guilty man with nothing to lose? You do not. Does a man, despite a doctor's diagnosis to the contrary, just suddenly up and decide, 'hey, I have terminal cancer?' No he doesn't. Please don't be deceived. Trust your eyes, the video, the blood on Mr. Bullins's pants and your common sense. Don't go looking for a solution to a legal problem that doesn't exist. We'd ask you to return a murder conviction."

Judge Leventis dismissed the two alternates and sent the remaining twelve jurors to start their deliberations at noon. The lawyers shook hands and exchanged well-wishes, and Morley, his vanity quickly revived, re-moussed his hair, pinned his own campaign button to his lapel, and gabbed with the press while Stella sat stoically at the commonwealth's table, occasionally swiping her phone. A deputy brought in cases of bottled water and boxes of pizza for the jurors, staff and attorneys. Andy and Kellie snagged waters and two pizza slices and holed up in a basement storage room, an intricate, complicated spider's web attached to the light fixture, water damage staining the far wall.

"No matter how this ends," she told him, "you squeezed out every ounce you could for Bullins."

Andy smirked. "I'm sure he'll be appreciative." He was eating his pizza from a flimsy, greasy paper plate, and he set it on a cardboard box of printer-ink cartridges stacked three high. He and Kellie were sitting in faded red cafeteria chairs. "I'm tired. I hope we can take a long vacation soon. Very soon."

"I hope so too," she said. "It'd be nice if we could go somewhere warm, like Nassau, but the pandemic has put the kibosh on most everything Caribbean." She sipped her water. "Or Savannah would be fun. You could meet my sister. I love Jones Street—the tree-tangle tapestries with light tumbling through, the Spanish Moss, the slender row houses, the red-brick street, like the road to Southern Oz. Growing up, it was as if I lived in the grandest blanket fort ever built."

"Well, I assume the plague has landed in Savannah as well, and December's pretty blah in Georgia." He grinned. "I thought you only lived there for a few years. You're a Tidewater girl. Why the sudden nostalgia?"

"Yeah, fifth and sixth grade, but it's such a marvelous city. You'd have a ball."

"Honestly, I was in the market for something a little more prosaic. A modest hotel suite with a view, room service, a king bed, a fireplace,

Guinness and Netflix. Last I saw Longmire and Henry Standing Bear, they were in quite a pickle. I have a full season left to watch."

"Could we spring for champagne and mix in a *Virgin River* episode every now and then?"

"Definitely. Maybe we could see what's available in Charlottesville. The Boar's Head or—" A knock on the door interrupted him. "Damn, they can't have a verdict—it's barely been fifteen minutes."

The door opened and Bailiff Howell stuck in his head, grinning. "I have a VIP visitor I figured you'd wanna see." He beckoned behind him, and Noah came scampering into the room and hugged his dad, who lifted him off the ground and kissed his cheek.

"What're you doing here?" Andy asked, his son still suspended.

"His mom snuck him in to watch the closin' arguments," Howell explained. "I think he was right proud of his dad."

"You were awesome," Noah said. "You're already on YouTube."

"Where's Brooke?" Andy asked. He kneeled and put his son on the floor.

"She's upstairs," Howell replied.

"She's welcome to hang out with us here in the cushy storage room if she'd like." He eyed Kellie.

"Yeah," she said. "More than welcome."

"The man next to me," Noah gushed, "well, sorta next to me 'cause there's Covid, he said you were the best lawyer he's ever seen."

"I doubt that," Andy demurred. "I'm not even the best lawyer in this room."

"Hey, Kellie," Noah said, slightly shy around her since they'd only seen each other twice before.

"Hey, Noah," she answered. "I like the new haircut."

Andy texted Brooke, and she joined them several minutes later, standing in the doorway but going no farther. After they visited for a while, she told her son it was time to leave, and he fussed about wanting to stay until the jury decided the case.

"Might be hours," Andy explained. "Pretty boring. I'll call you as soon as I hear, okay?"

"Okay. But I still wanna come to your house tonight like I'm supposed to. I don't care if it's late."

"We'll see. Thanks so much for being here. What a great surprise." He peeked at Brooke. "Thanks to your mom as well."

"Not every day your old man goes to work and it's national news," Brooke said.

"Even if it's midnight, you promise you'll call?" Noah asked.

"Midnight, no." Andy smiled. "And it might be bad news. Never know. Give me a hug before you go."

The boy gave him a high-five instead, and when Andy told him he loved him, he replied, "You too. Don't forget to come and get me tonight."

"He's a determined little fellow," Ralph remarked.

And then...they marked time. There wasn't a peep from the jury by three o'clock, and at three thirty, the lawyers met and had some tentative discussions about a plea, a better offer for Bullins, but he wasn't interested, just cackled and threatened, "Those sons of bitches are gonna get what's coming to them."

Andy sighed and slumped. "Just when I thought you couldn't be any worse, you find a new bottom," he muttered.

At four thirty, the jury sent a note inquiring about a phrase in one of their instructions, and Judge Leventis brought them into the courtroom and patiently explained the words and the law. Mr. Morris, now dressed in a tasteful Christmas sweater, thanked her and told her the twelve of them were enjoying each other's company as much as masked folks in a tight space possibly could. Several jurors chuckled, and the lady next to Morris mentioned something about "new friends."

"They seem pretty jolly," Vikram remarked to Andy. "Probably a positive sign for us."

"I quit trying to predict juries years ago," Andy replied.

At six o'clock, the jurors asked for a dinner break, and they were loaded into a small school bus and driven to a local sub shop, SUBstitution, where three deputies babysat them.

At eight fifteen, Ralph opened the door to the storage room and announced: "They have a verdict, Andy."

CHAPTER TWENTY

ANDY AND KELLIE MET Vikram on the stairs, and they hurried into the buzz and hubbub and anticipation, spectators hastily taking their places, cops ringing the room, laptops opening, cameras beginning to stir, the clerk arranging files. Bailiff Howell, his voice resonant, his hands clasped behind him, announced court was in session, and everyone stood as Judge Leventis walked to her seat on the bench, poised and stern. "We're back in session and on the record," she said. "Please bring out the jury."

"We got this," Damian whispered. He touched Andy's elbow. "Don't worry, my man."

The twelve men and women, somber and inscrutable, filed into the gallery, and Mr. Morris handed the verdict form to the bailiff, who delivered it to the judge. She silently read the decision, her reaction a blank, obscure, revealing nothing.

"Please rise, Mr. Bullins," she directed him. "Ladies and gentlemen of the jury, listen as your verdict is announced. 'We, the jury, find the defendant, Damian Bullins, guilty of obstruction of justice.' Signed by Hobart Morris as foreperson, dated December nineteenth, twenty-twenty. So say you all?"

The jurors nodded, and most responded with yeses. The judge polled them individually, and each panel member confirmed this was his or her decision. Damian located his new lady friend among the spectators, looked at her, smiled, and tapped his heart with an open hand. He hugged Andy, who struggled not to appear repulsed and wedged his forearm against Bullins's chest to separate them. Nothing else mattered now. The maximum sentence available to the jury was twelve months of misdemeanor time, which required only six months of actual incarceration, and Damian Bullins would be set free by midnight, home for the holidays.

Next, the jury received Damian's abysmal criminal record, brief evidence and subdued comments from the lawyers. They returned to the law library for deliberations and swiftly agreed on a twelve-month sentence. Morley vanished and sacrificed Stella to read a short statement to the media, disingenuously thanking the people of Patrick County for delivering the commonwealth a guilty verdict.

Hobart Morris and eight of his fellow jurors agreed to a one-time meeting with the press, after which they'd have nothing else to say, ever. The other three jurors, eager to fade away, left together in a hurry, arms linked, eyes downcast, accompanied by a cop, and kept mum. Wearing masks, five men and four women stood in a semicircle in the law library and answered questions.

Andy watched the entire interview online the next morning, and he expected the jurors to feel scammed and snookered, angry because they'd been hoodwinked by a slippery lawyer and a court system that diced up the truth and allowed them only shards and tidbits. He'd observed their expressions during the sentencing, seen their reactions when they'd learned about Bullins's criminal history, the prior felonies and crimes of violence. Upon hearing from the judge the most severe punishment for obstruction of justice was twelve months in jail, a young man, a college kid taking virtual classes from his parents' home, said, under his breath, sadly bewildered, "Wow."

Oddly though, by the end of their first-and-last national interview, these nine people were anything but disappointed or publicly dissatisfied with their verdict. Damian had confessed and was high on meth and was a racist who'd directed the N-word at the victim, the reporters kept repeating, and the more they politely questioned and prodded, or sympathetically inquired as to regrets, the more the jurors dug in and defended their decision.

"So what if he confessed?" a juror blurted. "He was *supposed* to take the blame, wasn't he?"

"It ain't our fault we didn't hear nothing about his confession and him using bad language or the drugs," another juror volunteered. "We made the correct decision based on what we were shown. Maybe you should be complainin' to the judge."

A welder from Woolwine said, "Reasonable doubt, like the judge told us. How was this not reasonable doubt?"

"I read about the alleged confession in the papers," a woman responded. A retired school teacher who'd moved to the county from Chicago, she'd been a conscientious note-taker. "But the judge and lawyers told us what we'd seen *before* coming to court didn't count, to forget it, so I did, and hey, you can't believe half of what you hear in the media these days anyhow."

"Well," Morris protested, the last comment before they all left, ill and defiant, "isn't a man like Damian Bullins, a criminal, the kind of person you'd hire to help you do this? His record helps prove our point, okay? Saints don't get hired to cover up a murder. Yeah, I wish we could've given Bullins more time, but we couldn't. We gave him the max, the twelve months. We went through the case with a fine-tooth comb, and everybody agreed. There's somethin' real hinky about Mr. Benson and his story. He's an odd duck. Why would he give money to a kid he doesn't know if he barely has any relationship with his dad? That check proves they'd talked and discussed things, way more than you'd have dealings and conversations with some basic hired-hand stranger."

The jurors exited the library with the press still raining questions, and as the bailiff and several cops escorted them to the parking lot and their vehicles, cameras and reporters in tow, the night black and freezing, Morris hesitated on the sidewalk and faced the newswoman and tape recorder closest to him. "Occurs to me, we did our job and followed the law, and maybe you people oughta start focusing on the bigger picture in this murder situation."

CHAPTER TWENTY-ONE

Sunday evening, Andy and Kellie arrived at The Greenbrier in West Virginia, where they stayed in a cottage not far from the main building. Despite the pandemic, the resort was festive with lights and decorations. A huge Christmas tree sparkled at the entrance, and oodles of sleighs, candy canes, nutcrackers and snowmen illuminated the grounds, as bright as could be. Inside, red bows and poinsettias bedecked the lobby and hallways. Their cottage was pet friendly, so Patches made the trip, and the concierge arranged for both *Longmire* and *Virgin River* to be streamed on the television. The view wasn't much, but there was a fireplace and a king bed and room service, and they only left their lodging to bundle up for walks with the dog and a single trip to the fancy formal dining room for a meal, coat and tie required.

Monday at dusk, they were buzzed, close to drunk, and they sat on their winter porch underneath a wool blanket, the holiday lights starting to come alive as the sky drained, and they sidled up to talk of love. He said it first, then she said it back, and they sealed the bargain with Veuve Clicquot straight from the bottle, and the next morning, as soon as they were awake, she made him repeat it, sober and groggy, made him tell her he loved her in case he'd just been champagne-struck the night before.

Driving home to Henry County on Tuesday, they broached the possibility of moving in together, living at Andy's, and he suggested, after several quiet, contented miles, right before the speed limit dropped at Fincastle, she might want to consider bringing over some of her clothes and so forth in January, but they'd have to stay separate whenever Noah visited, at least for a while.

"Sure. Yes. I'd like that," Kellie said. "I think we should. A lot of changes are coming our way. Let's hope we don't strangle each other."

❈❈❈

THE OFFICE WAS OPEN until noon on December 23, and Andy was at work early, eight o'clock, dressed in jeans and a chamois shirt. Patches was quickly in his favorite spot, sprawled beside a corner register, enjoying the heat. Andy and Kellie had turned off their phones, avoided the news, and made themselves scarce for three blissful, oblivious days. A tall stack of pink messages was on his desk and a yellow "SEE ME" Post-it note from Vikram was stuck to his chair. He'd brought a thermos of coffee from home, and he was unscrewing the lid when he heard loud, insistent banging on the locked front glass door. He peered out from his office, and through the door's stenciled letters and numbers, he recognized Damian Bullins and his bedraggled fiancée, Misty. "Damn," he said. He considered ignoring them but realized he'd have to deal with Bullins eventually and might as well put the shit show behind him as soon as possible.

"Where the hell have you been?" Bullins demanded the moment Andy clunked the deadbolt open.

"I took a short vacation after working my butt off for months to save you from your crime." He pulled the door toward him, allowing Bullins and Misty into the lobby. They were both impaired, high and disheveled, though it was impossible to tell whether they were on the climb or riding the meth-and-liquor jitney down the incline, but for certain, they were wired and had probably been rolling for days. "What can I do for you?"

"Well, yeah, thanks again for fightin' so hard for me. I never doubted you."

"I'm glad you're satisfied," Andy said. "You've already thanked me. We're good."

"I wanna thank you too." Misty had tumbled onto a sofa and her head was resting against the wall. "Sorry I was rude to you."

"We alone?" Bullins asked.

"Nobody around but us," Andy informed him. "And Patches, my dog." The mutt was parked next to Cindy's desk, ears perked, watching.

"Misty's your responsibility. No lawyer-secrets with her listening. I assume you don't care what she hears. Of course, she might grow very vindictive and talkative once she discovers your South Carolina connections."

"Soof Carlina," she responded, her eyes shut. "Huh?"

"She's a moron," Damian said, slightly slurring the last word. "Man, we've been tryin' to find you for days."

"Why?"

"Since you're leavin' and goin' out on your own, me and you need to take this to the next level and cash in."

"Cash in?" Andy repeated, incredulous. He noticed Misty's eyes were shut, her mouth gaped. She was wearing a tie-dyed thermal shirt but no coat and no socks.

"I've been in touch with other lawyers, mainly this dude Buck Simpson from Danville, and we need to sue the piss outta Cole Benson. I wanted to give you first dibs on it. We're lookin' at millions." He wiped his wrist across his nose. Then did it again. And again. Shuffled his feet, almost jogged in place.

"Lord, you don't have any civil claim against Mr. Benson. None. In a correct world, wouldn't he be the plaintiff suing *you*? Leave the man alone; you've done plenty already."

"What about my boy, how about what he's due from—"

"You can't sue to collect on an illegal contract, and besides, Damian, we both understand why that's not something I want to be involved with."

"Don't matter what we sue for, just need some excuse. The trick is ol' Cole'll pay me off to keep me from testifyin' against him when he's charged for murder." He stuck out his hand, his thumb and index finger pinched together. "I got the key to his jail."

"That's despicable, Damian. Totally shitty. You—"

"How's it any more shitty than what you're doin'? You knew I was guilty—hell, I confessed—and you knew all the crap you told the jury was lies, and we played this kinda game, and you can get rich and famous off Alicia Benson's Black ass, but I can't?" He was so agitated he nearly panted.

"I didn't kill anyone. Nor did I do anything illegal or unethical as an attorney. Every fact and piece of evidence I gave the jury was legitimate."

"What's done is done. She's dead. Hell, seems like I probably did Cole a favor." He smirked. "I may as well make the best of it. She ain't comin' back. A positive from a negative. Lemons to lemonade."

Misty made a noise, somewhere between a groan and a snore. Spit was dribbling over her chin. Her eyes were still shut. "Ahhh, Damian, ahhh," she gurgled, "let's go. I'm ready. Quit arguin' with him."

"Stupid meth whore," he snapped. He looked at Andy, his lips a tiny, thin slice. "She's history. I got a real lady in my life now. Meetin' Becky in South Carolina tomorrow."

Andy had his fists at his waist and his shoulders angled, but he spoke normally. "Damian, I want nothing—nothing, zero—to do with you, your sociopath's sick, bogus, extortion lawsuit, or your girlfriend. My work for you is finished. We have no reason to see each other or be in contact. Never bother me again. Are we clear?"

"Yeah, asshole, we're clear. We're clear you're missin' the biggest chance of your pitiful life." He leaned closer to the sofa and smacked Misty on the shoulder. "Get up, bitch." As she was wobbling to her feet, he pointed at Andy. "Don't forget. I made you, little loser boy, and I'm just as famous as you are."

***

"Oh, BELIEVE ME," VIKRAM said an hour later, "I'm not surprised. Mr. Bullins was so high and belligerent yesterday that I almost had to call the cops. He was determined I should give him your cell number. Poor tagalong Misty was a thousand miles deep, could barely walk." Vikram, Andy and Patches were in the breakroom. "Hope your vacation went well. Welcome back to paradise."

"Couldn't have been better, thanks," Andy replied, grinning. "I found your note on my chair—what's up?"

"Lots. Most important, Brooke was trying to locate you. But she insisted it wasn't an emergency and didn't concern your son."

"Strange," Andy said. "I spent the morning before we left, Sunday morning, with Noah, playing video games at my house and saw Brooke twice. She knew our phones were shut off and how to locate me at

The Greenbrier if it was important. I've dreaded dealing with all the calls, so I haven't listened to them yet. Maybe she left a voicemail."

"Well, Rosencrantz has delivered the message," Vikram said. "On a melancholy note, I suppose we need to set a date for your leaving and process the paperwork."

"Will February first be okay for you?" Andy asked. "What we discussed?"

"March one would make my life easier."

"March one it is," Andy said. "Seems so...so sad, I guess, to be actually quitting, to put it in writing."

"Never too late to change your mind."

Andy laughed. "Ah, not *that* sad, Vik." He reached down and scratched between the dog's ears. "You think Damian will sue Cole Benson?"

"He's a career criminal with a black-hole conscience and nothing to lose. If he can find a lawyer willing to file a complaint, I'm sure he will."

"He mentioned Buck Simpson. From what I've heard, Buck's respectable. Hard to imagine he could possibly file a suit in good faith. Of course, the whole issue might be moot soon—at his current clip, Damian better hope Santa's keeping him on the Narcan list."

Vikram chortled. "Indeed. Which brings us to the final item on the agenda. Stella Hespell wants you to call her about our case and Cole Benson."

"Why?"

"I doubt she's calling to convey Morley's heartfelt congratulations."

"Yeah," Andy said. "Big of Morley to skedaddle and leave her holding the bag. He's the worst. The cowardly, goateed movie villain who cuts and runs while Liam Neeson's pummeling the hired henchmen and about to kick down the door."

Vikram punctured a clementine with his thumb and began peeling away the orange skin. "Let me bring you up to speed, since you've been living at a resort for three days. The epilogue. I'm not certain if the jury members were truly so wedded to their verdict, but the press interview— which seemed tame and respectful, even sympathetic, to me—got their backs up and made them crusaders for their decision. If you watch media snippets of their comments and hear some of the basic facts, you definitely get the impression more work needs to be done in this case—a murderer is walking around free. A rich, powerful murderer from the fringe sect that gave us Warren Jeffs, television shows about devaluing women by marrying as many as you please, and a book of apostate scriptures that contradicts the holy Baptist Bible."

"I'm not surprised. It sells newspapers—or whatever it is the media sells to make money these days. A perfect storm. The Eldorado Fleetwood convertible."

"Yep. Given the choice, I'd rather be a middle-class Hindu than a wealthy Mormon—generally we're viewed as harmlessly misguided, not as heretics and dangerous interlopers." Vikram smiled. He ate a clementine section. "I imagine Stella and Morley are debating what to do about a jury verdict that essentially names Cole Benson as his wife's killer."

"But *they* understand the verdict doesn't capture the truth. Bullins confessed. He was high on meth and has a history of violence, especially where women are concerned. He won on loopholes, quirks and an impossibly friendly jury making the wrong inferences. He's guilty. Cole Benson is innocent."

"But," Vikram said, separating another section of fruit, "we're dealing with Peter Morley. Liam Neeson's about to kick in the door and thrash him. You think the senator plans to make the honest, but difficult, decision?"

Andy went to his office and tried Stella on her cell number, but she didn't answer, and he left a message. She phoned ten minutes later while he was sorting through his own message pile.

"Congrats again," she said and sounded sincere. "And happy holidays to you."

"You too," Andy replied. "I enjoyed working with you. Dunford County will be in great hands come 2021."

"I assume you know why I'm calling."

"Maybe."

"I have a decision to make," she declared. "I need to determine what comes next for my office and Mr. Cole Benson."

"True," Andy said. "But you already know Bullins confessed. You already know he was high and violent and why, according to the confession, he did

219

what he did. You think he'd make a good star witness? You want to pin your credibility and hopes on him? Seriously?"

"Mr. Morley is very, very uncomfortable with the public perception of the jury verdict."

"Ah. Peter the Great is worried the loss will affect his fundraising and committee appointments and poll numbers, and doesn't have the guts to simply hold a press conference and put this to rest."

"I don't have the same low opinion of Mr. Morley as you do. Thanks to him, I'll be the commonwealth's attorney in a few weeks. He's a friend and mentor, and public perception of how the system operates is important to some extent."

"Exactly! Exactly! You'll be in charge soon. What the hell difference does it make what Morley wants?"

"None, in the long term. I want to follow the truth. I have no desire to ruin an innocent man, which is why we're having this conversation." She hesitated. Exhaled. "I understand and respect your attorney-client privilege with Mr. Bullins." She hesitated again. "But let me ask you this, without getting into any particulars or private communications: If you were in my shoes, what would you do?"

"I'd remind the naysayers and conspiracy theorists and bloggers and pundits and Facebookers and religious bigots of the full facts, highlight the *correct* ruling Judge Leventis made decimating your case, and set Mr. Cole Benson free to raise his girls in peace. Not even close."

"I understand, thanks," she said quietly. "Message received. So you'll know, there may be some kind of civil suit in the works. I had a call from a Danville lawyer, a Mr. Simpson, hoping to, as he phrased it, 'coordinate our efforts.'"

At noon, Andy left Patches dozing in his office, and he visited the Wendy's takeout window and then waited in the parking lot, kept the engine idling. A few minutes later, Brooke pulled in beside him and climbed into the Jeep. He handed her a bag of food, but they didn't drop their masks to eat.

"Thanks," she said. "Both for lunch and meeting with me."

"No worries. I'm not trying to be a jerk, but why couldn't we just talk on the phone?"

"This is definitely face-to-face stuff," she explained.

"Okay. I read Noah the riot act again about being more appreciative, and he's seemed a tiny bit more agreeable the last couple of visits."

"He *is* in a better mood," she said. "The reason being we've potentially located a new house."

"Oh, great. I'm glad—"

"Careful," she cautioned him, "the grease is seeping through the bag and will stain your pants."

"Thanks." He moved the bag to the floorboard. "Tell me about the new house."

"It's nice, and he can walk to the Aarons' and visit his buddy Mike, and there's a treehouse. Well, more of an elaborate room on stilts attached to a tree, and he, naturally, loves it. I'm closer to work. New HVAC, newish roof."

"Sounds like you've hit the jackpot."

"Here's the catch," she said. She clutched her bag tighter, crunched the paper. "Thank god I have a job and a work history—my credit rating is strong enough I can qualify for a loan at the bank. But the owners will finance the property for me at a much cheaper interest rate and no closing costs if I give them a down payment. They're asking me for thirty thousand, which is twenty percent of the total price."

"That's a helluva fair deal."

"The house belongs to Dr. Philpott, the president at the college. He and his wife bought it for their son and daughter-in-law, and the son's accepted a job in Kansas City. The Philpotts are friends and generous people and are trying to give me and Noah a break."

"Okay."

"Problem is, Andy, I don't have enough cash right this moment to pay them." Every word was dismayed, frustrated. "Howard is stonewalling me and dragging this out, which makes no sense, unless you just want to be an asshole. We weren't married long, and I'm not trying to be vindictive or looking for big dollars from him. I offered to settle for a hundred grand, my

Explorer and a no-fault divorce. No spousal support, none of his pension. His lawyer hasn't so much as responded to Ms. Jacob."

"If I were in his shoes, I'd take your offer and run like a bandit."

"I can withdraw a chunk from my 401(k), and I have my savings from before we were married, but I'm ten thousand short. You offered to help when this all began, and I wondered if you'd loan me the money, with interest, for nine months? Certainly the divorce will be settled by then and I should be able to repay you."

"Yeah, I can—"

"Ms. Jacob will do the paperwork. It'll be formal and legal. I'm not asking for charity."

"Okay," he agreed. "You're positive the house's sound and in good shape?"

"I've already had my cousin, Ray Stanley, inspect it. He's a contractor. Remember him? Years ago, he helped you with some rafters."

"Ray's a pro," Andy said.

"So, thanks. Thank you. Ms. Jacob will let you know when the papers are ready."

"I consider it an investment in our son," Andy replied. "Hope this will put him in a better frame of mind." Above his mask, the skin around his eyes crinkled. "Of course, I'm probably shooting myself in the foot. Now he'll want to stay in the rickety treehouse with his pal and will refuse to visit with *me*."

"I hope not. I could use some harmony and cooperation where he's concerned."

"While we're discussing plans and Noah and what's next for everyone, I...well, since you're here, I'll go ahead and let you know Kellie and I have decided she's going to stay at my house, except of course, when I have Noah. She's keeping her place. I'm not sure this is a great time to deliver the news, not sure there'll be a great time, but...there it is."

"I've told you before, Andy, I don't have any claims on your personal life. Unless it impacts my son. I didn't feel the need to comfort you with a five-star production when I got married, as if I thought you were losing some wonderful treasure and soulmate and I was crushing your heart.

I recall when Howard and I announced the news, your former girlfriend had recently fled to Florida. You're Noah's father, and I wish you well. No more and no less. We're friends with a child." She stared at him hard. "But do not let her spend the night if he's there. Do not. He's still a boy."

"Isn't that *exactly* what I just explained?" he said, peeved.

❋❋❋

ANDY TOOK VACATION TIME and was still not working on January 6, a Wednesday. School—or what remained of it—continued to be held online following the holidays, and Andy loaded up his son and the dog at dawn and traveled to Chesapeake to buy several pieces of mahogany wood from a specialty lumberyard. He planned to build an armoire for Kellie, a surprise, so he swore Noah to secrecy. Noah slept for the first fifty miles, and they stopped twice for snacks, and they detoured to visit a Stuckey's after Andy saw a billboard advertisement and reminisced about the store's *amazing* pecan log, his favorite childhood treat. Noah tried a bite and decided the candy was "gross and too salty."

As they drove through South Hill, the boy never looked away from his iPad while his dad described *his* journeys to the Great Lakes with *his* parents, how his mom always kept the folded tissue that smelled like Certs, perfume and Wrigley's Spearmint in her purse. And who could ever forget the ice chest in the Hughes station wagon, full of sandwiches and orange sodas? Or the big paper roadmap that was such a chore to refold?

Andy paid for the wood, and he and Noah wrapped it in old sheets and carefully arranged it in the Jeep. They left the lumberyard and followed the interstate to the Cape Henry Lighthouse, where they leashed Patches and walked around and peeked into the gift shop but didn't sign up for the tour. Their motor-court room was tidy and Covid sanitized, and they were asleep by nine, bushed, the TV flickering and chattering until Andy turned it off in the middle of the night.

The next day, they headed to Virginia Beach and saw the cold, stern ocean and hunted shells and sharks' teeth beside a pier. They spent the night in a swank Hyatt House suite, billed at winter rate, and had a ball sneaking in the dog, laughed and giggled at their mischief and rule-breaking as they dashed from the stairway to their room. Friday morning, Noah enjoyed blueberry pancakes on the boardwalk, an amiable passerby snapped pictures of dad, son and mutt in front of King Neptune's statue, and they started for home. "I wish we could stay longer," Noah said.

"I do too. Maybe we'll make this a yearly tradition."

"But without all your long, boring stories."

**

ANDY WAS EAGER TO begin crafting the armoire, so he was in his shop the next morning after a quick breakfast, the pot-bellied stove filled with wood, the propane heater at full blast. He studied and measured and puzzled the mahogany pieces on a worktable. He hummed along to Charlie Parker. Patches kept him company. He was so engrossed and content, he didn't hear Lynn Dylan-Haley until she was well past the door and called his name in a loud voice, startling him.

"Sorry," she said when he wheeled around. "I knocked and kept trying to get your attention. I didn't mean to scare you."

He laughed. "Well you did. Good morning, Boss."

"Must be nice to have something that can hold you so fully. A genuine passion."

"I'm building an armoire for Kellie. And yeah, there's nowhere I'd rather be, nothing I'd rather be doing."

"Can I interrupt you?" she asked. "I wouldn't bother you at home on a Saturday unless it was urgent."

"No bother. You're always welcome." He turned down the jazz. "You want to go in the house? My first investment from my new salary will be a mini-split to keep this place warm in the winter and cool in the summer, though I have to confess I like the whole woodstove vibe."

"Me too. I'm fine here."

"Coffee?"

"Thanks, but no," she said. "You're still not smoking? Made it through the trial?"

"I think it's behind me—if Damian Bullins didn't push me over the edge, nothing can."

"Congrats."

"Have a seat." He swung open the stove's door, chunked a shimmering orange log with a poker, clanged the door shut, and sat down across from her.

"So," she said, pulling off wool mittens, "here's where we are. I'm extremely concerned about Cole Benson. I fear he's about to become Peter the Great's sacrificial lamb and Damian Bullins's personal piggy bank. We both realize that's horribly unfair."

"Definitely."

Lynn balanced the mittens on her knee. "For what it's worth, I think Cole's positives far outweigh his negatives. He's not the first powerful man to cheat on his wife. At least he owned up to it and didn't lie to her."

"You don't have to sell me on your client. I feel sorry for him."

"I'm worried he's going to be indicted," she said.

"By whom?" Andy answered. "I spoke to Stella before Christmas, and my impression was she's planning to close the book on this and leave Benson alone."

"Stella's bright and incredibly principled. I talked with her yesterday, sort of a courtesy call. A warning. Morley's still not resigned—the legislature hasn't convened, so he doesn't need to yet. My sense is he plans to empanel a quick January grand jury and drop an indictment in Patrick County. He can save face, beat his chest at a press conference, boast how he's not afraid to tackle the rich and privileged, then leave his protégé with an impossible nightmare. The best of both worlds for him."

"My lord," Andy said. "In a certain sense, he and Bullins are the same person, just on opposite sides of the coin."

"In Morley's defense, I'd say Damian Bullins is in a league of his own."

"How can I help, Lynn?"

"Can you talk with Bullins? Persuade him to leave well enough alone? He killed this man's wife, now he wants to get paid for the crime? Seriously?"

"Seriously." Andy grimaced. "I wish I could reason with him and make him disappear, but I've already tried. No luck, I'm afraid."

"Did you mention the possibility of perjury?" Lynn suggested.

"No, but we both realize that's a major longshot and wouldn't matter to him anyway."

"You think you'd have any influence with Morley?" she asked. "Perhaps you could arrange some kind of joint statement blaming the judge and jury and legal system, and you could praise Morley's brilliance and sort of give him public permission to not charge Cole."

"Whatever I can ethically do and not lose my law license, I will. We've seen the law at work, so now I'd welcome all the justice we can scrape together. Of course, even if Morley indicts Benson, who's to say Stella won't dismiss it?"

"The indictment's arriving soon," Lynn said, "maybe Monday. Or so a little birdie tells me. Whether or not Stella ultimately dismisses it, I'm sure a civil suit will be right behind, the Trojan Horse for Bullins to extort cash from my client. You never truly recover from a murder indictment, and who knows what can happen—Damian Bullins is free and a minor folk hero, and a crime victim is regularly vilified in the media. I hate this for Cole. Hell, there're twelve jurors who heard the evidence and believe he had a role in his wife's death. Conceivably, that could happen again. I'd like to stop the bleeding now."

"I'll call Morley this morning. See if I can make any progress."

"Thanks, Andy," she said. "Much appreciated. Enjoy the hammer and nails." She stood.

He stayed fast in his chair, looking at her, his fingers laced together on his lap. "This has never settled well on my conscience, Lynn. I've not mentioned it, not even to Kellie or Vik, but I think anyone would struggle with enabling a remorseless murderer—"

"You did exactly what you swore an oath you'd do. The judge did what she was duty-bound to do. I imagine she's upset by this also. Every defendant is entitled to due process and a quality lawyer. It's a core value in an occasionally imperfect system, and you'd be a fraud and a cheat if you didn't do the best you possibly could."

"I suppose. But all the abstract rules and noble rationalizing—just highfalutin excuses, really—seem small and impotent when I stack them up against Alicia Benson's photo, this sweet lady, already mistreated by her husband, lying dead in her kitchen, with her *very real* blood poured onto the floor. Now this bullshit. I can't help but feel corrupted to some extent."

"You didn't have a vote as to whether Bullins was guilty or innocent."

"No, but we seem to have turned Blackstone upside down."

"Sorry?" she said.

"He's famous for reminding us it's better to let ten guilty men go free than to convict one innocent defendant. We've managed to let one guilty killer go free and risk destroying ten innocents. Well six, if I'm being accurate: Benson, his dead wife and his four daughters."

As promised, Andy phoned Morley at nine sharp, then again an hour later. He never received a return call. His text was also ignored. By noon, he was so preoccupied he couldn't focus on the wood and the design, and the stove was broiling the room. He went into his house, microwaved a plate of leftover meatloaf and vegetables, and mindlessly turned on the TV. Noah had cut off a DVD before it finished, and Andy hit play and watched the last fifteen minutes of a Christmas movie, and he knew the tale would be sad and tragic, that snowmen are never gifted with happy endings.

✸✸✸

"HAVE YOU HEARD?" CINDY asked him Monday morning, as soon as she spotted him in the lobby.

"Heard what?" he inquired, but he had an idea why she was so excited.

"It's a circus over in Patrick County. The news media's there for round two, and Mr. Morley's brought in a grand jury to indict Cole Benson. Another lawyer's suing him for ten million. Mr. Kapil says Stephanie Katt's absolutely livid."

"She should be," Andy replied. "Did you catch any details about the civil suit?"

"Third-party beneficiary," Curtis Matthews remarked as he came into view, walking briskly, his forearm wrapped against a bulky file. "The clever theory is that Bullins's son, who's the intended beneficiary of the alleged million-buck agreement, is himself innocent, so the contract is not void for public-policy reasons. The other nine million is…wait for it…." Curtis was even with Andy, and he made an okay sign with his thumb and index finger. "Punitive damages. We live in a house of mirrors these days." He butted the door open with his shoulder and was gone.

CHAPTER TWENTY-TWO

Saturday, January 16, was sunny and pleasant, warm enough that Andy decided to return home and collect Patches and jog the Smith River Trail after he finished stretching and lifting weights at the gym. He let the pooch follow along off-leash, and the dog was so smart and so well-behaved that he just trotted right past a yapping, growling teacupper who was straining against his harness and baring his miniature teeth. They finished their loop, and Andy drove them into Martinsville. The city was static and empty, so he was able to park on the street directly in front of Lynn's office.

"Your coffee's already made," she said as he was walking in, "and I picked up some treats from the bakery in Collinsville. I didn't forget the pup—I brought a dog biscuit, just in case he came too."

"We're both grateful. Thanks."

"Thank *you* for calling last night. And for meeting on a Saturday—seems I have a bad habit of spoiling your weekends."

"My weekend'll be just fine."

"I'm in hopes you have some ideas and possibilities for my client."

"I do." Andy took his coffee mug and sat on a small leather sofa. The sofa was stiff and smooth and smelled new. "Even though you told me the indictment and civil suit were coming, I still…it's almost impossible to believe Morley would actually indict Cole Benson. The civil suit, well, okay, yeah, the lawyer, this Buck guy, doesn't necessarily have the full picture and evidently has a legit theory of recovery. But a criminal charge? Especially when Morley had such an easy exit. This is a new slimy rock bottom for him."

"Are you familiar with some South Carolina woman by the name of Becky Adams? She was on the national news last night lecturing viewers about poor, pitiful Damian and how the judicial system is bought and paid for by the rich and powerful. She claims to be his 'redress advocate,' whose job it is to ensure he's made whole because of his mistreatment by Cole Benson and the 'Mormon Mafia.' Not once did the hideously fawning plasticine interviewer remind her that Damian, if you accept the very best about him, helped facilitate a murder and failed to report the would-be killer to the cops when he knew in advance Alicia Benson was in danger."

"She's Damian's new girlfriend," Andy said.

"How bizarre. She was articulate and seemed sane. I took her for a grifter or publicity hound."

"Ted checked her out. She's a nurse and has lived a vanilla life until now. Suddenly she's a Gilmore Girl."

Lynn canted her head, blinked. "Meaning?"

"Another Tedism," Andy explained. "Frequently, your high-profile, depraved murderers somehow attract otherwise ordinary women who become enamored of them. Gary Gilmore's girlfriend—I can't recall her name—tried to kill herself in a joint-suicide pact with him while he was jailed. Manson had his female fans. Ted Bundy had a gaggle of groupies. They're still in line for O. J. Simpson."

"At any rate," Lynn said, "the network took some janky poll—I'm certain it was rigged and skewed to push their narrative—and according to their numbers, sixty-three percent of people interviewed think Cole Benson should stand trial for murder. Any wonder a whore like Peter Morley wanted a press conference to announce his handiwork?"

"Nope," Andy said.

"The best was how he kept hinting this was part and parcel of his big, genius plan to catch the small fish first then move on to the big target, as if you didn't beat him like a rented mule at the trial. As if he always knew Cole was guilty, which makes zero sense if you give it a second's thought."

"I'm at the point nothing surprises me."

"Yeah," Lynn replied. She was aimlessly pacing, her expensive hiking boots squishing on the shiny hardwood.

"I thought about this most of yesterday. Didn't sleep worth a damn. Let's try the obvious route first. Would Benson pay anything at all? A million to him is equivalent to a thousand dollars for you and me."

Lynn stopped her wandering, stood firm. "No. Absolutely not. Even if he were willing to, what'll keep Bullins from raising his hand and swearing to a lie? Trusting a murderous sociopath isn't a sound legal strategy."

"I assumed as much but thought I should ask." Andy's coffee was sitting untouched on a table, a white napkin underneath. "I don't blame him, not one bit. I wouldn't pay either."

"His reputation's already been dragged through the mud, so there's nothing to keep quiet or secret, and he's repulsed by the idea of rewarding the wicked monster who killed his wife."

"Here's what I can do," Andy said. "Technically, there's no attorney-client privilege if other people are intentionally made privy to the conversation. On December twenty-third, with his local girlfriend Misty present, Damian essentially told me he killed Alicia Benson and the whole trial defense was a lie. I'd agree, if push comes to shove, to testify regarding our conversation. Not that I didn't strongly suspect this truth before of course, but a supreme convict like Damian always understood, as he informed me, exactly how to play the game so I was legally obligated to present the guilty-spouse defense."

Lynn dragged a chair across the floor so she was close to Andy. She sat erect with her arms folded. She started to speak and caught herself. She scooted to the end of the chair's cushion. "There'd be massive repercussions. Potentially, career-altering damage to you."

"The law—the *Clagett* case—and our ethics rules allow me to reveal his statements under these circumstances. There's also the mandate *requiring* me to intervene to prevent fraud on the court. I'd be doing the correct, righteous thing, just like I did when I went to battle for him and pulled every available legal lever and pushed every courtroom button for his guilty ass. Different songs from the same hymnal."

"No doubt. But while you and I understand the same set of rules that delivered Bullins his freedom also allows you to break the seal on attorney-client privilege, ninety-nine percent of the public doesn't realize the privilege isn't absolute—even the experienced felons like Damian. They believe you can tell your lawyer anything, anytime, and it'll always remain confidential. You'll come off as untrustworthy, crooked and the commonwealth's toady. Nobody wants a blabbermouth lawyer."

"Yep," Andy said. Patches was at his feet. The dog scratched his neck with his hind leg, shook, then licked and gnawed at the fur on his hip.

"Did you caution Bullins?" she asked. "Remind him the privilege was gone with Misty there?"

"Basically, yeah. He *brought* her and was obviously aware she was with us. He inquired as to whether we were alone. I warned him she might overhear us and not be too trustworthy, especially since he was planning to dump her. I told him there was no secrecy."

"Hmmm." Lynn was up and pacing again. "He'll probably still squeal malpractice and maybe even file a bar complaint."

"I'm not worried about the bar," Andy said. "They don't punish lawyers for following the rules." The couch was uncomfortable, and he arched his back. "As for your client, my revelations should tamp down the torch-and-pitchfork crowd and stop the criminal charge. This'll provide Stella plenty of cover to dismiss the indictment. And if she doesn't, I'll testify against Damian at any trial."

Lynn lit for a moment, rested against her desk. "Thanks." She looked away. "Not much more I can say. You're a good lawyer and a better man. I'll give Mr. Benson the news, and I'll have a draft of an affidavit to you Monday."

"I had an excellent teacher," he replied. "I've already written a draft. Finished it at three in the morning. I'll email the file to you in the next hour or so."

***

"ARE YOU OKAY?" BROOKE asked him fifteen minutes later. "You're actin' very mysterious."

He was standing on the stoop of her rented house while Noah hunted for his coat and a missing iPad charger. "I'm good. Work issues. Thanks for keeping him extra. Sorry if I inconvenienced you."

"I was happy to have the time with him."

"How's the new house coming?" he asked.

"Ms. Jacob should send the loan papers to you Tuesday. The closing's scheduled for the twenty-sixth. January twenty-six."

"Remember, today is the big meeting and transition day for Kellie and Noah. She'll be with us until eight tonight."

"Thanks for letting me know in advance," she said matter-of-factly. "She'll be wearing a mask, please."

"Yes. I just wish we weren't so pandemic limited—there's nothing special for us to do, and we're kinda stuck at the house."

Noah was chatty during the drive, sat in the rear with the dog, and he seemed indifferent when his father reminded him Kellie would be spending the day with them. "I know already," he replied. "I'm not a little baby." At the house, he said a polite hello to her, shed his backpack, plundered the cabinets for nuts and chips, and invited the dog to join him on the rug in front of the couch, their typical routine. He was soon engrossed in a video game, then he started watching a Spider-Man movie for the umpteenth time.

Near the clamorous, frenetic end of the movie, Andy informed Kellie about his decision to testify against Damian Bullins. They were in the kitchen making sandwiches at the counter. "Yeah," she said, "you have to do it. Legally and morally you do. It's bad enough the lowlife is free as a bird and unrepentant, but he shouldn't be allowed to profit from lying and killing."

"Well, it is what it is," Andy said.

"I'm proud of you." She glanced toward the den to make certain Noah couldn't see them and kissed his cheek. She smeared Duke's mayo across a piece of toast and pushed the bread down onto bacon, lettuce and tomato to complete her sandwich.

For the first few hours after lunch, Noah was prickly and sweetly jealous, and he made it a point to tell Kellie *he* helped his dad build Patches's house, and the door threshold needed *three* coats of poly, and he had his *own* tools in the shop, wonderful tools his dad bought him, not Chinese *junk*.

"Your dad tells me you're a natural, a great builder," Kellie praised him.

"We're carpenters," the lad corrected her.

"Sorry. Thanks for setting me straight."

"There's a rule too, for *our* workshop: No phones ever allowed. Like church."

"A rule I agree with," she said. "And will follow."

She asked him to teach her how to play *Fortnite*, and she gave it a brow-knitted try but wasn't a gamer, had never touched a controller before, so she was slow and thumb-clumsy and barely made it off the Battle Bus before her skin perished. To his credit, Noah was mostly kind and empathetic. He didn't belittle her, but he did lose interest when she was quickly eliminated for the third time in ten minutes. He told her he was bored and switched to something or other on his iPad. She left at eight and thanked him for sharing his day with her. "Okay," he mumbled noncommittally.

***

JANUARY 21, ANDY HAD tried three public-defender cases in general district court—a DUI, a trespass at Walmart, and an assault and battery—and he was at his desk, completing timesheets for those clients, some of the last he'd ever file with the state. He was wistful, reminiscing, in no hurry to finish. The door opened so forcefully that it bounced against the stop, and Cindy bolted into his office, flustered.

"Sorry, Andy," she said, "but crazy Damian Bullins is on the phone, and he's drunk or high or both, and he's raising Cain and demandin' to speak with you."

Andy signed and dated a timesheet before responding. "This office no longer represents him. Mercifully, my work for him is done. Tell him we have no business remaining and no need to speak. Don't argue with him or try to placate him. Hang up if you need to."

"You're sure?"

"Positive," he replied.

"With pleasure," she said. "Can't stand him. Also, I'm starting to get reporter calls, wanting to talk to you."

"You can ignore those too."

She returned a few minutes later to report Damian was enraged and making threats. "He said you were a traitor and a liar. I wrote down most of his BS on the message and his number." She laid the pink paper on his desk. "His new girlfriend, this Becky witch, also called earlier."

The next morning the firestorm hit the media. Stories described how Bullins's lawyer had turned on him and sworn to an affidavit that revealed damning confidential conversations, and the cable news experts, most of whom hadn't so much as sniffed a courtroom in years, weighed in and opined and blathered at the top of every hour. *USA Today* headlined its piece "Superstar Lawyer Flips on Client Found Innocent."

"We knew this was coming," Andy said to Kellie as they sat at the kitchen table scrolling through their phones.

"At least most of the stories are fair," she suggested. "Accurate. They describe how it's your legal duty to not let him blatantly lie once he admits his crime. A safety valve in the system—that's how this reporter explains the situation in his article."

"I have no doubt the discerning public will read past the headlines and appreciate the nuances and my professionalism."

Kellie swiped her finger across the screen and was briefly quiet. "I hate Peter Morley," she fumed minutes later, bent over her phone. "Here's his quote. 'It's difficult to imagine how any attorney could so mishandle a case from start to finish. My heart goes out to the Benson family. They have suffered repeatedly because of Mr. Hughes's bad choices. If we believe his recent affidavit, his actions directly contributed to a murderer walking free and the subsequent unnecessary charge against Cole Benson. I assume the bar and courts will be carefully investigating this and will take appropriate action.'" She slapped the phone against her palm. "The worthless shitbag opportunistic prick! Hell, he indicted Cole Benson, not you, and he damn well knew Cole didn't kill his wife. The truth is you've done the right thing at every turn, even when it's been difficult. Screw him."

"What're you doing?" Andy asked.

"Sending the asshat a text."

"Don't, please," he said.

She kept at it and punched the send button with a fierce finger. "I told him he was a lying, dishonest piece of shit."

"'Politician' would've conveyed the same message with fewer words," he said. His phone brightened and played the factory-installed ringtone. "That was quick. I'll bet Pete's calling to apologize."

"Not likely," she said, still boiling.

"D, good morning, sir," Andy greeted DeMarcus.

"Not so sure I'd categorize the day as 'good,'" he said. "Seems we have ourselves a nasty tangle, Andy."

"Yep, sorry. Did you get my email yesterday?"

"Not until this morning. I was in court until nine thirty and you sent it to the office account, not my personal address. But I appreciate the courtesy and the heads-up."

"You were entitled to know."

"Listen—as an attorney I understand you've played this ethically and righteously and straight down the line, and everybody in the bar ought to commend you for how you handled the circumstances. This is textbook, law-school training. No doubt you're one hundred percent justified. But—"

"You don't have to—"

"But, Andy, I'm already sensing cold feet and resistance from some of my partners. Our clients don't give a damn about how well you follow the silk-stocking rules. They'll pick effective over ethical every day of the week, always choose a devil with dark skills over a saint with a conscience, and since most of our defendants are guilty, they want to feel certain their lawyer can hold a secret if they pay him enough."

"I understand," Andy said. "Don't blame you or your firm for being concerned."

"So while I love you as a friend and admire your guts as an attorney, as your potential employer, I'm probably going to have to put the brakes on and let your hiring cool for a while, then we'll recalibrate."

"Fair enough," Andy replied.

"And yeah, again, I'm so sorry, and I respect you more than you can imagine, and I hope this blows over and we can sign a deal, and in the meantime, I'll fight to bring you here. Absolutely."

"I know you will. Thanks."

An hour later, at the PD's office, Vikram bear-hugged Andy in the hallway, and he told him, for everyone to hear, loud and emotional, he was lucky to be his boss and friend, and if Andy wanted, he'd phone Richmond and withdraw the paperwork, and they'd just keep on as if nothing had ever happened. Vikram's voice never wavered, but he was teary by the time he finished and hugged Andy a second time. "As long as I'm in charge, you'll always—always—have a job here," he promised.

CHAPTER TWENTY-THREE

ANDY REALIZED *EXACTLY* WHO was at his house the instant he saw the new red Corvette with a temporary cardboard tag parked in his driveway. It was Monday, January 25, and he'd stopped at the gym on the way home, only to be turned away because the facility was at Covid capacity. Damian Bullins was sitting in a rocker on the front porch, Patches pacing nearby. The winter sun had started to wane, so Bullins was tucked in to shadow and weak light, mostly shrouded. Andy stopped beside the car, yanked the Jeep's parking brake tight, and took his .38 from the glove box. He exited with the gun apparent but at his side, pointed at the ground.

"What the fuck are you doing?" he demanded, striding toward Bullins. The dog trotted to meet him.

"Come on now, Andy," Bullins said, grinning, the words a taunt, "can't two friends visit without a gun bein' drawn?" He displayed his empty hands. "'Specially since I'm unarmed." He sounded normal, sober. He rocked backward, paused the chair, then brought it forward. "Good to see you. We need to talk, okay? And since you ain't takin' my calls, here I am. Just like old times."

"Leave," Andy said. "Get off my porch, get in your car, and drive away." A coherent, malevolent Damian struck Andy as much more menacing than the sloppy, impaired version.

"Or what?" Bullins laughed. "You gonna shoot me?" He peered at the Corvette. "Nice wheels, huh? Sweet Becky's helpin' me with the payments 'til my lawsuit money arrives."

"I'll...call the cops, and you'll be arrested for trespassing." Andy was frustrated by how feeble he sounded. A brazen criminal was goading him on his own front porch, and he was left lacking. "Or maybe I'll just kick your ass. I'd enjoy that."

"Threatenin' me," Bullins jeered. "Wow. I doubt you're gonna fight me or call the police—you've had enough bad publicity already. I kinda think your hands're tied where I'm concerned. You want *more* bad reports and to lose your lawyer card for sure?"

Andy stepped onto the porch. He slid the gun into his hip pocket. "Leave now, Damian," he said, his voice steely.

"Sure, Andy, I'll leave, and once I do, you'll regret it for the rest of your life, I can promise you. Here's all I wanna say: How 'bout you just keep the hell outta this? I'm not askin' you to help me or to lie for me, but how 'bout you mind your own business and not screw up my payday? What's your interest in a cheatin' bastard like Cole Benson? What kinda crooked lawyer betrays his client and reveals his personal secrets? You ease off, keep quiet, and me and you mend fences, and I tell the media you're the best lawyer ever. You can say you've reconsidered that affidavit you signed for Cole and maybe misunderstood some things. I might even throw a few dollars your way."

"Damian, you're a dumbass and a sociopath. An idiot. A waste. I plan to continue to do what's right. Last thing I'd consider is negotiating with a piece of shit like you." He advanced until he was directly in front of Bullins.

"Okay, but don't say I didn't warn you, Andy."

Andy reached down, clamped a hand on Bullins's shoulder, and jerked him up. The chair lurched forward when his weight left the seat. Andy spun him around, bent his wrist behind his back, and began marching him toward the Corvette.

"Andy, Andy, Andy," Bullins said, "I can see I'm not welcome—no need to assault me. Just wanted to give you a chance and fair notice."

They'd passed the porch's small step and were in the driveway gravel. Andy pushed Bullins, shoved him in the back with both hands. "Keep walking."

Bullins continued silently to his car. He opened the door, and the key warning buzzed, the interior lights shone. He turned and spoke from behind the red door, a tiny speck of illumination glinting in the window glass.

"So you pick wrong, Andy. Your choice. A lot can happen, right? Like poor Aunt Jemima Alicia Benson. Never know. One minute you're peelin' apples, next minute you're gone. Poof. You take care and think about my offer, you hear?"

He climbed in the vehicle, pulled the door shut. The engine started and the headlights brightened. The car whipped a tight half-circle so it was aimed for the highway, spinning gravels and rutting the drive, then sat idling. The window lowered. "Give my regards to your boy," Damian said, his neck and head visible as he spoke. "Little Noah. Hope he stays safe and healthy."

Andy was so blindly angry that he charged the Corvette—instinct and a fool's errand—and Patches loyally came along with him, barking at the taillights as Bullins departed, the engine chugging loud and powerful. Andy halted and Patches kept running, and seconds later, the car slowed to a roll and Andy saw an arm extend from the window, and he saw the muzzle flash, and he heard the bang. Patches yelped when the bullet tore in to him and collapsed his legs and sent him to the ground.

CHAPTER TWENTY-FOUR

ANDY RACED TO THE veterinarian's office, speeding to almost a hundred on the rare rural straightaways. Patches lay limp across the Jeep's rear seat, swaddled in a white sleeveless gym shirt, the toe of a tube sock wadded into the exit wound, blood spreading through the shirt so thoroughly that the fabric was half crimson by the time they hit Route 58. The bewildered creature's windpipe seemed to be shrinking, and he breathed in gulps and gasps and wheezes, his eyes closed.

Andy was trained to improvise, to ad lib, to turn on a dime. Courtroom lawyering is all about resets, invention, nimble thinking and stitching together a plan on the stressful fly. He was furious and anguished, his stomach roiling, his hands trembling, but his mind was in perfect order—balanced, sharp, efficient, methodical—as he began calculating how best to punish Damian Bullins, the gas pedal occasionally mashed to the floor.

Dr. Clint Thomas's mom, Cheryl, worked in the Henry County court system, and Andy had phoned her immediately after loading the dog, hoping she'd answer her cell. She did, cheerful and sunny as always, and he informed her of his dreadful emergency, and she called back minutes later to confirm her son was en route to his clinic on Kings Mountain Road and would be there soon. She added she was praying for him and the dog and promised she'd be in touch with her church's pastor so he could include them in his prayers as well. "I can't thank you enough," Andy said sincerely.

Dr. Thomas was younger, only three years graduated from Virginia Tech, and he was posted outside his office door when Andy arrived. Wearing jeans, muddy Muck Boots and a ball cap, the doc sprinted to the vehicle, and Andy was quickly pushing the seat forward to make space for him to examine Patches.

"Mom says he was shot," Dr. Thomas stated as he maneuvered the bloody dog from the Jeep and cradled him, both arms underneath Patches's belly.

"Yes. About twenty minutes ago. Thirty minutes max. My guess is a .22 pistol from the sound of it." They were rushing toward the building. Andy swung open the door for the vet. They went straight into a treatment room, where Patches was arranged on a stainless-steel table, a bright light glaring from overhead. The dog opened his eyes, licked his lips, exhaled, and closed his eyes again. His lips didn't completely cover his teeth, seemed stuck and incomplete. His tongue drooped. His breathing was still choppy. The doc began peeling away the shirt and removed the sock plug from the abdomen wound.

"Who in the world would shoot him?" Dr. Thomas asked.

"No idea, Clint," Andy replied. "None. I caught a glimpse of a pickup with a Carolina plate, but I can't even say for certain the shot was fired from there."

"You think this might be connected to the whole Benson thing?"

"I really doubt it," Andy said. "Not sure how or why it would be." He cleared his throat. "But you never know, I suppose."

Owing to either professional habit or an effort to keep Andy calm and informed, Dr. Thomas recited exactly what he was doing to treat the dog, announced every detail and medical procedure as he went. "Appears we have an entrance and exit wound, no bullet remaining as best I can see. I'm packing these wounds with sterile gauze to stanch the bleeding, then I'm going to give him a bolus of IV fluid for shock. For the blood loss." The vet inserted an IV needle into Patches's front leg and began draining a bag of liquid into him.

"Okay," was all Andy could summon. "Thanks," he said hoarsely.

"I'll draw a smidge of blood to test, then grab an X-ray." He punctured Patches with a needle, and the syringe began filling with dark red blood. He moved and spoke confidently, but Andy was discouraged when the pup didn't stir or flinch or crack his eyelids during the needle stick.

"He's not very alert," Andy observed. He caught himself wringing his hands and stopped. "Do everything you can for him, please."

"I'm gonna roll him for an X-ray and run the blood. Be right back. You can take a seat over there." The doc gestured at a chair beside a keyboard and computer screen near the corner of the room. He kicked off the table's brakes and freed the wheels.

"Can I do anything to be helpful?" Andy asked.

"Sit tight and cross your fingers." He pushed Patches out of the room and turned left into a hall, disappeared.

Andy sat down, glum, waiting. Soon, he checked his watch. Not even three minutes had passed. He walked to the door and peeked down the hall. Nothing. He glanced at his watch again. He wandered to the lobby, went outside into the cold air. Considered a cigarette and was glad he didn't have any. Traffic motored by on the road in front of the clinic, and a horn blared. A stoplight changed from green to yellow. He returned to the treatment-room chair and sat with his face in his hands, slumped and miserable. At least most of the early, high-octane adrenaline had burned off so his skin wasn't tingling.

Dr. Thomas reappeared seventeen minutes later. He parked the table in its former spot. He rested his hand on the dog's head, stroked his fur with a single sweep that stopped at his withers. "Here's what we have, Andy. The bullet's gone. Went through him. I think it might've clipped his spleen, but no bones or organs were involved or compromised. He's lost a fair amount of blood, and I'll give him a transfusion in a few minutes. Clean and disinfect the skin breaks and suture the larger exit wound. We'll hospitalize him here with us tonight, and once the blood and fluids take hold, he should start to revive and feel better. You were smart to cram the sock in him and come here so fast."

"Oh, thank goodness. What a relief. Are you sure? He still looks pretty bad."

Dr. Thomas laughed. "Well, that's my best medical opinion."

"Sorry," Andy replied. "I'm just worried sick. He's part of the family."

"I understand. No problem. I'm going to hang around for a while and tidy up and make my notes, and I'll examine him again him before I leave.

I'm scheduled for a morning of large-animal farm visits tomorrow, but my partner, Jon Adcock, will be here at eight. He's the best there is. You guys'll be in extremely capable hands. Just check with him first chance you have."

"A favor, please, Clint. Another one, I suppose. I'd like to stay here with my dog. Spend the night beside his cage." Andy smiled weakly. "His *kennel*, I mean. I realize that's probably not allowed for a number of reasons, but I'd be in your debt even more than I already am."

"Well, yeah, okay, if you want to and don't broadcast it. My mom would scold me to no end if I didn't accommodate one of *her* lawyers." The vet inclined his head. "And you want to bunk on the concrete, amongst the other animals and noise and smells? Not in the lobby? Or your own comfortable bed? There's no treatment reason for you to be here, and I'm predicting you won't sleep much."

"I wouldn't anyway. I'll call my girlfriend and have her bring a blanket and pillow."

"Okay."

"I can't thank you enough, Clint, for coming in after hours and the great care. Cheryl too—if you hadn't helped us, I'd still be on the road to Greensboro and the twenty-four-seven emergency vet. The dog might've died. I hope I can repay you someday. I'm beyond grateful."

"My pleasure. Rumor has it you're a good guy for an attorney."

Kellie arrived while Dr. Thomas was at the computer finishing his file notes. She dropped blankets and a pillow on a lobby couch and hugged Andy. "I'm so, so sorry. How is he?"

"Evidently, better than he looks and acts. Thanks to Dr. Thomas."

"Well," the vet said, "thanks to luck and providence and the good Lord and whatever else. The bullet missed everything vital, and my involvement was pretty basic."

"You think he'll be okay?" Kellie asked.

"I do. There're never any guarantees, but I'm optimistic. He'll be a week to ten days before he's completely healed, and we have to watch for infection, but yeah, this could've been much worse."

The doctor situated Patches in a kennel, said goodnight, and locked Andy and Kellie in the building. They sat against a painted cinder-block wall across from the dog, who was flopped on his side and breathing steadily. A square white bandage with a dot of seeped blood was taped over the bullet hole, the fur shaved to bare skin. The transfusing blood dripped into him via clear tubing connected to a pump that kept a regular rhythm of low, muffled clicks.

"Did you see who shot him, Andy?" she asked.

"Nope. Did not."

"I know who I'd put at the top of the suspect list—Damian Bullins. A guy who abuses women and leeches off his elderly aunt would have no problem shooting a dog. Just his style."

"Maybe, but…intuitively, I don't feel he's involved. I've known him and represented him for years, and I truly don't think he did this. He'd get high and call on the phone and make *threats*, and if he ran across us accidentally and was jacked on meth, he might impulsively kick Patches, might even lose his temper and shoot *at* him, but this would be too calculated and too much effort for him. And, jeez, how many enemies have I made practicing law? We're threatened nearly every week by some or other unhappy court customer. Also, this could be completely random. Yahoo kids shooting at whatever crossed their path. As best I can tell, the shot came from the road."

"Maybe you and I know a different Damian Bullins. This is sneaky, depraved and cowardly. Sociopathic. Fits him to a T. Tell the cops to investigate the hell out of him."

"I will, but I doubt he'll confess if he's in fact the shooter—I'm guessing he's learned *that* lesson—and there's nothing to connect him. Nothing. Plus, I understand he's mostly in South Carolina with his new lady friend and probably all alibied up. For what it's worth, the first name I thought of is Austin Emerson, the loose-cannon lunatic from Claudville who keeps filing baseless warrants against his neighbor. He cursed me and promised I'd 'pay' last time Judge McGarry dismissed his spiteful case against our client."

"Possibly," she said. "But the timing of this is so suspicious—right after you gave Lynn the information about Damian's guilt."

"I'm sure the cops will cover every angle. I'll keep my ears open too. I intend to find the guilty bastard, and once I do…"

"We need to make sure it's simply a dog event and doesn't become more. Are you and Noah safe?"

He put his arm around her shoulder. "I'll be careful. No need to panic. Let's concentrate on discovering who did this. Word'll leak sooner or later. Punks and criminals can never keep a secret."

"You're a lot more Zen about this than I'd be." She gave him a quizzical look.

"I wasn't an hour ago. I was so mad I could barely drive."

Ninety minutes passed before Andy finally persuaded her to go home. She wanted to stay, but he insisted she get a proper night's sleep and reminded her she had clients who needed a rested attorney the next morning. He walked her to the exit and kissed her, then returned to his vigil with Patches, the pillow folded in half and wedged between the wall and his head. Alone with the infirm animals, Andy tinkered on his retribution plan, blueprinted every detail, but around eleven o'clock, as he grew weary, his thoughts would detour and take him elsewhere, and he kept replaying the same scenes, looping the same story, sometimes as if he were at a distance, watching the vignettes projected onto a drive-in-movie screen in his mind, fluid and Technicolored, the soundtrack a mangled tomcat's persistent meows.

He recalled his son and the Van Buren Street Footbridge, which was a couple minutes' trip from the small house Andy had rented on Front Street while visiting Missoula. The bridge was old, with stout steel girders and rusty, zigzagging rivets the size of walnuts. Milky streetlight globes sat atop high poles along the length of the walkway, and strings of exuberant white bulbs illuminated the entire span at night. The off-leash dog park was across the bridge, bounded by the Clark Fork River. On their first morning in town, still accustomed to eastern time, Andy, Noah and Patches were awake early, at 6:15 a.m., strolling to the park, the bridge lights burning and dawn filtering in enough for them to see the far bank of the river.

"What're those?" Noah asked, fascinated, at a complete stop near the first walkway planks.

Chest-high chain-link panels—safeguards—ran from end to end on each side, and they were filled with padlocks, hundreds and hundreds of padlocks—gold, silver, black, red, purple, pink, big and tiny and in-between, keyed and combination. They were hung on the bridge's sides, dangling from the chain-link, like peculiar, mismatched jewelry.

"They're love locks," Andy explained.

"Are they holdin' the wire together?"

"No." Andy smiled at his son. Patches squirmed in his harness and pawed a wooden board, uneasy about the rushing water underneath him, foreign and scary. "People buy locks then hang them on here. It's a symbol of their being together forever. Of love and commitment. Taking care of each other. So they're called love locks."

"Do they ever come off?" Noah asked.

"No. You click your lock shut and throw away the key or combination. They're forever. That's the whole point." Patches pulled on his leash, whimpered. "I'll bet the river's seen a lot of keys."

"Can anyone put them up?"

"Sure."

"Then we ought to, you and me. We're like that." He looked at his father. "And Patches. The three of us."

"They're more for people who...well, yeah, absolutely, we should. We will. Great idea." Andy waited for Noah and the dog to mosey on ahead before he wiped his shirt sleeve across his wet eyes.

They were at the door when Ace Hardware opened. Noah selected a gold lock, and Andy, always the craftsman, spent eight bucks on a cheap micro-engraver and cut three sets of initials into the lock's face: NH AH PH. Noah then traced over the letters with a red Sharpie. They decided on a location, clicked the lock closed around the stiff wire, and Andy dropped the keys into the river, tossed them underneath the bridge, almost upstream. They barely made a splash, plunked a faint, slim slit in the big water. Noah had to tiptoe stretch so he could see over the panels and watch the keys disappear into the Clark Fork. "Okay," was all he said, and he swiftly hopscotched to other concerns, asked about a trip to the rock store in town.

After lunch at their rented house, Andy concealed the actual keys in a fast-food wrapper and buried them in an outdoor garbage can. He'd sleight-of-handed a small stone into the water, couldn't abide polluting the magnificent river but didn't want to diminish the ritual for his boy, and the keys would be gone forever just the same, the bond intact.

❖❖❖

"Damn, guys, you startled me," Andy exclaimed. He was in his shop three days later, a drab Thursday, bent over a drawer, his back to the door. He'd just located a used fifty-amp breaker, and after he'd spun to see who was there, he palmed the breaker and returned it to the drawer without revealing what was in his hand.

"Sorry, Andy," Brooke said, "we're an hour early for drop-off, but your son was pitching a fit to check on Patches. You didn't answer when I called, but we figured you might be in the shop since you never bring a phone in here, and anyhow, maybe we could see the dog even if you weren't around. Hence the drive-by. Hope it's not a problem; unannounced visits haven't always gone so great for us." She cocked an eyebrow.

"Yeah, left the phone in the kitchen. No problem. Always happy to spend extra time with my son."

"What're you looking for, Dad?"

"Oh...a T15 drill bit."

"Why're you lookin' in the electrical drawer? The drill bits are over there." Noah pointed. "And you just used a swear word."

"I thought I'd accidentally dropped one in the wrong drawer a while ago. Apologies for the bad language."

"What kinda gloves are those?" Noah asked. Andy was wearing blue nitrile medical gloves.

"They're sterile gloves," Andy replied, "for...changing the dog's bandage. But I was getting ready to use some epoxy, and they're perfect for that job too. Any more inquiries, Sherlock?"

"Yeah, can we see Patches? Mom said he's home."

"Sure. He's resting in the den. I bought him a fleece bed, and he's weak enough that he's actually using it."

"Mom told me he got shot."

"Yes," Andy said.

"Why?" the boy asked. "Why would anyone do somethin' so mean and hateful?"

"We don't know yet. But I'm determined to make it right, and I reported the crime to the police, and they're helping us find the bad guys."

"I hope they have to go to jail forever," Noah declared.

"Wouldn't be unfair," Andy said.

Patches was tailless, but his nub shook and vibrated the moment he saw Noah, and he struggled and rolled so he could sit on his haunches, and he licked the boy's face and neck while he was being hugged, his eyes, especially the blue one, awash with joy.

Brooke and Andy were standing well behind the boy and dog. She took a step backward, nearer to the kitchen. She crooked a finger at Andy. "Good news," she said quietly. "I can repay the money I owe you next week."

"Already? How? I thought you were expecting several more months of delay and battle."

"Seems Howard's new honey is a huge watersports gal, and the idiot purchased a freakin' *boat* while we were still living together. A hundred forty thousand, he spent. He put it in his name only, thought—"

"But under Virginia law, it's classified as marital property since you hadn't separated," Andy noted.

"Yep," she replied. "He basically hid it at her house and then lied on the papers you have to answer under oath—"

"Interrogatories," Andy clarified.

"Ms. Jacob doesn't play around. She somehow tracked down Captain Howard's new toy and now we have him in an enormous bind, so he's ponied up the hundred grand, plus I get the title to my vehicle. He pays for the divorce and pays my attorney, and as a bonus, I'll receive nine-hundred-a-month spousal support for two years. More than I asked for to begin with."

"Wow. That's an extremely favorable settlement. I told you Janine's an excellent lawyer."

"For me, 'extremely favorable' would mean my son and I were happily living with the man I loved and married and enjoying our lives. But this is what's left to me, and I have a clear conscience about prying away his precious money—he lied and cheated and hit me. At a certain point, your choices are limited and you make the best of what's available."

Brooke departed after a ten-minute stay, and as soon as he was positive she wasn't returning, Andy told Noah he needed a few moments to finish up in the shop, wouldn't be long. He covertly pocketed his phone, went to the shop, hurried to his drawing board, and removed several Google Earth overviews of Route 773 in Ararat. He'd located and printed the pages at the library in Roanoke, where he'd lingered and waited and watched and skulked until—finally—a kid left a public computer and didn't log off, so he was able to find the information without leaving behind his virtual fingerprints.

After deadbolting the shop door, he stuck the Google Earth sheets in a drawer underneath a Skilsaw's owner's manual. He took several full breaths, pulled his phone from his pocket, and slowly, deliberately punched in ten numbers, the numbers gleaned from a peek at the yellow carbon-copies in Cindy's message book. He looked through the window, scanned the driveway, yard and porch. He was definitely alone, except for his son.

The phone rang five times before Bullins answered. "My famous lawyer, Andy Hughes, has seen fit to call me," he sneered before Andy said hello or identified himself.

"Listen, Damian—"

"My lyin' turncoat lawyer would be more correct." Damian sounded only mildly high. His speech wasn't slurred or sloppy, but he spoke rapidly, in spurts, drugs or liquor—or both—squeezing his thoughts.

"I arguably have a legal duty to return your call."

"I'm sure you're recordin' me, settin' a trap."

"No, I'm not," Andy answered. "I've considered our situation, and I'd like to find a way we can reach an understanding."

"The understandin' we need, Andy, is for you to take back the lies you told in your affidavit so I can have a fair day in court."

"Damian, you and I both know the truth, and we both know there're no lies in my affidavit. You murdered Alicia Benson. But I've met with Mrs. Dylan-Haley, who's one of Cole's lawyers, and she urged me to try to persuade you to do the right thing."

"She needs to do the right thing and pay me, otherwise her client might be convicted of murder."

"Well, I've mentioned a financial option to her, a payment for you. How about you and I meet face-to-face, man-to-man, and we discuss amounts and see if we can close this book. My son, my dog, Cole Benson, his kids and I would all like for this to be resolved."

"Don't know nothin' 'bout you and your dog or your kid, nothing whatsoever, and this feels like a setup or trick to me. You must think I'm a total dumbass."

"How could it be a trick, Damian? Exactly what do you think I can pull off by seeing you and working on a settlement agreement? I'm not a wizard or telepath or voodoo priest. But negotiations are usually better when people sit down together and try to reach a deal. Let's see if I can take them a realistic offer. Maybe it won't be everything you want, but you're facing some significant legal impediments given my willingness to testify and the information I was obligated to reveal—"

"Nothing but a crooked lawyer's bullshit," Damian shouted.

"...and it's very likely Ms. Hespell will soon simply dismiss the indictment, and pfft, your leverage is gone. Even if Cole's somehow found guilty, you won't receive a penny, not a red cent, and any civil money that's paid—a helluva longshot—will go to your son and probably be managed by a trust or the court. Again, you receive *nothing*. All you really have, now that I've followed the law and come forward, is the potential to make Cole's life unpleasant and further injure his reputation. There's room for everyone to be reasonable."

"Just spit it out, Andy," Damian snorted. "What's on the damn table? What's the offer?"

"This isn't a conversation for the telephone. You pick the place and time, and we'll meet."

"Then I pick Becky's house. In South Carolina."

"Nope. I said the two of us, privately, Damian. You and I. And I'm not hiking to South Carolina as if I'm your lackey. Where are you now?"

"At the casino in Cherokee. You can gamble if you wear a mask. You wouldn't believe how many people recognize me. They all think you hosed me."

"How about the camper at your aunt's in Ararat? Your residence. Can't get more on your turf than that."

"What's in this for you, Andy?"

"I'll be rid of a sociopathic, dog-shooting, murderous asshole. Pretty strong motivation, wouldn't you agree? Patches survived, by the way. You and I will definitely be discussing how you'll make amends for that sick-ass stunt. What kind of a shitheel shoots a defenseless dog?"

"I know you're recordin' us, and that's why you're repeatin' a bunch of false crap. Cole killed his wife, and I was the fall guy. Jury decided in my favor. I served my time for what I done. I ain't never harmed a dog in my life. You're talkin' crazy. Nobody can believe anything you say."

"When do you want to meet?"

"Maybe I don't want to. Maybe you should be speakin' to my new lawyer, Buck Simpson."

"Then, fine, don't meet with me. You called me, remember? Ignore me, and you'll get a big fat nothing, and also understand you and I will be enemies in the future, and my day will come."

"Okay. I'll be there Monday. At my aunt's. The camper. I'll be recordin' us, and Becky'll know I'm goin' to meet you, just in case."

"Well, Mrs. Dylan-Haley will know I'm meeting *you*." Andy paused. "I'm not the violent felon with an eleven-page criminal record."

"Noon," Bullins said.

"Six," Andy replied. "I have a job, unlike you. I'll be there on Monday, February first, at six o'clock. Maybe you should write it down now before you take drunk on free casino booze. This Monday at six. Six at night, not in the morning. Try to be coherent."

"I'll be there, asshole. Bring a checkbook."

Andy disconnected the call, immediately phoned Lynn Dylan-Haley, and lied to her about the specifics of his meeting. "Per your request, Boss," he told her, "I have a get-together with Damian Bullins this Sunday at his aunt's. He contacted the office high as a kite several days ago, raging and demanding to talk to me about his case, and I finally returned his call. During a relatively sober window, he seemed as if he might listen to reason. Reason and a check."

Lynn sighed. "We've explored that option already—my client won't pay him anything, especially since you've contradicted his story, and we've gained some advantages legally. I also worry about you having a negotiation with Bullins. He has another lawyer, and you're factually at odds with him. A conflict."

"He called *me* and wanted to discuss the *criminal* case I represented him on. Buck Simpson represents him in a *civil* proceeding. If I refuse to so much as speak with him, can you imagine how I'd be raked over the coals if I ultimately have to testify against him in court? I can just hear the cross-exam: 'You wouldn't even accept his call and allow him a chance to explain or correct your recollection?' I'm damned if I do, damned if I don't, Lynn."

"Be that as it may, I simply don't see Cole Benson paying this guy."

"Every case has *some* value. It may be no more than nuisance value, so let me take a run at this, and I'll be in touch Sunday night. You can always decline, and it's certainly possible Bullins arrives impaired and irrational and we accomplish nothing. A comprehensive settlement would be a tonic for everyone, myself included."

"Well, thanks for the effort," she said. "You be careful. Bullins is dangerous and a killer."

"Believe me, I'm well aware who he is."

●●●

THE NEXT MORNING, FRIDAY, Cindy delivered several messages and a rubber-banded stack of letters to Andy, who was in his office, but oddly, not busy or preoccupied as usual. Instead, he was staring at the ceiling, reclining in his chair, his feet propped on his desk. "Thanks," he said, but didn't change his gaze or connect with her.

He didn't read the messages or open his mail. He left work early and dropped by the strip-mall salon to see Kellie. Once a month, she volunteered to pick up sisters Nora and Flora from Blue Ridge Care Village and bring them with her to have their nails done, her treat. Kellie had met the firecracker widows, both in their eighties, when she was at the rest home interviewing a client's grandma, and they'd been palling around ever since. As Andy walked in, Flora delivered the punchline to a joke, and the three ladies went on a laughing jag. He stayed with them until thirty fingernails were shiny and bright and the sisters' thumbs were finished off with yellow rose decorations. "Noah and I will miss seeing you this weekend," he told Kellie before he left, then kissed her cheek.

Flora grinned wide and remarked, "You are something else, Andrew. Always the gentleman."

That night, with Noah asleep, Andy disappeared into his shop at eleven fifteen and worked on the armoire for five hours, occasionally returning to quaff coffee and look in on the boy. He fashioned drawers and compartments until he feared fatigue would blunt his skills and he'd make a mistake he couldn't repair. He spent the majority of Saturday working on the piece as well, felt bad about leaving Noah to entertain himself but didn't have any other choice.

"I'll take a vacation day and finish tomorrow," he declared to his son as they rode to Brooke's on Sunday afternoon, though the furniture—beautiful and exquisite, with a secret hiding place—was already completed and draped with a mover's blanket. "I need around seven more hours."

"Yippee," Noah said sarcastically. "Big whoop. It's all you've been doin'. You didn't even let me help, and now I have to leave early and can't spend the night. I hope your girlfriend's happy."

"We'll make it up. I promise. I'm sorry about the furniture. It's not Kellie's fault. I have an important work meeting tonight, okay? My job. I wish I didn't. I love you and regret every minute I don't see you. I realize you can't understand, and I'm not always able to explain and tell you, but..." His voice stalled in his throat, and he blinked back tears. "I will do anything I can to keep you safe and take care of you. To be your father. Okay?"

"Whatever," Noah eight-year-old answered, and the perfect, childish response caused Andy to smile and grab the boy and pull him into as big a hug as the shoulder harnesses would allow.

Andy also regretted that he'd had to rush the armoire—the original plan was to surprise Kellie with a Valentine's Day present. Still, she'd been flirty and excited Sunday morning when he let it slip he'd be skipping work on Monday, sequestered in his shop, putting the final touches on a spectacular gift for her. "I'll see you Tuesday night," he said at the end of their call. "Come with high expectations and celebration champagne."

CHAPTER TWENTY-FIVE

As EXPECTED, CONNIE GATES was drunk and cloudy and surly when she answered the door at her dilapidated, crackerbox house in Ararat on Sunday evening. A faded Cub Cadet riding mower was junked in the front yard, half-covered by a tarp. The tarp was pinned to the ground by a brick on one side, a rotting wooden planter on the other. At least a dozen bags of trash, several open and spilled, were haphazardly heaped beside a single overflowing garbage can. A Chevy Cobalt with a dented, primer-colored fender and a cardboard-and-duct-tape rear window was parked in the drive, its front tire dunked in a mudhole.

"Whadda you want?" she asked, her speech labored. She swayed and grabbed the doorframe to keep her balance. "Oh, wait, nooo," she said. "You're Hughes, the lawyer, ain't you? Damian's lawyer."

"Yes ma'am. I am. Nice to see you again."

"Why're you here?" She was wearing pink terrycloth scuffs, sweatpants and a long-sleeve flannel shirt. The hair around her bald spot was thin, limp and oily. She leaned on a cane. "'Specially after you done him dirty. You're a common cook. *Crook*."

"Well, ma'am, I'm here to meet with Damian and try to make him some money," he replied. "We're on good terms."

"Say what?"

"I agreed to meet your nephew here today, Sunday, at seven. It's seven fifteen, and he's not arrived yet. Running late, I suppose. You think I could wait inside with you? I'd appreciate it. It's thirty degrees. Cold. Sorry to be a bother."

She walleyed inspected him, breathing through her mouth. She rubbed her cheek with her knuckles.

"I brought a peace offering for you, by the way. A bottle of wine. Least I can do after the misunderstandings and difficulties we've all been through recently."

"Wine?" she said. She pawed at her hearing aid.

"It's in my Jeep. I was planning to drop it off after my meeting with Damian."

"For me? Free?"

"Yes."

"You've come to see Damian?"

"Correct, Mrs. Gates. You'll recall I helped him beat his murder charge."

"Well, hell yeah, bring it on in. Time's a-wastin'."

The living room stank of cat piss, kerosene from the heater, rancid food, and a miasma of cigarettes, alcohol and neglected hygiene. The flat-screen TV was tuned to a *Bonanza* episode, but there was only faint volume. Gates tottered to the sofa and lowered herself onto a cushion. A nearly empty bottle of Aristocrat vodka was on a coffee table, evidently her only company until Andy had appeared. He sat adjacent to her in a recliner with black cigarette burns scarring its Naugahyde arms, mercifully five or six feet distant. He twisted off the top from a bottle of sweet wine and passed it to her. "Do you need a glass?" he asked.

She didn't respond. She turned up the bottle, sucked several lusty swallows. A trickle leaked from the corner of her mouth, and she chased after it with a clumsy tongue and finally wiped it away on her flannel cuff. Andy attempted to chat with her, but she wasn't the least bit talkative, so they were mostly silent and awkward, marked time, and watched Hoss and Little Joe prevail in a saloon brawl. She only grunted, her eyes shrunk to slits, when he told her he needed to use the restroom and would be right back. "Don't always flush like it should," she warned him.

He wiggled on fresh nitrile gloves as he walked down the hall, guessing and searching. After three tries, he found the panel in a closet. He pulled a string to illuminate the bare ceiling bulb, checked over his shoulder, slid into the musty space, pulled the door almost shut, and went to work. He finished his task without any complications, turned off the light, and stepped into the toilet and flushed the commode for show.

"Well," he said after returning to the living room ten minutes later, "seems Damian isn't coming. It's seven-forty."

"You can't count on him for nothin'," she griped. The wine bottle was trapped between her thighs, the neck resting against her stomach. "Selfish little shit won't even buy me a car as famous as he's got. After everything I done for him." She focused on Andy. "Can I bum a cigarette?"

"No, sorry. Gave it up."

"Wiped his nasty *ass*," she rambled, agitated. "Put up my place for his bail." She wrinkled her face. "Where you been, Hughes? Seems you was gone a long time."

"Bathroom, remember? The flush was A-okay, no problems."

"Right, yeah."

"Thanks for the hospitality, ma'am. If you hear from Damian, just tell him to text me."

She gripped the bottle with both hands, relaxed deep into the sofa, and coughed. "Yeah. Uh, tell him what?"

Andy didn't answer her question or speak to her again. He left her and drove home, had to brake and swerve a mile into the trip to avoid hitting three deer darting across the country road.

"No luck," he reported to Lynn once he'd ducked into his shop, changed clothes, filled the dog's water bowl, and poured himself a cold beer. "Damian didn't come. I should've known better. He's completely erratic and unreliable."

"Probably for the best," Lynn replied. "You've covered your bases by responding to him, and anyway, Cole isn't about to write a check. Not even a nuisance check. But I appreciate the effort. None of this can be any fun for you."

"The worst part is I had to take my boy to his mom's so I could go on this snipe hunt. Missed a night with Noah, thanks to Bullins jerking me around."

✦✦✦

ANDY DEPARTED HIS HOUSE early Monday morning. He could *not* be late. He was thankful for a clear sky and a dry forecast, though there was a favorable chance of snow flurries around midnight. He'd shredded the Google Earth printouts, then burned the crosscut scraps. His trek through the woods covered 1.9 miles from a parking spot behind an overgrown tobacco barn on a secondary road, and it would be slower and more arduous because he was wearing multiple socks and size fourteen hiking boots on his size twelve feet, a longshot, lawyer's precaution. He altered his license plates with colored electrical tape, changed a 1 to a 4, an S to an 8, and obscured the registration month, another one-in-a-million protection, but these days it seemed the sky was indeed lousy with satellite eyes. The cylinder in his .38 was full when he flipped it from the frame. A spool of twenty-pound-test Stren monofilament fishing line was in his jacket pocket, a failsafe if the wrong person approached the loaded door. He was dressed warmly in winter camo, including gloves and a face covering, anticipating a long wait. His cell phone remained on the kitchen counter, plugged in to an outlet.

He stopped at Fulton Brothers Building Supply, stripped off most of his outfit, and bought sandpaper and dowels he didn't need and told Harold, the manager, he was taking another break from lawyering to finish his girlfriend's armoire. "Man, you need to send me a picture," Harold said. The receipt in the brown bag showed the purchases were made at 7:49 a.m.

He was back home at 8:15 p.m., sweat-damp underneath the heavy clothes. He unlocked the shop and returned a Phillips-head screwdriver to its slot in a drawer; it was third longest in a set of five. He went to the kitchen, tapped his phone, and read Kellie's response to his automatically generated text at 4:30 p.m. telling her the gift was nearly finished. "No rest for the wicked," she'd replied and added a winking yellow emoji.

As he showered, he braced for the wallop, expected a revelation—or something, anything—to take hold of him, and he put his face in the water spray and spread his arms crucifix-style, but strangely, nothing changed, nothing came on him, not a twinge, not a hot bolt of remorse, not a deliverance, *nothing*. He was neither lifted nor weighted. He only felt the dull, familiar assurance he occasionally experienced at the end of a difficult court trial, a workman's simple satisfaction when he'd gained a fair result for a client. He finished with a long, cold stream on his neck and shoulders, then stood naked and trembling, wanted to make sure his small, fierce war hadn't rendered him senseless or left him broken inside.

"Your surprise is ready," he cheerfully informed Kellie a few minutes later, wrapped in a towel, watching his lips move in the bathroom mirror, seemingly a surreal tick out of sync with his words. "I think you'll be pleased."

"Well, you've been at it all day. This must be something spectacular, but don't sabotage yourself by hyping my expectations too high."

"I've been at it for nearly a *month*. I wanted to finish this week—it's the anniversary of the first time I saw you at the office. Technically when we first met."

"That's as sweet as it is obscure," she said.

"I'm not positive of the day, but this is the week," he said, and it was true. "First of February." He quit watching his reflection. "You want to come by tonight?"

"It's almost nine and not everybody has tons of vacation days and a retiree's lazy schedule. Will it hurt your feelings if we stick with tomorrow as planned?"

"No. I'm tired too. See you at the office. I love you. I'm lucky we're together."

Snow began falling earlier than expected, before ten o'clock, and it was far more than flurries, unfurled thick and heavy from a bottomless sky. Andy flipped on the house's floodlights, dividing up the outside world into a stage of bright, radiant flakes and endless black backdrop. The yard was soon white, the driveway gravel covered. He poured a bourbon, which he sipped once and then abandoned, and he rearranged the furniture so he could sit at a window and watch the world erased and cleansed and reborn. Patches joined him. The snow finally stopped around four in the morning, and there were easily eight inches of accumulation. He *might've* dozed for a moment, but as best he could discern, he never truly slept, never faded away, just remained in an out-of-place chair, numb and forever different and receptive to whatever he was next due.

The Jeep was built to travel in snow, and the courts were closed because of the weather, so at seven thirty, he was able to fetch Kellie and bring her to his house for a breakfast of biscuits, gravy, eggs and sausage patties, and she brought the celebratory champagne and they uncorked it early for mimosas in front of the fireplace. They weren't through with the drinks, but Kellie claimed the snow and anticipation and promise of a fantastic present were too much like Christmas morning for her to wait any longer, so they put on boots and coats and stamped footprint holes from the porch to the workshop.

"You seem sort of distracted," she mentioned as he was kicking away snow from the front of the shop's door. "Kind of, I don't know…elsewhere. You barely ate."

"Sorry. I'm fine. I'm just tired. Didn't sleep well." He smiled at her. "I'm excited too. Anxious about the big reveal."

Andy didn't fool around with teases and speeches. He'd positioned the armoire in the center of the shop, and he held Kellie's hand and led her to the furniture, which remained covered. He removed the blanket, lifted it straight up. "Hope this makes you happy," he said.

"Oh, Andy." Kellie kneeled and touched the armoire's sides, and she began opening drawers and small cabinet doors so she could see inside the compartments. "It's absolutely beautiful. Gorgeous. Thank you. And look at the cute little carved feet. I couldn't love it more. And I love you and your talent and all the work you did for me." Her breath registered in the frigid air.

"Here's the encore," he said, grinning. He showed her how to access the secret compartment.

"I'll definitely have to find something worthy of the space." She stood and kissed him, and when her chilly hand rubbed bare skin under his shirt, he jumped, and she pinched him and said, "Let's go inside where it's warm and properly celebrate the week we met each other."

They went to the house and had sex in front of the fire, and after they finished, he kidded her because she'd kept on her wool socks and a T-shirt from a Chris Stapleton concert, and she was telling him a funny yarn about the show, how she and her girlfriend had accidentally landed in VIP, and while she was talking, he fell sound asleep on nothing but a thin blanket and a rug, and she let him be, his face beatific, for three hours, until she woke him, concerned he'd have a crick or kink from the hard floor.

⁕⁕⁕

THE PRIMARY ROADS WERE clear by Wednesday, and Andy drove them to the PD's office, where everyone was snow-day cheery and dressed in casual clothes since the courts remained closed. He kept to himself as much as possible and was concerned he might've seemed too chipper greeting Cindy or chatting with Curtis about possible fixes for a balky heat pump. He'd been there for thirty minutes and was scrolling through emails when Vikram cornered him in his office, entering without a knock and shutting the door behind him.

"Morning," he said.

"Morning, Vik."

"Lynn told me you tried to meet with Bullins and work out some kind of settlement. She felt I should be in the loop—didn't want me to think she was meddling with my lawyers."

"Yeah," Andy replied. "I planned to tell you as well, and I've already documented everything in the file. We were scheduled to meet at his camper Sunday night, and naturally, the worthless fool didn't show. I then had the pleasure of watching *Bonanza* with his drunken aunt in Dante's innermost circle."

"I'd be careful if I were you. I can think of several reasons, both practical and professional, why you'd be advised to avoid Bullins completely."

"No worries. We're on the same page. I have no intention of speaking with him again. I got this very same lecture from Kellie last night—I also filled her in. I'm satisfied I've honored every obligation I have where he's concerned."

Vikram was standing. His hands were clasped behind him. He wore a red corduroy shirt. "I agree. From start to finish, you've had nothing but difficult choices in his case, and you never once took the easy exit or avoided doing the right thing, no matter what. You are, Andy, the kind of lawyer we should all hope to be."

"Yeah, well, maybe, but of course, while my law license is festooned with ribbons and gold stars, my *reputation* is slaughtered."

"As I've told you before, the offer to remain here is always good. Your reputation with me is as excellent as it ever was."

"Thanks." Andy scratched his temple. "Oh. Have you seen my cell phone? I've lost it. A Samsung Galaxy?"

"No," Vikram answered.

"I can't find it. I worry I might've dropped it at Kellie's apartment yesterday morning when I picked her up." In fact, the phone had been gutted, beaten with a hammer, then blasted with an acetylene torch, the melted lump stuffed inside a milk carton and dumpstered along with two trash bags at the Henry County public green boxes. Any records in the scheduled-text feature were destroyed. "What a pain if it doesn't turn up. I think I'd rather lose my wallet if I had a choice."

※※※

IT WASN'T UNTIL THURSDAY, as Andy and Kellie were donning face coverings and wiping their boots on a saturated doormat at the entrance to the PD's office, that Cindy rushed into the waiting room, arms flapping, and asked, breathlessly: "Did you guys hear yet?"

"Hear what?" Kellie was unwinding her scarf. "Has Seamus the Rainbow Leprechaun finally located me? Was he carrying a pot?"

"Damian Bullins is dead."

"Wow," Andy said. "Ding dong."

"Do we know what happened?" Kellie asked. "How?"

"Ted talked to the cops in Patrick County. He and Vikram and Curtis are in the breakroom. According to Ted, the monster was electrocuted."

They followed Cindy down the hall, and they could hear Ted's voice, lively and animated, as soon as Andy shut the lobby's security door behind them. They went into the breakroom and stood next to a puny microwave.

"We hear the world might be slightly improved today," Andy remarked.

"I have some *shocking* news for you, Mr. Hughes," Ted said, an arch flicker in his eyes. "Your best buddy, Mr. Bullins, has moved on. Patrick County deputy found him dead in the snow early this morning."

"I would've guessed a drug overdose," Andy replied. "Or a random stranger who pulled a knife in a bar fight, but Cindy said he was electrocuted."

"So do you know the details?" Kellie asked.

Ted nodded. "Yeah. Some. Damian was jackleggin' power from his aunt's house and runnin' it to his little camper. The wire come loose from the connection on the camper and was still hot and touching against the metal side. That energized the whole shootin' match, so evidently when he took hold of the door he was fried. Adios and goodnight, Irene."

"Couldn't happen to a more deserving person," Cindy stated.

"Still need an autopsy," Ted cautioned, "but they're pretty sure he was zapped."

"Since he's such a celebrity these days," Curtis said, "I imagine this will headline the, uh, *current* events news." He chuckled at his own wit.

"Even with that kind of half-ass rig, the breaker should've flipped," Andy observed, "and the power shut off."

"Yep," Ted agreed. "Unless you're the druggie idiot who's hooked to a fifty-amp breaker. You could burn that camper to the ground and a fifty-amp ain't even gonna twitch."

"When did it happen?" Cindy asked.

"Don't know exactly yet," Ted said. "Snow's a complication for calculatin' time of death. Sheriff Smith said Damian was at the Cherokee casino down in North Carolina until Monday morning. No specifics so far, but the casino people reported the late Mr. Bullins had 'an incident' Sunday night involvin' a female, and they booted him Monday once he'd sobered up."

"You were there Sunday, right?" Kellie asked. "At his aunt's?"

"I was," Andy answered. "Seven o'clock as scheduled, but evidently Damian had more important business at the casino."

"Thank the Lord," Cindy said, "you didn't somehow wind up same as him. What if you'd grabbed the door?"

"There was no vehicle other than his aunt's, no light in the camper, and no sign of Damian—I would've felt very uncomfortable entering his 'home' when he wasn't around. Anyhow, who knows when the wire came loose."

Ted tugged his mask to his chin and sipped from a *Columbo* coffee mug. "Deputy told me the wire had slid plumb off the camper by the time the police got there. Was lyin' beside it, curled up through the snow, real obvious. The snow or wind or maybe Bullins fallin' against the camper probably knocked it totally on down. Too bad for Damian he didn't come at a different time. For what it's worth, his aunt claims she heard his car pull in Monday evenin', and she spoke a few words to him, but they'd had a nasty feud, so she didn't think it odd he wasn't sociable. Then she was snowed-in—along with Jack Daniels, I'm bettin'—and she assumed he was in his camper. She found him dead and notified the cops this morning."

Andy shrugged. "Can't say I'm too sorry."

"It's weird," Vikram said, "isn't it, how luck seems to get distributed, how fortune's doled out? This guy enjoys the most incredible run of impossible, undeserved breaks I've ever witnessed—the Miranda error, the dishonest investigator, the missed appeal deadline, the adultery, Benson's trip home for lunch, the check for DJ, the sympathetic jury panel, Judge Leventis's ruling, Andy's amazing lawyering at trial—and you just get the feeling things *have* to turn on him at some point. How many winners can one man draw in a row? He'd accumulated some misfortune, and the bad karma evidently arrived in one giant dose."

"Exactly," Curtis said. "Like flipping a coin. I understand, statistically, if you hit ten heads in a row, in theory, the next flip is still fifty-fifty, but man, after a while, you just have to *know* a tail is coming and maybe a string of 'em.'"

Vikram's smile wrinkled his paper mask. "There's a silver lining, I suppose. I took your advice, Kellie, and watched the YouTube videos. It's reassuring that on rare occasions, the Plinko disc bounces all over the board but finds the big money in the middle. The ricochets and rebounds aren't *always* a disappointment. You could argue this particular fluke benefits lots of people."

"Yep." Kellie leaned against the counter, searching her phone. She read from the Internet: "Only four hundred people a year are electrocuted. Win big on the long odds, lose big on the long odds."

"This is great—and deserved—for Cole Benson," Cindy said. "He's free and clear, as he ought to be."

"Well," Vikram replied, "he's free and clear *legally*. The conspiracy theorists and Internet harpies will have a field day." He glanced at Andy. "The Eldorado will be making laps for years."

"The Mormon Mafia does have a long reach," Curtis cracked. "To go along with an army of young bicycling operatives in snappy attire."

"Let's not forget," Andy reminded them, frowning, "Damian Bullins murdered an innocent mother of four girls, and he was only emboldened by the whole trip through the judicial system. Me, I'd like to think the universe has some immutable conscience and the ability to discharge its will and intervene if need be. *Everyone's* scrutinized by an inevitable, mandatory reckoning. Somewhere there has to be a barricade and checkpoint."

Vikram nodded. "According to our Rig Veda: We call the truth by many names. Ironically though, Andy, you're the only person who doesn't gain from the...uh...immaculate electrical reception. Sadly, the real damage from your courageous choice will continue to be determined by the star chamber of public opinion."

"Hope you change your mind, Mr. Hughes," Ted offered, "and stick here with us."

"Who'll be my general-district-court sidekick?" Curtis asked. "I vote you should stay, my friend."

Andy felt Kellie push against him, felt her arm wrap around his waist. "Me too. We're a good team, all of us."

"Same here," Vikram said.

CHAPTER TWENTY-SIX

JULY WAS BLAZING HOT, and almost-daily showers kept the air humid, even in the morning. The chiggers were as pesky as they'd ever been, and tomato plants were plagued by sickly yellow leaves and withered and failed. The toads and lightning bugs, though, flourished, filled the skies with blinking dots and driveways with obstacle courses of round, brown bumps. The pandemic had eased thanks to the arrival of a vaccine, and Andy had received his shots and quit wearing a mask at the end of June.

On July 22, the temperature was nearing seventy when Andy woke and dressed at dawn. He made coffee for himself and Kellie, ate breakfast, fed Patches, and filled a thermos with ice and tap water. He kissed Kellie's forehead, whispered he loved her, but he couldn't tell if she sensed him there or would remember the moment. He'd decided to leave Patches behind because of the heat, but the mutt trailed him to the truck and seemed determined to go, so he relented and opened the door, and the dog bounded into the cab.

The drive to Smith Mountain Lake via Figsboro Road took forty minutes. The dirt access into the lot was washed and rutted, and the truck dipped and bounced through a patch of woods until the lake came into view. Andy stopped but didn't switch off the engine, kept the air conditioner blowing and Pat Metheny on the speakers. The sun was discovering the blue sky, the water calm, not a single boat to be seen. Andy was, as always, the first on site. He sat in the cab while "Third Wind" finished playing, didn't lock the doors when he got out.

The house wouldn't be very large, certainly not by the ritzy standards of this part of the world, but the location was spectacular. His signs had arrived last night, and he removed one from the pickup's long bed. He walked beside the truck and forced the thin metal legs into the ground several feet off the dirt trail. HUGHES CONSTRUCTION was at the top. BONDED AND INSURED came next, then a phone number. A graphic-artist friend of Lynn's had done the design and it was superb.

The signs were an indulgence, really not necessary, but he delighted in them, and he and Kellie had celebrated the milestone with a cold-beer toast. He was booked solid for the next year—word of mouth from his lawyer pals and trips to behold the expert carpentry at his own home had gained him all the customers he could handle. His second-draw check for this project would net him more cash than fifteen months' toiling at the PD's office—not DeMarcus dollars but not too shabby, either.

The house was only framed, so it was a skeleton of boards—joists, supports, studs, headers, plates and rafters—above a plywood floor. They'd just begun the rough plumbing, and scaffolding climbed up a side. Andy walked through the rectangular entrance, underneath weight-bearing, tripled two-by-sixes. He relaxed on a makeshift bench he and the crew used for lunch and breaks. A blue jay was squawking from a pine tree.

As he did most mornings, he took in what he'd accomplished. Every cut was spot-on, every angle was exact, every board was leveled and precise. He found a singular, sublime truth in his work—there was no need for misdirection, technicalities, closing argument or slick, dodgy words. A plank was on bubble or it wasn't, a length was 16 1/8 inches or it wasn't. There was no gray, no wiggle room, no hiding the ball, and the conclusion was something to be *proud* of, not rationalize and explain away. Well satisfied, he smiled, then laughed, his chin tipped skyward, grateful to be in the midst of so much certainty. He patted the dog.

He heard Max's truck motoring in from behind, the cracked muffler becoming louder and louder, and soon Ace and "Nails" Nelson would appear in Ace's Impala, and they'd all begin another day. Andy rose and stretched. Tonight, he'd see Noah, and they planned to pitch a summer tent in the yard, and it would be spectacular fun, and Andy wouldn't be worried about a devil finding the wrong mix of meth and liquor and taking a craven shot at them. To wall off his son, he'd lent the statutes and law books an uncommon hand, and he might've shaved a corner round in doing so, but the complicated architecture of that choice—just like the flawless wooden bones surrounding him—lay square and perfect on his conscience. He slid his hammer from a tool belt and went to work, true-struck a tenpenny nail.

ACKNOWLEDGMENTS

SOMEHOW, I'LL BE SIXTY-FOUR years old when *The Plinko Bounce* is published, and, all things given, this seems like a good time for an alpha-to-omega thank you to all the people who have helped me and my books along the way.

I'm indebted to Mrs. Ann Belcher, Dr. Tony Abbott, Mr. Tom Wolfe, James Crumley, Nancy Olson, Henry Clay Clark, Chris and Karen Corbett, Dave Melesco, David V. Williams, the marvelous Charles F. Wright, Frank Beverly, Smilin' Ed, Julia Bard, Rob and Margo McFarland, Chris Duggan, Eddie Nicholson, Jack Morris, Charles "The Baron" Aaron, Edd Martin and Sterlyn Lineberry, Chip and Christina Slate, Eddie and Nancy Turner, Ward and Pam Armstrong, Larry Cowley, Nelson Stanley, Junior Taylor, Gary Sheppard, Derek Bridgman, Skip Burpeau, Jack Murphy, Jenette Kahn, and Wood Brothers Racing.

My Heath family has always shown up for me and never let me down, and I've had a great in-law ride—sometimes literally with Nephew Caleb behind the wheel. I'm lucky to be a part of such a fine clan.

Big thanks to Sara Eagle, Joe Regal, Tiffany Regal, Markus Hoffmann, Josie Freedman, Jennifer Simpson, Lukas Ortiz, Gary Fisketjon, Sonny Mehta, and my gifted pal Gabrielle Brooks. Richard Howarth and Kelly Justice gave me a start over two decades ago and have been kind to me ever since. I've never met Brian Sweany, but I'm fairly certain he's responsible for taking great care of me and my novels.

Tyson Cornell, Guy Intoci, Hailie Johnson, and Alexandra Watts have been so very smart and such a pleasure to work with, rare birds indeed, and their insights and remarkable talents made this book better from start to finish. Thanks for finding a place for me.

A big tip of the hat and a deep, humble bow to Anne-Lise Spitzer. In some form or fashion, we've been working together since 1999, and no one has ever done more for me. I'm grateful and hope you realize how much I appreciate your skill, determination and wise words. Cheers.

You don't hear this every day: Dr. Nick Kipreos saved my life, and Dr. Stacey Wolfe patched up my head and saved my life a second time. For my money, there are no better physicians—and people—on the face of the planet.

My mom and dad stuck with me and encouraged me through the long run of rejection letters and closed doors. They were steadfast, and I could not have asked for more supportive parents. My sweet mom got to see my first book in print, my dad was around for three.

Finally, my wife's mention is always the same, never changes, and still holds true in 2023: Deana Clark has been the best possible wife and remains "the hottest girl in the joint" no matter where our travels take us. Once again, this is for her.

Printed in the USA
CPSIA information can be obtained
at www.ICGtesting.com
JSHW031312070224
56832JS00007B/8

9 781644 284308